INSIDEOUT

Marvin McIntyre

Copyright © 2013 Marvin McIntyre
All rights reserved.
ISBN: 0615663494
ISBN-13: 9780615663494
Library of Congress Control Number: 2012943272
GraMac Press

DEDICATION

To Cathy, Jamie, Jon, and Cristin...Mom made you perfect.
And to Kay, tireless editor and fabulous sister.

Previously by Marvin McIntyre

Insiders

PROLOGUE

THE NAKED MAN'S SLOW-MOTION DESCENT stopped in mid flight—at the precise moment that his facial expression was caught by the camera. The man sitting in front of the screen studied the image, appraising the artistry of the shot. It was a sublime portrait of abject horror, captured in the instant of recognition. He breathed deeply and closed his eyes, savoring her work.

Unlike the movies, real life often affords only one take of a classic moment. He slowly clicked forward, relishing the victim's expression as it morphed from disbelief to instinctive hope. In mid somersault the man's arms rose and fell in a pathetic attempt at flight. Again the reviewer paused the frame, admiring the predictability of man's survival instincts.

Once more, he advanced the scene. At the moment of impact, the victim's eyes were squeezed shut, perhaps in prayer. The screen went dark.

The aftermath, images of the victim's splattered and broken body, held no allure for him. It was the acting, the dialogue, all that transpired prior to the execution, and then the visual beauty of the man plunging through space, hurtling to certain death. That was his passion.

In the solitude of his private room, he reflected: she had created such perfection on her maiden voyage. Finally, a woman worthy to share his life.

No light was necessary to hit the requisite keys on his computer to restart the sequence. He scanned the frames, searching for that moment of truth, when his personal Judas came to realize that his life was never his own.

CHAPTER 1

"THE RAPE TRIAL OF CHAD Alexander, III will begin tomorrow in the Fairfax County Circuit Court. Why is this the hardest ticket in town to get? Because Alexander, whose father is the founding partner of the prestigious law firm of Alexander, Gentry, and Sharp, is listed in *Forbes* magazine as one of the wealthiest people in the DC/Maryland/Virginia area."

The anchor woman leaned forward and spoke in a voice as buttery smooth as a therapist's , "Folks, the father of the accused has to be really rich, because he hired the flamboyant James Kersey, the top defense attorney, in the country to represent his son." She shook her head. "Kersey thrives on high profile, money is no object cases, and he has *never* lost. If this weren't a rape case, the prosecutors might just save the state some money and run up a white flag. There are sure to be fireworks, so stay tuned, and we'll keep you up to date. This is Jackie Mayfield saying good night from your Fox news station."

"And out!"

No other reporter in America had the latitude to cover news as if she were having a conversation with her viewers. Jackie rolled her eyes at the cameraman and said to no one in particular, "Where did we go wrong in the news business? Now even a rape trial needs to be a sideshow."

The Fairfax County Courthouse is located on Chain Bridge Road, not surprisingly in the city of Fairfax, Virginia. The picturesque thoroughfare is marred only by the threat of traveling too close to the rush hour from hell. The neighborhood surrounding the relatively new courthouse is an interesting mishmash of old and more recent construction. Tiny houses, vintage circa 19th century, cohabit with new condo developments and strip malls that reflect more of the old Colonial style. As would be expected, opportunistic law offices and bail bondsmen are strategically located on adjacent streets.

As visitors walk up the hill from the public parking garage to the Judicial Center, the sign identifying the Public Defender's Office appears to magically rise up and shout the basic tenet that everyone has a right to an attorney.

In the security-conscious world of this century, visitors expect the two-lap serpentine lanes leading to a conveyor belt for package and briefcase x-ray scans. Deputies manning walkthrough metal detectors efficiently seize cell phones and other electronic toys that might contain cameras.

By its very nature, any felony trial resembles a stage production. Drama comes not only from the fact that a defendant's life can be irrevocably changed, but also from the interaction of the main characters. Both the prosecutors and the defense attorneys attempt to be master storytellers, selling the elixir of their perceived truths.

Witnesses become transitory players, and their impact varies, depending on their performance and their significance to the plot. The twelve men and women who sit in the two-tiered jury box serve as the players' harshest critics and as ultimate arbiters of the play's ending. Finally, in one of the very few instances in which the director remains on stage for the entire production, the judge's word is law.

In Fairfax, Virginia, all major crimes are tried in the circuit court, and the most impressive courtroom in the Fairfax County

Courthouse is 5E, the venue for the Chad Alexander trial. In this massive theater, the standing-room-only audience of spectators and reporters conversed in whispers as it awaited the opening of the grand play.

Judge Michael Ford measured jurisprudence evenly without prejudice or bias and in strict accordance with the law. Through years of practice in his monthly card game, he had developed an inscrutable poker face. As a result, the odds of a successful appeal on his verdicts were higher than drawing to an inside straight flush.

The good judge was enormously well respected, a pillar of his Northern Virginia community and perhaps the best-liked jurist on the East Coast. In a miscarriage of biological justice, his 5'6" frame, strengthened by a rigorous five-day-a-week workout regime, nevertheless housed a not inconsequential belly. Fine food was the only discernible weakness of this highly disciplined man.

Only in rare circumstances did the judge have to consciously focus on maintaining a placid demeanor. His years on the bench immunized him against the horrors of humanity, the blustering protestations of judicial advocates, and what, fortunately, was only the occasional erroneous verdict.

While he waited in his chambers, Judge Ford concentrated on his breathing. As the father of two boys and two girls, rape trials were repugnant to him. Even though required, it was difficult to be dispassionate. The swashbuckling Kersey and his filthy rich client, who reeked of arrogance, guaranteed that the courtroom would be a circus. The judge sighed, reached up and massaged the back of his neck, and put on his game face.

As the players and spectators filed into the courtroom, a prickle of danger ran through the body of Chad Alexander, III like an accelerated heartbeat. His pupils dilated, and a slight flush appeared on his cheeks as he fought to control his ragged breathing. His eyes half closed as he felt a pleasant stirring in his loins. He blinked, as if waking from a daydream. Reluctantly, he focused on his lawyer's advice to observe the trial rather than become immersed in it. But Chad Alexander, III lived for the moment, particularly those moments in which he felt most alive.

CHAPTER 2

"I DO," SAID MEGAN O'BRIEN, reluctantly removing her hand from the Bible. She wanted to grab the Good Book and clutch it to her breast. God didn't protect her then. Maybe He would now.

"Megan," Virginia Perry said gently, "I'm sorry; but, well, you're going to have to relive that night."

Megan took a deep breath and nodded. After the excruciating rehearsals, when the Commonwealth's Attorney had viciously peppered her with questions and innuendo, having this brilliant, but sympathetic second chair ask the questions was a gift.

"On the night of the incident," Perry began, "had you seen any warning signs from the accused?"

"No."

"And prior to his alleged attack, had there been any suggestive behavior or sexual advances?"

"No," Megan answered again.

"So you had no clue as to the accused's intentions?" "No. There was nothing that led me to believe he was a predator."

Judge Ford stole a glance at the defense table. That statement should have elicited an objection. If the defense attorney had been a rookie, the judge would have asked him or her if there was an objection. But the great James Kersey was sitting there smiling, his hands resting comfortably on the arms of his chair.

Trying not to tread too heavily on her layer of legal ice and possibly kill the golden goose, Perry asked, "Did you buy anything for the accused that night?"

"Yes," Megan answered. " A toothbrush. We were going back to my apartment for a quick cup of coffee. It was late."

Megan turned and looked at the jury. She had that girl-next-door look: light red hair worn in a ponytail, light blue eyes, and an upturned nose sparsely sprinkled with freckles. It would have been difficult to typecast a better picture of innocence.

"Why would you buy a toothbrush for a man you barely knew?"

"He asked me to," she said, as if that explained everything.

"So he couldn't afford to buy his own toothbrush?"

"No. Of course he could. He was driving a brand-new Mercedes convertible. He asked me if it was OK if we stopped so that he could buy a toothbrush, and then he didn't have change, so he asked if I would mind paying for it."

Perry shook her head knowingly. "I know it will be difficult for you, Megan, but please describe what happened after Chad Alexander entered your apartment."

Megan nodded and gulped a breath. "I-I asked him if he wanted coffee. He said no. Then it was like he leaped on me. He slammed his hand over my mouth. He said he had brought duct tape, and if I made him use it to shut me up, he would torture me." Her frail voice faltered, and she gritted her teeth to steady herself.

"Do you need a moment, Ms. O'Brien?" Judge Ford asked kindly.

"No, sir," she said, with tears running down her pale cheeks. "I want to finish."

The judge nodded as Megan continued.

"He's unbelievably strong," she said, glancing at Chad.

The jurors' eyes also went to the accused. His handsome face had such a look of hurt and confusion that it became painful to watch. Almost in unison, their attention returned to the witness.

"What exactly did he do to you?" Perry asked

Neither Virginia Perry nor the defense attorney interrupted as Megan fought through sobs to describe the graphic details of the rape. When she finished, Perry gave her a few moments to collect herself and then asked her final question: "Megan, why didn't you call the police?"

Megan's chin hit her chest, and she answered softly, "Because he threatened me, and because I was ashamed."

Perry looked at her sympathetically, letting the jury feel the moment. "Thank you, Megan," she said softly. She walked back to the prosecution's table. "No further questions, Your Honor."

Judge Ford looked at his watch. "It's 11:45. Unless counsels object," he glanced at Kersey, who shook his head, "court will adjourn until one o'clock."

As she forced down her third, and what would be final, bite of her tuna sandwich, Megan gave a brave smile in response to the caring faces of her attorneys. She gathered up the remains of her barely consumed lunch, wiped the wooden table with her napkin, and closed her eyes for a moment. She tried to pray, but thoughts of her next ordeal would not be denied.

CHAPTER 3

THERE IS A PHALANX OF defense attorneys who will dress down, speak in monosyllables, and do whatever they can to relate to the jury. James Kersey took the opposite tack. He was outrageous, over-the-top dramatic, a better-dressed George Clooney clone; and every woman on the jury, along with a few of the men, wanted to sleep with him. Low baritone voice, dark bedroom eyes, and swept-back silver hair were accented by $5,000 custom-made suits, blinding white shirts, and amazingly colorful, bright ties that were never worn more than once.

It was not as if the country's most renowned defense attorney needed special effects to mesmerize a courtroom. James Kersey was a hired gun. He took only high-profile cases, primarily ones that were televised, and he never charged less than a seven-figure fee. He'd been doing it for 25 years. Part actor, part showman, he had no peer.

Light reflected off of the defense attorney's Patek Philippe wristwatch. As it synchronized with his graceful, sweeping gestures, it produced a slow-moving, almost hypnotic light show. It added dramatic punctuation, as if God Himself wanted to know the answers to the questions asked by the great James Kersey.

"Ms. O'Brien," he began, "may I say that you look very nice today, quite sensible."

"Objection," said Virginia Perry, rising quickly.

"Sustained."

"My, my." Kersey turned to the jury. "Back in my day, it was okay to compliment a woman's attire."

"Mr. Kersey," said Judge Ford, pulling the leash.

"Okay, okay," said Kersey, raising his two tanned hands *sans* wedding ring in a placating manner. He turned from the jury back to the witness and studied her for a moment. She looked like a patient about to undergo a root canal without anesthesia.

"I'll try not to upset you, but you do know that it's my job to get to the truth."

"Yes," she replied uncertainly, not sure she if was supposed to answer.

He nodded. "I hope that your attorneys have told you that the rape shield law precludes me from grilling you about every sexual experience you've ever had."

"Objection!" The prosecutors stood in unison.

"Sustained!" barked Judge Ford.

Kersey moved closer to the witness and smiled reassuringly. "Did you notice that I did not object even once during the time Ms. Perry was eliciting your testimony?"

"Yes?" Megan answered, suddenly confused.

He nodded. "I thought that it was the polite thing to do," he mused. He turned his body toward the jury. "Sometimes these trials are difficult for jurors."

Kersey shrugged, "He said, she said. Who exaggerated? Who changed their mind?"

"Objection."

"Counsel, approach," said the judge angrily.

After a brief discussion, in which the entire courtroom knew that the defense attorney was being scolded, Kersey turned and gave a perfect imitation of a little boy with his hand caught in the cookie jar.

The jury smiled and tittered in response.

Abruptly, Kersey spun toward the witness. "Ms. O'Brien, was this your first date with my client?"

"No."

"Do you claim that he was rough with you on other dates?"

"Objection."

"I'll rephrase. Did you go to the police after your previous dates?"

"I... I only went out with him once before."

"I'm sorry. Did you answer my question?"

Megan blinked rapidly and shook her head.

Kersey looked at the judge.

"You will need to answer the question audibly, Ms. O'Brien."

"No. I didn't call the police after the first date."

Kersey nodded his head as if that answered everything. His left hand went to his face, and he tapped his index and middle fingers on his chin. "So you all didn't have sex on the first date."

"No," she answered softly.

"Whose idea was that?"

She looked at him strangely.

"I mean, did he try to get frisky?"

The jury tittered again.

"No."

"Did you?"

"No!" she said more forcefully, with a hurt look in her eyes.

Kersey turned and walked back to the defense table, ostensibly to look at some notes. Then he slowly walked back toward Megan, appearing to be trying to work something out. "You two have a date. Did he take you out to dinner?"

"Yes."

"A nice dinner?"

"Objection. Whether it was a nice dinner or not is not relevant."

10

"I disagree. There is a substantial difference if a gentleman takes a lady to a fancy restaurant instead of a Burger King."

"Overruled. I'll allow it."

The jury smiled and nodded in agreement.

"Yes. It was a nice dinner."

"Thank you." Kersey nodded again. "So would you say that he was a gentleman that night?"

"Yes." Her answer was barely audible.

More nodding. "Did you invite him in for a drink or coffee?" he asked in a stage whisper.

Tears welled up in her eyes. She raised a hand to wipe them away. "Yes. I asked him if he wanted a cup of coffee."

"Did he accept?" Kersey's voice was louder and held a mixture of incredulity and implied accusation.

Megan recoiled as if she'd been slapped. Her head went back, she squeezed her eyes shut, and the tears flowed more freely.

"Counsel, does your witness want a short recess?" Judge Ford asked gently.

"No. I just want to get this over with," Megan answered quickly. "No. He did not rape me that night. He didn't come in for coffee. He gave me a kiss at the door and left." Her hands flew to her face, and she sobbed.

This time Kersey turned to the jury and nodded sympathetically. He waited until Megan collected herself. This had the dual benefit of demonstrating his compassion and reinforcing the illusion of his client's gentlemanly behavior. "Do you feel better?" he asked, sounding like a kindly grandfather.

The prosecutors felt bile in their collective stomachs. His faux concern carried the implied truth that confession was good for the soul.

"Not really," she said, looking at him with hurt and anger.

"Now let's move to the night in question. You testified that my client spent the night with you."

"Objection," the lead prosecutor said wearily. "Ms. O'Brien testified that he raped her throughout the night."

"So he didn't spend the night with her?" Kersey interjected before the judge could rule.

"Counsel, approach!" After a sidebar conference, during which the judge warned against editorializing, the cross-examination resumed.

"I guess we'll have to backtrack." Kersey shook his disappointedly. "Was there alcohol with dinner?"

"Yes."

"What variety, and how much did you each consume?"

"We shared a bottle of wine," Megan responded listlessly.

"I won't ask who had three glasses and who had one," he said pointedly.

"Objection! Foundation."

"I'll withdraw," said Kersey with a casual wave of his hand. "How did you get back to your apartment?" he asked.

"In his car."

"With the top down on the convertible?"

"Yes."

There was another nod. "Did anyone see you two enter your apartment together?"

"I... I don't know."

"Would friends have commented? I mean, you're 26 years old. You've had men friends in your apartment before, correct?"

She exhaled. "No. No one would have commented; and yes, I've had male friends in my apartment before."

"How about when Chad left the next morning? Did any friends mention it to you?"

"No, they didn't."

He raised his eyebrows. "Handsome guy leaves your apartment the morning after, and no one saw him and commented to you?

"Objection. Asked and answered."

"Sustained."

Kersey looked at his notes and pretended to read them. "I believe you testified that he threatened to use duct tape to silence you."

"Yes."

"How big a roll of duct tape did he bring with him into your apartment?"

Megan gave him a confused look.

"He didn't have a gun or flash a knife, so he must have held out a threatening roll of duct tape, right?"

"Objection! He's testifying!"

"Sustained."

"I'll rephrase."

"Did you see any duct tape, Ms. O'Brien?"

"No," she replied, on the verge of tears.

"No? Did you think that my client had it in his car? Did he ask you to wait while he went to the car to get it?"

"Objection!"

"I'll withdraw. Maybe he was going to borrow the duct tape from you?"

"Objection! He's badgering the witness, Your Honor."

"Sustained!" Judge Ford ruled forcefully.

"Did you call the police the minute he left?" Kersey asked with a sense of urgency.

"No," Megan answered in a small voice.

Kersey raised his voice and his level of incredulity. "Did you call your dad? Did you call a friend?"

If possible, her negative response sounded even smaller.

"Normally," Kersey went on, "I'd agree that a woman has the right to change her mind, but ..."

"Objection!"

"Sustained. Mr. Kersey," Judge Ford admonished, "you have been warned."

Kersey raised his hands, and the light again reflected off his watch, making it seem like he was performing an exorcism. "I'm sorry," he said, giving Megan a confused look. "I'm just having a hard time figuring this out." He spread his hands in a gesture of hopelessness.

"Objection! Mr. Kersey's inability to understand rape is not our problem."

"Your Honor!" cried Kersey with indignation.

"Counsel, approach," said Judge Ford. It was obvious to the jury and all in attendance that he was not happy.

"The objection is sustained, and the jury is reminded that the accused is innocent until proven guilty."

Kersey stared at the witness. "My client rejected you before. You were obviously attracted to him. On the night of the *alleged* incident you bought him a toothbrush before going back to your place!" His words clipped, accusing, battered her.

"Objection!" screamed the prosecutor. "Counsel is both testifying and badgering the witness! He is giving his closing, and he didn't ask a question!"

"Sustained."

"Sorry, Your Honor." Kersey walked over and looked each juror in the eye, then turned quickly and asked, "Did he not call you back after the night of sex?"

"Objection!"

"Were you afraid that he might never call you back?"

14

CHAPTER 4

A TELEVISED TRIAL WAS A smorgasbord for James Kersey. All strategies and tactics were on the table. Even preparation was secondary, as the adrenaline of the moment heightened his world-class improvisational talents.

In the live arena of television, the presiding judge would attempt to reign him in; but too many interruptions would open the judge to criticism. Without television, placing any defendant on the stand is risky. However, with the cameras rolling and proper coaching, Chad Alexander's movie-star looks and aura of innocence would render his words meaningless.

James Kersey walked slowly up to his witness. He knew that Chad was not happy in his off-the-rack navy blazer; light gray, pleated trousers; and button-down, light blue shirt. He did let the young man wear a nice silk red tie with a blue stripe that matched the color of his shirt. Add his thick blonde hair cut short for the trial, his tan skin, and his sculpted body to those guiltless green eyes, and the boy wouldn't be convicted if the jury saw him in the act.

"Chad," Kersey said gently, "I didn't want you to testify, did I?"
"No, sir."
"Why not?"
Chad gave an apologetic half smile.
"Objection. Relevance."
"I'm just laying some foundation, Your Honor."
"Sustained."
"Chad, were you surprised when you learned of this accusation?"

"Yes, sir," he replied, wide eyed.

Kersey nodded sagely. "The three women that previously testified on your behalf. Did you remember them before this trial?"

"I did," he said.

"Each one testified that she had sexual relations with you. Were they all long-term relationships?"

"No, sir," Chad said, and actually blushed.

"No?" said Kersey, raising an eyebrow and feigning surprise. "Did you date any of the three women more than twice?"

"No, sir," Chad responded in a low voice.

"In this world of speed dating, I guess it's not that unusual. Do you have a problem with relationships?"

Chad sighed. "I guess I'm still looking for the right woman."

Kersey did not need to shift his glance to feel the daggers from the prosecutors as he asked his final two questions. "Was Ms. O'Brien the right one?"

"No, sir."

"Why not?"

Chad grimaced as though he didn't want to answer. Reluctantly, he said, "She was nice, but she was real aggressive."

The lead prosecutor decided that his co-counsel could handle the cross. He could have enumerated the facts, but they needed the jury to feel empathy. Virginia Perry approached the witness, smiling to hide her disdain. An attractive woman with a broad face, dark hair pulled back in a professional bun, she had a natural smile that put people at ease. Other than her intellect, her greatest attribute was her believability.

"Mr. Alexander, you look nice today," Perry began, mimicking defense counsel. "Is this normal attire for you?"

"Ah, yeah, sure."

"In our search of your home, we noticed that all the suits and sports coats in your closet were custom made. Except for that expensive-looking tie, I believe that you dressed down for us."

"Objection. Relevance," said Kersey from his seat. "Is there a question?"

"I'll rephrase, Your Honor," Perry said smoothly. "Did your attorney pick out your outfit today?"

Chad gave her a bored look, "Yes."

"Have you had previous acting experience?" Perry asked.

"Yes. I had the lead role in *Damn Yankees* in high school," Chad said proudly.

"Oh, did you play the part of the devil?"

"Objection!"

Before the judge could rule, Chad frowned and answered. "No. I was Joe Hardy, the hero."

Perry turned to the jury. "It's nice to see that your acting skills haven't diminished."

"Objection," said Kersey in a tired voice.

"Sustained."

"Did it bother you that Megan suffered bruises?"

"Of course," Chad answered contritely.

"As well as vaginal tearing and a partial tear of her rectum?" Perry continued, bearing down.

Kersey stood slowly. "Did Counsel ask a question?"

"I'll rephrase. Did it bother you that her insides were ravaged?"

"Objection. Foundation, Your Honor. The bruises were reported three days after she was with my client." Kersey raised his hands. "We have no knowledge of what transpired during those three days."

"Sustained," said the judge.

Perry took Chad through the paces, scoring minor points, but failing to light the fire of anger she knew was underneath the schoolboy charm. He'd been well rehearsed.

After exhausting her questions, she started to walk away and then turned. "Are you familiar with the term 'date rape,' Mr. Alexander?"

"Yes."

"Have *you* ever been raped, Mr. Alexander?

"No!" he replied indignantly.

Perry shook her head, now looking at him with obvious disgust. "Well, there is a major difference between consent and terrified acquiescence."

"Objection!" shouted Kersey as he stood.

Before the judge could rule, Perry shouted, "If you don't know the difference, any woman can tell you."

Points scored by the prosecution on cross-examination included Megan's bruises, the insinuation that the rich kid takes what he wants, and the allegation that Chad's father had tried to throw money at the rape charge. Yet juries are human. They want their rapists to look like monsters, not like Chad Alexander, III.

CHAPTER 5

"THE WORLD IS RIPE WITH possibilities. It is possible, for example, that this literary journey you are undertaking is a tale of fiction rivaling J.K. Rowling's Harry Potter series. Or that the uncanny accuracy and precision of the prose is compelling evidence that you are witnessing the unfolding of historical achievement, and thus, every word is glorious truth.

"In order to understand the artistry and symmetry of my accomplishments, it is necessary to disregard conventional thinking. If you are unable to suspend your brainwashed perceptions of what is good and what is evil, give my epistle to a more enlightened soul.

"If you are reading this after my death, pause and reflect with profound sorrow, for genius is not replaceable. If I am alive and being persecuted by misguided, inept authorities, I invite you to be my champion. For, of course, I am innocent."

Mac McGregor could not believe that he was reading Jeremy Lyons's book, *Survival of the Fittest*, for perhaps the tenth time.

The proverbial train wreck, a serious traffic accident, Lawrence Taylor breaking Joe Theismann's leg. The conscious mind begs you to look away. Instead, you watch with morbid fascination, unable to tear your eyes away from the carnage. The masochistic futility of these thoughts only added to Mac's frustration.

At 57 Mac was still in decent shape. Part of that had to be attributed to heredity. A shade under six feet tall, brown hair that had just recently received a splash of gray at the temples, and a refusal to allow the emergence of love handles, at least for the time being, had ensured that body image was not a concern. His dark brown eyes reflected not only his desire to squeeze joy out of every day, but also his ability to react to crises calmly while seeking solutions.

The fact that he was reading this deranged narcissist's unadulterated crap guaranteed that Mac, a highly regarded financial advisor, was currently not cool, calm, or collected. On the surface, it would appear that nothing fazed the 30-year industry veteran. He benefitted from a terrific 32-year marriage, having his four kids living within 15 minutes of his home, and managing the top-ranked investment group on the East Coast. Also, it's a good rule of thumb that any advisor who survived the global financial crisis of 2008 with his clients and sanity intact has definitely been battle tested.

Yet who could conceive that a request to help a friend would turn into a year of terror for Mac and his family. Even though it was never proven, Mac was convinced that Jeremy Lyons had run an illegal hedge fund and that he was a stone-cold killer. It was three years later, but the hangover from that time had not faded.

Mac closed the book. On the front of the book jacket, Jeremy Lyons's hands grasped the sides of a small desk, and his intense eyes glared at his readers. From the waist up, his naked, tanned body, hairless and muscular, projected a formidable image.

From his supine position on one of the black, aluminum chaises by his pool, Mac angrily frisbeed the book onto the lawn. Of course, it didn't land open, with the pages creased and the spine torn and bent; instead, it settled as if he had gently laid it on its back on the grass.

It was early fall, the back-yard rectangular pool was closed, and the four identical chaises were perfectly placed in the center of the decking. Mac always sat on the second from the right as you looked from the house, and there was a small, circular, black mesh table equidistant between his chaise and the one usually occupied by his wife, Grace. She was out grocery shopping, so he was wallowing in his masochistic moments in solitude.

Gold and red maple leaves whispered on the large flagstones as if moved by a gentle broom. He closed his eyes and imagined the serenity that could have been his if he had resisted yet another reading of Jeremy Lyons's now infamous best seller. Or more accurately, he thought ruefully, if he hadn't stuck his nose into the devil's lair in the first place!

Mac's was an advance copy, signed by the author. The book had become an overnight best seller, and anyone else might have been flattered by the attention. However, Mac reasoned that no one else's personalized copy included a not too subtle death threat. The threat could not be taken lightly, because the author had the curriculum vitae to make it happen.

Mac removed his sunglasses, which included a magnifying lower half for reading, and placed them on the table adjacent to his chaise. He lay back, closed his eyes, and folded his arms across his chest as if he were lying in a slightly elevated coffin. As the afternoon sun caressed his face, Mac tried again to figure out what he was missing. He retrieved the book and turned to the final chapter. Until now he had thought that this chapter was just more pontificating.

"Another misconception is that desires are insatiable. Admittedly, for the small segment of society that is clinically deranged, this statement may not hold true. But for those seeking riches, pleasure, or power, too much of a good thing dulls the appetite.

"The careful reader has noted that with a mere snap of my fingers, extraordinarily beautiful women whose sole objective was to give me sexual pleasure were always available to me. Whatever fantasy I could conceive with any number of women would be enthusiastically fulfilled. Regrettably, without the challenge, the allure diminished, and I was sated.

"Imagine an endless buffet and the ability to ask for any food or libation perfectly prepared to your liking. Would not your taste buds ultimately lose appreciation?

"Financial success came too easy for me. In less than twenty years, I became a multibillionaire. If the thirst for riches is not insatiable, why would I continue after my first hundred million? Fame? I walked in the shadows, exchanging fame for fortune. Did the challenge become greater with new regulations for me to consistently overcome? Again regrettably, no.

"The answer, dear readers, is that no other challenge interested me ... yet."

Mac closed the book. His head was throbbing. There was no logical reason for Jeremy Lyons to tantalize his precious readers with the possibility that his autobiography might be fiction ... unless he wasn't finished!

CHAPTER 6

THE SNIPER RIFLE FELT COMFORTABLE in his hands. In the not yet light morning, the man held the wooden stock to his cheek as if he were a father holding his child close. The single-shot bolt action rifle had a massive telescopic scope with a laser sight underneath.

The rifle had perfect accuracy, no damage ramp-up or fall-off. The zoom display featured a charge meter and a small laser dot in the middle. When zoomed in, the charge meter increased gradually from 0 to 100 percent, indicating the amount of damage that would be done by the shot.

The rifle was his weapon in war – and old friend returning to its master. Reunited. Now as the shooter perched on the side of the Bethany Beach water tower, his field of fire would be pristine.

Intel was irrefutable. The subject would enter Route 1 from the ocean subdivision of Sea Del Estates. The assassin would come from the south in a nondescript vehicle.

The shot was challenging. A moving target required either a hit through the windshield, killing the driver, or a shot that disabled the car or discouraged the assassin from his mission. Failure was not an option; the subject was too important.

As the ambient light of dawn crept from the ocean towards the bay, the subject appeared—a kindly old man graced with an unforgettable smile. His companion, a white handful of Maltese, strutted by his side.

Behind the man, the shooter saw the approaching black car of death. Braced for the shot, he aimed, and fired. Miss! He fired again. Miss! Each time he fired, he missed the target completely!

The unearthly screams caused David Grant to sit bolt upright in bed. He opened his squeezed- shut eyes to a mass of tangled, sweat- soaked sheets. He wasn't there. An assassin had run his father down, and his warrior son couldn't save him. George Grant, the sweetest man who ever walked the earth, was exterminated, and there was no retribution. So the son paid, in his dreams. The screams had been his own.

Mac McGregor and his partner Artie Cohen had first ventured into the Elephant and Castle Pub when Mac and his family had been shadowed by full-time security. After a few months with the ever-present guard, both Mac and Artie had felt a lessening of the tension. To Artie this meant that he would naturally act as if the security was for him. Particularly when an attractive woman was nearby, Artie would whisper to the formidable man accompanying them as if to say, "He's with me."

On a number of occasions, Mac had suggested that his friend might want to participate in the cost of the service. As expected, Artie was content with just the perks.

Artie was a gifted tax attorney whose appearance and facial expressions allowed him to get away with anything. He looked totally harmless: bald with just a Friar Tuck fringe and a pleasant, unlined face highlighted by blue eyes that saw humor everywhere. A serial kidder, he was the only sober animal in the over-60 crowd.

As Artie and Mac walked to the restaurant, a light rain played a soft percussion on their umbrellas. Mac had snagged a black golf umbrella, while Artie, who was an abuse masochist, had borrowed a female associate's smaller version. His was a manly shade of pink.

The restaurant was crowded, so they missed the more comfortable booths and sat at a table. Immediately, a dark-haired waitress, dressed in black, her top revealing the required cleavage, asked what they would like to drink. Mac made eye contact and said, "I will have an Arnold Palmer, please." Artie started to speak, but Mac pre-empted him in a singsong voice, "and he will have an Arnold Palmer also, but he wants his a little heavier on the lemonade."

The waitress gave a polite laugh as Artie threw his hands out in a calming manner. "Please," he whispered, "be tolerant of him. He forgot to take his meds today." She walked away, shaking her head and still laughing. Familiar faces who tend to overtip a bit always seem to have a captive and amused audience.

As they haphazardly studied the menu—a reflex, not to determine choice—Mac looked curiously at the coveted booths. He nodded his head towards one of them. "David is sitting up there with someone I don't know. I'm going to introduce myself. You'd better stay here. If the guy had to meet both of us, he would probably bolt."

Artie nodded in acknowledgement. "Order my usual," instructed Mac, wagging his finger as he got up from the chair. "No funny business. I'll be right back."

The look of innocent hurt was not an unexpected response.

"Is this seat taken?" Mac asked pleasantly of David Grant, another one of his partners, as he approached the booth from the rear.

David apparently hadn't seen him, and he reacted with a start. "Oh, hi, Mac," he said with what seemed like feigned enthusiasm.

Mac paused and studied the two men. He smiled, masking his awkwardness. It felt like he had interrupted an intimate conversation.

David recovered quickly and started to slide out of the booth.

"No, no. Stay there," Mac said. "I'm just playing. Sorry to interrupt. After all, it's been over twenty minutes since I've seen you."

David gave a more relaxed chuckle. "Mac, I'd like you to meet my friend Blake Stone. Blake, Mac is my boss."

David's luncheon companion reached out a deeply tanned hand attached to a wiry, superbly muscled forearm. In contrast to David's prototypical investment banker attire, the man had on worn jeans; scuffed, dark brown boots; and an untucked, faded blue shirt. A Wall Street executive and a testament to the good works of the Goodwill organization—an unlikely pair.

"Uh, we were in the service together," David offered quietly, answering the questioning look Mac had tried to keep out of his eyes.

Mac took a mental step back. He wanted to say that he wasn't judging, just curious. Instead he said, while looking Blake in the eyes, "Thank you for your service."

Blake nodded as he held Mac's gaze. Blake's assessment of Mac felt like a CAT scan, and from his annoyed persistent stare, the results had come back negative. Blake still had not spoken.

"As David will attest, I'll use any excuse to spend less time with our partner Artie Cohen." Mac nodded towards the object of his derision.

No smile or acknowledgement from David's friend. Now Mac knew how stand-up comics felt when all attempts fell flat.

"Are you still in the service, Blake?" asked Mac.

Blake shook his head negatively.

It was challenging enough for Mac to try once more. "What are you doing now?"

Blake shrugged, looked at David, then turned back to Mac and gave a sardonic half smile, as if to say, "Why are you still here?"

"Whatever David wants me to do," he said.

"We have the same job!" Mac responded enthusiastically, jousting to regain a semblance of control. Raising his hands, he started to leave. He thrust out his hand and again felt the strength of the man's grip. "Blake, nice to meet you. Sorry to have intruded."

As Mac started walking back to his table, he heard the man's soft voice call after him. "Mac." He turned back to the sound. "Nice to meet you, too."

David watched as Mac sat back down at his table and started conversing with Artie. He turned back to Blake, linked his fingers together, and laid his elbows and hands on the table. He spoke in a low voice. "Seriously?"

"Why, what would be the problem, my captain?"

"Did you overdose on testosterone this morning? Mac is my boss, and my friend."

Blake rolled his eyes. "Come on, man. I know the type. His suit cost more than my whole wardrobe. I was just messin' with him. He's cool."

Relationships forged in battle have no boundaries. "Let me tell you what you don't know, Snake," David said evenly. "In 2008, our financial system was circling the drain. It was the worst panic since the Great Depression. Every day, Mac McGregor came into the office with a smile on his face. He reassured his clients, encouraged his associates, and provided strong, unflinching leadership. Grace under fire; I know you understand that."

Blake continued to hold his gaze, but showed no emotion.

"Oh, and by the way," David continued, "while our financial world was crumbling, Mac had a minor distraction. A friend in government asked him to help find a man who had been a former colleague of Mac's. Thanks to the FBI and Mac's investigations, the man was found. Unfortunately, he escaped. The man was a vicious, crooked hedge fund manager who employed a trained assassin to expedite profits.

"Mac doesn't need to be intimidated; he doesn't need the snake-eye stare. He needs some peace." David stopped talking and looked down at his plate.

"Got it," Blake said quietly. "Sorry, man."

David blew out a breath. "It's okay. I overreacted." He looked up at Blake. "One more thing. You were on assignment, but Mac and his wife drove three hours to attend my dad's funeral." David's eyes glistened. "Mac gave the final eulogy. Three years later, members of our church in Bethany Beach still come up to me and tell me how moved they were by his words."

CHAPTER 7

IT TOOK CONSIDERABLE SELF CONTROL for Chad Alexander, III to maintain the mask of the wrongfully accused. Almost imperceptibly he nodded in silent agreement as his eloquent advocate began his closing argument.

"I'm still trying to make sense of this," said James Kersey, as he addressed the jury as if he were starting a conversation in a bar. "Why are we here? Have you ever worried that political correctness might go too far?"

Kersey considered the unanswered question, then turned his back to the jury and took two steps away from them. He turned again and walked slowly toward the jury box. "It's almost insulting to have to list the facts of this case again." His frustration was evident, and as if he were reminiscing, it morphed into a humble smile. "Will you allow me to digress for just a moment?"

To the chagrin of the prosecutors, a number of the jurors nodded.

"When I was in college, my roommate was , , ," He paused. "Well, back then we called him a lothario. I'm not sure what the term would be in today's vernacular, maybe a player, but he was irresistible to women, and believe me," Kersey said, nodding for emphasis, "I envied him. Anyway, above his bed, in bold letters, there was a message that simply said, 'Give me a sign if you change your mind.'"

Kersey let that be absorbed. "Isn't that what we have here?" he asked softly. In rapid-fire manner, the flamboyant attorney ticked off the salient facts of the case, bombarding the jury with his logic.

"Ms. O'Brien admits that my client was a gentleman on their first date and refused her invitation to join her in her apartment.

"Three beautiful former lovers testify that my client *never* made an unwelcome advance.

"Ms. O'Brien testifies that a bottle of wine was consumed during the second date.

"Ms. O' Brien says that she was threatened with invisible duct tape.

"The walls of her apartment are paper thin, yet no one heard screams.

"There were no witnesses before, during, or after sex.

"Ms. O'Brien told no one – not her father, not her friends, not the police about that night for *three* days."

Kersey paused, closed his eyes, and massaged his brow with his hand. "Why did she wait? Hoping my client would call?"

At the conclusion of his staccato rendering of the facts, Kersey's eyes widened, and his handsome face took on a look of bewilderment. He lowered his voice, leaned close to the jury, and seemed to make simultaneous contact with each member. "I don't know," he sighed wistfully. "I may be too old to understand the new rules of sex."

The jury tittered in response, and Chad surreptitiously canted his emerald green eyes to check the prosecution's reaction to this response. The Commonwealth's Attorney, a slim, rather pale man with milky eyes and an ill-fitting blue suit, was squeezing his thin lips together. He was obviously not a theater buff.

"I wish I could turn back the hands of time," Kersey continued, as his hand rose reluctantly to his tanned forehead. His wistful tone was synchronized with the longing look in his eyes. The jury, on cue, leaned forward, awaiting his next thought.

"Not just because of this case, but because society has moved far beyond my Midwestern values." He smiled ruefully. "There is pornography on the Internet with universal access. Sexual practices that were against the law in some states are now accepted as normal. Incredibly, our society has turned into a buffet of all-you-can-consume perversions."

Kersey stopped, looked at the jury, and shook his head. "There are bondage fantasies, women in rubber suits with whips." He wrinkled his face like he smelled something putrid, "And even rape fantasies."

Kersey walked purposefully to the jury rail. He leaned in and said with solemnity. "There is one final fact that everyone in this courtroom knows. This fine young man," he said, pointing dramatically at Chad, "should not have been subjected to the scurrilous accusations of this ..." His large hand rose like a stop sign as he shook his silvery mane with heartbroken disappointment. Then his voice softened, and the words came out like a benediction. "This tragically mistaken young woman."

Chad walked out of the courthouse into bright lights and huddled masses. There were enough microphones poking at him to make him feel like he was being attacked by a porcupine. After his Oscar-winning performance during the trial, this part would be a layup.

"I don't know why she did this to me," Chad told an attractive CBS reporter. The injured angel act played perfectly in Northern Virginia. Tears on command filled his eyes. "Thank God the jury knew the truth."

After answering many of the reporters' inane questions, Chad raised his hands. "I'm sorry. As you might imagine, this has been quite traumatic for me. I'm sure that I'll be a better interview when it hits me that this nightmare is finally over."

Chad turned and walked down the steps towards the waiting black stretch limo. His father couldn't be bothered to show up during the trial, but Chad knew he would show up today for his share of the limelight. He smiled. If the verdict weren't enough to send dumb-ass Megan over the edge, his injured puppy-dog puss on every TV station would definitely be the final nail in her coffin. What the hell was she thinking?

Chad reached for the car door. He knew that his father's driver got out of the car and opened the door only for his father or his father's clients. At first he felt, rather than saw, eyes staring holes through him. He looked over, and there was that hot reporter from Fox staring at him and shaking her head. Another Fox reporter had been in the gaggle that had shoved mikes into his face, but that one had been a guy. Little Miss Jackie Jerkoff was too big time to interview him. Besides, she'd been railing all along about how she thought he was guilty.

Now she just stood there staring at him. A quick glance assured him that the media's focus was now on Kersey. Chad's eyes swept back to Jackie. He mouthed "Blow me," winked, and got into the car.

CHAPTER 8

"MAC, THERE'S A MR. ALBERT Lahr on line two. He read about you in *Barron's*."

These were the phone calls Mac's team loved to get. He grabbed his phone. "Mac McGregor."

"Yes, Mr. McGregor. So good of you to take my call."

The heavy British accent made Mac smile. He glanced at the caller ID and saw that the caller's number was blocked. "Of course, Mr. Lahr. How can I help you?"

"Well, you have had some bloody nice things written about you, and I wondered if you would consider helping me with my money."

Although the top management of Johnston Wellons had designated Mac's team as the High Net Worth Group, Mac had purposely never established a minimum account size. He felt that the quality and expertise of his partners and associates gave him the flexibility to have any client work with the most appropriate advisor. Plus, that sort of exclusivity felt pretentious to him.

Still, the odds were that if a caller had researched him, that person would be aware that he worked primarily with affluent clients. After 33 years in the business, Mac felt that his instincts about whether a person sounds wealthy were pretty well honed. He considered that he might be seduced by the accent, but this felt like the mother lode. On the other hand, a successful relationship between advisor and client is not guaranteed simply because of a large portfolio.

"Can you tell me something about yourself, Mr. Lahr?" Mac asked. "We want to find out how we might best be able to help you."

"Oh no!" the caller responded teasingly. "It sounds like you must determine if I am worthy to become an account. And please call me Albert."

Mac laughed politely. "Actually, the worst sin would be for you to be disappointed in us. I am not concerned about your financial eligibility, but I do want to make sure that we're a good fit for you."

His new best friend, Albert, squealed out a high-pitched laugh. "Nice escape, Mac. I think that it may be fun, as well as profitable, to work with you."

"I can only guarantee the fun part."

"Fair enough," Lahr guffawed. "I have an upcoming meeting, so I will have to jump. What time on Monday can we have a chat?"

Mac checked his computer. "I'm free from 10:00 till 11:30. Would that work?"

"I will call your office at precisely ten o'clock," Lahr responded. "And I will probably start with one hundred."

Mac paused, not sure what to say. He had assumed the prospect would want to sit down with him.

"Is that satisfactory?" Lahr asked.

"Albert, our methodology works best when we're able to get a relatively comprehensive look at your situation. Is there a time when we might be able to sit down and roll up our sleeves for a bit?"

"Hmm," Lahr answered, and Mac could imagine the wheels turning. After a moment Lahr continued. "I'm always so tightly scheduled. If I said that I would come to see you, I would have to cancel numerous times, and your affection for me might diminish."

Mac rubbed his forehead. Charming had been replaced by frustrating. If an individual wants to invest a lump sum, but is reluctant to disclose his or her net worth, objectives, or fears, it dramatically decreases the advisor's ability to add value. In addition, when someone wants to invest only one hundred thousand dollars, it limits the opportunity for diversification. Mac was about to suggest that Lahr would be better served with another advisor.

"Even though you are adorned with the highest credentials," Lahr said reassuringly, "I am not giving you all of my liquid assets. However, I do reserve the right to send additional funds. Would one hundred million be a respectable start?"

Mac's pulse quickened. He had to work to control his breathing. "Of course," he said with forced casualness. "We're flattered, and we'll do a good job for you."

"Splendid! I won't micromanage you, and we will make a lot of money," Lahr said excitedly.

Mac ruminated for a moment. If he insisted on a full financial exam, the prospect might be insulted. He decided to approach the situation as if he were managing a mutual fund for the man. In that case, only eligibility and legitimacy would be required.

"If you're comfortable with a hundred percent equity allocation." Mac said, "our normal portfolio consists primarily of large cap, dividend-paying stocks. We add to that companies where we personally know management."

"No inside information, I would hope. We British always play by the rules."

Mac laughed. "So do we. sir. I promise."

"I will leave everything to you, but I would prefer to be your most aggressive investor. So if you want to add leveraged derivatives, IPOs, ETFs – in fact, anything speculative, as long as it's liquid."

"We can do that for you," Mac cautioned, "but it *really* steps up the risk."

"Not to worry," Lahr interrupted. "I may have many failings, but I do not lack courage."

Mac exhaled. The more aggressive the strategy, the more cover-your-behind paperwork was required. "Do you have time now for my associate to get the new account information from you?"

"Not at the moment, dear boy, but I promise that I will call back by tomorrow at the latest. To whom shall I give the information?"

"Ask for Wade Larson. He heads the operations for our group. Would you like me to send you his contact information, along with mine?"

"Why Mac McGregor, you are considered a financial wizard. I know everything about you. That is why I am trusting this money to you."

There was a teasing, challenging familiarity that felt a bit off, but the last time Mac's group had had a call-in who offered to have them manage 100 million was *never*, so eccentricity was definitely overlooked.

"OK," Mac said with a forced short laugh. "If you call my number and ask for Wade, he will help you."

"Splendid. Ta ta," Lahr said and disconnected.

"Ta ta?" Mac thought. *"That's too flighty even for a rich Brit."*

Mac stared absently at his computer screen, looked to his left at CNBC, and noted that the markets would close in twenty minutes and that the high-frequency traders were accelerating downside momentum into the close. He leaned back in his chair. *Was it that long ago when just people traded stocks and the stock market rose or dropped because of value or news events?*

Mac blinked back to reality. Reminiscing doesn't pay the bills. He looked back at his computer screen and answered a few e-mails. Then he wrote an e-mail to the group, asking everyone to gather at his desk at 4:10 for a quick meeting.

There were no business secrets in Mac's lovably dysfunctional group of fifteen—open architecture, open communication, free exchange of ideas. Mac's mantra was that he ran a benign dictatorship, but in reality he had very bright, caring people, and there was no monopoly on good ideas.

"I've just had an unusual call," Mac began.

"The President wants advice on how to fix the economy," R.J. stated sagaciously.

"No. Grace called and wants you to fix the plumbing," quipped Lena Brady.

"You're both wrong," offered Danny DeMarco helpfully. "Grace did call, but she wants you to hurry home so you can play hide the salami."

That broke everyone up.

Trying to regain a semblance of seriousness, Mac said, "If any of you ladies would like to file against Danny, I will be a witness."

"Yeah, Danny Demento," said Lena, turning to him. "He said unusual, not unimaginable. Get with the program."

It started again, and Mac held up his hands. As he described the call, collective eyes widened. "I don't know if the guy is legit. He sounded strange, but substantive." Turning to one of his key associates, he said, "Annie, Google Albert Lahr and see if you can find out who he is. He sounded British. Try all reasonable spellings."

Mac's eyes scanned the faces of his second family. There were no disinterested parties working with him. Each face reflected the excitement of landing a big account. "If this pans out, I may have to buy a *Barron's* subscription for anyone in the group who doesn't have one. Class dismissed, although some of you should have to stay after school for insubordination."

"I will! I will!" said Danny, running over to climb onto Mac's lap.

CHAPTER 9

WITH LESS THAN A WEEK left of Daylight Savings Time, Grace McGregor expertly navigated around the crater-sized potholes that littered the makeshift road to Pennyfield Lock on the C & O Canal. Her husband had his head back against the headrest of their five-year-old white Toyota minivan; his eyes were closed. She looked over at him with patience and understanding, yet she was tempted to zerbert his exposed neck.

Grace was glad that she could almost always drag Mac on an evening walk, regardless of the stress of his day. She also appreciated the fact that nature was allowing them to grow old together. If her mom was any indication, she would not have to worry about coloring her brown hair, and she thought it unlikely that her blue eyes, which Mac claimed she had used to snare him, would ever fade.

Mac was finally showing a faint hint of graying temples, and his current self-assessment included admitting that he was also slightly tonsorially challenged. He had mentioned to Grace, as well as to R.J. and Artie, that if it would not be disrespectful, he would be the only Christian wearing a full-time yarmulke.

While Mac fought with an occasional hair landing in his bathroom sink, Grace fought with the scale. Ten unwanted and unappreciated pounds clung to her like a suction cup. Exercise generally maintained that as the high-water mark, but decreasing that frustrating number might require lowering her quite reasonable wine consumption. Obviously, that would be too radical.

Fortunately, neither Grace nor Mac considered their partner's appearance issues as possible impediments to their mutual attraction to each other. He could be bald, she could expand like a balloon, and they would still think each other sexy.

Mac did not bring business home. However, a wife of over 30 years notices a bulging vein in the neck, a slight abruptness in speech, or a forced smile. "Are we gonna walk that market's ass off?" she asked as she pulled straight into a parking space.

He smiled, head still back, eyes still closed, as she opened her car door. "I would hate to be that towpath," he said, revving up. "I'm gonna punish that bitch." Mac opened the passenger door, unfastened his seatbelt, and jumped out of the car.

"Remember," Grace admonished, "my legs are shorter than yours, and it's your job to match my stride, not the other way around."

"Regulators still aren't regulating, Greece can't get out of its own way, the market was down a friendly 300, it's every man for himself!" Mac ran backwards for a moment and then spun around. "Catch me if you can!" He headed towards the towpath, lurching left and then right in grotesque parody, as if he were eluding tacklers on a football field. Small stones crunched under his Nike Free black athletic shoes in spastic cadence.

After crossing a small wooden bridge, Mac began jogging in place in front of a white stone house. The house, built in 1832, had recently been renovated and was available for rent by those venturesome enough to spend the night. Even though neither McGregor had the urge to give a house that looked like it was covered with designer mold a go, they did appreciate its quaintness and its history.

Mac and Grace had gone inside the house shortly after the renovation was completed. Grace only made it to the first floor, claustrophobia preventing a climb up the narrow wooden stairs to the second level. Not that they needed further convincing, but that confirmed the decision that the couple would not be lock keepers for a night.

Particularly in the hours just before darkness, the C & O Canal was an oasis of serenity, a gentle embrace from nature. On weekends, or during prime usage time, the hikers' tranquility was often interrupted by, "On your left!" as bikers whizzed by. But tonight the canal belonged to the McGregors.

Vertical cliffs of rocks housed trees jutting out at sharp angles, almost as if they were javelined into the imposing wall of stone. On this crisp fall day, leaves of burnt red and pale gold waved greetings to any remaining hikers determined to breathe in the last gasps of beauty before nightfall.

Grace shook her head as she stared at her husband. The fact that he looked utterly ridiculous would not only not bother him, but he would feed on it. He was now running in place, knees pumping high in the air, arms moving like pistons, head turning from side to side. There was a big grin on his stupid face. She was used to his shenanigans, but what continued to amaze her was that if someone approached him, he would just take the goofiness up a notch.

"If you pass out, don't count on me for mouth to mouth."

"That's cold, woman," Mac said as he stopped, put his hands on his knees, and panted like a dog. He lifted his head and grinned. "Ready to go back?"

Grace gave him an eye roll and walked past him, heading on down the path. "Follow me, but stay a step behind. I don't want anyone to think that I know you."

As usual, he listened poorly, and they began their walk in earnest. Although their usual strategy was to walk fast enough to get their hearts pumping, but still be able to converse, the beauty of the evening required silence. The friendly, cushiony consistency of the towpath made walking a pleasure rather than a chore. Only the threat of darkness deterred a more lengthy sojourn.

As Mac and Grace continued along the towpath, they searched for fat turtles absorbing the sun's last stand while they lay on the rocks or the banks of the canal. To their right, the squirrels scampering through the phalanx of trees reminded the McGregors that they were the guests here. Then the prize: a great blue heron perched at the water's edge turned its head slowly, as if to acknowledge and accept their presence.

They stopped for a brief moment and marveled as the sun seemed to highlight the shallow canal waters, turning them into a glorious mirror. Then they turned to head back. At this point, the trees on the side of the canal that borders the Potomac River thinned, presenting a magnificent view of the seemingly calm, but notoriously dangerous, churning water.

Grace spoke first. "It's not just the markets that are bothering you, Mac. After 2008, this is just a blip to you."

Mac blinked, startled for probably the hundredth time that she could read him so well. He turned his head towards her. "You think you know me, huh?"

The question was rhetorical to her, so she just looked at him.

Mac looked straight ahead. "You know that feeling when you suspect something, but you also know that what you're imagining is ridiculous?"

He turned his head slightly to see her reaction. She nodded, understanding. "So logically," he said, gesturing with his hands while he walked faster, "you have an absurd idea, but you can't get it out of your head?"

This time Grace gave him a sympathetic smile of agreement while she struggled to keep up.

"A prospect called," Mac began. "He said that he read about me in *Barron's*. Nothing too unusual so far."

He sounded like he was trying to convince himself, but Grace said nothing.

"He either doesn't want to come see us, or he's too busy to come see us."

"Don't you have other clients who live out of town or out of the country that you work with but have never seen?"

"None who give me a hundred million dollars and tell me to have at it." Mac shook his head. "Nothing shows up on Google or LinkedIn. I know nothing about him. I ask him what his objective is, and he says it's to make money, and he is convinced that I know how to do that."

They were silent for a good minute. Then Grace offered, "Aren't some people adamant about their privacy?"

Mac blew out a breath. "Yeah, I guess. I hadn't considered that. The paperwork is all signed, the Compliance Department doesn't seem to have an issue, and the money's good."

"So what's your concern?" she asked.

He looked over at her again. "I told him that I would charge him fifty basis points." She wrinkled her nose in confusion. "Charge him one half of one percent annually to manage his money." Mac raised his voice. "He says, in his thick British accent, that a fee of one percent would be more equitable!"

Grace waited a few moments before responding. "Maybe *he* thinks you're worth more than *you* think you are."

Almost as if he were talking to himself Mac continued. "Sure, if I had already made him money or done something brilliant, he could say I deserve more. It would be a first, but if you're rich enough to give that much money to a stranger to manage, I guess it doesn't make much difference."

Grace stopped like a horse that doesn't want to go over a jump and grabbed Mac's arm. "Mac McGregor, you are not a stranger to anyone! There is enough material about you on the internet for someone to write an unauthorized biography."

Mac smiled and took her in his arms. She was so cute when she was protecting him. He felt lucky that it was not just the kids that she would kill for. "If you put in some stuff from your diary, my biography might be juicy," he teased.

"Sorry," Grace responded. "You may be well known, but you are waaaay too boring for me to have a diary."

"Damn, woman, you are a freak of nature. The farther we walk, the colder you get!"

They were almost back to the white stone house, and Mac felt that his time on this conversation was about up. Still, he wanted to put a period on it. He stopped, faced her, and placed both hands on her shoulders. "Here's the real crazy thing, babe," he said softly as he looked into her eyes. "When he told me to raise his fee, it felt like he was laughing at me."

CHAPTER 10

THE RESTON TOWN CENTER, AT less than 100 years old, is a relatively new addition to the Northern Virginia landscape. On the southwest corner of the Town Center, near the Hyatt Hotel, is an extremely popular restaurant/bar called Jackson's, which bills itself as "Mighty Fine Food & Lucky Lounge."

The Lucky Lounge is actually two bars. In the summer, one opens through three garage doors out to Library Street and is known as the garage bar. The décor of this warm weather bar, like the rest of the restaurant, is 1940's art deco, with red frosted globes around lights suspended from the ceiling and chrome-framed bar stools. Although Chad Alexander, III was not particularly pleased that the stools were without backs, they were large, round seats, and they were covered in naugahyde of a color that was just a shade away from fire hydrant red, almost like a warning sign.

The second bar, which is about the same size, is just inside the revolving door that opens to Democracy Drive. Straight into the restaurant, about 20 feet from the door, is the hostess stand and a generous foyer for waiting crowds. Mosaic tiles inset into the marble floor spell out "Jackson's" in contrasting colors. The interior is quite similar to the garage bar, except there are ledges fronted by stools along the walls to the left and right of the large oval-shaped bar.

Because the ledges are a good four feet from the bar stools, Chad considered that area as a grandstand, where his legion of admirers could wait for a possible audience with him. With all of the working stiffs in suits crowded into the bar and the dining room booths, the atmosphere was consistently noisy, just the way Chad liked it. If he motioned a woman to come over, he did not want what he said to be overheard.

Chad's favorite bar stool should have had his name engraved on it. Instead, no matter how crowded the place was, whenever he entered, there was a "Reserved" card on the stool waiting for him. In Chad's mind, trust-fund babies, particularly only sons, had to be big tippers. Wouldn't want to cheap out on the old man. On numerous occasions, the bouncers had been called to ensure that the seat was ready for their best customer.

For the third time in as many nights, the petite, pigtailed blonde with the halter top barely harnessing two perfectly sculpted breasts sidled up to Chad and rubbed them against his arm. Twice before he had not acknowledged her, not spoken to her, and just shook his head dismissively when she came on to him. However, at the moment he was bored.

Chad looked at the woman appraisingly. No other man in the bar would turn this shit down. Each night her shorts had ridden progressively higher on her well-formed butt cheeks. *Tight body, no fat, hungry dark eyes, face probably an 8*, he mused, *to go along with a 9 body.* "What's your name again, bitch?" he whispered seductively.

Her eyes fluttered, her face reddened, and she licked swollen lips. "Felicity," she whispered back in a parodied attempt at sexuality, "and I want you."

Chad moved his head back and stared at her as if he were considering the offer. He could smell the nervous sweat coming off her body. After a few moments of silence, he leaned forward. "Here's the deal. One time offer. You know my wingman, Matt, who joins me every night at nine?"

Felicity's head bobbed up and down like she was auditioning for a porn movie.

Matt had been Chad's friend since grade school. A curious contrast to Chad, he was 5'6", ambitious, driven, and the original Boy Scout. To him, Chad Alexander walked on water. His reaction to Chad's indictment on rape charges was to burst into tears. Whatever Chad told him, he believed.

"Give my little pony a ride around the ring, and then maybe you'll get a shot at the thoroughbred." To emphasize, Chad moved slightly on his stool so that his crotch rubbed her arm.

Felicity blinked rapidly, gave him a disbelieving look, saw the certainty in his eyes, and recovered quickly. "Uh, okay," she stuttered, looking desperately at him for approval.

"That's a good girl," he said, leaning over to whisper in her ear and simultaneously rubbing his thumb over a nipple. "You go on now, so it doesn't look obvious."

Felicity gave him the smile that an abused child, begging for love, gives a parent. Then she walked away.

Due to the barrage of media attention. Chad Alexander, III was the most requested item on the menu at Jackson's. Half the women wanted to jump his bones, because they had always known he was innocent. The other half wanted to try him on so they could brag to their friends. Chad wasn't particular. Either way worked for him, and if you brought a girlfriend, you moved to the head of the line. No ugly bitches need apply.

As Chad signaled the bartender for another drink, a woman walked into the bar—rather, glided into the bar—and sat at the far end. As she moved past him, Chad felt her presence even before he saw her.

His first thought was that she was African royalty. Her long black hair, tied back, shone in the lights. From behind, her body was perfect; he could rest a beer can on that ass. She walked by too quickly for him to get a serious look, and she was angled so that all he could see was a high mocha cheekbone.

He waited about ten minutes and then motioned for the bartender to take her another drink. The bartender complied, and when she looked at him curiously, he pointed back at Chad. She turned and looked at him, and she was so gorgeous that Chad almost fell off the stool. She held the glass of white wine up as a salute, then shook her head from side to side. She handed the glass back to the bartender and turned her back to Chad.

Chad was pissed, but he didn't push it. She finished her wine and left through another exit, thereby totally avoiding him. He was fuming, and for the first night in two weeks, he went home alone. Consolation sex just didn't cut it.

The next day Matt called Chad at 12:01. The rule was never before noon. Words spilled out excitedly as he told Chad about the amazing girl he had met.

After about a minute of Matt's unrestrained excitement, Chad lost interest and interrupted. "You're welcome, dude."

"Huh?"

"Who do you think set this shit up, Mattie Boy?"

"No! No! You're playing me, man. She liked me. I could tell."

A long sigh. "Felicity? Right?" Chad was getting annoyed. "You were a means to an end."

If Chad were capable of empathy, he would have felt Matt's silent pain over the phone. When he heard nothing, he added, "Dude, when someone sends you a present, a thank you is in order."

"Thank you, Chad," came the wooden response. "I, I have to get back to work."

As he hung up the phone, Chad shook his head. The poor schlep worked two jobs to put himself through Georgetown Law. Being poor was a sin.

CHAPTER 11

TONIGHT THE BLACK GODDESS WAS back again, same seat, still ignoring him. Just like last night, she was alone, talked to no one, drank her wine, and looked straight ahead. The bartender stood in front of her and chatted her up for a minute. She smiled, and the man actually swayed as if she had emitted a force that made his legs weaken.

Chad crooked a finger, and the bartender rushed over to him. The man nodded vigorously as Chad gave him instructions. He walked away, then returned to her with a bottle of Dom Perignon and uncorked it. He poured it out, and Chad saw her ask him something. He nodded.

She picked up the glass, held it out in front of her, and walked toward Chad. He smiled and stepped down from the bar stool. A hot-pink silk blouse with two buttons undone barely contained her creamy smooth breasts.

That was as far as he got, because she walked right by him. Chad turned his head in confusion. Two heavyset girls were sitting at a small table. The goddess handed the less attractive one the champagne, pointed to Chad with a smile, and walked back to her seat.

Every instinct cried out for him to grab her right there in the bar, slam her to the floor, and butt-fuck her into a coma. Instead, he gulped breaths, steadied himself, and pasted on a phony smile that said, "We're just playing a game."

It seemed like hours, but was probably only thirty minutes, until she left the bar. He followed her.

"Hey!"

She whirled and glared at him. Chad raised his hands, trying to placate her. "I'm harmless. I was just trying to buy you a drink. Can't we talk?"

"Listen, 'Harmless,' I'm not interested."

"Do you go the other way?"

"That would work well for your ego. No. But I don't have time to play with boys."

"Boys? Do you see any boys here?"

She rolled her almond-shaped eyes and turned to walk away.

"Come on," he said in a pleading voice as he grabbed her shoulder.

She spun around so quickly that he stepped back, almost falling. Her right hand held a can of pepper spray six inches from his face.

"Whoa, whoa!" he said, backing up more. "No need to go there!"

She shook her head and turned away slowly.

"What can I do to just get you to talk to me?"

She turned back to him. After what seemed like an eternity, she said, "Be guilty."

"What? What did you say?"

She leaned toward him, and her scent was intoxicating. "You were either wrongly accused, or you're an extraordinary actor. In the first case, you're boring. In the second case," she paused and studied him, "you might be interesting."

"What do you want me to say?" he whispered frantically.

She looked at him for a long time, then cocked her head to one side and gave a slight shrug. She sighed. "Get in your car. Follow me. It's probably a mistake. I think you're a child."

Chad couldn't help watching her as she walked away. He pumped his right arm. "Game fucking on," he whispered to her wake.

Chad hopped into his black Mercedes convertible, which he had parked in a handicapped space. He figured that he'd be able to sniff her exhaust, no matter which car was hers or wherever the hell she was leading him. When she jumped into a fire-red Ferrari that he'd eyeballed earlier, he about shit in his pants.

Her car shot away from the curb. She punched it and never looked back. Chad was used to driving fast, but this bitch was insane, taking corners like she was running from the devil.

Screeching to a stop in front of the Ritz Carlton in Tyson Corner, Chad jumped out of his car almost before it stopped. She was going towards the door of the hotel. The valet looked at him curiously.

"Hey, Ms. Andretti!" Chad called after her. "I need to know the room!"

She looked back at him, debated again, then said, "Fairfax Suite," turned and went through the door.

Chad smiled at the valet, who was looking at him wide eyed. He handed the kid twenty bucks and asked where he could get some condoms. Then he leaned in close to the valet and said, "Can you believe a broad this gorgeous picked me up in a bar, told me to follow her, and she's staying in this place?"

The valet shook his head.

"She promised to teach me shit I haven't even dreamed about." He gave the kid an exaggerated wild-eyed look of terror. "She scares the hell out of me. Any way you could sub for me?"

The valet emptied his pockets like he was getting robbed, held out a fist full of cash, and said, "And I'll write you a check, too."

CHAPTER 12

"MAC, A JIM MADISON IS on the phone for you."

Mac McGregor was studying his computer from a semisupine position, and the name did not ring a bell. He preferred to take all calls personally; but the industry was rife with unfamiliar wholesalers and head hunters, so at least a modicum of scrutiny was required. "Please ask him if he was referred to us."

A few moments passed before his assistant spoke again: "He said he's a close friend of Rod Stanton." Rod was Mac's friend and his largest client.

Mac reached forward to grab the receiver: "Mac McGregor."

"Did you miss me?"

Mac sat up so quickly in his black ErgoFlex ergonomic mesh office chair that he almost toppled forward. He closed his eyes and listened, his imagination running wild.

"Cat got your tongue, old fella? I thought you brokers were never at a loss for words."

Heartbeat accelerating, blood pressure rising, beads of sweat popped out on Mac's forehead. He forced himself to take deep breaths. Dear God, it was not his imagination; that level of arrogance was as exact as a DNA sample. He hit the **Mute** button and motioned for R. J. to pick up on his line. Almost immediately, the caller responded, "Ah, Mr. Brooks, so nice to have you on our party line."

Through the glass that separated their offices, Mac saw R. J. raise both his hands in bafflement and mouth "WTF" at the caller.

"Mr. Brooks, I hear that you're quite bright. Perhaps you were also helpful in tracking down that evil hedge-fund manager."

R. J. looked at Mac for guidance, but Mac shook his head slowly from side to side as if his head weighed too much to warrant significant movement.

"Well," the aristocratic voice said, displaying a tinge of frustration, "I would hope that you can be more loquacious than my old friend, Mac. Although he does like to be the center of attention, so you may be just a silent partner."

Mac shook his head and looked at R.J., whose eyes had widened in alarm. He quickly typed an e-mail: "Get off the phone, call Joe, and tell him that Lyons is on the phone now!" He hit **Send**. R.J. gave him a momentary questioning look, and Mac shot him a "do it," look that brooked no argument.

"Even though I do enjoy not only the sound, but also the intellectual content of my own voice, it would be polite to respond."

The last phrase had the unmistakable tone of a threat. "What do you want?" Mac asked evenly.

"There is life!" Jeremy Lyons responded gaily. "I would like to have a word. Oh, and by the way, your friend, Agent Joe Sebastiano, will not have time to trace this call, because I don't have time to dawdle. But perhaps Compliance will let you set up something for our future chats. As you might guess, neither the FBI, the CIA, nor any of the other initials have a snowball's chance in hell of locating me. However, they certainly have my permission to call upon Big Brother and give it the old college try."

"Need I repeat my question?"

Jeremy laughed. "See! I like that! You have spunk! For some strange reason, you have acted like you're afraid of me. Yet when I call, your blood pressure doesn't rise, your heart doesn't beat out of your chest. No. You just ask me what I want."

Mac felt like there was a fire raging out of control in his belly. He bit hard on the inside of his lip. "If you're not gonna tell me what the hell you want, I'm gonna go back to work."

"Really?" came the menacing reply. Jeremy paused for effect. "Then perhaps I'll need to make a house call."

"*Fuck you, asshole,*" Mac's mind screamed. Biting back a reply, he forced himself to wait and draw out the silence.

Jeremy continued as if he had not expected a response. "Life is all about choices, although only the truly gifted make the right choices all the time. But you'll make the right one this time. What is the best day of the week for our weekly conference call?"

"Our weekly conference call?" Mac felt like his head was spinning. He was in an alternate universe.

"If you're just going to repeat what I say, we won't get anywhere. Okay, I choose. Wednesday. Every Wednesday I will call at exactly four o'clock. Keep your calendar free. And, Mac, old boy, try to be a little more responsive next time."

Jeremy disconnected. Mac continued to hold the phone limply in his hand. Finally, the sound of the phone off the hook roused him from his stupor. He threw the phone on his desk, got up from his chair, ignored the questioning looks, and went into the men's room.

In the men's room Mac slowly undid the top button of his white dress shirt, loosened his tie, and rolled up his sleeves. For probably 30 seconds he splashed cool water on his face. Then he moved with his eyes half closed to the automatic paper towel dispenser. He ran his hands across the front two or three times until the machine spit out the towels. He patted his face, threw the towels in the basket, and walked into the farthest stall from the door. Still fully clothed, he sat on the toilet seat, placed his elbows on his knees, cradled his forehead, and tried with all his might to hold back the tears.

CHAPTER 13

IF THE FBI HAD A mafia, Special Agent Joseph Francis Sebastiano would be the don. As he liked to say, he was born into the business. An interesting comment, since the males in his family had been either construction workers or construction workers. All it took was one summer of laying bricks for Joe to decide that he'd rather lay down the law. A born-again agent might have been a more accurate description.

In the movies, Joe would not have been able to play himself, because the typecasting would have been too perfect. In serious moments, his stone-faced look of intimidation demanded respect. At other times, his flamboyant gestures, dark olive skin that molded into expressive faces like his skin was Silly Putty, and a Bronx accent that went from thick to incomprehensible gave an entirely different picture.

Joe had been Mac's client for twenty years. The man's competence and professionalism were evident in his demeanor. But his ebullience, and particularly his perverse sense of humor, guaranteed that he'd become one of Mac's closest friends.

"Mount Gay rum, caffeine-free Diet Coke, a couple of limes in a tall glass."

Joe looked at the waiter, raised a skeptical eyebrow, and said, "Miller Lite, please." He turned to Mac. "I'm not sure that I'm endowed with enough testosterone to order your drink."

Uncharacteristically, Mac shrugged and did not respond. The fact that he passed up a whole host of easy retorts told Joe that this was not a social get-together.

Mac had chosen the familiar confines of what used to be the Men's Grill at Congressional Country Club before political correctness forced the conversion to the Senate Pub. The more popular alternative for social or serious drinking was the club's newly constructed Founders Pub, with its rich dark woods, abundance of natural light, and magnificent views of the fairways of the fabled golf course.

It wasn't just that his friend was a creature of habit, which he was. Joe knew that Mac met potential clients in the Founders Pub for breakfast. The psychology of walking into the pub and being surrounded by photos of Congressional's first five honorary presidents, Taft, Wilson, Harding, Coolidge ,and Hoover, on one side and industry titans Henry Ford, Walter Chrysler, William Randolph Hearst, and John D. Rockefeller on the other side reminded a visitor of how close this club has always been to the nexus of American power. Mac and Joe were meeting in the Senate Pub because Mac was really troubled about something, and he did not want to be disturbed.

"Jeremy Lyons called *you?* Not the 800 number? On your personal line?"

"Yep."

"What the hell did he want?" Joe's voice was hard.

"To set up a weekly conference call, a fireside chat with me."

"Okay. I've gotta get a handle on this. He didn't outline his agenda?"

"No."

"Just conversation?"

"Yes."

"Did he threaten you?"

Mac paused. "He threatened to make a house call if I didn't respond to his ramblings."

Joe was silent for a moment. "Did the threat sound serious?"

"Serious enough to get me to capitulate."

"Other than the threat, how did he sound?"

"Like Josh Groban singing 'You Raise Me Up.' Joe, nothing changes with him. He is the same cocky, arrogant, officious bastard that he was over twenty years ago when I met him."

In a voice coated with remorse, Joe said, "Mac, I'm so sorry that I let him get away. I really thought that after all this time he would leave you alone."

"I know. But we've agreed not to waste time trying to create a more perfect past."

"We need to re-engage the security for you."

"Nope. I'll handle it."

"Sure you will. You're the Chuck Norris of the financial world. You'll portfolio-manage him into submission."

Mac nodded his head approvingly. "I like that. You're cute when you get testy."

"I'm serious, damn it."

"Of course you are." Mac leaned across the table. "So am I. I may be forced to talk to this asshole, but I'm not gonna live in fear, looking over my shoulder anymore. I'll bounce any strategy off of you, because you're my friend, a trained operative, and smart as hell. He said that his calls can't be traced. Is that true?"

Joe leaned back, winced, and massaged his fingers across his brow. "I'll double-check, but I believe he's right. If he uses Skype or a similar program to link to his final destination using multiple private communication nodes, he should be untraceable. I'll e-mail you the more scientific explanation."

Mac blinked. "I'm impressed. How does an Eye-talian know this technical stuff?"

It was the first sign of the old Mac, and Joe smiled. "R.J. taught me."

Joe finished his beer and declined another. Both men seemed to be contemplating the next step as Mac signed the check. He crunched the dregs of ice with his teeth, a habit that had been the only serious issue in his 32-year marriage. "It's a chess match, Joe. If I could take my family out of the equation, I'd love to engage."

CHAPTER 14

CHAD ALEXANDER KNOCKED ON THE door of the Fairfax Suite and stood there with his best smile. Not a sound from inside. He knocked again. If this bitch was playing him, and some old broad opened the door ...

The door opened, but the security chain remained on. She peered out the door with a bored look. "Break the chain."

He gave her a puzzled look, then stepped back, ready to slam his shoulder into the door.

Before he moved, she unlocked the chain. "I wanted to test your level of commitment," she said, walking away from him.

He moved toward her.

"Stay!" she commanded, holding up her hand. "Sit on the couch and wait for me. Remember, I call the shots. Otherwise, there will be unpleasant consequences."

"I've got it, I've got it," he said as she walked through the French doors into the bedroom. *You can call all the shots,* he thought to himself, *until you run out of bullets.*

It was only about five minutes, but it seemed longer to the man who was staring at a blank plasma TV while his dick was about to explode out of his jeans. She opened the doors, and Chad's jaw dropped to his chest.

When she walked into the room, it was almost as if she floated. Her beauty was both unnatural and breathtaking. Her black lace teddy was tied loosely across her swelling breasts and then crisscrossed to end up hanging loosely at her sides, just above her thighs. Even in the muted light of the room, her impossibly flat abdomen seemed to glisten. The brief, sheer panties covered her in a way that was more erotic than her nakedness would have been.

Chad was mesmerized. She needed no jewelry, no fuck-me high heels, no makeup except for the blood-red lipstick covering her full, sensuous lips.

She stood, regal and proud, and gave Chad a look of disdain. For him it was the ultimate aphrodisiac. "Do not embellish," she began. "Recite every action as best you can remember it."

He nodded, adrenaline pumping through his body.

"Come and stand in the doorway of my bedroom."

He followed her to the bedroom like a puppy looking for a chew toy.

"Stay there," she said as she stood about ten feet away, by the side of her bed. "Take off your clothes."

Chad took off his clothes and stepped toward her.

"No." She threw a Ritz Carlton bathrobe, emblazoned with its distinctive lion-headed crown emblem, on the floor in front of him. "Put this on. I will tell you when to come to me, and when I do, your penis will be engorged with blood and your body inflamed. You will make me pay for any indignity a woman has ever done to you. Remember," she admonished, "if you break my rules, you will pay."

CHAPTER 15

"SHOW ME. I WANT IT all. Not the crap in the news. Ev-er-y detail. Take me there," she whispered, "or I don't need you." Her eyes seemed to liquefy with desire.

The heat emanating from her body inflamed Chad. His breath came in short bursts as he began. "Her place," he rasped. "Asked if I wanted coffee. I shook my head no.

"'Would you like something else?' she asked.

"I nodded, my head rising slowly up and then down. She looked at me with those trusting blue eyes." His smile spread slowly in remembrance, and his face began to flush.

"Go on," she said huskily, as she gracefully reclined onto the silver satin sheets of her circular bed, her back propped against two enormous, blood-red pillows."

He stepped towards her.

"No," she hissed. "Go on."

He nodded, impatient. She wanted a show. He took a breath and leered at her. No holds barred. "'Don't worry about me,' I told her. 'I take what I want.' The simple bitch had no idea," he said, shaking his head derisively.

Getting into it, he pantomimed the gestures, adding drama and intensity. "I reached over and in one bear swipe ripped her flimsy blouse open. She screamed and backed up frantically, falling back over the couch. I was on her like a fucking panther, clamping my hand over her mouth. Her head was shaking from side to side, tears spewing from her eyes. I put my mouth next to her ear. 'One sound that is not a moan of pleasure, and I will tape your mouth shut, and I'll be so pissed that you can't suck me off that I will hurt you more than you can ever imagine.'"

Like the slow dance of a cobra, his penis swayed as the story increased in intensity. "I made her strip, slowly. Then she had to touch herself, put her fingers inside and then taste it." He leaned forward. "I rammed my cock down her throat. She gagged and tried to pull away. I grabbed her by the hair and shoved her into my crotch. I told her, 'You better make me come, bitch. You better make me come.'"

"Is that enough detail for you?" Chad asked. He threw his robe on the floor.

"Go on," she rasped, her left hand reaching down to caress her dark nipples.

Her act only inflamed Chad more. The clock was running out on the black beauty. In a raspy voice of his own, he added, "Are you ready for an instant replay?" He took three long strides and stood next to the bed. Reaching down, he grabbed his blood-filled penis. His smile turned to a snarl. "Your choice, bitch: the easy way or the hard way."

"No!" Her scream was unearthly. It was the last sound Chad Alexander, III heard before a powerful forearm across his throat rendered him unconscious.

When Chad came to, he was naked, on all fours at the foot of the bed. His mouth was taped, and an unbelievably strong arm was wrapped across his chest. The massive hand gripping his left arm was squeezing with the ferocity of a boa constrictor. Panicked, he attempted to struggle.

"No, no, no," a voice lightly scolded.

Chad's eyes rose to the voice. Sprawled at the head of the bed was an enormous, grotesque man waving a sausage-like finger at him.

"You are looking at me," the man said as if he were talking to a child, "but it is my twin brother who has you secured in the classic wrestler's position. Probably not the first time a pretty boy like you has been with twins," he added, sounding amused with himself. "So if you struggle...." The man pointed over Chad's shoulder.

Instantly and effortlessly the man holding Chad flipped him ninety degrees to the left and then back on all fours. Chad's body shook with fear. His captor was obscenely pressing his genitals against Chad's naked buttocks.

"By the way, do these really work?"

Chad's eyes returned to the man at the head of the bed. It was the first time he had really focused on the animals who held him captive. The sight was so terrifying that he thought he would vomit into the tape over his mouth. Long, stringy, filthy strands of black hair framed a mashed-in face with a nose spread over half of its surface. When the man talked, rotted yellow teeth seemed ready to fall out of his mouth. Small, piglike, noncompromising dark eyes looked at Chad with amusement. In his meaty hand the man held one of Chad's Viagra pills.

Chad turned his head from side to side as if he could shake himself awake from this horrifying nightmare.

"You like what you see, Goldilocks?" asked the man. "Hey, whaddaya think? I'm down to 360. Lookin' good, huh?" The animal motioned to his bulbous, sweaty body. He lifted a hairy, arm and sniffed his armpit, which was as greasy as an oil slick. "Whew," he said making a face. "We didn't have time to shower first."

Chad's head bobbed up and down, and his eyes frantically beseeched the man to remove the tape from his mouth so that he could talk.

"Don't worry, Goldilocks," said the man, bringing his face close to Chad's. "We're going to be taking that tape off. Why, to us," he pointed to his brother, "it's just another happy place."

The man sat back on his haunches, laughing as the sweat of fear christened Chad's body. "But I'm afraid that there's no daddy buyout today. Now," the man moved on the bed until he was whispering in Chad's ear, "do we do this the easy way or the hard way?"

In abject horror, Chad watched the monster swallow the Viagra. He heard the click of a remote and watched as the smile lengthened on his tormentor's face.

A single banjo began a familiar song. Then another banjo joined, then the banjos took turns, and the duel commenced.

CHAPTER 16

FOR ANYONE OTHER THAN JEREMY Lyons, renting Castillo del Reyes would have been a jaw-dropping experience. It is located in Siboney, which is the most prestigious neighborhood in all of Cuba. This sprawling, gated compound was built just after the turn of the 20th century by a captain of the tobacco and sugar cane industries and stands as an opulent monument, befitting both its first owner and its namesake kings. Previous guests included Yasser Arafat and Pope John Paul II. Ironically, the town of Siboney is also the town where Castro gathered his troops on a farm before he attacked the Moncada Barracks, a raid that is widely accepted as the opening salvo of the Cuban Revolution.

Two years earlier Jeremy had commissioned his associate, Max Parnavich, to rent the nicest, most secure mansion in Cuba. He overpaid the requested rental by 50% and got permission to construct, at his expense, a gym and workout space on the property. In addition, he left a security deposit that could be kept if the owners later wanted to reconfigure the mansion. Although the probability of Jeremy's ever staying there had not been high, the Cuban hideaway had been his storm shelter.

Compared to the amenities, convenience, and security of his Naples, Florida, compound, an upgrade would have been difficult, if not impossible. A contingency plan was a necessity, but by its very nature, it was less than optimum.

Jeremy knew that for him, success was always inevitable. Yet he tried to anticipate adverse outcomes, because he believed that without pre-emptive precaution, man was an untethered kite.

The extremely high ceilings of Castillo del Reyes, the communication system, and the security features were all acceptable to Jeremy, as was the fact that there was direct access to the ocean via his private cove, complete with yacht. He often ventured out on the yacht with the extraordinary Sabine to clear his mind and mentally test his strategy.

The master bedroom was serviceable, and the bathrooms had all been upgraded, but he had been through three chefs, and the cuisine was still not up to his standards. From a decorating perspective, the mansion was entirely too formal, certainly more appealing to heads of state and older guests. The notable exceptions were the patios highlighted by hand-painted, gold leaf drop ceilings that had been created by true craftsmen from an earlier era.

Jeremy sighed. Still, in his limited excursions outside of his temporary abode, he had yet to see a comparable property. There was beauty in the turquoise waters and silky white sand, but the self-described "heaven in Havana" fell short of his expectations and his stature. In English the name translated to Castle of Kings, but it took more than a name to impress King Jeremy.

As much as Jeremy loved old movies—the acting, the plot, the sheer artistry of the times—a movie was still a fantasy. He preferred to create, to be immersed in his own fantasies, to develop, direct, and marinate in them. That choice was far preferable to being a spectator or a voyeur.

When Max Parnavich served as his instrument of coercion, Jeremy would watch the recorded results of his missions in solitude. It was not until Sabine replaced the sadly departed Max that Jeremy welcomed a viewing partner.

"Prior to this classic," Jeremy said drolly, "I was not aware that I had a limit." He shifted, savoring the feel of the soft black leather recliner on his naked body. "At what point does the artistry of the staging, the cleverness of the dialog, and the graphics of the cinematography cross the line into revulsion?"

Resting between his spread legs, Sabine's lush body in repose seemed to glow in the ambient light of the TV screen. "Does this mean that my work will not become one of our favorites?" she asked teasingly. A kindred spirit to Jeremy, she relished their private time.

"If judged solely on its merits—timing, execution, and the theme of the punishment fitting the crime—it would indeed rank near the top, my dear."

"Thank you," she responded, modestly bowing her head.

"And the carnal joy expressed by the largest two participants is intellectually interesting. But if one is not wired that way," he paused, "then other forms of torture hold more allure."

Sabine smiled, aware how her lover was wired. She turned her head and kissed his inner thigh. "I will accept that Wrestlemania pushes your visual boundaries. Just as long as you continue to have no limits with me."

CHAPTER 17

JACKIE MAYFIELD COULD BARELY STAY still in her chair. She had checked herself in the mirror so many times that she almost expected to hear, "Yes, you are the fairest of them all. Now leave me the hell alone."

She knew that it wasn't just her conservative leanings that had gotten her the coveted anchor spot on Fox News. How many ugly women do you see as anchors? Still, some angel had dropped this story in her lap. It was an exclusive, and it was orgasm worthy.

Jackie was a strong advocate of women's rights, and she had watched every minute of poor Megan O'Brien's witch trial. She could smell phony bullshit a mile away, and Chad Alexander was as guilty as O.J. During the trial, Jackie had called on all her sources to try to find some evidence exposing the scumbag, but she had come up empty.

She had picked up the phone three times to call Megan, but her reporter's instincts, ingrained and nonnegotiable, forced her to lower the phone each time. No matter how improbable, a premature leak would be disastrous. She sighed. *Oh, well,* she thought, *waiting another fifteen minutes is not the end of the world.*

Pills measured the length of her existence. What a profound thought. Megan O'Brien would not have considered herself capable of profound thought after three glasses of Yellow Bird Chardonnay. She reflected, *Yellow Bird: how symbolic, a coward's way out.*

As much as possible in matters of this sort, everything was taken care of. "Oops," she giggled audibly. *Can't end a sentence with a preposition, even if it's only in your mind.* The sound of her giggle was unrecognizable, as though it came from a stranger. Less than an hour ago, she had finally extricated herself from her father's home. After her mom died, her dad was close to being walking comatose. He lost all confidence in himself and in how to be with Megan. She knew that she reminded him of Mom, and that just made the situation worse.

"Dad, I'm all right. I'm fine. O'Briens bounce back. No, I'm not gonna move, I'm not gonna hide. Then he will win." Who was she kidding? He already had won. Finally, she had convinced the parental parole board of one that she would be better off in her own apartment.

She decided that she needed to add specificity to her profound thought, thereby making it more profound.

The pills, lined up exactly one-half inch from each other, accurately measured the length of her remaining time on earth. As a tribute to her dead mother, who had made OCD an art form, Megan O'Brien had a checklist for everything—even ending her life.

She fuzzily revisited her list. *Dinner with Dad, check.* She blinked away a tear. He would be heartbroken. It was her one regret, but unavoidable. Better the surgical slice than living the rest of his life with everyone thinking that his slut daughter was crying wolf because some rich guy pulled a "wham, bam, thank you, ma'am."

An involuntary laugh turned into a snort that almost made the wine go up her nose. That million-dollar lawyer had made her look like a gold digger. She had wanted to scream. The bastards had offered her $500,000 to just go away; but no. She raised the wine glass to her forehead and felt the cool wetness. *Just think, I will never feel anything again. If I had taken the money, no one would ever have known.* She sighed. *Who am I kidding? The result might have been the same.*

Who knows how many other women would have been raped by that brutal psychopath? So I did the right thing; Mom would have been proud, that is, until the vultures started shredding every fiber of my self respect. Thank God Mom was not alive to see the abomination they called a trial. "Oh well," she spoke out loud as she toasted the air with her wine glass, "no good deed goes unpunished."

Sweet letter to Dad – not an e-mail; I know better—telling him how much I love him, check. His faith in her never wavered. Megan's eyes teared. It had been somewhere between sweet and pathetic. He had tried to act like it didn't affect him, but he had gotten older before her eyes. The pain and humiliation would never go away.

That TV reporter, Jackie Mayfield, had stood up for her all during the trial. An army of one. An e-mail worked for her. Megan had already typed it on her iPad, and the game plan was that she would struggle to the iPad and hit **Send** with her last dying breath ... but she couldn't count on it. She had left the same e-mail on her computer as backup. *The police will find it if I don't make it. Maybe it will provide a tragic epilogue to my ruined, wasted life. Check.* Finally, she had on clean underwear. *Check, check.*

Forty-five minutes ago, Megan's weathered and scarred old coffee table had housed twelve perfectly positioned soldiers. It had been easy getting prescription Ambien. She did have trouble sleeping. *No more,* she smiled ruefully. *Now I can sleep for eternity.* She tried to figure out if that was a profound thought, then decided that it was too trite to count.

One pill every ten minutes with the cheap wine chaser. Isn't that how washed-out whores do it? I'm fighting sleep as if my life depended on it, she thought. *How ironic. I have to wait until I'm dying to become so damned profound.*

Megan laboriously lifted her left wrist to her face. The delicate, inexpensive watch that her parents had given her on her 25th birthday stared back at her. Through blurred eyes, she saw the time: 10:58. The remote was in her lap, and she pressed the power button for the TV. *What if* ... adrenaline stirred her senses. *What if Jackie is not on the news tonight?* Megan took a ragged breath. *She never misses a night.*

Her go-to move: her iPad was on her lap, insisting on telling the truth about that awful night in graphic detail. Jackie would be the only one who would get the story first hand, a dying declaration of innocence. *Maybe,* she thought ruefully, *some other girls would be spared.*

My dad and a TV reporter I don't even know—the only two people in the world who care. She struggled and finally produced a lopsided smile. Jackie Mayfield deserved an exclusive.

Gratefully, Megan watched as Jackie's face filled the screen. She reached for the pills, placed another one on her tongue, and put the wine glass to her lips. She thought absently, *Jackie sure looks serious tonight.*

"Shocking new developments in the Chad Alexander, III rape case!" Jackie Mayfield's dramatic opening built in intensity. "An hour ago his father, Chad Alexander, II filed suit against the Ritz Carlton hotel chain. He accused them of improper supervision, failure to respond, and harboring a criminal element. The plaintiff alleges that his son was brutally attacked in one of their rooms. The sadistic, perverted attack went on for over twelve hours. Currently, Chad Alexander, III is in an undisclosed medical facility. That in itself would be a whale of a story and a tragic ending for a man exonerated from the hideous accusation of rape."

Jackie leaned into the camera, her emerald-green eyes demanding that everyone watching pay attention.

Somehow Megan's hand managed to find her swollen tongue, and she removed what remained of a dissolving pill. She was confused. Had she heard right? Jackie's tone sounded like she felt that Chad *deserved* the attack. Megan blinked her eyes, begging them to focus as Jackie began speaking again.

"Within thirty minutes of the filed complaint, Fox News received a flash drive, delivered personally to me, that sheds a little different light on this allegation." She leaned forward again, and this time the genuine compassion and tenderness of her eyes caressed her viewers as she paused dramatically. With the quietness normally reserved for a precious child, she said, "Megan O'Brien, this is for you, girl. Justice delayed, but justice repaid."

As the startling image of a nude Chad Alexander, III filled the screen, Megan grabbed her cell phone. Her numb fingers punched once, then twice; finally 911 connected. The phone dropped from her fingers onto the couch. Her mind was fuzzy, her eyes were closing against her will, and her head felt like a gigantic watermelon forcing its way onto her chest. With her last cogent thought, she rammed two fingers down her throat.

Patrick O'Brien was sitting in his favorite armchair, sipping his nightly Miller Lite, worrying about his only daughter, and watching the 11 o'clock news in a half-assed manner. All of a sudden it was like he had been hit with an electric cattle prod. The woman on TV that Megan liked was talking about Alexander again. But she had a gleam in her eye. *She's reporting that the big-shot father is claiming that his rich prick son was mugged in the Ritz Carlton in Tysons Corner and that he is suing the hotel!* With increasing excitement, Patrick said a quick prayer, hoping that they had beaten the bastard within an inch of his life.

He knew he wasn't supposed to ask God to hurt somebody, but in the next few moments it felt like his prayer had been answered. Unconsciously, as the unbelievable story was unfolding, Patrick was holding his breath. When the angel on TV said, "Megan O'Brien, this is for you," it felt like his heart was coming out of his chest. He almost didn't hear Jackie Mayfield's warning that the video she was about to show might be disturbing to some viewers.

As the partially nude image of Chad Alexander wearing a Ritz Carlton bathrobe appeared on the screen, it was as if evil itself possessed the television.

With the first words out of the boasting rapist's mouth, Patrick's mood changed dramatically. He stood up, fists clenching and unclenching unconsciously at his sides. A sledgehammer hit his gut as the venomous words poured out of Alexander's mouth. Angry veins popped out on his neck, and his face turned blood red. His cry of anguish, like that of a wounded grizzly, seemed to shake the foundations of his apartment.

Patrick bent over, hands clutching his knees, and forced himself to breathe. He had to call Megan. Stuffing his fury, he staggered to the phone and dialed.

After five rings he shouted, "Call me baby, call me! I have to see you!" He waited five minutes and called again. Still no answer. He left another message. Then, throwing a jacket on over his pajamas, Patrick snatched his keys off the kitchen table, and ran to his car.

Twenty minutes later, Patrick pulled into a no parking zone, jumped out of the car, ran through the lobby, and took the elevator to Megan's apartment. He rang the bell and beat on the door. No response. He inserted his emergency key into the lock and burst inside. He screamed for her, "Megan! Megan!" The oak coffee table. A half-filled wine glass and pills. He couldn't comprehend what had happened, The place looked like a war zone, and Megan always kept her home immaculate.

Pills! He picked one up, looked at it, his imagination piercing his heart. He staggered to her bedroom. Empty. He collapsed on her bed, his head flew into his hands, and he let out an unearthly wail. His cell phone rang. He fumbled it out of his jacket pocket, dropped it on the bed, flipped it open, and with his eyes shut and his face contorted in pain, gasped, "Megan?"

CHAPTER 18

"DID YOU MISS ME?"

Mac McGregor's gut clenched when he heard the silky tone of his adversary. "So much that I'm taping this call so I can hear your dulcet tones whenever I'm lonely. But that was your opening the last time we chatted, and I'm going to need a little more originality to stay interested."

"Ha! See, this is more what I expected from you. No curling up in a ball with your hands over your head. A little light repartee instead. I do hope you noticed the spontaneous and clever rhyme I just made."

"I did notice," Mac responded. "And because it was off the cuff, I won't chide you about the meter being off."

"Oh, of course. I did forget. You're the Poet Laureate of the brokerage business, and I *dared* to pass a rhyme by you."

A chill went through Mac. For years he had written songs and poems for clients' birthdays and anniversaries. He had no idea how Lyons could possibly know that. It was like the man knew every intimate detail of Mac's life. This personal invasion was more frightening than physical confrontation.

Mac looked up from the phone and noticed his partners and associates looking at him, either directly or discreetly. Everyone knew that this was the first scheduled call, that it was being taped, and that their friend and senior partner was extremely anxious. He smiled, nodded, and went back to the business at hand.

"Hello? Knock, knock!" Jeremy rapped his phone with his hand. "You haven't left me, have you?"

"Is that an option?" Mac asked dryly.

"Of course, dear boy. Everything in life is a choice. Free will is a gift from God. We would all like to be able to foresee the consequences of our choices, but that would remove all mystery from our lives."

"Is it possible to have a conversation with you that does not include a veiled threat?" Mac asked.

"You misinterpret," Jeremy said abruptly. In a tone laced with arrogance, he asked, "Did you confirm my assertion about the futility of trying to trace my call?"

"Yes. Not that I had any doubt. Let me read you the FBI's conclusions."

"Have I somehow given you the impression that I have unlimited time?" asked Jeremy.

"Sorry. Most retirees love to talk."

"Too many ineffectual attempts at levity are tiresome."

"Got it. I'll try to up my game."

"Or," Jeremy said lightly, "we could just Skype our calls and add an intimacy to them."

"Sounds perfect."

"But I believe the intimacy would be lost if we did it at your office." Jeremy paused as if waiting for the implication to hit home. "And how do you get any clients with that bedside manner?"

"My warm, engaging dialogue is reserved for clients that we think would be good fits for our practice."

"Really? You stockbrokers don't still cold call, scrounge up anyone who has a pulse? Just think, if I opened an account and sent you a billion or so, it could catapult you to the top of the *Barron's* rankings."

"One of the benefits of having done this for a while is that we have the freedom to accept or reject clients."

"Wouldn't it be interesting if you put this opportunity to a partnership vote?" Jeremy challenged.

Mac felt like he should have been practicing Lamaze techniques; the man was insufferable. "How can I help you, Mr. Lyons?" he asked with feigned patience.

"Respect. That's a good start. Ready for your first assignment?"

"Assignment?"

"Yes. And you must learn not to interrupt. Have your friend stumbling Joe find out if I will be harassed, charged, or prosecuted in the event that I make a triumphant return stateside. One week should be sufficient time to get me an accurate answer."

The next sound Mac heard was a dial tone.

CHAPTER 19

THERE WERE FEW SECRETS BETWEEN the two friends. Mac McGregor knew that the Jeremy Lyons saga was the most frustrating case in Joe Sebastiano's otherwise storied career. As a special agent with the FBI, Joe had considerably more successes than failures, but this was the first time that he felt he'd let down a friend.

As Mac looked at Joe, he realized for maybe the first time that the signs of age were stealthily sneaking onto his friend's face. The lines in the corners around Joe's still vibrant, dark brown eyes were pronounced, as if there had been some artistic chiseling on his granite face. What used to be a perpetual tan now looked more weathered, and his silver hair, while still full, was cut shorter. Exercise still kept excess body weight at bay, but even Joe's outrageous behavior had been tempered from its previous manic state. *I hope that Joe is not doing the same inventory assessment of me,* thought Mac.

Starting slowly, Mac pulled up the picture he had saved on his iPhone of Jeremy Lyons's inscription in Mac's copy of *Survival of the Fittest*: *"To my inspiration – I have enjoyed playing hide and seek with you. The next time it will be your and Grace's turn to hide. All the best, Jeremy."*

Joe had seen it before, of course, but Mac held it out to him again and said, "In case you're wondering why I called this meeting."

"You keep it on your phone?"

"Yep. Reminds me to be vigilant. Take nothing for granted."

Joe sighed. "I don't know how you're ever going to get past it when you have that constant reminder."

"I'll get past it when it's life without parole or the son-of-a-bitch is wearing a toe tag."

Immediately after Mac's four o'clock call with Jeremy Lyons, a tape of the conversation was sent to Joe's office. Mac had opted for a primitive method of recording the call because he did not want to get the compliance of the firm involved. A few moments of silence passed, and then Mac asked, "Did you run the tape up the flagpole already?"

Joe had stopped at Mac's home in Potomac, Maryland, on his way home. Mac wanted to have this conversation face to face. They were seated across from each other now, and Grace was discreetly out visiting with one of the kids. Joe nodded and lowered his eyes.

"Oh, for crap's sake!" Mac yelled as he got up from his chair and threw his hands in the air. His face was flushed. "Lyons knew! Some million-dollar-a-minute shyster told him that the authorities didn't have enough evidence."

Mac paced around the room. "Why the hell did he assign me to intercede for him? He didn't need me."

Joe was silent.

"Of course," Mac said, sitting down across from Joe again. "He knew that, too. He just wanted to screw with me. He forced me to ask you to find out what charges he would face if he resurfaced, knowing that I would feel like shit even asking the question. And he wanted to be sure I knew that, of course, the smartest man on the planet is also bulletproof."

Mac snapped his focus to Joe. He narrowed his eyes and spoke. "The FBI must be the most efficient government agency in the world. Twenty-four hours was all it took to determine whether Jeremy Lyons was still on your Most Wanted List." His suspicion and bitterness hung in the air.

Joe returned Mac's accusing gaze with expressionless respect.

"Really?" Mac asked in a wounded tone. He lowered his head and put both hands on his forehead. Gradually, he lifted his head, his eyes burning with accusation. "You've got nothing. My paisan, my loquacious, never at a loss for words, dear friend and protector never thought to say, 'Sorry, pal, the manhunt has ended. Jeremy Lyons has passed GO and picked up all the money.'"

Joe let out a breath. "I'm sorry, Mac. There are circumstances..."

"No! No! There are not circumstances!" Mac shouted, interrupting. "From day one my deal was that I was to be kept in the loop! Remember?"

Joe's swarthy face reddened with anger. "Will you just sit down so we can talk about this?"

"No. I can't," said Mac in a more controlled voice. He walked to the door and opened it. "Go home to Barbara. You're of no use to me."

For a full minute the two men stared at each other, neither moving, as if they were statues. Finally, Joe said in a choked voice, "Mac, I'm not going anywhere. I'm asking you as a friend to please hear me out. If after that you don't think I'm still your friend, I will walk away."

Mac glared for another moment and then sat down. He rested his elbows on the table, interlocked his fingers, and waited.

"It was about three months ago," Joe began. "I'd like to tell you it was a week ago, but I'm not going to bullshit you. I went nuts. The limp dick bastards said that the odds were against charging Lyons and making anything stick."

Mac had decided to just listen and not offer a comment unless it was asked for.

"Then they added the addendum," Joe continued, "that sent me through the roof. I took it as high as I could to get it overruled.

Mac, they said that I could not tell anyone, including you. Their cock-a-mamie logic was that as long as Lyons didn't know he could safely return, he would stay out of the country."

"During our initial investigation into Lyons, the Bureau had no sense of humor about granting you access. I did it anyway. In this case they were more specific. 'Tell McGregor and you're looking at early retirement.'

"You and I never talked about it, but right before we initiated the high-risk takedown of Lyons's operation, your largest client and best friend withdrew all his money from Lyons's hedge fund." He shrugged. "No coincidence. You gave your man a heads up, which could have screwed the operation and had you facing charges of obstruction."

Mac's expression did not change.

"But you put it all on the line for a friend. You're the brave one." Joe blinked hard and gave Mac an unfamiliar look of shame. "I caved. I'm sorry as hell."

Mac looked back at his friend for just a moment. He blew out an exasperated breath. "If it works, you're brave. If it doesn't, you're an idiot. The real lack of insight belongs to your supervisors at the Bureau who would think for a minute that Jeremy Lyons wouldn't figure this out before they did."

Joe gave him a begrudging half smile.

"Run it down for me, Joe. What are the holes in what you have?"

Joe nodded. "Let's examine the areas where we believe there's criminal activity. First, the insurance scam. It's legal to buy life insurance policies from individuals. Yes, an inordinate number of insured folks on the policies that his company purchased died from unnatural causes. We all believe that he used Max Parnavich to expedite death, thereby dramatically increasing his return on investment.

"No witness, no physical evidence or DNA evidence was found at any of the scenes, although it might have been possible to place Max at the oceanfront home in California. But he's the only suspect, and the only one who could tie Lyons in, and he's six feet under. You can't indict on statistical anomalies; you need a witness, physical evidence, or a confession."

"But we know that Lyons ordered the hits," said Mac. "David Grant still walks around like a zombie half the time. Can you imagine knowing someone killed your dad for money and that he's walking around free?"

Joe shook his head.

"Can't we follow the money trail?" Mac asked. "It had to all funnel back to Lyons."

"The best people in the Bureau haven't found the smoking gun."

Mac sat back and shook his head in disgust. "The regulators have to have him dead to rights on insider trading. You invaded his office with every acronym in the industry."

Joe gestured futilely with his hands. "We've tried to get the traders to roll over on Lyons, but we've got no leverage. Mixed in with what we suspect were illegal trades were a number of legitimate trades. The CEOs and CFOs all lawyered up, and none of the women who were the receptacles for the information ..."

"Receptacles?"

"You know what I mean. Anyway, none of them ever bought or sold stock or talked to Lyons about the information. And Lyons waited long enough after he got the inside information that there wouldn't be a computer-generated flag from the SEC, NYSE or NASDAQ. Still, there was a pattern."

Mac spoke mostly to himself. "Martha Stewart sells a few days before an adverse announcement, and the computers light up like somebody won the jackpot. Wait a while, and it's like there's a statute of limitations on cheating. The computers see no evil, hear no evil ..."

"There's more, Mac." Joe went on. "There were white papers written on every one of his investment decisions detailing the rationale for the purchase or sale."

"Damn, he's good."

"The people who could testify against him, Max Parnavich and Frank Griffin, are both dead. Shortly after Lyons went into exile, Griffin took a header off his balcony. It was undetermined whether he jumped or was thrown off. He was an employee of Lyons's operation, and he had been turned by the FBI."

"What about Margo Savino?" asked Mac. "She was his first employee."

Joe shook his head. "The prosecutor didn't rule that out." Joe spoke quickly. "Hers wasn't your garden variety aggravated assault. The heinous results of the torture, the body branding, and the miscarriage ... " He shrugged.

"Well?"

"It's still a close call. Do you think Margo would testify against Lyons?"

"I don't know. The only hope would be to have Sam ask her." Mac blew out a breath. "You know, the only positive that has come out of this whole mess, other than that sadist Max taking a dirt nap, is that Sam is head over heels in love."

Joe raised his eyebrows. "It's that serious?"

Mac gave him a smile of incredulity. "Sam is so completely goofy over her that you can't look at him without cracking up."

Joe nodded and returned the smile. "The other question is what does a crack defense attorney do with the fact that Margo has been paid a comfortable pension ever since the incident. She didn't report it. And she told you that she had the option to walk away."

Joe's face wrinkled in disgust. "So a sleazebag attorney suggests to the jury that she gets fifty grand a year for the rest of her life in exchange for being disfigured."

Mac felt a wave of nausea. He looked at Joe through eyes he was sure had aged ten years in just the last three. "In this economy, how many people would turn down a deal like that?"

Their shared silence did nothing to dissipate their frustration. Mac's hand went to his brow, and he massaged it as if he were trying to knead an answer from his brain. He looked his friend in the eye. "Joe, just so I'm clear. We know, but can't prove, that Lyons killed old people to collect on their insurance, had hookers seduce corporate executives for inside information, tortured his employees, and threatened me and my family. And our system is so broken that Jeremy Lyons is as free as a bird."

Joe managed to meet Mac's gaze, but his eyes held no answer.

CHAPTER 20

MEGAN O'BRIEN FELT THE GENTLE pressure on her left hand—the warm familiar feel of calluses holding not tightly, but firmly, and with an urgency of concern. The antiseptic smell so indigenous to hospitals invaded her nostrils as she fought to regain consciousness. As she struggled to open her eyes, bright lights threatened to penetrate her brain. Pain eased slightly, helped by the damp, soft kiss on her pale brow.

She heard her name whispered in reverence. Fighting against the instinct to disappear into sleep, she opened her eyes a fraction of an inch, just enough to see the large head and tear-stained face of her father. Her eyes closed again, and she shuddered. She was alive. Thank God, she was alive!

As if they were part of a slow moving orchestra, parts of her body randomly regained feeling, independently, but in sequence with her concert of pain. Although the IV was already attached to her left arm, she imagined that she could feel the multiple stabs as a nurse searched for a reluctant vein. Her stomach felt like she had been disemboweled. Her throat felt like her tonsils had been sanded off.

But Megan O'Brien, the unjustly accused Megan O'Brien, was alive. A weak smile almost managed to catch the solitary tear wending its way down her freckled cheek.

For at least the hundredth time, Patrick O'Brien massaged his forehead and continued upward, running his hands through the still thick white hair that covered his scalp. His eyes went back to his daughter. For the past 48 hours he had not left her bedside.

Several nurses and a doctor had ordered him to rest, but nobody moves an O'Brien when one of their own is down. First his wife with breast cancer, now his daughter. Stick a fork in his big Irish ass; if Megan had died, too, Fightin' Paddy would have been done.

He reached a big hand over the hospital bed and tenderly rubbed his baby's arm. *Sleep until you are ready,* he thought as he glanced at the ceiling and thanked his Savior once again. The doctor said she should fully recover. *I will never let anyone hurt you again.*

Patrick closed his eyes as the nightmare he'd been through resurfaced in his mind. But now that he knew Megan was going to be okay, his heart felt like it might finally be recuperating from the punching-bag-like pummeling it had received over the past few days.

The flickering, but silent, TV mounted on the wall caught his attention. Fortunately, the other bed in the hospital room was not occupied, so he was alone with his thoughts and his beloved daughter. Almost three days later and they were still showing clips of poor Megan's trial. It was Patrick's fault. Not that the smug bastard had raped her, even he couldn't take the blame for that, but as soon as he heard, he should have taken a socket wrench to Chad Alexander's nuts. Then there would have been no trial, and he wouldn't have almost lost his reason for living.

Stuart Bowers had been the lead detective, and he was the one who had arrested Alexander. After that slick Hollywood lawyer got the bastard off, the detective had spoken to both Megan and Patrick. "Off the record," he said, looking right into Megan's eyes, "the justice system got it wrong." He knew that she had been raped, and he apologized as if it were his fault.

Then yesterday, Detective Bowers came to the hospital to see Megan. He had brought her flowers, and he asked Patrick if he could speak to him privately. "I need you to identify your daughter's handwriting on this note that was found in her apartment.

"If it is not your daughter's handwriting, then my reading of the episode is that she is here as a result of too much stress and too much alcohol." The detective paused and then continued in a voice that would have intimidated a hardened criminal. Only the compassion in his eyes betrayed his tone. "And Mr. O'Brien, I am rarely wrong. I am sure that this is a bogus note. If I am correct, you may just dispose of it."

When the detective walked out of the room, a confused Patrick looked down at the folded note and opened it.

Dearest Dad,

I am so sorry. Mom was strong, and I am so weak. I cannot live my life with the stigma of this trial. Wherever I go, people will stare and whisper behind my back. Every time you hear someone mention my name in a bar, you will get in a fight. You will spend the rest of your life defending my tarnished honor.

I have sent the truth to Jackie Mayfield, the TV reporter who has been one of the few people on my side. I'm too tired to run, and I have to stop the pain.

My beloved father, you can do no more than what you have done. My final wish and prayer is that both you and God will forgive me. You are the greatest father on earth. I love you.

Megan

Patrick O'Brien, a large, genial, man with a booming laugh, loved by many and feared by some, crumbled onto a nearby couch. As sobs wracked his body, he cried, "Thank you Jesus, thank you Jesus," and stuffed the note into his pocket.

CHAPTER 21

BEFORE JOINING JOHNSTON WELLONS, WADE Larson had run the operations for a local branch office of Merrill Lynch. He was tall, genetically thin, with a shaved head, an easygoing smile, and a deep baritone voice that inspired confidence. His organizational skills were unrivaled, he had a quick grasp of systems and technology, and most importantly, he was a diehard Redskins fan.

Like free agency in sports, movement within the brokerage industry is frequent, just not as lucrative. Wade had been looking for a less bureaucratic environment, and the prospect of working as a zookeeper for Mac McGregor's group was too enticing to pass up. Circumstances dovetailed nicely, because Lena Brady, who formerly held the position, wanted to concentrate on her clients, and whatever Lena wants ...

"You're good to go on the Lahr account, boss. Option paperwork is approved."

Mac looked to the left at Wade, whose desk was close enough for conversation. In addition to his other duties, because of his expertise in the strategy, Wade was responsible for supporting Mac's managed accounts. Danny DeMarco also worked with them in a research capacity and as another set of eyes.

Since the beginning of the 21st century, financial advisors have migrated to the role of consultant rather than that of money manager. After all, it is easier to blame an underperforming mutual fund manager, separate account manager, or hedge fund than to take the blame yourself.

For over 25 years, Mac had personally managed a portfolio of high-quality stocks for clients using what he felt was a more conservative strategy than simply picking stocks. And if a portfolio did underperform, he would rather take the heat himself. It was a strategy he knew, and he had established a good track record over the years.

Furthermore, Mac felt that having a hands-on strategy differentiated his organization from others and made the client feel like his or her advisor was more engaged.

"How many different stock positions will Mr. Lahr own in the portfolio?" Wade asked.

"The goal will be fifty to sixty stocks. I want to go in slowly and have some cash reserves in case the market hiccups and we can get some better numbers. One hundred million is a large portfolio for this strategy. We'll need to be sensitive to price, but it should work."

Mac paused with a strange look on his face. Wade asked, "Is everything all right?"

Mac shook it off. "Yeah. It's still hard to believe that a guy wires in that much money just from reading about me in *Barron's*."

"You've got street creds, boss," Wade said, as if that removed all the mystery.

Mac threw him a skeptical look. "For that kind of money, you trust, but verify." He paused a minute. "I wonder how often we will hear from Mr. Lahr."

"Maybe never," Wade replied matter of factly. "He's designated an intermediary. Her name is Alcina. I've talked to her, and she seems really smart. Lahr has signed off so that she can handle everything. I guess a hundred mil is too little for him to bother with."

Mac smiled. "Then let's do a killer job and get more.

"Good afternoon," Jeremy Lyons said cheerfully to start the conversation.

Mac rolled his neck backwards, closed his eyes, and waited for the mental Novocain to start working. Clients appreciated Mac's financial discipline and his emotional balance, regardless of the tenseness of the situation. He was completely comfortable in his ability to listen, remain calm, and offer comforting advice, even in the most stressful or painful moments.

Yet with Jeremy, Mac had been totally incapable of emotional detachment. He was all in, and he felt every dig of the sadist's words as if they were knives slicing his soul.

"Are you ready for your next assignment?" Jeremy asked.

"I've been counting the minutes."

"Good. You did an excellent job on your first assignment and ..."

"Yes," Mac said, interrupting the flow. "Are there other things that you already know but want me to double-check for you? Would you like to know who's playing in the Super Bowl?"

"Ah, football: gladiators in combat. Don't you prefer our little sparring? It's so much less vicious."

"Not sure that I'd agree, but if you want to level the playing field, I'll be happy to engage in a winner-take-all game."

"Really? Level the playing field?"

"Please. Don't bullshit both of us," Mac said, venting some of his frustration. "You remember MAD, Mutually Assured Destruction. That's a level playing field. How am I a threat to you?"

Jeremy was quiet for a moment, and Mac wondered whether he was savoring Mac's anger or becoming annoyed. He hoped it was the latter.

"Your whining is becoming tiresome. Just pay attention to your assignment," Jeremy said, feigning boredom.

"Jeremy, you know everything about me. Let's have some sharing time. I know nothing about your background. Were you close to your parents?"

"My insipid mother and reluctant sperm donor father are no concern of yours."

"You seemed open to leveling the playing field. Give me something. If your family life was painful, the *last* thing I want to do is cause you pain."

"I don't feel pain, you idiot, I inflict it!"

"I get that. I feel it every time we talk."

The ensuing silence made Mac wonder if he had pushed too far. Finally, he heard Jeremy exhale.

"Write this down," Jeremy commanded. "Ask your friend Sam Golden the following question and be precise in your reporting of his answer. Does he believe that the Dodd-Frank reform legislation and the proposed Volcker Rule are sufficient to prevent another financial meltdown?"

Mac was silent.

"Read the question back to me."

Mac felt like he was a kid again being forced to write "I will not poke the hornets' nest" on the blackboard a hundred times. He did as instructed.

"Good. I am not interested in your opinion, only Mr. Golden's. You should ask him when you have dinner together."

The next sound Mac heard was the dial tone.

"You looked like you were gonna pass out," R.J. said, walking over to Mac's desk.

R.J. was one of the most authentic people that Mac knew, and his friend's concern was written all over his face. "Good call. Try this one on: 'I don't feel pain, you idiot, I inflict it.'"

"Whoa! You don't have to prove it to me, Mac. I have the scars," said R.J., backing up.

"You are such a wuss," Mac said, surprising himself with a smile.

"And I don't need a replay of your Snideley Whiplash voice," R.J. said with mock terror.

"Snideley Whiplash? That might just become the new nickname for the inimitable Jeremy Lyons."

"Glad I could contribute," R.J. said with a bow.

Mac's smile faded as his brief respite of levity wore off. "He wants me to ask Sam Golden a question for him," Mac said haltingly. "He told me to ask him at dinner. The man is a human nanny cam. I don't know why I should be surprised that he knows we're having dinner with Sam and Margo."

CHAPTER 22

"YUM!" MARGO SAVINO TOOK A major-league sniff of Grace McGregor's heralded spaghetti sauce.

"I hope you like it," Grace said, stopping mid-stir.

"Guaranteed," said Margo, smiling at her new friend. "You do know that I'm Italian."

"Uh-oh; that means you'll be a harsh critic."

"No way, Grace. I'm just so delighted to meet you, after all Sam has told me about you and your family, that I'd love it even if you scraped it off the road."

Grace laughed, a sound that was like a wind chime to Mac, who was sitting in the family room with his old friend Sam Golden. Conversation wasn't flowing as it usually did between the two men, because Mac wanted to be sure that Jeremy Lyons was not a topic of discussion.

Sam was still in the "I have to tell her everything, because love requires full disclosure" mode with Margo; so if Mac told Sam about Jeremy's re-emergence, he would tell Margo and cause her needless worry. In the early years of Lyons's hedge fund activity, Margo had not only worked for him; she had also been his lover. In return, Jeremy's associate, Max Parnavich, had taken a hot branding iron and seared a dollar sign into her flesh as a constant reminder that she was Jeremy's property. She, more than anyone, knew how dangerous the man was.

Mac decided to put Sam on the defensive. "Did you bring a calculator with you?" he asked.

"No," answered a puzzled Sam, whose career path had taken him from successful attorney to Chairman of the Securities and Exchange Commission to working in the Obama administration.

"Well, there's no way we can add up how much you owe me without one," added Mac.

Sam gave an uneasy chuckle. Grace's call of "Dinner!" saved him from an awkward response.

"Your table is gorgeous, Grace. Did Mac help you?" Margo said as Sam held out her chair.

"I'd sooner ask him to perform surgery on me," Grace muttered.

"Hey!" Mac responded. "Although, come to think of it, these hands," he held them up for inspection, "have been known to do wondrous things." The absurd look of rapture on his face was enough to cause everyone to laugh, even if the line had fallen flat.

They held hands around the table as Mac bowed his head and spoke. "Lord, we are thankful for our many blessings. Tonight we are especially grateful for our guests and the love and affection that they share. Bless this food to the nourishment of our bodies and us to Thy use. Amen."

Both Sam and Margo's first bites of spaghetti elicited the same reaction: their eyes widened in amazement. After the effusive compliments were finished, Mac addressed Margo. "So, young lady, the last time I saw you, you were suspicious and accompanied by your bodyguard brother, who looked at me like I was something he should clean off the bottom of his flip-flops. It's nice to see you without a scowl on your face."

She laughed heartily. "Well, when I saw you in Florida and noticed how much older you had gotten in the 20-plus years since the last time I'd seen you, I was concerned that you might be an imposter," she countered.

"Ouch," Mac said as everyone laughed. "It's easy to throw stones when you have five-percent body fat and look even more gorgeous than you did when I first knew you."

Margo might have blushed through her dark Florida tan if she hadn't been sure that Mac was going to fire another shot.

"So it's great that your beauty is still intact. I guess it's only your judgment that's seriously out of whack." Predictably, Mac nodded in Sam's direction.

Table laughter again, and then Margo leaned towards Mac and whispered loudly, "He gives me good drugs."

After dinner, the women handled cleaning up while Mac and Sam adjourned to the family room. Neither was a cigar or brandy type, and, unfortunately, Mac had an agenda.

"I can't tell you how much I appreciate ..." Sam began.

"Are you kidding me? She's so great, she almost compensates for you."

Sam smiled, and Mac asked quickly, forsaking a segue, "Do you think that the enactment of Dodd-Frank or the Volcker Rule would prevent another financial meltdown?" The two friends discussing financial regulations or the status of the markets was a natural as two Green Bay Packers fans discussing football.

"Now we're getting serious?" Sam asked with a sly grin on his face.

"Yep," Mac replied, nodding. "I'm picking your brain, but don't let it go to your head."

CHAPTER 23

"JUDGE FORD, PLEASE."

"May I tell him who's calling?"

"Yes. It's the president of his fan club."

She paused for a moment. "Which district would that be, sir?"

Mac laughed. "You could take it to the bank that the king of pranks, scams, and misdirection would have only smart, quick-witted folks around him to make sure that his game stayed razor sharp."

A polite chuckle. "You obviously know him well, sir. One moment."

In his most serious voice, Judge Michael Ford spoke. "Mr. Chief Justice, how good of you to call."

Mac laughed again. He always looked forward to sparring with his old friend and client of 30 years. "So close. If I'd gone to law school instead of the school of hard knocks, I definitely would have been a contender."

Now it was the judge's turn to laugh, low, guttural, and then building like a wave breaking. It was probably the most contagious sound in the universe. "To what does a lowly jurist owe the honor of having a bona fide financial wizard and semipro poker player call him?"

"Whoa! I take issue with the semipro comment. I'm just learning the game."

"Of course you are, and I am just learning the law."

Mac shook his head and smiled into the phone, remembering the many times that the judge's warm, honeyed voice had provided soothing counsel for him. "Your humble servant wondered whether we might conduct your financial physical early this year."

"Is there a problem?"

"No, your honor. You're in good shape. Losing money for a judge is definitely a capital crime."

The judge paused momentarily, then raised his voice for emphasis. "Continue to let that fear weigh heavily on your heart and your brain."

"I also thought that if you could meet me at eleven, I could entice you to stay for lunch at the Prime Rib. Of course, I would call ahead to make sure that they would fix up that special salad for you."

"Perfect," the judge chuckled. "Remember, only vegetables and no dressing."

"Thanks, Michael. I appreciate it. I'll e-mail you some dates. Let me know what works for you."

Whenever Mac McGregor walked from his office at 1735 Pennsylvania Avenue toward the restaurants on K Street, in this case, the Prime Rib, his actual path was determined by the traffic lights. Similar to navigating a maze, he knew where his destination was, but he zigzagged depending on which lights were green.

Judge Michael Ford canted his head to the left and gave Mac a skeptical look. "I assume that there is some method to your madness. Walking straight up 18th Street and turning right onto K Street must be a more treacherous route than I'd imagined."

"Michael, Michael, Michael. The straightest route would have no adventure, no challenge. We are men who need to test ourselves."

"Is it not test enough to drive into this wretched city? Add to that the problem of meandering through the mendacious maze of lobbyists and influence peddlers. And can one really be truly immunized against the power-hungry, self-absorbed, pontificating politicians who infest our nation's capital?"

Mac laughed at his friend's not atypical tirade. Because it was the day after Thanksgiving, the stock market closed at 1:30. Judge Ford, well aware of his advisor's control tendencies, had purposely opted for this date. And even though the judge was not working today, the 68-year-old man was never underdressed. A dark silver pinstriped suit, perfectly tailored to disguise his shelf like, loveable girth, was highlighted by a pale blue shirt and a silk red and light blue striped tie. The perfect V of his half-Windsor knot was held in place by an old-fashioned gold tiepin. In his jacket pocket, a folded, four-toothed, starched white handkerchief peeked out. Every time Mac saw his friend, he thought about the tragedy of judicial robes covering this epitome of sartorial splendor.

Although the judge's legs were shorter than his friend's, he nevertheless easily matched Mac's now purposeful stride. As they walked, Mac thought about the gift of competency his friend exuded. Behind the rimless glasses and dark, warm eyes, perpetually set on twinkle, there was a uniquely facile mind. Turning towards him, Mac asked, "Michael, have you ever considered running for office?"

Rather than responding glibly, the judge gave him a long look. He answered seriously, "So many of us enter the law because we feel that we can make a difference." He shrugged. "A few actually do. Politics is a masochist's game. It's like a slow-moving terminal cancer: strident confrontations carried on behind the illusion of civility by stubborn, ethically challenged, entitled bureaucrats."

He shook his head. "When only 10% of the people approve of your job performance ... " The comment lingered.

"So you don't think you could make a difference?"

"The odds are long, my friend, and even the possibility that my soul could be compromised terrifies me."

They walked in silence for another block. "Michael, do you discuss this with other people?"

"Ha! Never, my friend. But as my financial guru, you are bound by the tenets of confidentiality. Now, do hurry," he said as he raced to open the restaurant door, "as my meager repast of this morning yearns for good company."

The Prime Rib is old school, from the décor and the conventional dress of the patrons to the formal service and clubby atmosphere: dark draperies that blot out natural light, black lacquered mirrors, and a leopard print rug. Mac was surprised to recognize a few of the patrons at the bar. He ate here infrequently, yet it seemed like every time the same crowd was there. It reminded him of the older gentlemen at the country club always playing gin at the same tables, as if they had no place else to go.

When the expressionless, tuxedoed waiter laid the senior cut of rare roast beef in front of him, the judge gave an Academy Award presentation of calm, cool and collected.

"Michael," Mac said as he leaned across his grilled salmon, "you seem to be a little blasé about that bleeding side of beef. Would you rather share my salmon?"

The judge looked up from his prize with half-lidded eyes. "Do you see the lovely Mrs. Ford here?" Sophie Ford, his adorable, energizer bunny of positivity wife, would never condone this meal.

Mac clasped his hands together and looked around. "No, sir. I do not."

"Then saddle up, cowboy. This is how real men eat," he said in stentorian tones. "And please do not distract me with small talk or banalities."

Mac waited patiently as the judge dissected his meal. Finally, Michael tenderly laid down his fork, and Mac spoke. "I need you to do me a favor."

The judge picked up his black napkin, patted his mouth, folded the napkin neatly and put it down again. Then he nodded, smiled, and fixed Mac with his full attention.

"Something's gnawing at me about the Chad Alexander affair – he confesses and then winds up in the hospital. Sort of sounds like a coerced confession with the reward being some sort of beating. If you ask me why I care," Mac raised his hands palms up, "I don't know. Whatever punishment he received would not elicit my sympathy. But over the last few years I've developed a healthy dose of paranoia. I need to know what happened to him that night at the Ritz. Was he randomly attacked, set up, brutalized? Whatever specifics you can find out."

Judge Ford waited a full minute until he was sure his friend was finished talking. He did not ask why Mac wanted the information or what he would do if he got it. He simply nodded and said, "I will get you whatever I can."

Shortly after Mac and Grace finished dinner, Mac paused the TV to hit the bathroom when the phone rang. As he washed his hands, he heard Grace laughing. When he walked back into the family room, he saw her coming toward him holding the phone. She smiled and said, "Here comes the judge, here comes the judge."

"What took you so long?" Mac asked, looking at his watch. It had been six hours since his request.

The smile quickly left Mac's face. The description was detailed, graphic, and nightmare inducing. As Mac hung up the phone, Grace came back into the room. "Whoa," she said. looking at him.

"Let's go for a walk," he said, taking her arm. "I need some air."

CHAPTER 24

STANLEY LIPITZ COULD FEEL HIS blood pressure rising, his heart beating erratically, and sweat forming large oval rings on his wrinkled, striped shirt. Overleveraged and underloved, he had not been afraid since the day he received his Ph.D. from Yale.

His success as a biotech pioneer compensated for his obvious physical liabilities. A few strands of thin red hair failed to cover his oversized cranium and only accentuated his porcine features. High, puffy cheeks seemed to pinch his mud-brown eyes together, giving the impression that Stanley would be totally incapable of peripheral vision.

He had no illusions about himself and did not need phony reassurances that his Pillsbury Doughboy body was appealing in any way. He had no motivation to eat well or to exercise. His only goals were to be filthy rich and famous.

For years, he had lived as if his Alzheimer's drug, Celebra, had already been approved by the FDA. A ridiculously large house, fancy cars that he rarely drove, and not one, but two ex-wives who would have been considered trophies by all but the truly discriminating.

Fortunately, neither woman knew the other, and both were so anxious to spend Stanley's money that they had signed prenuptial agreements. It did cost him a bit more for each extrication, because at certain times they both had bruises that did not look accidental. Stanley imagined the conversation. "Hey, he did the same things to me. Your bruises look just like mine." He actually got off on the fact that a streak of violence was carefully hidden under the veneer of his harmless visage.

Beneath the façade of the brilliant scientist whose only goal was to save mankind lurked an ugly little boy consumed by naked and reckless ambition.

Six months ago, his fortune was written in the stars. Cerebrepharma stock was selling at $35 a share. His three million shares and options were worth well over $100 million.

Stanley's collaborator on the drug, a man 20 years his senior, had contracted the targeted disease himself before any of the Phase III testing had begun. When Stanley approached the man's wife and offered her ten percent of the value of his fellow scientist's holdings in cash, she accepted. Now both the ownership of the company and the scientific accolades would reside where they belonged, with Stanley.

Particularly when banks are reluctant to lend, advancing funds on concentrated stock positions is rare, and for Stanley Lipitz, the only equity he had anywhere was in his company's stock position. However, any fool could see from the amazing results of the Phase II trials that success in human trials of Celebra was inevitable. Thus, the investment banks had fallen all over themselves to lend Stanley money. It was common knowledge that whoever took care of the founder, CEO, and largest shareholder of the company would get the investment banking fees when a large pharmaceutical company tried to buy Cerebrepharma.

Yes, six months ago, on paper, Stanley Lipitz was in fat city, sitting on a blockbuster drug.

A tentative knock on the closed door of his office startled him back to the present. Stanley analyzed everything. A forceful knock would have indicated hope. He gagged, shut his eyes tightly, and fought back nausea. "Come in!" he screamed angrily.

Juan Alvarez opened the door halfway and peered around it. Juan was a small man with black hair, horn-rimmed glasses, and a pocked face with a patchy moustache. The very sight of him infuriated Stanley. He represented failure.

The side effects of drugs are always a question mark. Acceptable levels of risk vary with the efficacy of the particular drug. Adverse side effects for a drug that could actually cure pancreatic cancer, for instance, would be tolerated, because otherwise the prognosis is grim.

Stanley's drug stopped Alzheimer's in its tracks. It did not just slow down the progression. Taking it meant that whatever your condition was, it would not get worse. It was the company's wonder drug, and it was priceless. However, six weeks ago, prior to the scheduled announcement that would ensure FDA approval, a peculiar side effect was discovered.

For Alzheimer's patients, the drug worked as advertised for about six months. After that, the same dosage produced a feeling of supreme euphoria, followed by a devastating crash. In other words, the patients got high as a kite, then crashed and burned.

"What happened when you decreased the dosage?" barked Stanley.

"The disease progressed. Anything less than full dosage is a placebo."

"Increasing the dosage?"

"Severe headaches, uncontrollable hypertension, heart irregularities, violent nausea."

Stanley waved his hand angrily, dismissively. "And you couldn't find a way to block the effects, you idiot?"

"No... no, sir, please. Perhaps if we had more time."

"More time? You've had more time. Our stock has already fallen to 25, and the banks are all over my ass. If we delay again, they'll know we're screwed." He grabbed Juan by his shirt and pulled the man's face to his own. "If I go down, you go down. I'll tell them you were giving me false information all along."

Spittle covered Juan's face. He cowered in the bigger man's grasp, and his body began to shake. In disgust, Stanley threw him across the room. "You're a fucking idiot, you Spic bastard. They ought to deport your worthless ass."

"I ... "

"Shut up! I'm thinking!" Stanley paced the room, and Juan stayed as far away from him as the room allowed. "What are the side effects in the non-Alzheimer's cases?"

"The same thing, sir."

"What does that mean, you moron? Did they fly like saucers after six months of use, also?"

"No. No, sir. The effect on them was immediate."

"Immediate?" He paced again. "Did they make noise about suing because of what the drug did to them?" he asked quietly.

"No. Just the opposite. We had to wean them off of it. It was awful, like heroin withdrawal."

"So even with the crash from the high, they wanted the drug again."

"Yes, sir. I'm sorry, but it is quite addictive."

Stanley looked at the contrite man. What Juan didn't understand was that success is never a straight line. Sometimes you have to change course to achieve your objective. "I'll handle the press release in due time. Keep working and find a way to block the fucking side effects!"

CHAPTER 25

IT TOOK JUST THREE DAYS for Stanley Lipitz to make a decision. It had required some extensive digging on his part, but as he expected, everything came together perfectly. The probability of success increases in direct proportion to intellect.

At Cerebrepharma, Sudeep Patel was the sharpest knife in Stanley's employee drawer. In most things Stanley's opinion was the only one that mattered; but in this case, the facts backed him up: perfect SATs, full scholarship at Stanford, MBA from Wharton. And Sudeep was currently within sniffing distance of a Ph.D. in science at Stanford. He was the real deal.

As Stanley peered down at Sudeep from the other side of his massive desk, he was pleased to see that the man seemed calm and relaxed. Obviously, he had to be curious as to why he had been summoned; but the fact that Stanley's desk chair rested on a level one foot above the opposing visitor's chair did not seem to intimidate him. Stanley was additionally pleased to see that frequent rumors of his employee eviscerations also did not seem to faze this particular individual. Calm and fearless, exactly the way Stanley liked them.

Stanley clasped his hands together and fixed Sudeep with a friendly smile. "How are your parents, Mr. Patel?"

"Uh ... they are well, sir."

"Interesting. Most individuals of your ethnicity would show evidence of an accent, and most young men would incorrectly answer, 'They are good.'"

Sudeep smiled and nodded at the compliment.

"Your parents must be prescient. I believe that Sudeep means 'bright' in your language. Is that not correct?"

"Yes sir," came the proud answer.

"Are your parents well off?"

"No, sir, not really."

"How about your three brothers and two sisters?"

A flicker of surprise crossed Sudeep's face, but he answered, "No, no, sir. All are struggling a bit."

Stanley nodded as if he were not aware of this. "Have any of them visited you in America?"

"No, sir," Sudeep replied with a puzzled look.

Stanley nodded again. "Do you send part of your compensation to help them out?"

Sudeep hesitated, then answered, "Yes, sir."

"Quite admirable." Stanley paused and looked upward, as if searching for a question. "Yet the majority of your compensation is in company stock options. I'm not sure how you can afford to send much."

Sudeep shifted in his chair.

Stanley reached into his desk drawer and withdrew a pack of cigarettes and a box of wooden matches. "Would you like a cigarette?"

The building was nonsmoking, so Sudeep was totally confused. "No, sir," he said firmly.

Stanley took out a wooden match, held it between two fingers and snapped it. "Isn't it amazing how easy it is to break things, destroy their essence and value, with just a snap of the fingers?"

The non sequitur just added to Sudeep's confusion.

Stanley leaned towards him. "You said that you didn't want a cigarette, right?"

The man nervously shook his head.

Stanley nodded once again and leaned over the desk. "How about a blindfold, then?" he said ominously.

"I ... I don't ..."

"Another subject." Stanley waved a dismissive hand. In a taunting voice, he asked, "Do you think my appearance has been a help or a hindrance in my career?"

"I don't know."

"Of course you don't," Stanley said with exasperation. "I merely asked what you thought. You're not being graded. This face, this body," he pointed to himself, "an asset or a detriment to my career?"

"I guess it probably didn't help, sir."

"In school, no. It was my cross to bear: 'Hey, Assface! It looks like somebody laid their dick and balls in your face and forgot to take them off.'" He sighed. "Children can be cruel. Yet, we who are mocked have choices. We can wallow in self-indulgent pity, or we can decide to pay them all back, to refuse to lose." He raised his arms in triumph. "I'm in that camp."

Totally perplexed, Sudeep just stared at his boss.

"Do you know the story of the Trojan horse, Mr. Patel?"

"Yes, sir."

"You see, the fact that I am unappealing visually and unpolished socially allows my enemies to discount me." His face assumed a look of helplessness, creating a rather startling likeness to the old comic book character Baby Huey. "Don't you agree?"

Sudeep nodded tentatively.

His boss slowly leaned over his desk. "Yet, not unlike the Trojan horse, when you are asleep, I rip out your entrails."

The viciousness and force of his words felt like a slap in the face to the young man, and for the first time he looked frightened.

Stanley was quiet for a moment. Then he sighed audibly. "You had such promise, Mr. Patel." He waited a beat. "You are very, very smart and creative: two qualities that I admire. But," he shook his head and waved a fat finger in admonishment, "you underestimated true genius."

He stared at Sudeep, enjoying the sight of the man's flaccid face and breathing in the smell of sweat pouring off of him. "It took me two weeks to discover what you were doing. I must be slowing down. Or more kindly, perhaps I'm just too preoccupied with Celebra."

Stanley gave a slight laugh. "I must apologize. There are times when I do veer from the subject at hand, but I adore a play on words. So I shouldn't, but I must. Can you imagine if your last name were Inshit. Then, at this particular moment in time, I could refer to you by your full name. Perhaps Sudeep Inshit is only funny in western humor."

Sudeep squirmed in his chair.

"I may also be off a tad, because I don't know how much of the profits you keep; but I figure that you cleared around $300,000. Am I close?"

Sudeep's mouth gaped open.

"Close enough for government work?" Stanley hammered. "Close enough for twenty years in the slammer, having your pretty little ass be a sexual pincushion?"

Sudeep jerked as if he had been tasered. Stanley's loud accusations bounced off the soundproof walls of his office. "Do you think they'll give you a sabbatical on your doctorate or reduce your sentence because you, very cleverly, I might add, wired the money through almost untraceable means to your dirt-poor family in India, Mr. Patel?"

Sudeep's head fell into his hands, and his body shook with sobs.

Like violins accompanying the percussions of a broken man's wails of despair, Stanley's matter-of-fact voice was timed in perfect cadence to his victim's moans. "Our work involved combining polycontin, which, coincidentally, is the new collegiate drug of choice, with our drug to test the effects. I must give you credit. By varying the amounts that you tested in the combinations, you were able to surreptitiously siphon off what should have been an unnoticeable amount for your illegal distribution."

Stanley interlocked his fingers, placed his elbows on his desk for support, and leaned his large head on his hands. He paused dramatically. "Oh, and it required an excellent judge of competence on your part to assume that my CFO would not pick up on the discrepancies. But, unfortunately for you Mr. Patel," he lowered his voice to a whisper, "*I* notice everything."

Stanley motioned for Sudeep to come closer. He motioned more urgently until finally, gritting his teeth and setting his face in a measure of defiance, Sudeep leaned over the desk. In a whisper so soft that Sudeep had to strain to hear it, Stanley said, "And you tried to fuck me."

With a violent thrust, Stanley's meaty arms shot out from his body and slammed Sudeep's shoulders. The man fell backwards, toppling over his chair, and landing heavily on the Italian marble floor.

Stanley walked around his desk and stood over the fallen man, who was sobbing uncontrollably and lay curled in a fetal position. Calmly, he unzipped his pants, pulled out his penis, and urinated on him.

CHAPTER 26

MAC PICKED UP AFTER THE first ring. "Before you entered the life of crime and you were a lowly broker just like me, how did you attract clients?" he asked.

After a moment of silence, Jeremy responded, "I was *never* just like you."

"Okay, like me but much, much better. Does that help?"

Jeremy let out a short, cruel laugh. "And I have no need for your help."

"Apparently, you do. I don't call you," Mac answered quickly.

"Bravo," said Jeremy, clapping loudly into the phone. "There is a hint of testosterone there."

"Thanks, but you still haven't given me an answer. How did you get so many clients and generate so much revenue in such a short time period?"

"Now I'm supposed to give you a tutorial?"

"Obviously not. As in every other aspect of your life, you must have something to hide. So I'm going to ask another question, one that is much more relevant to today.

"I've wasted too much time trying to figure out why you chose to engage with me." Mac went on. Let me run a theory by you. I've been blessed in so many ways—great clients, a great team, and in my tiny world, a wonderful reputation for doing the right thing ..."

"Could you be more tedious?"

"I'm on to something here. I'm married to a wonderful woman who shares my bed each night, and I have four amazing,

112

productive children. I have no other worlds to conquer, and I thank God every day for these blessings."

Mac paused, curious to see if he'd be interrupted again. "Maybe with all you have—money, endless women, fame or infamy, take your pick, you're unfulfilled. You keep throwing dirt into the empty hole of your ambition, but it's never filled."

"If your analytical skills are as flawed as your psychological hypotheses, I could never have you manage any of my assets," Jeremy said.

"What the hell *is* your endgame?" Mac asked. "I can't believe that your obsession is just to keep torturing me, or to pick my brain for economic pearls of wisdom, or even to get the whole world thinking that you're a prince of a guy."

After another moment of silence, Jeremy spoke . "Of course you can't figure me out. Your lack of creativity makes you myopic, content to exist in your comfortable world of incompetent stockbrokers, surrounding yourself with unimaginative, visionless cretins, and your insipid family."

"You didn't answer my question."

"Nor do I have to answer any of your fucking questions."

Mac raised his fist in silent victory. He could hear Jeremy breathing. Every second of silence felt like uninterrupted points in a basketball game.

Finally, Jeremy spoke. "I'm going to give you something. You finally showed a bit of spirit today. Unfortunately, what I give you will fester like a growing cancer inside your gut." He paused, obviously for dramatic effect. "So, how does *Senator* Lyons sound to you?"

"Mac, ya got a minute?" It was the end of the day. Mac had been jammed with appointments, two reviews, two new clients. He was tired and he wanted to go home.

As the High Net Worth Group's newest partner, David Grant was given a wide berth by Mac. In Mac's opinion, investment bankers were wired differently, and that provided them with a different set of skills. David was analytical, serious, and quiet. Only the first trait was consistent with the rest of the team.

Each of Mac's other partners was an open book to him, but with David, he was taking time peeling back the layers of complexity. Instinctively, Mac felt that if he pressed with personal questions or questions about David's military background, his friend might close up like a clam.

Nevertheless, Mac gave David a grin. "Sure. Let's go into my conference room."

Mac sat down first. David closed the door and sat next to him, an earnest look on his face. "I feel like I'm not earning my keep."

Mac didn't respond.

Gesturing nervously, David continued. "I haven't done a great job of bringing in new clients. My investment banking skills are rarely needed, and I ..." He stopped speaking and looked down.

"Go on," Mac encouraged gently.

"Ever since my dad was killed, I haven't been a hundred percent. Hell, probably not even fifty percent!"

Mac waited until David looked up at him, then said, "Am I normally reluctant to tell someone when I think he's underperforming? It's early. No way you're going to be keeping up with R.J. and Danny out of the gate."

"I've been here two years!"

"Talk to me when it's five. Sorry, but you're still a rookie. All of us have baggage that weighs us down. None as tragic or frustrating as yours, but you'll work through it."

"So you're not unhappy with my work?"

"Asked and answered – subject change. I'm curious about something, and if I'm getting too nosy, noneya is an acceptable response. You and your friend Blake probably saw a lot of things in the army you'd like to forget. Were you both badasses?"

"I was in the bush leagues. He's all pro. Snake could wipe out an enemy company, place small crosses on their bodies, and then eat a steak dinner sitting on the corpses. The man's a machine."

"He placed crosses on the men he'd killed?"

"Yes. He was a committed Christian."

"So am I," Mac said as he thought about how he wanted to phrase the next question. "Does he feel that placing a cross on the bodies makes it God's work?

"Before you answer," Mac stopped David, whose mouth was open, "I'm not judging him. I understand war. I understand that it was your duty to protect your fellow soldiers and fight for your country. Not only do I appreciate everything you did, but I'm honored to know you and to have met Blake." Mac leaned forward. "What I don't understand is the crosses."

David nodded. "Blake feels that everyone should get a chance to go to heaven. He started out as a sniper, but strangely enough, that bothered him; it was too remote. His talents were up close and personal. And if the situation allowed it, he would place a cross on the dead man's body, which was his way of asking God to forgive him."

"Which him?"

"Sorry. The dead man."

Mac thought for a few moments. "So he is not burdened by remorse over his kills?"

"No."

"One more question," Mac said. "Actually, two, The first is, do you see how you started this conversation with your agenda and now the agenda is mine?"

115

David smiled.

"The second question is, when I shook hands with Blake, I noticed a strange tattoo on the knuckles of his right hand. What's the deal with that?"

David nodded. "Yeah. That's another ritual: 👁 4 N 👁 . When he was a sniper, he would close his eyes and kiss his knuckles after every kill."

"Remind me not to piss him off."

CHAPTER 27

LIKE MOST SMALL BIOTECH COMPANIES in the Palo Alto area of California, Cerebrepharma's money was not wasted on the surroundings. In the area adjacent to Stanford University, affluent neighborhoods and high-end retailers were the norm. But travel five miles or so to East Palo Alto, head to O'Bannon Drive, and you end up at what Stanley Lipitz liked to call "piece of shit biotech row." Each building appeared to have been built and owned by a corporation whose imagination stopped at concrete and tinted glass construction.

Every cloned building on O'Bannon Drive was involved in some form of drug research: specialty pharmaceuticals, ranging from enhancing existing pharmaceutical products, including a pill aimed at Parkinson's disease, to genetic research, to the elusive diet pill. The researchers inside the buildings couldn't care less about their environment, their clothes, or their lifestyle. It was all about the science.

Their neighbor had a slightly different philosophy. Stanley Lipitz had the only office in his entire 76-person company, and although he would be loath to check, it was undoubtedly the only office on the entire street. The remodeling that had been performed to his strict specifications had been justified by the significance of his celebrity status in the biotech community and what appeared to be the certainty of his discovery.

Stanley's office was a secured inner sanctum, complete with hidden video and audio recording devices, and a hidden private

117

elevator. Purposely, the opulence of his office was in stark contrast to the Spartan surroundings of his underlings.

After a while, Stanley was tired of hearing Sudeep's stifled cries. The man had not moved from the floor, and the smell of his urine-covered clothes had lost its appeal.

"You should feel comfortable, Mr. Patel," said Stanley. "The Italian marble floor that you are trying so desperately to disappear into was imported from RMR Marmo. It's the most famous showroom in India."

Sudeep moved slightly, but his head remained cradled in his arms.

"Here." Stanley threw him a royal navy plush towel, which he had gotten from his private bathroom. "Dry yourself off. I'm afraid that you're a bit odoriferous."

Still averting his eyes, Sudeep listlessly wiped his left cheek.

"Sit up, *now!*" Stanley demanded. "Or I will call Security and have the police here in five minutes."

Slowly, Sudeep rose to a sitting position and glared at his tormentor through swollen eyes.

Stanley walked behind his desk, reached up, and switched on the Fanimation's Bourbon Street set of three-belt-drive, 52-inch ceiling fans. It was not ideal décor for his office, but the fans were able to disperse unpleasant odors quickly. He began pacing. "I have to decide whether you are redeemable. At the moment, your appendage is inexorably stuck in the guillotine of life, and I must decide whether to slice ..." His voice trailed off.

"What can I do?" It was a hoarse, desperate whisper.

"First," Stanley spun around, "get a backbone. Refuse to lose, remember?"

"Yes."

"Would you like a bottled water?"

"Yes, please." Sudeep ran the towel over his hands and face.

Stanley reached into the small refrigerator by his desk, pulled out two bottles, and tossed one to Sudeep, which he caught with one hand. "Tomorrow morning at eight o'clock, you will come to me with all of the information on your distribution line. In addition, I want the data on every school, from high school on up, within a 100-mile radius that could be a possible location for future sales."

"I ... I don't understand. You want the names of all the schools where we sold the polycontin, and ..." His face contorted in confusion, "you also want to know what high schools are in the vicinity?"

"Did I stutter?" Stanley glared at Sudeep and shook his head with impatience. He began pacing again, rubbing his hands together. "How many people know the results of the Phase III testing of Celebra?"

"I believe only you, Juan, and myself, sir."

"Believing is for fools. Knowledge, absolute certainty rule the world. Find out. And if that is indeed a certainty, put a lid as tightly on that information as you'd like to have on your asshole if you end up in jail."

Stanley stopped pacing and walked toward Sudeep. He leaned down, and the man did not flinch. "Within 48 hours, I need to know how quickly and how widely you could distribute a new drug. It will be called Euphoria. It causes an incomparable high, unfortunately followed by a devastating low. But that is meaningless, because," he whispered seductively, "it is so fucking addictive."

The two men stared at each other for a solid minute, then Sudeep rose slowly from the floor and stood erect. He folded the towel and looked up at Stanley. "Is there a hamper?"

Stanley nodded and pointed to his bathroom.

A few steps before the bathroom, Sudeep turned. "How about a shirt?"

Stanley gave him an amused look. "A shirt?" He shook his head, reached into his right front pants pocket, and pulled out a roll of cash. He plucked two hundred dollar bills and offered them to the man. "Buy a new one. You're going to be busy, and you'll need to look like you're prosperous."

Sudeep reached out, took the money and then walked into the bathroom, opened the hamper, and dropped in the towel. Then he gently closed the top of the hamper, walked back, and stood in front of his boss. "And if I ..."

"Yes," interrupted Stanley. "If you follow precisely my every instruction, execute perfectly my every order, and keep your filthy fingers out of my money, you will be a free man. And perhaps even a moderately wealthy one. Layers and layers of protection must be in place." He paused. "Do you think that Juan could be compromised for the right price?"

"I don't know."

Stanley nodded. "Find out. Be certain of your conclusions."

Sudeep stared at him and said nothing.

"There is less than a six-month window, and you have much to accomplish. I have devised a way to get you the product. We'll discuss that after you make your reports to me. Any questions?"

Sudeep shook his head.

Stanley picked up the broken match. "When you break something, there is often the opportunity to fix it." He paused. "Sometimes you can rebuild it, even make it stronger."

He tapped the box of wooden matches. He counted out six, studied them for a moment, and then held them out towards the man. "Six in your family. Isn't that right Mr. Patel?"

The man nodded in response.

"On the other hand, there are some changes that can't be fixed. The chemistry is altered, the very make-up of what you deemed solid is questioned, and thus the truth becomes warped and changed forever."

With a flourish, Stanley struck all six matches at once. "You have six months to right your path and keep your world intact. I am confident that you will act with wisdom, alacrity, and precision."

CHAPTER 28

A FEW DAYS AFTER STANLEY Lipitz relieved his bladder on Sudeep, Sudeep sent him an e-mail: "Do you have a few minutes to discuss progress on Celebra?"

Stanley e-mailed a simple reply: "Now works."

Less than five minutes later, Stanley ushered Sudeep into his office. He raised a finger to his lips and motioned for the man to stand still. Walking back to his desk, he opened a drawer and removed a device that resembled a fat, rectangular remote. Stanley placed the device on his desk. Then he picked up headphones, which he placed over his ears. Flipping a switch on the device, he listened, nodded, and returned the equipment to the drawer.

"Less invasive than a full-body cavity search. Proceed."

Stanley sat down in the chair behind his desk, but he did not ask Sudeep to be seated.

Without preamble, Sudeep spoke. "Juan is agreeable to an arrangement."

"Agreeable?" Stanley asked, raising a threatening eyebrow.

"Yes, sir. He wants ten percent."

"And I want to be handsome. Do you think I will get my wish, Mr. Patel?"

"No, sir. I do not. However, I believe that I've analyzed the situation correctly. If Juan resigned or was terminated," he paused and looked his boss squarely in the eye, "it could bring attention to our operation."

Stanley nodded, pleased with the man's thought processes. "I concur. Perhaps all you needed was a little watering to have you grow."

Sudeep's jaw clenched, but he said nothing.

Stanley stood up and began pacing around the room. Finally he stopped, walked over, and sat on the front of his desk, which put him at eye level with Sudeep, who was approximately three feet away.

"Inform him that if he looks the other way, you will pay him $100,000 a month, surreptitiously wired to an account of his choosing."

"*I* will pay him, sir?"

Stanley looked at Sudeep as if the man had lost his mind. "Of course, you will, Mr. Patel. And if he doesn't agree, *I* will ring his scrawny neck."

CHAPTER 29

CORPORATE AMERICA IS INSTITUTIONALIZED. A strict game plan with precise rules and regulations guides its every movement. Corporate news is disseminated under strict guidelines. Press releases are vetted, often by both inside counsel and outside attorneys. In a world where a misplaced or erroneous word could cause significant harm to a stock price or be chum to hovering class-action lawyers, it is impossible to be too careful.

The myriad safeguards put in place to protect a company's stock price and its coffers were ignored by Stanley Lipitz. To acknowledge them, abide by the prescribed rules, would have given credence to the axiom that two heads, or in this case multiple heads, are better than one.

As he read his press release, Stanley smiled. Intellectually he had not yet met his equal, and when it came to spin, he knew he had no peer. With the stock price hovering at 22½ and his personal net worth under water, according to the now-frantic bankers, Stanley knew that a bold move was required. Litigation risk was acceptable, because if the highly motivated Mr. Patel performed as expected, Stanley would have a fortune hidden in Swiss banks before any judgment could be rendered.

Criminal risk, however, was unacceptable. Thus, there was an extremely fine line in inferring that his one-drug-wonder company had the answers, while walking the high wire of fraud. Emphasize the unimpeachable, exude confidence that time will solve any minor glitches. Fortunately, there were no instant fact-checkers in the biotech industry. In reality, all Stanley had was a blockbuster street drug.

A case could be made that there would be a market for a drug that froze the deteriorating mental faculties of a loved one for a finite period of time: a reprieve, time to get affairs in order, right your past wrongs and ask for forgiveness.

Stanley mused. Perhaps he should give it an evangelical name. He shook his head. All the warnings in the world wouldn't get a caregiver to stop pill-pushing after six months. Stanley closed his eyes, imagining the poor patient's distress: "I'm slipping. I know I'm losing it. Where's my pill?" Perhaps this patient would be the exception. Either guilt or hope would cause the caregiver to continue dispensing the drug.

So, it was not Armageddon for Cerebrepharma. The stock would eventually suffer, because it was a Band-Aid and not a cure. In fact, Stanley estimated that after the stock plummeted because of the dashed hopes for a longer-term cure, it would likely settle in the ten-dollar range. For Stanley, it would be meaningless; he would be broke, ruined, and still ugly.

If he were an honorable man, he would tell the truth about Cerebra, file for bankruptcy, and screw the bankers. He smiled again. What a ridiculous hypothesis. While he was at it, why didn't he just tell Mr. Patel to cease and desist, that he hated the idea of young men and women becoming addicted to drugs? No; his path was clearly chosen. After the third reading, he was convinced. It was a masterpiece.

"Hey, Mac, did you see this?"

Early in his career, R.J. Brooks had decided to get the Chartered Financial Analyst accreditation. It was the most onerous of designations in the financial industry, requiring three years of study. Only about a third of the candidates who began the program actually passed all the tests and received the designation.

R.J.'s accreditation ended up being more of a testament to his intellectual gifts than a highly utilized addition to the team. Partly because he was more valuable working with clients than analyzing stocks, his skills in that area were rarely requested. In addition, the firm's research department was quite capable, so Mac felt that the talent was a bit redundant. That did not decrease his pride that his partner had persevered, and he found the designation quite useful on those occasions when investments did not work out as planned. Mac informed clients up front that when certain stocks did not do well, it would be R.J.'s fault.

R.J. had printed the press release he had just read online rather than e-mailing it to Mac and possibly subjecting it to a quick glance and delete. In addition, it had more personal interest than business interest to Mac. About a year ago Grace's father had died after a long struggle with Alzheimer's, and that had just added to their already full plate of stress.

Mac took the sheet of paper and looked at it.

"In human trials, Cerebra has proven effective in delaying the progression of Alzheimer's in 97 percent of the studies. The trial covered 300 people in various stages of the disease. For a six-month period, cognitive functions did not decline at all, and in twelve individuals, testing showed a slight increase. Further studies will be required to extend the efficacy beyond six months; however, the company believes that freezing a loved one's cognitive degeneration is the first step in curing the disease.

Cerebrepharma will submit its drug for final FDA approval at the completion of its studies."

"What's the symbol?" Mac asked automatically.

"CRBE; stock's up 6 to 29¼."

Mac nodded. "If a patient could get this drug soon after being diagnosed ..." He looked up at R.J. "Thanks. Part of me doesn't want to tell Grace about this, because the first natural thought for anyone who's gone through it is, 'Why didn't they discover this years ago?'"

"You were close to her dad, too, Mac."

Mac smiled and looked at him. "You bet. He was one of the sweetest men on the planet. Listen, the important thing is that they're finally making progress on this damn disease."

Mac looked down at the press release again. "Ninety-seven percent is off the charts in effectiveness in a human trial. I love the statement about 'freezing a loved one's cognitive degeneration.' Still," he looked back at R. J., "it does take a lot of balls to make a statement like that in a press release.

CHAPTER 30

"WHAT THE HELL NUMBER IS this?"

"It's a throwaway."

"Really? As far as we know, this guy's still out of the country, and you think he has ears on you?"

Mac blew out a breath. To his credit, Joe Sebastiano had not given him crap for being overly secretive when they were originally closing in on Jeremy Lyons's location. In retrospect, Mac's paranoia at that time turned out to be justified. Cautious by nature, he did not want this predator any closer to his thoughts than he already was. "Are you really going to pimp me about this?"

"Nah," said Joe. "I was just hoping that you had a side business dealing drugs and could get me some of that Euphoria drug; it's supposed to be better than sex."

It was too easy. "Instead of that, why don't I just give your Barbie doll a laxative? Even that would be better than sex with you."

"That's better. You've been morose for too long," Joe replied, chuckling. "You're out of practice. Do I need to bring out my bug detector?"

"No. Keep Little Joe in its holster. I have a better idea. I'll talk, you listen. Then gather all the expertise of the FBI and figure out a way to stop this madman. And Lyons is living inside of *my* shorts, not yours. So please don't question my decisions. I'm trying to have at least a semblance of privacy in my life."

After a moment of silence, Joe filled the void. "Is it okay if I say something before I go into mute mode?"

"Sure."

"I'm worried about you. If I were in your shoes I'd be going nuts, and I'm trained for this shit. But Mac, you've become caustic and short tempered, and stress is coming off your body like cheap perfume. I miss the days when I could count on you busting my balls."

Mac smiled into the phone in spite of himself. With his left hand, he reached up and massaged his brow. "Me, too, pal. Okay, you've softened me up, and you didn't even need an anal probe. Let me run it down for you. Remember the Chad Alexander trial and the subsequent YouTube confession?"

"Yeah. His father tried to sue the Ritz and then got sucker punched."

"Do you know what happened to Alexander?"

"No; just that he was mugged."

"I've got a little more detail. Actually, the rapist got some of his own medicine, courtesy of two men."

"Ouch." Joe paused. "Why, other than it's nice to see the bastard get what he deserved, do we care?"

Mac seemed to chew on this before he spoke again. "I'm not sure we do, but have you thought about this at all—thought about who was behind this elaborate sting operation?"

Joe considered the question. "It is intriguing. If this happened in an alley or a flophouse and the father of the girl who was raped was smiling, I'd understand. But how do you lure a heterosexual predator into the Ritz, where he ultimately gets gang-banged by two guys?"

"Maybe by using a hot woman," Mac suggested. "The valet at the Ritz identified Alexander, said he was gonna hook up with this amazing black woman. Apparently, Alexander kidded with the valet about how she was gonna rock his world."

"I'm not sure how you got this information, and I'm not sure that I want to know, but I still don't get it," Joe said.

"Think of the precision of this operation. Lure the victim; pay the men assaulting Alexander; it happens at the Ritz, which is sure to incense the pompous father."

"That's a lot of variables."

"Exactly," Mac agreed. "No way the plumber dad of the raped girl pulls this off. It's like a military operation or one out of the CIA. So, bottom line, we have an avenging angel out there, and nobody takes credit."

"You think *Lyons* had his hand in this? asked Joe.

"Work with me on my hypothesis for a moment. Lyons arranges vigilante justice. How many times does a stranger evoke such extreme retribution?"

"It would be an aberration." Joe admitted.

"So if we can connect this to Lyons, I don't know, assault and battery, intent to maim, you could charge him."

Joe waited before responding. "I understand why you might see Lyons in every well-orchestrated criminal act."

"Joe," Mac interrupted. "There must be some consequence for what this man has done and his intrusion into my life. I've committed his damn book to memory. When he expands on battlefield strategies, he describes seemingly random events, which, when stitched together, provide a road map to victory. I don't know where the hell Lyons is going, but couldn't Alexander's gang rape be a first step?"

"I'm not denying that this appears to be the work of professionals. But who is Megan O'Brien to him? How does Lyons profit?"

"Open your hand and extend it flat in front of you."

"Uh ... okay."

"Did you feel it?"

"What?"
"The buck being passed."

CHAPTER 31

ALEGRIA LOPEZ WAS NOT AN attractive woman. Her total lack of physical appeal to members of either sex was attributed partly to unfortunate genetics and partly to the fact that she couldn't care less what she looked like. Her dark, stringy hair was washed only when she remembered; she dressed only because it would be uncomfortable to work without clothes; and cosmetics never touched her face.

When Jeremy Lyons decided to disband his hedge fund, all his traders except Alegria had been instructed to stay in place. Alegria surmised that those traders had also been instructed to stick to the script when questioned by the authorities and that any deviation would be harmful to their health. She had no illusions about Jeremy Lyons.

Jeremy never discussed the main focus of his operation with Alegria. It was her job to find legitimate trades, execute them, and make money for the hedge fund. She was proud of her record of success, and Jeremy never criticized her when a trade went wrong.

When Jeremy left Naples, he asked Alegria to go with him. If she had declined, she knew that she would still be safe. If her mentor were capable of any human feeling, it was because of Alegria, who had become his surrogate daughter. When she had accepted his offer without hesitation, a flicker of genuine affection had floated through his eyes.

It was not the financial opportunity associated with continuing to work for Jeremy that had caused her quick response. He had paid her quite handsomely during her tenure with him, and she was confident that her skills would be sought after by any fund manager in the country. Although her environment and the freedom to make trading decisions without judgment were compelling, they were not the impetus. To Alegria, Jeremy Lyons was a god. No other individual had ever challenged her intellectual gifts. He mentored her. He pushed her. He was provocative, demanding, and impossibly uncompromising. Not only was Jeremy brilliant, he was also ruthless. Absolutely nothing stood in his way. He eliminated incompetence and required perfection.

Alegria fed off his teachings like a starving baby on her mother's breast. Although Jeremy had never discussed any unlawful methods he employed to accomplish his objectives, Alegria was not naïve; however, it fell outside of her area of responsibility, so she did not judge. The first copy of his book, *Survival of the Fittest*, had been given to her with the inscription: "To the child I'll never have." Over the last eighteen months, under his tutelage, she had perfected her craft, and now she knew that she was his equal. Yet, she continued to look at him with reverence and awe.

As Jeremy walked into the trading complex, Alegria nodded acknowledgment. For the past eighteen months she had followed Jeremy's instructions to the letter. "It's difficult for me to understand your emotional detachment," she said.

Jeremy sat down in an adjacent ergonomic black leather swivel chair, folded his hands in his lap, and smiled with amusement.

Undeterred, she continued. "For some reason, you are no longer engaged."

He raised an eyebrow to concur.

"You are not burned out; your skills have not diminished in any way."

"Do go on."

"I never imagined that you would relinquish control."

"Control? The word is nebulous. Is it not possible to lend control of a particular situation or operation? Control is only relinquished when it cannot be regained. Is that the case here?" he asked pleasantly.

"No, of course not. And I appreciate the confidence you have in my abilities. I share your confidence, and I am proud of my performance. But you have gone from analyzing and discussing every trade, even micromanaging, to now showing little interest in my trades or my performance."

"Do I need to scrutinize more closely?"

She shook her head in frustration. "You know what I mean. How can you go from a trading perfectionist to a casual bystander?"

Jeremy unfolded from the chair, stood up, and walked over to Alegria. He reached down and placed his hands gently on her shoulders. She looked up at him. Her frown turned to curiosity.

He held her gaze for a moment, then smiled and turned away. He walked slowly towards the exit of the trading floor, then turned around and looked at her again. He raised a contemplative finger. "I enjoy engaging with you, but only if it has a productive end. We have scaled down the financial side, and I want to be sure that you continue to be intellectually challenged."

Alegria nodded enthusiastically, like a child being asked if she wanted to stop for ice cream.

Jeremy returned to his chair, sat, and leaned forward. "You can do the amount of trading required in your sleep. It is time to test your intellect in more creative ventures."

She leaned forward, focusing hungrily.

"This is far outside your area of responsibility," he warned. "And once you are under the tent, you can't go back to the familiar."

"I'm aware that you have no restrictions on achieving your goals," she said with confidence.

"And does that bother you?"

"It is not my place to be bothered."

"That's a non-answer."

"If you want me to say that I agree with your methods or condone illegal acts, I won't say it. On the other hand, unless you're asking me to commit felonious acts, I will not judge you." She fixed him with her gaze. "And under no circumstances, even under the threat of death, will I betray you."

CHAPTER 32

FOR A MAN WHO HAD experienced the majority of acknowledged pleasures in his life, a genuine feeling of what most would describe as joy was rare. Although Jeremy Lyons still enjoyed hedonistic pleasures, the phrase "there's nothing new under the sun" had become applicable. Financially, his success was not only legendary, it was also chronicled.

He had no heirs, so his legacy had to be created and preserved in his lifetime. It was not enough to garner astronomical riches. It was not enough to become a highly successful author. When he amassed the power of Hitler, demonstrated the charisma of Bill Clinton, and presided over a rebuilt world like Franklin Delano Roosevelt, *that* would be enough.

The tropical sun bathed his lean, muscular, perfectly toned body as he lay motionless on the chaise on his balcony. He was clad only in black silk running shorts, and the ultraviolet rays acted like a steam bath as he ignored the bubbles of sweat that covered his hairless body and continued to cook his skin to an even golden brown.

As religious as he was in his daily workouts, it was important for him to be browned to perfection, like a loaf of freshly baked bread. He rolled from his stomach to his back after exactly thirty minutes of exposure. Only on rare days when clouds obscured the sun would he deviate from his routine.

Lost in thought, it took Jeremy a moment to determine that his iPhone had received a text. That in itself was unusual, and the fact that it occurred with still five minutes remaining on his back annoyed him. He had disciplined himself to ignore any disruption to his routine.

After exactly five minutes, he rolled back over onto his stomach and grabbed the phone from its position beneath the chaise and read the message: "I think I found it."

He smiled. Alegria. The accuracy of his instincts was once again confirmed. As he had expected, bringing her into his confidence had caused her young, facile brain to accelerate to warp speed. If she said she thought she had found the information he needed, it was a certainty.

Jeremy turned over and sat up, then reached for a towel from the adjacent table and dried his body. He looked out across the railing of the balcony and breathed deeply, filling his lungs with air. He exhaled slowly. Alegria had always been an eager student, and now she was also a devotee – a disciple, fully engaged in his quest. And as a contrast to the late, great Max Parnavich, he would never have to worry about her wandering off the reservation.

As Jeremy had anticipated, Alegria was nervous. When he texted her to come to his suite at 6:30 that night and have dinner with him, he waited ten minutes before he got her response. Alegria was not a social person. During her entire tenure with him, she had not communicated with any male or female except for purposes of business.

While Jeremy carried out operations from his Naples complex, he had maintained both audio and visual surveillance on all his employees. He knew that Alegria had called her parents every week, but she had shown no interest in banter, flirting, or sex with any of her co-workers. The woman paid no attention to her appearance; she was the perfect intellectual machine.

The contrast between Jeremy's black silk karate robe and bare feet and Alegria's food-encrusted blue jeans and wrinkled long-sleeved work shirt, complete with unattractive Crocs shoes, was stark. He was pleased that she appeared to have washed her self-cut dark, stringy hair. The obvious reason for her nerves and unconscious fidgeting as she waited for her master to speak was that she had information that she felt would please him. The less apparent reason was that Jeremy had never asked her to have dinner with him before.

"Sit, please," Jeremy said as he motioned to a comfortable leather couch the color of a strong latte.

Alegria seemed to mentally debate for a moment and then sat on the edge of the couch and wrung her hands.

Jeremy sat down across from her on a matching couch and reached for the menu that was lying on the glass coffee table between them. "Would you like a menu?" he asked pleasantly.

"Uh ... no. Anything is all right."

"I know you don't drink, so I've taken the liberty of ordering you a Diet Coke. Is that okay?"

She nodded her head up and down like a bobble-head doll.

An extremely attractive, diminutive Asian woman appeared with a glass of red wine for Jeremy and a Diet Coke for Alegria. Jeremy turned to her and spoke in Chinese. She smiled, nodded twice, and then left the room.

Jeremy leaned forward, placed his elbows on his knees, and steepled his hands. "Tell me about your discovery."

"The origin of the street drug Euphoria interests me," Alegria began. "It has unique characteristics, which produce what is apparently an unparalleled feeling of bliss."

Alegria was in her element, and all signs of nervousness and lack of confidence were gone. "However," she continued, "the subsequent crash is devastating. My research indicates that the duration of the high is, on average, twenty minutes, whereas the gut-wrenching, depressing side effects last approximately an hour. The drug is highly addictive.

"There have already been three apparent suicides from overdoses," she added somberly. "Two college students and one high-school student. And the distribution in the California school system appears to be accelerating at an alarming pace."

Jeremy nodded, not interested in the maudlin. "So it's unlikely that some run-of-the-mill chemist cooked up the formula in his home meth lab."

She nodded.

"Is it just regional?"

"Yes," she responded.

"Big pharma can't be involved." he said thoughtfully. "The supplier has to be indigenous to the region and in league with the distributor."

Alegria's eyes shone like a hungry cat's.

"Sorry. Please continue. I was just trying to work out the logic."

"No, no," she said. "I love seeing you process thoughts."

Jeremy smiled and lowered his head with a slight bow of acknowledgement. He gestured with his hand for her to proceed.

"So my first question was, where was the first dissemination of the drug? It is illogical to think that the distributor would begin selling the drug at schools that were far away from the source. Also, as you said, a drug this powerful was not home grown. So the likely supplier is a biotech company."

"And that led you to biotech companies that had large pipelines or were profitable."

"Yes!" she said excitedly. "There is a huge risk in producing, processing, and of course, disseminating a drug with side effects that can lead to fatalities."

"So, your next step?" he prompted.

"Which company would be desperate enough to risk obliteration, and which control person would be desperate enough to risk incarceration?"

"Excellent."

"I started with twelve possible biotech companies, and after running them through probability scans, I ended up with three."

"And what did you do to determine our winner?" Jeremy taunted, knowing that she had the answer.

"I used the hacking software that you created to analyze the financial situations of the three CEOs. If that hadn't worked, I would have gone to the CFOs." Alegria said this softly, with a bowed head, and she blushed with embarrassment. "One company stood out like a sore thumb."

Jeremy waited a moment to add drama to his next words. "To commit a crime in order to save the lives of children," he said soothingly, while mentally welcoming her to the dark side, "is God's work."

CHAPTER 33

IT HAD TAKEN SPECIAL AGENT Ellen Williams a long time to recover from the trauma of her shootout with Jeremy Lyons's hired assassin. Having a killer bleed out on top of you is not just another day at the office, even for a trained FBI operative.

At least with that incident, it seemed like there was an expiration date on the psychological damage. Not so with her dad's disease. When Charlie Williams was 64, he was diagnosed with early-onset Alzheimer's. To have this happen to her father, a brilliant scientist at the National Institutes of Health, just didn't seem fair.

Charlie had spent his whole life giving to Ellen, her mom, his friends, and his community. Now her mom traveled daily from their home in Bethesda to the Alzheimer's facility at Arden Courts in Potomac, Maryland. On this Saturday morning, Ellen was making the trek from her apartment in Arlington, Virginia, to meet her mom there.

Ellen had become an authority on Alzheimer's, the irreversible, progressive brain disease that slowly destroys memory and thinking skills. Eventually, as was happening with her dad, even the ability to carry out the simplest tasks disappears.

When her dad became incontinent, Ellen persuaded her mom to move him to Arden Courts. She had done her research, met the managers, interviewed the staff, and threatened everyone with jail if her dad wasn't given first-class treatment. Because Ellen had been told that her appearance belied her profession, she wasn't sure that anyone took her threats seriously.

In spite of her athletic build, dark hair, olive skin, and blazing green eyes, Ellen might not accept the "beautiful" tag that most people threw at her; however, she did not argue that she was easy on the eyes. She had lost count of the times she'd been asked if she was an actress on television or in movies. The disadvantage of her good genes was that it was hard to be taken seriously as a kickass FBI agent.

Every other time she visited her dad, Ellen played the role of an actress: smiling, joking, hugging him like he was a producer who had just given her a starring role. This time was different. This time there was finally hope.

As a result of some heavy politicking by her boss, Joe Sebastiano, who seemed to know everyone, Ellen got her dad involved in a clinical trial being run by a California biotech company. Job assignments had precluded Ellen from seeing her dad more than once a week in the last month, but her mom swore that the disease's progression had stopped. If he still maintained the ability to carry on a conversation and send out his heartwarming smile, then Ellen's prayers had been answered.

Arden Courts was a lockdown facility. Ellen's chest tightened. Not her dad. He was too gentle, too happy, too innocent to be caged. She gathered herself as she stood outside the main building. She understood the logic, even though she hated the fact that her dad was a patient.

Visitors entered a code when they wanted to leave, and they were advised to make sure that a resident was not close behind them. *So far no escapes,* Ellen thought ruefully.

Every time she visited, part of her wanted to grab her dad, take him home with her, and take care of him, because whenever she had to leave him, it felt like a vise clamping her heart. Hellos were a rush of hugs, kisses, and fierce embraces. Hellos held the possibility of a smile, a laugh, or a giggle of glee. Goodbyes felt like abandonment, seeing his face fall, and in the worst of moments, seeing a tear slide down his cheek. Yet Ellen knew that someday, some horrible, unimaginable day, she would leave to a blank stare.

Ellen brushed a tear from her eye with the back of her hand and walked through the doors. A middle-aged woman with a sweet smile looked up from her desk and said, "Nice to see you, Ms. Williams." Ellen nodded, smiled, and thanked her. In spite of her misgivings, this was a lovely facility. The residents all had their own rooms, and although they could not exit the premises, they had access to a beautiful courtyard.

Ellen first looked for her dad in his room. It was clean and, of course, filled with pictures of her and her mom. She turned, and an attendant pointed outside. On this warm, sunny spring day, several residents were enjoying the courtyard. Her dad's back was to her, but the slight build, light gray hair, and grand gestures were unmistakable. He was holding court, to the delight of his small audience.

"Dad," Ellen said tentatively as she touched his back.

"Ellen!" Charlie Williams said with excitement. He spun around and threw his arms open wide enough to encircle the world. Tears ran down her face as she hugged him. The disease had taken weight from him, and she felt his shoulder blades. He hugged her so long, it felt like the first slow dance with her high-school crush.

Finally, she pulled away to look at him. One of the most insidious effects of Alzheimer's is that it acts as a one-way rheostat on the eyes. The incandescent light that shone so brightly with cognizance continued to dim, as if Satan slowly turned the knob.

Ellen took her dad by the arm and walked him over to a bench, where they sat together. As she faced him, his sweet face beamed up at her, and he began to sing softly, "Twinkle, twinkle, little star."

Ellen lost it. She grabbed him and hugged him again, so that he wouldn't see her tears. He had sung that song to her when she was a little girl, and he always claimed that it was written about her, because she was his star.

"How are you doing, Dad?"

"Good," he said, smiling. He gave her a knowing look and whispered, "I have the pill. Can't tell."

Ellen gave him a more analytical look. It wasn't just wishful thinking. He definitely had not deteriorated since her last visit, and his mood was great.

"I won't tell, Dad," she whispered.

"Mom gave it to me," he said proudly. He looked around first, then leaned over so that he was almost nose-to-nose with her. Whispering even softer, he said, "I think it will make my penis big."

CHAPTER 34

JEREMY LYONS WAS COMFORTABLE WITH solitude. During his short career as a stockbroker, winning clients had been tempered by the necessity to associate with inferiors. He was always four or five steps ahead of whoever he conversed with, and it was painful waiting for them to catch up. Why wouldn't he prefer to be alone with his thoughts and his creativity, rather than trying to educate hapless investors?

The typical man's dream is to have more money than he can spend, total autonomy in his work, and an infinite supply of beautiful women at his disposal. Jeremy Lyons had that, but he needed more. He needed intellectual stimulation, a mind to mold, a soul to inspire.

At first he thought that Alegria Lopez was too moral, too religious to become a convert. Yet, to Jeremy her mind was energy itself, and it was intoxicating. The adverse side effects of manipulating a person's mind normally were of little consequence to him. Often, playing Max Parnavich to the breaking point had been a rush for him. But Alegria was different. For some reason, he needed to preserve her integrity as he delicately turned her. It was a challenge, and challenges were aphrodisiacs to Jeremy.

The answer, of course, was forgiveness, for that leads to redemption. And there is no greater honor than leading a sinner to the path of righteousness.

He gave her a paternal smile. "It seems that you've become more relaxed having dinner with me."

"Yes," Alegria replied, smiling tentatively.

"And your insights are helpful to me in navigating my path."
Her smile broadened.

Jeremy leaned forward and clasped his hands together in his lap. He laced his voice with sincerity. "It's not easy for someone of your background to forgive misdeeds as serious as mine." He lowered his eyes, and his face became a picture of humility. "But you have the ability to see beyond the fragility of man." He opened his hands and stretched them out in a gesture of love.

She spoke softly. "Thank you." She bowed her head.

After a moment she raised her head and looked at him, concern evident in her eyes. "I sometimes feel guilty about taking this time from Sabine."

Jeremy nodded, touched by her honesty. "Sometimes an affair of the heart must take second place to affairs of the mind. Sensual pleasure is transitory. Progress is forever."

At this point, Alegria was positively glowing. She was all in.

After savoring the last bite of his sea bass with a coconut reduction, Jeremy looked up at his contented student. "The difference between failure and faith is focus," he began pedantically. "If you were to collaborate with me in the next phase of my quest, wouldn't it distract from your financial endeavors?"

Pushing her plate aside, Alegria unconsciously put her index finger in her mouth and gnawed on the nub of her fingernail. A moment later she realized what she was doing and hastily removed the finger from her mouth. "I'm sorry," she said nervously. Then her words rushed out. "If I had to choose, I would spend *all* my time helping you. There can be no higher goal."

"I'm not asking you to choose. I'm really trying to gauge your degree of commitment."

"One hundred percent!" she blurted.

Jeremy nodded and smiled like a lawyer whose witness has produced the perfect answer. Resting his arms on his thighs, he moved forward. "Now that we've identified the cancer, how would you suggest we cut it out?"

CHAPTER 35

UNLIKE HIS BOSS, A DICTATORIAL prick, Sudeep Patel hated subjecting young people to addictive drugs. But he had no choice. His boss had him by the balls. If he could disappear and return to India, extricating himself from this cesspool, he would do it in half a heartbeat. His father had terminal cancer. His mother and siblings were full-time caregivers, and their only means of support was the money Sudeep sent to them.

Initially, he rationalized that he had done everything possible to solve his family's crisis situation. When he told his father that he was going to quit school and take a second job, his father had told him that he would be dishonoring his family.

So Sudeep pleaded with his employer to compensate him with increased wages, and in return, he would forego any stock options. His search for compassion had resulted in Juan Alvarez, his immediate superior, saying that he had run it up the flagpole. Whether Alvarez had actually had the courage to approach Stanley Lipitz was in doubt. Still, the bottom line was, if Sudeep did not like his compensation arrangement, "Don't let the door hit your ass on the way out."

For Sudeep it was a difficult decision to start distributing drugs on the black market that could be obtained legally through prescription. The fact that he had a talent for it only shamed him more.

Sudeep sighed. In the last month he had been able to send $50,000 to his family. Even that had a significant element of risk if his level of compensation were ever analyzed. If anything happened to Sudeep, the Swiss bankers would alert his family, and the $900,000 currently in his bank account would provide for them for life. Still, he could not rationalize continuing to destroy young lives.

Sudeep knew that living on Sacramento Street would only sound reasonable to those who were not familiar with East Palo Alto. The seedy complex of three nondescript, two-story buildings spoke volumes about the residents. The unpainted gray concrete exterior matched the cracked cigarette gray of the parking areas between the buildings. There was no landscaping, and the crop of satellite dishes on the corners of the building was the only evidence of life within. The redeeming features for Sudeep were that his apartment was walking distance from the office, and it was cheap.

After climbing the black metal steps from the ground to the second floor entrance, Sudeep was bone tired. It was midnight, and all he wanted was to collapse on the bed in his efficiency apartment. He kept telling himself that he could do anything for six months. Then it would be over, and he could spend the rest of his life atoning for what he had done.

As he looked down at the threadbare, stained red/brown carpet that covered the dingy building hallways, a wave of depression made him stagger against the door. Tears of exhaustion involuntarily trickled down his cheeks. He took a breath, reached into his pocket for the key, and opened the door to his apartment.

Out of nowhere, a strong arm wrapped around his throat, constricting his airway. Sudeep had no time for coherent thought. As he rushed into blackness, the assailant carried him into the room.

Sudeep awoke slowly, as if becoming aware of his surroundings after excess sleep. He blinked his eyes, struggling for clarity of thought. He was lying on his drab Goodwill couch, which had been crammed into his tiny apartment and still showed the effects of previous cigarette burns. There was no reason to believe that his rusted refrigerator held anything but expired milk or that his ten-year-old TV was hooked to cable. In fact, the only discernible change was the man standing with his arms folded in front of the apartment door.

Sudeep's mouth formed a question, but the stranger spoke first. "The taser is sooo overused. I prefer a more personal method."

"What? Who are you?"

"At the conclusion of our brief meeting," the man said, looking around the dingy apartment with obvious disdain, "I believe that you'll determine that I am your guardian angel."

The smile that accompanied the intruder's proclamation sent a shudder through Sudeep. "What did you do to me?"

"Oh, that," the man said with a dismissive hand wave. "A simple sleeper hold. Significantly less residual discomfort than being shocked senseless. It's only dangerous in the hands of amateurs."

Sudeep was sitting up now, but afraid to move. The man was dressed as a jogger, complete with a Lakers cap. He had made no attempt at disguise. The latex gloves he wore ratcheted Sudeep's fear up even further.

Feigning composure, he studied the stranger. Incredibly fit, perfectly tanned, he apparently had no hair on his body, and his age was indeterminable. In spite of himself, Sudeep swept his eyes over his apartment, looking for an escape or a weapon of defense.

The man took a half-step toward him and gave Sudeep a start. "You do remember that I promised a brief meeting. Unless I have drastically underestimated your intellect, there will be no need for violence. However, I would like to move this along," he said impatiently.

"What do you want?"

"Your employer."

"What?"

"You're not deaf, are you? That could complicate matters. I would sit down somewhere ..." The man's eyes took in the room's lack of decor as his face registered disgust. "But I'm afraid I'm too much of a germaphobe. Would you like me to run this down for you to save us both some time?"

Sudeep nodded.

"You are in charge of illegally distributing the dangerous street drug Euphoria. You obviously do not spend your ill-gotten funds on yourself. Either willingly or through coercion, you have performed this function admirably and under an almost impenetrable shroud of secrecy. If it were not such a reprehensible venture, you could be commended for your organizational skills and devotion to duty."

Sudeep listened in horror to the man's recitation.

Leaning towards Sudeep, the man's eyes lasered into him. "Cerebrepharma is a house of cards." The stranger's right hand lashed out with thumb and forefinger less than a quarter of an inch apart. "And I," he pantomimed a pulling gesture, "will extract the essential card that will collapse this insidious company.

"My fa-family," Sudeep stammered.

"Of course. Your concern for your family has always been paramount." With Sudeep's mention of family, the man's tone changed instantly from what had sounded like a death sentence. "Do you Skype them?"

Sudeep nodded dumbly.

"Then let's go to your computer," the man said as he took Sudeep by the arm.

As if he were a robot, Sudeep got on line.

"We moved your father to Artemis Hospital. I believe they are the most highly regarded for their cancer treatment. I hope you don't mind."

Instead of responding, Sudeep gave the man a blank look of wonderment. It was the best hospital in Delhi. Sudeep stared into the screen as a small boy might have done in the 1950s when he saw his first television program. His father was propped up in a hospital bed, and his mother and siblings were smiling as they surrounded him. What appeared to be two bookend American Marines were standing on either side of them, arms crossed.

The voice behind Sudeep spoke reassuringly. "Your father is getting the best of care. My men will ensure your family's safety. In fact, your family believes that you have not only provided the upgrade in their conditions, but that the men assigned to them are responsible for making sure that the level of care is maintained. A little of the 'might makes right' theory. Now please stand up and turn around."

Sudeep did as he was told and looked up at the man. It felt like a staring contest until the stranger spoke for a final time. "Your family will be provided for, and you will be free if you testify and tell the truth. But if you ever commit another crime, then you are like the vermin who made you do this, and you will be exterminated."

CHAPTER 36

"OH, I DO SO LOVE a detente," said Jeremy Lyons.

Mac feel like he was unable to pass a giant kidney stone. "Is that what this is?" he asked in a bored voice.

"I'm shocked that you don't look forward to our verbal jousting. Who else could possibly compete with your rapier wit?"

Choosing not to respond, Mac decided to go on the offense. "You have to be jerking my chain with your bid to be a senator."

"Why do you say that?"

"Your priors. That would be my first thought."

Jeremy sighed theatrically. "Those of us born in the '50s tend to be stuck in the *Father Knows Best* generation. Assume that a fraction of the hyperbole associated with my exploits is indeed correct. Forgiveness is a tenet of all Christian faith."

This bastard knew that faith and family were the surest ways to needle Mac.

"The question from voters," Jeremy continued, "is not what *did* you do, but what *can* you do for *me*."

"And you have the answer?"

"The key to success is strategy. You may want to write this down. 'Find an issue that inflames your audience.'"

Although he felt like he was being roped in, Mac couldn't resist. "You're speaking at the Barron's Top 100 conference. There will be 500 attendees, all potential voters. What is your issue *du jour*?"

The silence that followed gave Mac a flicker of hope that he wasn't being reeled in. It was short lived.

"Before I grace you with the perfect answer to your question, let me ask you one. What do you feel is the number one attitudinal or systemic problem confronting our country?"

"Partisanship, incompetence, misinformation, apathy…"

Jeremy interrupted him. "The number one problem is *entitlement*. When 50% of your citizens are not paying taxes, are they being encouraged to be more productive, or in some cases, to be less productive? A capitalistic society only flourishes when there is incentive to create, to innovate, and to prosper."

"Welcome to the GOP. Maybe there is hope for you."

"Permit me to enthrall you and all your brilliant money managing colleagues at your precious conference. Have there been any repercussions from the credit default swaps, AKA the weapons of mass destruction, as your friend, Warren Buffet, called them?" Jeremy asked.

"No," Mac answered tersely.

"Have post-crisis regulations corrected these problems?"

"No."

"AIG's Financial Products Unit underwrote more than three trillion dollars worth of credit default swaps with zero dollars reserved for paying potential claims. As a student of history, you must know that the Commodity Futures Modernization Act of 2000 completely unregulated these babies. Here's the punch line: The logic behind the radical deregulation of these risky derivatives was that the banks and markets would never do anything to put their franchises at risk. If they did, the shareholders would surely punish them." Jeremy's laugh took obnoxious to a new level.

"Thanks for the history lesson," Mac responded to stop the cackling.

"So why will there be 500 people on their feet applauding?" asked Jeremy.

"Because you finally finished talking?"

"Because I propose that credit default swaps should be regulated as insurance products. Insurance companies require reserves. Lots of money on deposit to ensure that payments can be made if required. On the other hand, the swap requires not one penny to be put up against billions in potential losses. It's like you being able to bet me a billion dollars on a football game. What happens when you lose?

"Remember," Jeremy continued, "in this illustration of my readiness to govern I am enlightening a specific audience. And we both know that the public wouldn't understand that a problem exists or that the regulators should have already focused on the problem and corrected it.

"Simple solutions for complex problems. The true visionary must choose the appropriate antidote for the most pressing problem that is bothering a particular constituency. Help everyone, but one at a time. Am I a natural, or what?"

Mac refused to answer.

"So, Mr. McGregor, can I count on your vote?"

CHAPTER 37

LELAND FOLTZ WAS A CONSUMMATE professional. Even at 69 and currently unattached after three failed marriages, the legal icon could still get it done. His white, wispy hair was painstakingly combed and sufficiently sprayed so that it barely managed to cover the California sun's induced age spots. His face had been frozen so often that on those rare occasions when he wasn't tan, it looked like he was covered with brown polka dots. Still, his presence commanded both respect and attention.

"Let me get this straight," said Marci Finestein, the wafer-thin. intense Assistant DA in the Palo Alto Office of the District Attorney for Santa Clara County, California. "Your client siphoned off polycontin from his employer and sold the drug in the California school system. The employer caught him in the act, but instead of calling the authorities, he told your client to stop pilfering his supply of a legal drug and instead use and expand his distribution network to sell the highly illegal drug Euphoria in colleges and high schools?"

As she waited for a response, the 34-year-old, hard-charging woman encountered only Sphinx-like demeanor. Not a blink, not a twitch. Leland Foltz's impenetrable expression remained stoic.

Finestein leaned forward. "Just between us, Mr. Foltz, do you really believe your client's story?"

Foltz nodded slightly.

Finestein continued as if she were trying to wrap her head around it. She spoke first as if she were talking to herself. "Boss catches criminal, says, 'Stop, bad man. If you don't do what I say, and that means upgrade your criminal activities to a Grade Three felony, I will have you arrested. By the way, I am comfortable with my personal risk, because I can claim plausible deniability, so they'll just fry your ass.' Did I get that right, Mr. Foltz?"

This gambit did not merit a nod. In fact Foltz's eyelids dropped, and what could be seen as a look of boredom appeared.

The prosecutor shook her head dramatically in frustration and raised her voice. "I can't imagine that my boss will let this despicable piece of garbage walk. The 'I was just following orders' defense didn't work at the Nuremberg Trials and it hasn't worked since then."

Finestein knew that the defense attorney could not be goaded into conversation, so she implemented Plan B. She acted like she was deep in thought; she crinkled her face as if she were solving the problems of the universe, and she looked skyward. After five minutes of professional silence, she offered, "Maybe I could get my boss to go with ten years. You said your guy's young. Maybe he's out in six on good behavior. It's a hell of a lot better than life with no parole. Three kids have died from this crap!"

Her impassioned plea fell on uninterested ears. Foltz felt like he was watching a movie for the hundredth time. He could have recited the dialogue by heart.

"Could you help me here, Mr. Foltz? What possible mitigating circumstances could your client have for committing this series of reprehensible crimes?"

Foltz looked at her for a moment as if he were still lost in thought. "Ms. Finestein," he said kindly, "the man's initial crime, not unlike that of Jean Valjean, was simply trying to support his family. Had he not complied with his boss's every order, he would have been turned over to the police, who would have jailed him, and his family would have starved. I know that you have children, Ms. Finestein. How far would you go to save their lives?"

Finestein started to speak, and Foltz raised a finger. "In our initial conversation, I informed you that unless my client had full immunity, your investigation would continue aimlessly with no arrests in sight. Perhaps you mistake me for someone who would compromise his client's explicit instructions." He shook his head, implying that only a fool would think that way.

"For the rest of his life, my client must remain in the shadows, because by coming forward and indentifying the monster behind this, his part would be revealed, and his family would suffer. I don't for a second condone any of the actions this man has taken. But I *know*," his eyes glowered with intensity, "that there is a bigger malignancy out there, and *you* have a responsibility to this community, to the State of California and to this nation to stop it! Stop it now! We can eradicate this evil drug, cut it off at the source." He lowered his voice. "I implore you to act before another child dies."

As Leland Foltz walked down Grant Avenue, he turned his face to the sun and smiled. A quarter of a million dollars for an hour's work; it doesn't get any better. Maybe he should have negotiated his payment in Euphoria. Even with Viagra, at his age the real thing was almost more trouble than it was worth. He laughed out loud, drawing the attention of a few passersby.

CHAPTER 38

"UH, MAC." R.J. BROOKS KNOCKED on the door and scrunched his face in a 'Don't Shoot the Messenger' look. "You may have a bigger problem than clients' last-minute tax planning."

"What's this?" asked Mac as R.J. handed him a printed page.

"As you know," R.J. replied, "I'm notified with a Google alert whenever there's a mention of Mac McGregor, either praising or maligning, in the news."

"And this would be in the latter category?" Mac responded dryly while raising an eyebrow.

"Not exactly. It's actually quite flattering. But unless you're holding out on me, it's just, let's say it's probably unexpected."

Lena Brady interrupted Mac's confusion with a shout-out on his intercom: "A Colonel Jacobs for you. And that's right: fifteen years later and I'm still answering your phones."

"It's been fifteen years for me, too, and I'm still taking crap from you," Mac countered.

"You're welcome. Do you want him?"

"Name doesn't ring a bell, and R.J.'s dropped some nefarious article on my desk. Have somebody do a search on him, and I'll call him back."

Mac picked up the article and started reading as R.J. waited patiently. It was from the *Naples Daily News*, dated today:

> *The Wounded Warrior Project's largest donor will be honored April 21 at Freedom, a popular club and restaurant in Naples. Many of the wounded warriors will be present, and all active-duty military*

personnel are invited. The guest of honor is one of America's leading financial advisors, Angus "Mac" McGregor. The Wounded Warrior Project recently received a $5 million donation from the Mac and Grace McGregor Family Foundation.

William McMahon, who heads the Wounded Warrior Project, said, "We received this extremely generous donation with no fanfare and no request for publicity. It was a gift straight from the hearts of a humble, extraordinary family, and we are forever grateful."

Mac's face drained of color, and a wave of nausea engulfed him. "Why?" he whispered.

R.J. didn't respond; he just stood by Mac's desk and waited.

Mac closed his eyes and breathed deeply. "How do I get out of this?" He looked up at R.J.

"Maybe Artie can figure something out," R.J. suggested.

Although it was a sunny, 55-degree day, and wind was not a factor, it was not warm enough for Mac to walk the six blocks to the Army and Navy Club without his black raincoat on over his suit jacket. It was one of those "See, I was right" Al Gore days in February, but Mac's partner, Artie Cohen, also had on an overcoat, so Mac did not feel like he was the only wimp.

As the duo turned left onto 17th Street, a familiar African-American street woman smiled at them. Mac had a dollar ready and dropped it into her jar.

"Thank you, honey. Have a blessed day."

Artie looked at him skeptically. "Booze or drugs, take your pick."

Mac shrugged. "I prefer more positive scenarios, but the combination of being called 'honey' and wished a blessed day is worth a buck to me."

With Mac and Artie, the strategy was to make sure that they were on the sunny side of the street as they navigated their way to lunch. The Army and Navy Club was just off Farragut Square and thus at a diagonal to their office.

The club made the select list of the intrepid partners for three reasons: The tables in the main dining room were far enough apart that sensitive financial conversations could not be overheard; the soup and salad buffet on the lower level was quick and delicious; and as a member, only Mac could pay.

In addition, the venerable club had an illustrious 80-year history. The club's original purpose was to provide an inexpensive dining and gathering place for military personnel. Today, the majority of the members still had a military background.

"Why didn't you ever join the Metropolitan Club?" Artie asked as they passed that historic club on their left.

"It won the proximity vote, but it just seemed so staid. Every time I go there, I feel like I should be wearing a tux."

"R.J. is a member," said Artie.

Mac shrugged. "He enjoys being a grownup."

A few steps later, he switched the subject. "Although the odds are against it, there may actually be something you know that I don't."

Artie nodded confidently, his stride now more purposeful. "I understand," he said, "and I'm here to help. I've got your back."

Mac gave him an amused look. At times, his partner was certifiable. "Your confidence is comforting."

Just before they crossed 16th Street, Artie stopped and placed his hands on Mac's shoulders in a fatherly way. He whispered sympathetically, "I've talked to Grace. I know the problem."

"Really?" Mac asked, raising a skeptical eyebrow.

"You're both uncomfortable with your performance. She asked me to give you a few pointers."

"Are you sure she didn't just ask you to go screw yourself?"

By the time they began their lunch, Artie's self-amusement had subsided, and he took on a look of serious contemplation. "What's the problem?"

Mac took a bite of salad, thought for a moment, and then spoke. "Lyons set me up. He gave five million dollars to the Wounded Warrior Project in my name. The charity called, probably wants to honor me. Can I just say, 'I didn't make the contribution?'"

"You could, but the consequences would be uncomfortable for you."

"I'm listening."

"Okay. In late September 2001 President Bush signed an executive order that froze the assets of any organization, including charities, that received funds that were linked to terrorist organizations. Because the U.S. Government doesn't regulate charities, charities then set up their own nonprofits or took advantage of unwitting nonprofits.

"So the Treasury put out a publication called," Artie made air quotes, "*Anti-Terrorist Financing Guidelines: Voluntary Best Practices for U.S.-Based Charities.* The concerns that arose from this publication prompted most high-profile charities to refuse contributions from individuals or organizations when they could not identify the donors."

"I don't like the sound of this."

Artie summarized. "If you deny ownership and Lyons doesn't fess up, the Wounded Warrior Project loses the five million. And you look like a schmuck."

"I might have known," Mac said wearily, "that the master planner left no escape route."

Artie shrugged and nodded affirmatively. He thought for a moment and then asked, "If you deny making the contribution, do you think Lyons is heartless enough to let the charity lose the money?"

"Hell, yes! The money is nothing to him. This whole exercise is to have me twist in the wind." In frustration, Mac's hand went to his forehead, and he rubbed his brow. "I also wouldn't put it past him to plant a story that I agreed to the donation and then withdrew it. God, I hate being manipulated!"

CHAPTER 39

"COLONEL JACOBS." IT WAS THE crisp response expected from a professional soldier.

This was not a call that Mac McGregor wanted to make. According to Artie Cohen, his choices were to go along with this ruse or risk the charity forfeiting the five million.

"Yes, sir. It's Mac McGregor, returning your call."

"Thank you. I want to apologize, because I'm afraid we've had a communication snafu."

Mac held his breath, hoping that the article was just a mistake.

"It seems that Mr. McMahon, who heads the Wounded Warrior Project, and I each thought the other was going to call you last week."

Mac's left hand rose to his forehead.

"Our function is on April twenty-first here in Naples at the Freedom Club. Obviously, it would be extremely awkward if you and Mrs. McGregor couldn't make it."

Mac started to respond, but the colonel pushed on as if he were rushing troops into battle. "Airfare and lodging at the Ritz have been taken care of, and we'll have a car pick you up at the airport," he said hopefully. Then he paused.

"Colonel, first I need to thank you for your extraordinary service to our country." The search that Mac had requested confirmed that Colonel Robert Jacobs was the rarest of American heroes. "I have not previously had the privilege of speaking with a Medal of Honor winner."

"I'm hoping that you'll soon get a chance to see one, too, sir."

Mac could not believe how tightly Jeremy Lyons had boxed him in. He had no escape. "Colonel, may I ask you a few questions?"

"Certainly."

"Tell me a little about the metamorphosis of this restaurant. How long have you been running Freedom?"

"Well, sir, pretty much since Mr. Lyons went AWOL."

"Do you know him well?"

"No, sir. I've never met him. But for some reason, he thought I'd be the right man for the job."

"How much has the place changed since it was a club called Someplace Else?" asked Mac.

"About 180 degrees. I'd be proud to show it to you and tell you all the good things we're doing for the military."

"You don't stop, do you, colonel?"

"No, sir," Jacobs said with a chuckle. "Please tell me we can count on you. It'll be a hell of an embarrassment if we can't."

Mac closed his eyes, trying to wish the situation away. His mind raced for about thirty seconds, and the ensuing silence assured his capitulation. "Yes, colonel, you can count on us. But we'll make our own plane and hotel reservations."

"But, sir ..."

"Thank you, colonel, but that's my deal."

"Of course, sir. And, Mr. McGregor, one more thing."

"Yes?" Mac answered warily.

"We also need you to give a short talk to our troops."

When a Medal of Honor winner speaks to a room full of military brethren, the hushed silence and reverent attention to his words are almost spiritual. Mac McGregor felt like he was in the holiest of places. He could not have been more undeserving of the platitudes in Colonel Jacobs's introduction, and he prayed for strength to get through this night.

The packed audience, overwhelmingly composed of military personnel in a colorful array of full-dress service uniforms, blended together like a kaleidoscope of solidarity. It was only the honoree who was out of place among these brave warriors. The faces of the wounded, those missing limbs or parts of their faces, or in wheelchairs, were the unkindest cuts. There were looks of appreciation and gratitude as they waited for the words from their new hero, Mac McGregor, the imposter.

In its heyday, Someplace Else had been an ultramodern, high-end, invitation-only private club run by Jeremy Lyons. On the eve of Lyons's hasty exit from his Naples compound, a call had been placed to Colonel Jacobs. For the two years before that, the American hero had been on retainer waiting for that call. He was to be in charge of Lyons's club, effective immediately. He was given the authority to hire and fire, and all profits were to be donated to the Wounded Warrior Project. Colonel Jacobs had since transformed a place that was accused of cronyism, obtaining insider information, and providing high-class hookers into a bastion of patriotic benevolence.

Now known for its fine food, excellent service, and predictably by-the-book behavior, Freedom had become the most popular restaurant in Naples. To further amplify its image, diners who were active-duty members of the Armed Forces did not pay for their meals. Jeremy Lyons's role as master puppeteer had enabled him to have the perfect contingency plan in place before his departure, and he had played with the strings like a virtuoso.

Part of Mac wondered if midway through his speech, Jeremy Lyons would emerge and take credit for the $5 million donation. In the entire audience, only Grace knew of his pain.

Mac stepped to the podium and thanked Colonel Jacobs for his kind introduction. During high school, college, and a brief stint of teaching, Mac had always been comfortable speaking to crowds. He spoke without notes and, like a trained actor, knew when to pause, modulate his voice, and add humor. But only God could help him now.

Mac took a deep breath, looked out at his attentive audience, and began to speak. "I'm flattered, humbled, and unworthy to speak to you tonight. You are the heroes." He paused and looked around the room. "And I am but one member of a grateful nation.

"Previously, this establishment was not representative of the best of America. It was probably one of the least likely candidates to be called Freedom. Yet, under the capable leadership of Colonel Robert Jacobs, it has become a place of honor and generosity.

"At the risk of being accused of pandering to my audience," Mac smiled, "I believe that it was not until 9/11 that the country regarded the military in a new light. My father, who was in the navy in World War II, spoke often of the feelings of nationalism, unity, and patriotism of those times. Fast forward to Viet Nam. Our citizens' reaction to the men and women who fought in that war remains one of our country's greatest embarrassments. It's okay to hate the war, but never the warrior."

Applause rose like a wave as the audience stood to give Mac a salute.

He gulped a breath to steady himself. *Hate the charlatan,* he thought, *but not the message.*

"But looking at the military in a new light should only be the beginning. We *must* take care of those whom we put in harm's way."

The crowd applauded again.

"I look around at you, our protectors, the heroes we are honoring tonight, and I have hope. And hope can be contagious. And with hope, change is possible. Not the politicians' change of empty promises and factual distortions, but change that happens when integrity takes charge."

Mac's left eye teared with emotion. He was the grateful one. These warriors kept our country safe. He threw his arms outward. "You, those who serve and protect, are the hope for our nation. I believe that the hope for America starts right here." He stepped back, and the audience rose for a sustained ovation.

CHAPTER 40

"MAC!"

Mac turned to the voice behind him. Everyone else had addressed him as Mr. McGregor, so the use of his first name caught him off guard.

The well-tanned, superbly conditioned Army captain held out his hand. "Blake Stone, sir, David Grant's friend."

Masking his surprise, Mac shook the man's hand and said, "Of course, Blake, I remember. Good to see you again."

He turned to Grace, who was standing beside him. "I met Blake when he was having lunch with David Grant in D.C. They served in the army together."

"Ma'am," Blake said as he stepped forward to take Grace's outstretched hand. "It's a pleasure to meet you. I've heard great things about you from David."

"Aren't you nice? Thank you, captain," said Grace, giving him her killer smile.

"I wondered if I might give you two a ride back to your hotel and then steal your husband for just a few minutes?"

"That works for me," said Grace, turning toward Mac for agreement. She was used to friends and strangers wanting to borrow her husband for investment advice.

"Sure," Mac said, nodding. "We're at the Naples Beach Hotel and Golf Club."

It was a warm night, so after Grace got in the elevator, Mac and Blake walked to the slatted wooden chairs and sat facing the gulf.

"Can I buy you a drink?" asked Blake.

"No, thanks. I'm not much of a drinker, and tonight took more out of me than I thought."

When the waitress came over, Blake said, "Two waters, please. That will be all," and handed her a ten-dollar bill.

"Thanks!" she said with a big smile.

The silence that followed could have been awkward, but the sound of the gulf and the soft breeze carrying the smell of the salt air seemed to relax them both.

Finally, Blake spoke softly into the night. "You're a warrior, too, you know."

Confused, Mac turned to look at him.

"David told me what was going on. You went into battle with no armor, no protection. Any second, your adversary could have pulled the rug out from under you and ruined your career. And yet, you made us all feel good about ourselves. You cared."

Mac gave a nervous laugh. "I'm not sure that I ever felt less like a hero."

"Anyone else would have passed, retreated. Why did you take the risk?"

"The charity could have lost the five million," Mac said softly.

Blake nodded. "Yeah, I figured. Tell me about Lyons."

Mac turned to look at him. "Why are you interested?"

Blake gave him a guileless smile. "After David chewed me a new one for playing Harry Hardass with you, I figured I'd better make nice."

"Is that why you were there tonight?"

"Yeah. I wanted to hear you, but ...," he paused, "I also wanted to have your back."

"How would you have done that?"

Blake smiled again. "I'm pretty good at extracting my fellow soldiers from dangerous situations."

Flattered, Mac cocked his head. "I hope this doesn't mean that I have to give David a raise."

Blake laughed. "No. But my buddy did say that you were resilient."

Mac blew out a breath. "Didn't feel that way tonight."

Blake leaned toward him. "So are you just a fly that Lyons has caught in his web, and he keeps playing with you till he's hungry?"

"That analogy sounds a bit too close to home." Mac leaned forward and rested his hands on his knees. "I don't want to be abrupt, but why do you care?"

"David's a part of you. I'm a part of David."

Mac nodded as if he fully comprehended the Buddha-like comment. "Jeremy Lyons joined Johnston Wellons about two years before I did. He was a star—smart, aggressive, fearless. By the time I got there, he was already the firm's top revenue producer.

"Jeremy and I were as different as night and day. I was told that almost from day one, he would dictate strategies and buys and sells for his clients as if there were no possibility that they would fail. In his mind, he was always right. And if anyone disagreed with him, he was insulting and dismissive to them."

"Was he that good?" asked Blake.

Mac shook his head. "I have no evidence to support or refute. However, I do know that the man got chalk all over his shoes."

"Chalk?"

"Sorry," Mac smiled. "Like on a football field: if you get chalk on your shoes, you're out of bounds."

Blake nodded his understanding. "So you don't see him admitting he was wrong, even when the results proved it."

Mac thought for a moment. "I can't imagine Jeremy Lyons ever admitting he was wrong. His book, *Survival of the Fittest*, is a testament to his narcissism."

"Unlike you," Blake quipped, "who probably fell on the sword every time you stepped on your dick."

Mac laughed. "I'd have to be extremely agile to not tread there, but I like to think that our group owns up to our mistakes. If we don't, how do we get better, and hopefully not repeat the same mistakes?

"I am different from Jeremy in so many ways. I love to listen, get to know people, find out what keeps them up at night. I love my business, because I love helping people find solutions. For Jeremy, the business was probably just a way to keep score. How much money could he make? How many clients could he get? Was he better than everybody else? Neither I nor my clients expect me to always be right. But they know that when I'm wrong, whatever I advised, it was for the right reason."

Embarrassed because he felt like he was bragging, Mac added, "I started out dumb in this business, but I hope I got smarter every day." He looked at Blake, who was listening intently. " Let me give you a quick snapshot of my favorite psycho.

"When I introduced myself to him, Jeremy told me politely to 'fuck off.' If you couldn't make him money, you were dead to him. About a year and a half later, the firm established an advisory council of their top producers. Even though Lyons was the top producer, I was chosen to lead the council. He went postal and left the firm.

"I thought that our paths would never cross again." Mac shook his head ruefully. He leaned his head back, closed his eyes, and breathed deeply.

"But they did," probed Blake.

172

"Oh, yeah," Mac said, sitting up straighter. "Big time. I'm the son of a bitch's soccer ball, and he's David Beckham."

A thought crossed Mac's mind. He leaned forward and placed his arms on his thighs.

"Max Parnavich was Jeremy's hired assassin. A former SEAL, he raped women in Jeremy's employ whenever they got out of line. In all probability, he killed anyone who was a nuisance to his employer."

Mac took deep breaths as he felt the tension threatening to constrict his throat. Blake waited patiently.

"Parnavich attended my church in a phony military uniform and introduced himself. Later, he called up my daughter and asked her out. She refused. He terrorized her."

Mac's hands were clenched, and his fingers were white. His tremors of rekindled rage seemed to lower his body temperature. He shivered.

Blake reached over and embraced Mac's shoulder. Mac looked up with glassy eyes. "All of this was at Jeremy Lyons's direction. It's the only time that I actually felt like I could kill a man. Part of me wishes I had the stones to do it."

CHAPTER 41

"TONIGHT IS A FIRST FOR Fox News. We are allocating a half hour of prime time to cover an address by Florida's controversial Independent candidate for United States Senator, Jeremy Lyons. In an original and innovative concept, Lyons has pledged that he will not engage in a negative campaign.

"As unusual and refreshing as that may be, it is a second promise that has focused the spotlight on this man: Jeremy Lyons has promised that he will offer a course of action that will not only help Florida's economy, but will also help get America growing again. We know that all Florida is watching, and we hope that Washington, DC, is watching, too. I'm Jackie Mayfield, and this is Fox News at the Freedom club and restaurant in Naples, Florida."

The restaurant was packed, although it was not serving dinner or drinks on this particular night. The main lounge, a large circular room highlighted by a stunning center bar, housed rows of tightly packed folding chairs. The same cheap-seats arrangement also covered the magnificent dance floor, which was laminated with a hard polymer ultra gloss surface. The comfortable dining booths were purposely left empty. It was a night of equality.

The crowd was an eclectic mixture of reporters, bloggers, everyday citizens of Naples, and men and women in uniform. The positioning of the chairs allowed each spectator to see the small temporary podium and the large American flag adjacent to it.

All eyes were on the current Governor of Florida, Antonio Martinez, as he waited to introduce Jeremy Lyons. The popular and charismatic Hispanic governor had no dog in the hunt.

However, he was not only pragmatic—the TV coverage of this event propelled him to offer to introduce the candidate—he was also intimidated by the man.

Instead of readily accepting Martinez's offer, Lyons had said that he would write what he wanted the governor to say. Here is where the pragmatism came in. Governor Martinez's instincts were to tell the arrogant son of a bitch to kiss his ass, but Lyons was obscenely rich, and Martinez's campaign coffers always needed refilling.

"That's an unusual request, Mr. Lyons," Martinez had said. "Most candidates would just trust my eloquence."

"I'm not most candidates," Lyons had replied, nonplussed, "and I do trust your eloquence, but you are not aware of my intent."

The governor had nodded, grateful that Lyons had allowed him to retain at least a semblance of his dignity.

"Ladies and gentlemen," Martinez began, "the candidate has asked me to give you a specific introduction.

"It could be because he is afraid that I'll take the whole fifteen minutes," he ad-libbed with a big smile as he cut his eyes towards Lyons. The man's eyes compelled him to quickly return to the script. "I'm not here to endorse Jeremy Lyons. He has indicated that he is not seeking endorsement from any politician, only from the people of Florida.

"Mr. Lyons," he said as he stepped aside.

Jackie Mayfield's expression registered surprise and respect. She exchanged a glance with her cameraman and shrugged her shoulders.

Jeremy Lyons, dressed in a dark-blue suit and a powder-blue, heavily starched shirt with an open collar, moved to the podium. The contrast between his shirt and his remarkably wrinkle-free, bronzed face and head and his heat- seeking eyes gave an undeniable portrayal of confidence.

"Thank you, governor, for your succinct introduction," Lyons said with a wry smile.

He leaned toward the microphone and spoke in a commanding voice. "I'd like to ask you all to stand, and my friend, Colonel Robert Jacobs, will lead us in the Pledge of Allegiance."

Chairs squeaked as if a drill sergeant had ordered his recruits to stand. The service people were at rigid attention, and they saluted as Colonel Jacobs, in full dress uniform, complete with the Medal of Honor around his neck, stepped to the podium. After he finished leading the pledge, which included raising his voice to emphasize the phrase "under God," he nodded to Lyons and returned to his seat.

"Thank you. I believe that too often we forget that even though we are Floridians, we are Americans first.

"Although my campaign will be run utilizing both national media and social media," Lyons continued, "this is not a campaign speech. As you know, the majority of those are filled with empty rhetoric and promises that will never be fulfilled.

"Additionally, a negative campaign is a scare tactic, an odious mixture of innuendo, distortions, comments out of context, and half-truths. Often, the charges are simply lies. Consequently, I will refute any scurrilous charges made against me, and I will not attack my opponents. It is the responsibility of the people of Florida to analyze the respective records and accomplishments of those other contenders and determine whether or not they would be more qualified than I to help them have a better life."

"Sure sounds like a campaign speech to me," Jackie whispered to a colleague in a disappointed voice.

"Any success that I've been blessed to have," Lyons said gently, as he gripped the podium with both hands and leaned forward, "was because I was able to turn possibilities into probabilities and then into certainties."

He motioned to the cameras. "Would you please turn the cameras toward the audience? I need to ask them a question." He waited for the cameras to shift to their target. "Will anyone in this room who believes that our current politicians will be able to get us out of this economic mess please raise your hand."

As the cameras panned, not a single hand was raised.

Lyons motioned for the cameras to return to him. "I'm not surprised," he said with resignation. "However, I am surprised that we, the American people, accept this embarrassing state of affairs. This country has already spoken," he said as he raised his voice and threw his hands skyward. "We give up!"

The audience sat in stunned silence.

As Lyons's bald head moved vulture like, it seemed as if he made eye contact with everyone in the room. He spoke again.

"In the past two presidential administrations, both Houses of Congress were off the wagon. They were and are spendaholics. Mind you, they're not *recovering* spendaholics. It's morning, noon and night, and they can't stop. And you, you, you, we all," he pointed into the crowd and at the camera, "don't send them to rehab, don't make them dry out."

The room quieted to the level of an empty church as Lyons captured the complete attention of everyone in the audience. There were no BlackBerries, iPhones, or whispered comments. It was as if they were waiting for a proclamation.

"I'm not a Democrat or a Republican; I'm an Independent. My only allegiance is to my country. The success of our country is built on hard work, sacrifice, innovation, integrity, and confidence. How can you be confident if you can't get a job? How can you be confident if the mortgage on your home is higher than your home's value? How can you be confident when our elected officials haven't given us one single idea how to *fix* this situation?" Lyons's right index finger shot up in fury.

He let the moment breathe and then fixed a kindly smile on the audience. "Less than two weeks ago, one of our country's top financial advisors addressed our service men and women in this very room. He said that the hope for America starts right here." The candidate's smile broadened, and he nodded. "I agree with him."

Lyons reached down and caressed the sides of the podium. "Here are three action items.   In addition, I have assembled an implementation team to make sure that my proposals, unlike those of career politicians, will be carried out. Nevertheless, everything I say here," he nodded at the cameras, "will be sliced, diced, debated, and rejected by a plethora of media pundits. But make no mistake. I am identifying real problems, and I will offer solutions. For I am confident that I will be Florida's first Independent senator.

"Idea Number 1: Do not tax the wealth creators.   How many jobs have been generated by small businesses and entrepreneurs? How many people have been hired by Apple Computer or Amazon since they revolutionized communication and marketing? Instead, tax those who abuse the system and create no value.

"High-frequency traders armed with computers working at warp speed trade hundreds of thousands of shares of stock in the time it took me to say this sentence. If the average holding period of a stock is less than three seconds, are they adding any value? No! Are they increasing volatility – those sickening up and down swings of the stock market? Yes! Their most profitable days are days when our stock markets get crushed. Tax them! If they can't hold a stock for 24 hours, they should pay!

"Idea Number 2:   Is another financial meltdown possible? Have we solved the problem of banks that are too big to fail? My analysis says no. Although I have thirty years of experience in all the intricacies of the markets, I opted for a second opinion. I checked with the most astute financial veteran on the President's advisory team. He concurred that neither the Dodd-Frank reform legislation that was passed nor the proposed Volcker Rule would absolutely prevent another earthquake in our economy. We have to do better. Our citizens should not be lulled into a false sense of security by our politicians and regulators."

Lyons paused as if to stress the enormity of his words. "If we allow a shadow banking system to exist, we are inviting risk takers to abuse it. My opponents will accuse me of having manipulated the financial systems in order to create wealth for my investors and for myself. Their assertions are correct. I used every legal means, every available loophole in a flawed system to increase wealth. If I wanted to, I could do it again. But I'd rather fix the system. Who better to do it?" He opened his hands and smiled.

"My final idea," he said, his voice rising with enthusiasm, "will get America growing. It is simple, actionable, and non-partisan. Empty houses are invading neighborhoods like locusts. People owe more on their homes than the homes are worth. Investors need a reason to take the money languishing in no-interest bank accounts and buy real estate. Let's give them one. Anyone who buys a house in the next twenty-four months and rents it out should not be taxed on the rental income.

"What will that do? It will create strong demand for homes, particularly in Florida, where there is no state income tax. In addition, it will create jobs in every area of real estate and home construction: property managers, mortgage brokers, real estate agents, construction workers, painters, plumbers, electricians, cleaners, handymen.

"Most important, it will increase the value of our nation's homes. Less supply creates demand—Economics 101." Lyons stopped, breathed in deeply, and his chest and shoulders seemed to expand with power. "Empty promises, glib excuses, and non-answers from our elected leaders have drained the spirit from our good people. Rest assured. As your senator, my actions will *always* be consistent with my words. What I say, I will do!

"Thank you, and God bless America."

CHAPTER 42

GRACE MCGREGOR ROLLED OVER, CIRCLED her arms around her husband's chest, and gave him a fierce hug. Mac knew her dual purpose was to remind him that she loved him and to let him know that the clock radio was on its third song. Only one of them needed to get out of bed. He reached back, patted her arm, turned off the alarm, and trudged to the shower.

Normally, Mac read the paper while he ate his shredded wheat with berries and black cherry Greek yogurt. But today he channel-surfed the news. Perversely, he wondered if anyone cared enough to research the identity of the financial advisor referred to in Lyons's coming-out speech. The all-publicity-is-good-publicity part of him watched with anticipation; the I-want-no-connection-to-that-criminal part watched with apprehension. Nope. Why bother checking out the throwaway advisor when you can focus your target on Lyons's new best friend, Sam Golden? No worries about preparing for the inevitable accusatory call from Sam, because Mac was defenseless.

Mac's blue silk striped tie hung loosely around his neck. The temperature was already 75 degrees when he got in his car, so he had eschewed coffee and instead traveled with a bottled water. Needing a caffeine burst to prop open his bleary eyes, he stopped for a Starbucks green iced tea before going in to work. He nodded to the building attendant, who gave him a million-dollar smile and a salute. Mac rolled his neck as he waited for the elevator.

As he had expected, R.J. Brooks was at his desk. He would want a postmortem of Lyons's speech.

"Everyone loved him except us," said R.J. as Mac sat down heavily in his chair.

Mac crooked an eyebrow. "I don't think Sam would give him a standing ovation."

R.J. grimaced. "How are you going to explain to Sam that you passed on his comments to Jeremy?" he asked painfully.

"Poorly, or not at all. I blew it. I should have known that Jeremy would use Sam's information to humiliate me."

"Plus, he stole the idea about tax-free rental income that you and I had discussed. Probably the most frightening thing about this psycho is that he seems to know all your secrets."

"When did we talk about that?" Mac asked.

"If I had to guess—maybe four or five months ago. We ran through a number of permutations about how to jump-start the real estate market until we ended up with that one."

"Did you discuss the idea with anybody but me?"

"No. You said, 'Let's wait till there's a change in administration.'"

Mac placed his elbows on his desk, closed his eyes, and supported his head with his fingers. After a few moments of silence, he said, "Get someone to check the phone."

"What?"

"Check the phone. See if it's bugged."

"Seriously?"

"He steals my idea, knows who I'm having dinner with, makes me look like a snitch to my oldest friend."

"Okay," R.J. replied skeptically.

Mac looked at him. "I have to be right. It's actually more comforting to think that Jeremy stole my idea. The possibility that we think alike is scary as hell."

CHAPTER 43

RICHARD ORTH STOOD RAMROD STRAIGHT as he waited for his boss, the senior senator from Florida, Alan Smathers, to respond. It was not that Orth, a Citadel graduate and highly decorated Marine, was intimidated. It was just who he was.

"He's money?" Smathers said. "This wannabe Captain America, who was a target of the FBI, throws out a few crazy-ass ideas, and you think he's money. No Johnny- come-fucking-lately is getting *my* seat!"

The square-jawed politician, who publicly was a laid-back Southerner with enough of a drawl to be charming and enough steel in his dark brown eyes to become a political force, could instantly go from zero to a hundred in private.

It was the morning after Jeremy Lyons's coming out party, and the senator's chief of staff had come to his office directly from the airport.

"Alan," Orth said, "you asked me to attend and take notes. I listened, and I am reporting back to you. My assessment is that the man is powerful, reasoned, charismatic, and pretty damn formidable."

Smathers did not digest this news any better than he had Orth's initial comments. In fact, he was angrily circling around Orth as if he were a tiger working up an appetite for lunch. Smathers stopped in mid prowl. "Does he have backing?"

"He's doing it all by himself."

"That's ridiculous. He'll fade like a year-old newspaper."

Orth shook his head. "I don't think so. Somehow, the man seems to be intimidating and mesmerizing at the same time. We need to consider him serious competition."

"Bullshit! You get a hard-on for this guy after one speech? Come on, Richard, this guy is a political virgin. Where's his ad campaign? Who's running his organization? How will he get exposure?"

Orth smiled inwardly at his friend's defiant face. Smathers was still as fit as when they were in combat together. His short brown hair never needed a comb or brush. No skeletons; gorgeous, girl-next-door wife. As long as nobody ever recorded their private conversations, the man could run for president. Orth sighed, knowing it would come to this. He reached down to the chair beside him and opened his briefcase. He handed the senator the day's *Naples Daily News*. The headline read, *"The Lyons No Longer Sleeps."*

CHAPTER 44

COULD ... THIS ... DAY ... get ... any ... worse? Lena Brady had sent a blast e-mail to the team: "Sam Golden on CNBC at 4:00 – Watch Mac Squirm!" Mac McGregor shook his head. It was definitely time to reconsider the team's credo of information sharing.

He glared at Lena, who responded with a Cheshire Cat grin and waved from her desk. Mac held up an ineffectual finger of admonishment. A bigger problem was whether he should send a preemptive apology to Sam: an e-mail or a call to his cell and hope he didn't pick up? *That fucking Lyons,* he thought and gritted his teeth.

At a few minutes before four o'clock, Mac's team assembled in the large conference room to watch Sam's interview. Danny DeMarco was front and center, because Carole Dell was interviewing Sam, and even though they suspected that she was the station's token liberal, she was smoking hot.

Although most of the team was standing, Mac sat at the head of the large conference table, because he wanted to be able to duck under it if the interview went too far south. He felt like the accused waiting for a verdict from the jury.

"Mr. Golden, good to see you again," the pixie-faced blonde said, flashing her perfect smile.

"Thank you, Carole."

"I have to tell you that we've missed having you come on our show."

"That must be the case," he responded as he opened his arms like a bird initiating flight. "Otherwise, why would you want to interview an old has-been?"

She laughed. "You are the farthest thing from a has-been in this town that I know, but life sure seemed simpler when you were chairman of the Securities and Exchange Commission."

"It was. We were blessed with a better economic climate and much less leverage in the system."

She gave a professional nod of agreement. "Did you watch Jeremy Lyons's speech last night?"

"Of course," Sam answered.

"Well, the whole world seems to think that *you* were the astute financial mind that agreed with his analysis of the Dodd-Frank reform legislation and the Volcker Rule. Did you discuss this with Mr. Lyons?"

"No. I have never met or spoken to the man."

"So you're *not* the astute financial veteran?" Carole asked incredulously.

Sam gave her a paternal smile. "Carole, I have no idea who he was talking about. There are a number of advisors to the President that I consider more astute and more seasoned."

"Really?" she said, raising a skeptical eyebrow..

"I'm surprised that your station didn't immediately contact Warren Buffett. There have been numerous discussions about the Buffet Rule, and some would say not enough discussions of the Golden Rule."

She laughed. "You are really nimble, Mr. Golden. No wonder we miss you so much."

Mac was hanging on every word. Miraculously, it seemed like Sam was breaking every tackle and heading for the end zone. "Say goodnight, Sam," he insisted out loud.

Bearing down, her cuteness temporarily tabled, Carole Dell continued. "Correct me if I'm wrong, sir; but as the head of the President's transition team, you initiated a search for Jeremy Lyons when he was running a hedge-fund operation."

"That is correct."

"And ultimately, there was sufficient evidence to close down his operation."

"You would have to verify that with the authorities, Carole. That's not my job."

"But your job was to help clean up Wall Street."

"That was our objective."

Unperturbed, she probed deeper. "Did you express your opinion of Dodd-Frank to a friend who then passed it on to Mr. Lyons?"

Mac slumped down in his chair and closed his eyes.

"To an old lawyer, that sounds like hearsay," Sam said kindly. "Besides, I don't know anyone who is a friend of Mr. Lyons."

She was obviously flustered. "I'm sorry, sir, we're running out of time. But please tell us this: Do you agree with Jeremy Lyons's stated observations on Dodd-Frank and the Volcker Rule?"

Sam turned his earnest face directly to the camera. "The purpose of the Dodd-Frank legislation is to identify and manage threats to the stability of the nation's financial systems. In particular, the rules were designed to curb the derivative instruments that contributed to our global crisis. The goal was to improve accountability and transparency in the financial systems.

"As of yet, the Volcker Rule has no teeth. Perhaps the real question should be: When regulators are trying to govern risk, what is the financial institution's level of risk relative to its capacity to bear that risk."

"Getting down to the nitty gritty, do you think we have done enough to prevent another meltdown?"

"Carole, we all know that lawyers, of which I am one, are quite skilled at playing whack-a-mole with regulations. But to answer your question honestly, I must tell you that I really don't know."

The session ended.

As Mac muted the volume, R.J. spoke first. "Mac, did you teach him to tap dance like that?"

"Are you kidding me?" Mac said in an awed voice. "I'm still taking notes."

Mac was putting the finishing touches on an apologizing/congratulating e-mail to Sam when a call came in from him. Mac spoke quickly without saying hello. "Sam, I am so sorry. I gotta tell you how freaking amazing you were; but, man, I really stepped on my appendage. How can I make it up to you?"

In the few moments of silence that followed, Mac felt like he could hear the wheels turning. Sam spoke softly. "Mac, when I first heard Lyons's reference, I'll admit that I felt betrayed."

Mac's heart sank.

"But that lasted about three seconds. I have no moral high ground with you. We both know that Lyons is the sneakiest, most manipulative bastard in the world. Give me a break. You wouldn't be locked into your weekly torture sessions with him if you hadn't agreed to help me."

Mac was quiet, absorbing his friend's words. "Thanks. I appreciate the pass. What really scared me about your being on CNBC was that they had to know about your relationship with Margo and her link to Jeremy."

"They were aware of the facts," Sam said in his typically placid tone.

"You've got to be kidding me!"

"I would only speak with the assurance that it would not be mentioned, now or ever."

"How on earth did you get them to agree to that?"

"Mac," Sam said, as if he were addressing a kindergarten class, "This is not my first day in Washington, DC."

CHAPTER 45

STANLEY LIPITZ DID NOT WANT to call attention to himself as he entered the lobby of the Four Seasons in East Palo Alto. No matter how improbable, a stop and search would find him in possession of illegal contraband.

The hotel manager, an officious man with a phony French accent, nodded and smiled eagerly. "Good evening, Mr. Lipitz. Your room is ready, of course."

Giving him a bored look, Stanley took a key card and walked through the busy lobby to the bank of elevators. The beauty of this hotel, a magnificent monument to hi-tech titans, was lost on Stanley. He was only interested in the beauty of the two guests who would be arriving shortly.

Stanley exited the elevator, walked to the Presidential Suite, and inserted his card. He was well aware that extreme caution was called for, due to the expected expiration date of his charade with Celebra, his company's Alzheimer's drug. All of his energies should be concentrated on whipping Sudeep Patel like a rented mule in order to accumulate and hide the maximum amount of money while there was still time.

Later, after Celebra was exposed as a drug that offered only a temporary respite from the effects of Alzheimer's, it might be possible to distribute a lesser amount of the street version, Euphoria. But the danger level would increase exponentially. Yes, prudence dictated that all of Stanley's energies should be focused on maximum profitability. But the beast must be fed.

Financially, Sudeep had not disappointed him. The market for Euphoria as a sex-enhancement drug had exploded, and Stanley already had enough money hidden to cover even his extravagant tastes. However, to Stanley, too much money was like too much depravity: an oxymoron.

Sudeep had shown talent in other areas, as well. For the third time this month, the man had procured two university students who might have been repulsed at the suggestion of prostitution, but jumped at the chance to entertain in exchange for a month's supply of Euphoria. If Sudeep's previous referrals were any indication, the young ladies would be beautiful, without inhibition, and eager to please.

As expected, both were striking: tan, blond, and apparently with matching boob jobs. After blinking a few times and swallowing nervously to get used to Stanley's grinning, unappetizing appearance, they ran around the world-class luxury playpen like scurrying mice. Just like his previous guests, they giggled over the Italian marble bathroom with the deep soaking tub, the glass-enclosed steam shower, and the gold bidet. Both the master bedroom and the living room offered expansive views of the San Francisco Bay, and of course, the women wanted to look out all of the windows and pose in front of them.

When the women had completed their unguided tour of the luxurious suite, they walked bravely over to the king-sized bed. Stanley was lounging back on the bed, a specifically procured extra-large black silk robe mercifully covering his naked body. The young women stood together in front of him holding hands and smiling nervously.

"Afterwards, you will get your rewards," he said silkily, "and if your performance is outstanding, you may receive additional love pills."

Both nodded their excited assent.

"Come, stand next to me," said Stanley, patting the side of the bed that he was on. "And undress each other slowly, only gently touching each other's skin."

CHAPTER 46

JACKIE MAYFIELD INSTINCTIVELY GRABBED THE pillow and smashed it over her ears. The ringing noise wouldn't stop. With her eyes still closed, she reached up with her left hand, searching for the bedside lamp. The ringing was incessant, angry. She gritted her teeth, turned her head to the right and looked at the luminous dial: 2:13 a.m.

"Give me a break!" She had turned off the light a few minutes before one o'clock, exhausted from another news-a-thon at Fox. Politicians were center stage this year, and it was Sound Bite City. She finally found the light switch, and pitiless light filled the room.

The landline. No one called on that line. It was an unpublished number. The only reason she still had it was that it felt a little weird to sleep with her cell phone. Jackie couldn't remember the last time her home phone had rung, and, of course, it had no answering machine. But whoever was calling must be drunk or had dialed wrong, because the phone was not going to stop ringing.

She snatched the phone from the hook. "What?" she said angrily.

"Sorry to wake you, Ms. Mayfield," said the mellifluous voice.

"Who are you? How did you get this number? What do you want?" Her anger rushed out.

"We can save time if I ignore your questions and just offer you some advice."

"Advice?"

"Or," the voice became threatening, "I could make a call to another reporter who might be more receptive to an outsider."

Jackie sat up in bed like a jack-in-the-box. "I'm sorry. What do you have?"

Even in her sleep-deprived state, his comment registered instantly. Someone had sent Jackie a flash drive that implicated Chad Alexander as a rapist. The anonymous donor had included a typed tag that read: "Compliments of an Outsider." She had told no one, not even the station manager. It was like she had been protecting a source. She was wide awake now.

The caller continued. "In the next fifteen minutes, in the Four Seasons in East Palo Alto, California, detectives will be making an arrest. The accused is Stanley Lipitz, CEO of the biotech company Cerebrepharma."

Jackie thought frantically, trying to figure out the relevance. Embezzlement, fraud, nothing seemed worthy of a call from this source.

"Do you know why this is important to you?" the voice asked.

Jackie's eyes widened. It was like he was reading her mind.

"Because he is accused and, my dear, he is guilty of manufacturing and distributing the drug Euphoria."

Her heart almost leaped out of her chest.

"Perhaps it would be prudent for you to get a news crew to the lobby of the hotel at the conclusion of our little chat. Oh, and Jackie, please note in your summary that this is the second call you've received from 'An Outsider.'"

There are situations in life where you want to be right and you also want to be wrong. Mac had delayed the verdict by going out to lunch with Artie while R.J. supervised the technician checking Mac's phone.

Because patience was not one of Mac's strengths, he hurried through their lunch, and they walked at a brisk pace back to the office. The technician was gone, so Mac and Artie both went over to R.J.'s desk. "Is there a bug?" Mac asked.

"Not anymore," answered R.J. sheepishly,

'Shit!" said Mac through clenched teeth. "I'd better have the guy go check out my house."

"Why would Lyons go to this much trouble?" asked Artie.

'Because he can," Mac shot back.

"Would it be helpful to know that it was the most sophisticated listening device the man had ever seen?" offered R.J.

Mac glared an answer.

"Are you going to discuss this with Joe?"

"No."

"Are you going to confront Lyons?"

"No."

"Really? He'll know you removed the bug."

"I won't bring it up, and neither will he."

CHAPTER 47

THE HOTEL MANAGER OF THE Four Seasons studied the detectives' badges for an inordinately long period of time.

Detective Brenda Rutgers, the smart-mouthed and less patient of the two, asked the concerned executive, "Are you looking for an excuse to do a strip search?"

The man blanched as he looked at the stocky detective who, at 5'2" and wearing a look of barely constrained annoyance, seemed more formidable than the large African-American man by her side. He had lost his French accent with the detectives.

"Yeah, that's us, dipshit, and here's the warrant," she said, slamming the paper down in front of him. "You've got thirty seconds to check it out and give me the key, or ..." she leaned halfway over the counter, " I'm gonna jump over there and make a keychain out of your balls."

Marvin White had been her partner for three years, and he maintained a look somewhere between amusement and boredom. He'd seen it all from Detective Rutgers. His only concern was that the hotel manager would vomit all over the warrant.

The man turned abruptly and with his hand shaking like he had palsy, he grabbed the key card. It was rare that anyone disturbed a guest at his hotel, and it was blasphemous to disturb a frequent visitor to the Presidential Suite. But he slid the key card across the counter like it was burning his hand.

Detective Rutgers grabbed the card and glared at him. "And just so we're clear, if you alert your guest in any way, I will personally make sure that you're sharing a cell with folks who are short on hygiene, if you get my drift." She raised her eyebrows lewdly at the quivering man, turned, and sprinted toward the elevators.

Stanley Lipitz was way too immersed in his pleasures to hear the click of the door as it opened. "Nobody move!" shouted Detective Rutgers as she and her partner entered the room with guns drawn. The first thought that popped into her head was that she had walked into a hideous Disney movie in which this giant beached whale was frolicking with a pair of finless mermaids. Bulbous body, white, mottled skin without a hint of muscle tone moved aggressively upwards.

"Don't move!" shouted Detective White, who in two strides had his gun about six inches from Stanley's head.

"How dare you!" Stanley screamed, his face, ears, and neck crimson with rage.

Rutgers turned toward one of the girls, who was wailing and crying uncontrollably. She waved her gun from one to the other. "And you, Kim and Kourtney, turn on your stomachs and lie next to each other on the bed. And shut the hell up." They quickly complied.

"You got him?" she asked her partner.

As he nodded, she walked into the opulent bathroom and grabbed two large towels. She walked back and threw one over each girl's naked body.

Rutgers turned her focus back to Stanley, who had continued to shout threats and invectives. "Now, here's what's gonna happen, Mr. Lipitz. We are going to place you under arrest and read you your rights. Hear that, girls? If you did, shout, 'Yes, ma'am!'"

She nodded at the resounding chorus.

"Before we arrest you, we are going to execute our search warrant. We have shown it to the hotel manager, but we would be happy to share it with you." Working hard not to grimace, she asked, "Would you like to pull the sheet up over your body first?"

"Fuck you!" Stanley screamed venomously.

"Not in my worst nightmare," she said politely. "Besides," her eyebrows raised and her face was a picture of skepticism as she pointed at his three overlapping bellies, "I don't have time to do a search *that* extensive."

As the elevator doors opened into the lobby, camera lights flashed, and the video camera displaying the Fox emblem caught it all. Stanley Lipitz, arms manacled behind his back, stared defiantly into the cameras while the two girls smiled, grateful for the face time.

The shaken hotel manager, who had had as much success discouraging the press as he had the detectives, threw his hands in the air as Rutgers took steps in his direction. "I swear, I swear, I did not call them," he cried in a voice so high pitched that only dogs should have been able to hear it.

CHAPTER 48

CINDY SMATHERS WAS NOT A Ritz Carlton kind of woman. Even after two years of marriage to a U.S. Senator, she was not jaded. Her fresh-faced, youthful innocence was a welcome contrast to the Botox belles who dripped sophistication and cynicism.

In some respects, Cindy was much too trusting to live in Washington, D.C. She'd never known a stranger, and she'd smile and wave at anyone who caught her eye: a Tennessee girl who didn't know she was far away from home.

With her husband, Alan, in Florida for a fundraiser, Cindy was looking forward to a quiet dinner and a glass of wine. In a University of Florida sweatshirt, jeans, and well-worn tennis shoes, the unassuming U.S. Senator's spouse would have been hard to identify.

Added to the image were the four canvas bags of groceries from the Whole Foods at Foggy Bottom that Cindy was carrying back to her apartment. It was a straight shot, less than half a mile, and she loved to walk in the city. At six o'clock in the evening, traffic was still aggressive, but to Cindy, it was just part of the adventure.

Waiting to cross 22nd Street, she shifted the bags in her hands. The light turned green; the walk sign appeared, advising 24 seconds of ambulatory leisure; and she stepped off the curb.

Suddenly Cindy's head jerked to the right. A sickening screech of tires confirmed the vision of a vehicle bearing down on her. A violent tug on her sweatshirt pulled her backwards as the car sped past, missing her by inches. Her hands had flown up in self-defense, and her groceries were strewn in all directions. In her horror, she saw a carton of eggs that had been obliterated by the speeding car's tires.

Cindy's heart was in her throat as the shock subsided and she realized that she was alive. She took stock of her surroundings. Half standing and half sitting, she was being held and supported by the person who had saved her life. She started trying to stand, and a gentle voice cautioned, "Let me pull you back until you're standing on the curb. You've had quite a shock, so let's take it slow."

Cindy nodded as she was slowly helped onto the curb. When she stood, she turned and saw a stunning African-American woman smiling sympathetically.

Random witnesses to the incident approached, asking Cindy if she was all right and if there was there anything they could do. "No," she answered politely as she fought for composure. "I think I'm in good hands."

"I don't know how to thank you. I could've died," Cindy said hesitantly. "You saved my life."

"You're quite welcome," said the woman. "My actions were simply reflex. Perhaps we should attribute it to divine intervention," she added with a smile.

"Amen," said Cindy softly as her eyes filled with tears. "What can I do to repay you?"

"Well," the woman said with an impish grin, pointing to the street, "I did lose a bottle of wine that I was planning to drink tonight after a tough day. But I think your day has been even tougher."

Cindy turned to the street and saw a broken wine bottle still half covered by a torn paper bag.

"I think the crazed driver ran over it, so maybe there's some chance for justice," the black woman added. "My name is Monique Adams ." She held out her hand.

Cindy ignored it and rushed in to hug the woman in a tight embrace. "I'm Cindy Smathers. My apartment is just a few blocks from here. Please say you'll come with me. We can order dinner from the Ritz and drink wine till we're silly."

"Oh, I couldn't."

"Yes, you can. I will not let you go until you say yes."

Monique laughed. "Okay, you win. Give me your hand and we'll brave this D.C. traffic together."

The room was spinning. Cindy needed to open her eyes, but if she moved a muscle, an eyelid, nausea was inevitable.

Panic. Where was she? What happened? Why did she feel this way?

She concentrated on her breathing. Gradually, she opened her eyes halfway, but was greeted only by blackness. Was she drunk?

Without moving her head, she felt around and touched the smooth sheets beneath her. Okay, she was in a bed. God, why couldn't she remember?

Her hands touched her body. She was naked. "Anyone here?" she called out in a frightened voice.

Silence responded.

Still fighting nausea, Cindy opened her eyes and after a few moments' rest, turned her head to the right slowly, painfully. She was in her bed. Thank God for that. The digital clock read 3:15.

Why was she so disoriented? Where was her nightgown? Where was Alan?

A shiver of relief rolled over her. She was remembering. A black woman, Monique, saved her. Cindy remembered pouring a glass of wine, then nothing.

It was no use. It was blank.

Cindy scootched her way towards the nightstand and flicked on the bedside lamp. She squinted until her eyes adjusted. Gradually, she sat up on the side of the bed. *Now, just walk to the bathroom,* she told herself.

She gingerly placed both feet on the carpet and pushed up slowly from the bed. That didn't work. She collapsed back on the bed. Her legs felt like rubber. Burying her face in her hands, she sobbed softly. *It can't be the wine. It can't be the wine.*

CHAPTER 49

IT SHOULD HAVE FELT EXTREMELY uncomfortable and awkward. Navigating his angular, uncoordinated frame down to a sitting position on a blue-and-white beach towel had been challenging. A 57-year-old former chairman of the SEC dressed in well-worn jeans, a sweatshirt, and borrowed flip-flops two sizes too small was not exactly a fashion statement. Sam Golden was here as a spectator, but what he really wanted was to get in the game. It should have been awkward, but when he was with Margo Savino, it never was.

Most of the time Sam felt guilty as hell for getting Mac McGregor involved in his mission to locate Jeremy Lyons. In an improbable confluence of circumstances, Mac wound up living a nightmare that had no ending. It was only at times like this, when Sam was alone with Margo, that he selfishly marveled at how it had changed his own life.

The beach was her ritual, her church. She sat cross legged next to him, her black wetsuit masking the morning chill. Through the warmth of her left hand, Sam could feel her meditative state. The black Mag flashlight that they had used to light their way was powered off and lay on the towel behind them. In the ambient light of the impending dawn, the sole inhabitants of Sarasota, Florida's Siesta Key Beach waited together, motionless.

With her right hand, Margo reached down and grabbed a fistful of pure quartz pulverized to a fine sugar-white powder. She brought it forward as if toasting heaven, reached across her body, and slowly, gracefully let the sand sift through her fingers over their joined hands.

Sam's heart opened all the way, and he felt a tear that he didn't know he had trickle down his cheek. As the sun peeked over the horizon, the clouds, like guards of pink cotton candy, surrounded the golden orb's soft glow. He looked again at her smile of childlike rapture and could not decide which of God's creations was more beautiful.

It had not been an easy road back for her. The man that Sam believed was Lyons's hired assassin had tortured Margo, and as a result, her flesh had been branded and she had suffered a miscarriage. Both the physical scars and the psychological scars of losing a child had exiled this beautiful woman to a bitter, loveless existence.

The snake that had poisoned her soul had been killed. Finally, the 20-year smothering python of guilt had begun to loosen its grip. The head of the snake had gotten away, but except for his Satanic manifesto, Jeremy Lyons had been a nonfactor. It was like her demons had been exorcised.

Sam was not sure what part he had played in Margo's rebirth. He just knew that he had loved her from the moment he saw her. How this free spirit could love a gangly, gawky, unattractive, Ichabod Crane lookalike was another miracle. But she did.

He saw her glance at her Reactor Critical Mass dive watch. She turned, looked at him, and smiled lovingly. She held up five fingers and, as if compelled, swiveled her head back to gaze at the ocean.

When she first tentatively discussed her morning ritual and asked him to join her, he knew that she thought he would immediately offer excuses: "It'll be dark." "It's cold." "Why don't we rent a room at a hotel and watch from there?" Instead, he had taken her hands, looked into her eyes and said, "I'd love to."

It could be much worse, Sam thought, as he felt the morning's slight rise in temperature. She could have been a gym rat and asked him to join her for daily exercises with other fanatics. He shuddered.

He couldn't take his eyes off of her. At 52, Margo looked 40. Her rigorous swim routine kept everything unimaginably tight. Thank God she had eventually seduced him, because he still couldn't get over the fact that she was way, way out of his league.

From her sitting position, Margo got to her feet with the grace of a dancer. She leaned down and took Sam's hands. Looking at him playfully, she asked "Are you sure you won't join me, my love?"

Sam put his hand on his chin as if contemplating getting into the ocean with jeans and sweatshirt and swimming with a dolphin.

"I might cut my 45-minute routine short," she said," and I could try that exercise that you seem to enjoy where I wrap my legs around you."

Her sexy smile made him feel eighteen again. "Have I told you lately that I love you?" Sam asked, moving his eyebrows up and down.

A quizzical expression crossed her face as she pondered the question. "No. I don't think so. Not ever, in fact."

In an awful Elvis imitation, he crooned, "Well, darlin', I'm tellin' you now."

She laughed and squatted down to take his face in her hands. "Then live with me here in paradise, my love. You are my heart." She kissed him hard on the lips, turned, and ran toward the ocean.

Sam put his hand on the towel and pushed himself up. He kicked off his shoes and ran after her, a big, goofy smile on his face. His long legs caught her just as she was wading into the surf. He touched her arm, and she turned. Tears running indiscriminately down his cheek, his smile extending to his ears, he bobbed his head up and down.

"You will?" she whispered.

"Yes, yes. I love you," he answered.

Margo leaped into his arms, wrapping her legs around him. When she stopped kissing him, she looked at him and asked, "Do you want to go home now?"

"No, no. I want to watch you experience joy. And some day," he grinned sheepishly, "maybe I'll have the courage to join you."

Her dark eyes shone with a love he could not envision. "Thank you. I'll be back, my darling."

As he watched her bounce into the water, Sam Golden knew that he had just experienced a perfect moment in time.

Arms reaching, feet kicking in a steady beat, synchronized breaths, Margo's classic freestyle pulled her far from the shore. Exertion, plus the wetsuit, filled her body with a familiar pleasant warmth.

The predator, clad in black neoprene, swam in shark-like circles, invisible under the surface. As the diver exhaled, the closed circuit rebreather captured any emissions, making for a lighter tank and ensuring that no bubbles escaped to alert the prey.

A Zodiac Cadet, a 15-foot, dark grey, heavily reinforced inflatable rubber boat, sat idle a little over a kilometer from the strike zone, invisible from the shore. It waited alone in calm waters for its master to return.

Fifteen minutes straight out, then a 90-degree turn as Margo changed to backstroke. Fifteen minutes later she would execute a 45-degree turn and head back to the shore. The final leg varied between breaststroke and butterfly. The new theory was that you were supposed to confuse your muscles. *I think that having sex after such a long, dry spell is confusing enough,* she thought and smiled.

The combination of the adrenaline spike that always preceded a kill and the requirement to maintain the slow, steady breathing necessary for the measured tank mixture preoccupied a portion of the diver's senses that were meant purely to enjoy the pleasure of the act. Each previous kill had been precisely choreographed to capture on video the exact moment when the shock of the victim transformed into the recognition of impending death. These were the elements of theater relegated to a personal library that would make Scorsese jealous. A high-speed, waterproof camera was attached to the diver's mask. The wide-angle lens would ensure that the mission would be captured in its entirety.

Margo glanced at her watch out of habit, checking the accuracy of her mental clock: 14 minutes, 56 seconds. Good, but not a record. About ten percent of the time, she checked her watch at exactly 15 minutes. She turned right, flipped to her back, and floated for a moment just to see if she could still see Sam's goofy grin this far from shore. It looked like he had rolled up his jeans and waded into the water. His arms were waving like a windmill. She waved back; then, fixing her eyes on the clouds, she smiled at the crystal blue sky.

The top of the predator's head broke the water's surface. The dark eyes behind the mask narrowed. A spectator complicated the mission. The prey had always been alone. With the aesthetics altered, the diver briefly considered aborting. Emotion was supposed to be compartmentalized to ensure rational decisions, but this was personal. This was in response to betrayal. This was to teach a lesson, to close loose ends, and to salve old wounds. This was for revenge.

With textbook form, her shoulders and chest rotating around the central axis of her spine in the same plane as her hips, her arms always 180 degrees from each other as she cut through the water, Margo executed the perfect backstroke. Her kick was a steady six beats.

The diver's weight belt contained a mixture of high-density material and naturally occurring sand. The elements, when dispersed, would be indistinguishable from other sediment. The titanium dive knife tethered to the diver's waist was only for insurance. Surprise, power. and force of will would be sufficient to complete the mission.

Suddenly Margo's head vanished under the water. Strong hands grabbed her calves from below and jerked violently. An involuntary scream cost her valuable oxygen. Her arms flailed as she fought against the unrelenting force pulling her down. As she thrashed, her lungs burned for air. Her mind struggled to determine what type of marine life this could be as strong legs wrapped around her torso, attaching like a permanent fixture. She pistoned her legs, seeking leverage as water filled her air passages. She struggled desperately, feeling her lungs being crushed, her heart bleeding into her rib cage. Her head was brought close to the diver's mask, and she could see the rapt desire to kill burning through the intense stare and bared teeth. She began to succumb, embracing the inevitable. Her eyelids fluttered. Warmth began to envelop her as her brain formed its last conscious, agonizing thought: *Sam!*

CHAPTER 50

"MAC... SHE'S..."

Grace McGregor gave her husband a concerned look. She was driving their Toyota minivan, and they were en route to an early Saturday evening movie and then dinner. His face was contorted and confused. It looked like he was trying to snatch clarity through his cell phone.

Mac shook his head as he tried to decipher who the caller was and what had happened.

"She's dead." Intermittent, heart-wrenching sobs disguised the caller's identity.

Mac was at a loss for words.

From the hopeless abyss of uncontrollable grief, the caller said softly, "I'm so sorry. I... I had to call someone. You're my best friend."

Mac's heart jumped to his throat. "Sam? Is it Margo?" Mac knew that Sam was visiting Margo in Sarasota.

"Ye, yes," Sam answered, breaking down again.

"I'll catch the next plane."

"No, not, noth, nothing you can do."

"Yeah, there is. I'll e-mail you my flight information. Just send me directions how to get to you."

"No. I'll, I'll pick you up. Thanks."

Mac turned to Grace, his face pale. "Margo's dead. Sam needs me." He started working his iPhone as she made a U-turn. "I need to get the next plane to Sarasota."

Mac's trip to Sarasota had been a nightmare. He'd felt like he was fumbling for words, but the hardest thing was to keep the shock off his face when he saw Sam.

It was as if grief had placed two meaty thumbs right under Sam's eye sockets until indentations occurred and then, once it had a good grip, just pulled down on his face. With his puffy, swollen eyes and elongated face, Sam looked like an abused basset hound. Mac had blinked away tears. He knew that grief aged people, but he didn't realize that it could happen overnight.

CHAPTER 51

MAC WAS A CAULDRON OF fury as he counted the minutes until his weekly dance with the devil. When the phone rang, his words flew out like battering rams: "YOU CALLOUS BASTARD! HOW COULD YOU DO THAT? YOU WERE SAFE. SHE WAS THE FIRST WOMAN YOU EVER SLEPT WITH. SHE WAS NO THREAT TO YOU. AND SOMEONE," he choked on the words, "SOMEONE I CARE ABOUT LOVED HER!"

Mac was gripping his conference room phone so tightly that his fingers were white. The door to the conference room was closed, but even that could not muffle the sounds of his outrage.

"Are you talking about Margo?" Jeremy Lyons asked gently.

"You know who the hell I'm talking about!."

"What happened?"

Genuine concern in his voice stopped Mac momentarily. "Don't worry, Sicko. This is not being taped. You don't have to pull that phony bullshit with me."

"How did it happen?" asked Jeremy, raising his voice.

"She was swimming in the gulf. She was a great swimmer, by the way. She had just started a backstroke and waved to her fiancé." The words spurted out of Mac's mouth, "It looked like something or someone grabbed her from behind and held her under water until her lungs burst!"

Mac could feel the veins popping out on his temples as he waited for a response. "Just so you know that your plan worked perfectly, Sam Golden, who had waded into the surf to watch the love of his life on her morning swim, frantically tried to rescue her."

The silence weighed too heavily on Mac, so he let it all spill out.

"Congratulations. A perfect operation. An old love who might decide to testify some day to your perfidy and the guy who started the investigation into your crooked hedge fund both destroyed. You got two for the price of one. That's efficiency, you sadistic son of a bitch!"

"Are the police sure that it wasn't an accident?" Jeremy asked softly.

"Oh, is this my next assignment for you? More due diligence?"

"Do you mind stopping with the baseless accusations? I'm glad that you decided to make yourself judge and jury, but I had nothing to do with her death." His tone was strident.

"Motive. Opportunity. Retribution." Mac spit the words out.

"I guess that I'll have to contact the authorities myself. It must be comforting to you to be so positive in your convictions."

Mac snorted. "I didn't expect you to admit it; you're far too clever. And you don't have to waste your precious time with the police. The evidence is inconclusive. You're in the clear.

"Actually, there are two things that *are* conclusive," Mac continued through clenched teeth. "This tragedy has your fingerprints on it, and the bloated body of that sweet lady was *not* an accident."

"I'm terribly sorry that she's dead." Jeremy blew out an audible breath. "Please give my condolences to Mr. Golden."

"I'm sure that will be consoling," Mac said. "Perhaps you could also send a sympathy card."

Jeremy sighed. "With your mindset and determination that I'm guilty until proven guilty, there is no way we'll get anything accomplished today. I'll ..."

"These calls are over. I'm done with you."

Charged silence ensued. Finally Jeremy said evenly, "I thought we had an agreement."

"What? That I'd talk to you to keep my family safe?"

"Your family is safe from me."

"Sure it is. And you had nothing to do with Margo's drowning."

"Your ability to reason is colored by your empathy for your friend and the tragic loss of Margo. Why would a senatorial candidate risk having someone connected with him be assassinated? In the unlikely event that Margo would have ever testified against me, her allegations would have been discredited by a first-year law student. Why would I have her killed?"

Mac felt an unwelcome sliver of doubt. Nevertheless, he replied, "Because you can."

"You will reconsider your accusations in time, but I repeat your *family* is safe. What do I have to do to convince you?"

"Meet me in person."

"You do understand that it would be fatal to my endgame if any harm befell your family?"

"Meet me in person."

The challenge hung suspended in the air. Mac knew it would never happen, but if it ever did, he knew that he would be able to read guilt all over Jeremy's face.

After a stalemate of silence, Jeremy said firmly, "It will be arranged."

CHAPTER 52

"YOU *WHAT*!?" JOE SEBASTIANO'S SHORT fuse was lit.

"I told him that I thought he was full of shit. He denied having anything to do with Margo's death and said that it was a complete and tragic surprise to him."

"Do you believe him?"

"Who fucking knows? He is so slick that his denial would pass a lie detector test quicker that you can pass gas after a pepperoni pizza. Who else had any possible motive? She had been a recluse for over twenty years. And the only accident here is Jeremy Lyons's accident of birth."

Joe's voice caught as he spoke. "This is a devastating loss for Sam, and it's magnified by the fact that there is no evidence of a crime. He needs someone to blame besides himself."

Mac's eyes watered. "I know, pal. Sam is inconsolable. He's paralyzed with grief, and now that he needs me, it seems like I'm incapable of helping him."

Joe blew out a breath. "So you're livid. I've got that. But daring Lyons to come see you is idiotic."

"He gave me that crap about how he wouldn't harm my family. I told him that I didn't want his bullshit assurances over the phone. I told him to look me in the eye and tell me that, and I'd believe him. Otherwise, I'm done, and I'll take my chances."

"What the hell do you hope to gain from this?" Joe asked.

"I've already gained something. When Lyons snarled, I handled it. No shiver of fear emerged. I'm tired of looking over my shoulder. It felt right. Do you really think he'll come see me? Have his person call my person and schedule a lunch?"

"He knows he's safe. We've got nothing on him," Joe responded. "What stops him? Maybe he's tired of terrorizing you long distance."

Mac paused. "Yeah. I thought about all that. Bottom line: I bluffed. Hopefully, my poker skills are still intact. But the fear of the Boogey Man is sometimes worse than the Boogey Man himself. I've always told my kids to face their fears. What kind of man am I if I run from mine?"

"I know your kids, Mac, and I'm not that sure they'd agree on this one." Joe's voice increased in intensity. "This isn't like trying out for a team or running for class president, or even facing a bully. This man could torture you and kill you and then sleep like a baby, and I can't watch you 24/7."

"I don't want you to watch me, Joe, and I think you're wrong. I don't think he ever warns a victim. Besides, I think Lyons needs me. I'm his foil. Somehow, and for some reason, he's created a history with me. He gets off on screwing with me. He's the spider who has a luscious fly in his web, but he's not really hungry, so he just wants to keep playing with it."

Joe stared at him, and his lips compressed in a straight line. "You *do* know that the spider always ends up eating the fly."

"Yeah. Maybe I will get devoured. But Joe, if I don't challenge him, then he just keeps taking bites out of me until there's nothing left."

After a few moments of awkward silence, Joe sighed. "Okay. I see your point. Actually, he may need to keep screwing with you. Why do you think he chose you as the target *du jour*?"

"I wish I were just the target of the day and not a lifetime piñata.. If I had to guess, he chose me for a number of reasons. A hundred years ago our CEO, James Wellons, picked me over him to lead the firm's advisory board of top advisors.

"I've legitimately managed to achieve some reasonable street creds in our business. He enjoyed the fact that my good friend and largest client withdrew thirty million dollars from me to give to him, and he knows that I will not back down from verbal jousting. Remember, he is the consummate control freak. He was already tired of running his hedge fund, and I think he wanted to release his book. But he wanted to control the timing. I've been lucky so far. Most people who cross him end up dead."

Mac could almost see his friend's face over the phone. It would be frozen in granite as Joe replied, "If he kills your ass, I will kill it a second time."

"I know, I know," said Mac irritably. "Goading him into seeing me was probably not a smart move; but if it reduces the risk to my family, I'd do it all day long."

"I'm still not buying it. That makes sense if you're dealing with a sane person. Why would he give up the leverage of your family?"

After a few moments, Mac broke the uncomfortable silence. "Because in order to function, I have to believe it."

"What can I do to help?"

"Other than pray? We're assuming that he'll follow through. I put that at about 50/50. And if he doesn't, the control has shifted."

"Have you decided which hero you're going to be: Mitch Rapp, Joe Pike, Jack Reacher?"

"I'm staying away from fiction on this one. I'm going with a real American hero: Joe Sebastiano."

This time the mood was better as the two friends ate lunch in Senator Smathers's office. "Remember, Alan, this information is off the record," said Richard Orth, his hands raised to punctuate his message.

"Yeah, yeah, but it's good shit. How the hell did you get Sam Golden to open up about Lyons?"

"My mom used to work for him ," his Chief of Staff replied sheepishly.

"Okay. Go over it again. I knew the son of a bitch was dirty. This shit is music to my ears."

"Keep in mind that there's not enough evidence to indict Lyons on any of this. But you should be able to bury him with innuendo and suspicion."

"Evidence is hard to get when the witnesses keep dying. Go on," said Smathers.

Orth laid out what was known, what was highly probable, and what was suspected about the Independent candidate. The senator's eyes sparkled with each delicious tidbit.

"And if we talk to the FBI agent who tried to track him down, we might be able to get a comment *on* the record?" Smathers asked.

"Mr. Golden didn't know, but the agent has no love lost for Jeremy Lyons."

"Hot damn," said Smathers, rubbing his hands together. "Do you think we should back-channel a threat to Lyons?"

"I don't know," said Orth with concern. "Mr. Golden thinks that Lyons is extremely dangerous. If you cross him, there's no limit to what he might do to retaliate The example he used was that Lyons would kidnap a child if it would give him an advantage."

"I've got no kids," Smathers said, spreading his hands. "At least none that I know of. And what are we? We are genuine Grade A, ass-kickin' combat warriors."

"I don't know, boss. I've got a bad vibe about this guy."

"Watch the polls. If he doesn't fade, we punch him in the face. Call the FBI agent. Get all you can."

CHAPTER 53

IT HAD BEEN A LONG day. Neither Mac nor Grace had wanted to watch TV, and their dinner conversation had been disjointed, with an underlying current of tension. After she rinsed the dishes and put them in the dishwasher, Grace walked over to the far end of the family room, where her husband was shuffling through some work papers. She sat down on the ottoman by his chair instead of her normal choice of the adjacent chair.

When it was light outside, their two matching chairs provided a panoramic view of their lovely back yard. Grace briefly recalled fond memories of them reading together, sharing a humorous insight, reaching out and holding hands. Then she sighed and poked the hornets' nest.

"It is what it is, Mac," said Grace while gesturing with her hands. Mac had lowered his papers and was looking at her with what she felt was an impatient curiosity.

"Quite profound. What is what it is?" he asked evenly.

"The Jeremy Lyons situation, of course. It's consuming you. If you could extricate yourself, you would have already done so. You're smart. Joe's smart. If Jeremy is trying to clean up his act, let him. And then he won't need you anymore."

Her exasperated tone upped the ante. "Now that you've figured everything out, I'll get back to my work!" He raised the papers in front of his eyes.

"No!" She slapped the papers out of his hand. "We have to discuss this."

Like a rattlesnake, Mac sprang forward. "*We* have nothing to discuss. *We* are not in this quagmire. *We* wanted to tell Sam Golden to pound sand, take care of our clients, and not help him find Lyons. But *we* thought that wouldn't be the right thing to do." His words came out in a bitter rush.

Tears sprang from her eyes. Blood rushed from her face. As if she'd been struck, Grace stood up and shakily grabbed hold of the other chair. "How long has that been festering in there, a cancer needing to be released? For a year I was afraid that I would hear it: 'It's all your fault, Grace.'"

"This isn't about you!"

"You're right!" she yelled back. "It never is!"

Every fiber in Mac's body screamed for him to jump up and take her in his arms. Simultaneously, the defensive instincts of his mind rationalized to create paralysis. He started to speak, but Grace held up a cautionary finger.

"It has probably been at least six months since I have not felt guilty about talking you into helping Sam. Now I will *never* get over it." She spun around and left the room.

Mac sat in his chair, a portrait of solitude, the papers discarded on the floor. He laid his elbows on his knees and slowly lowered his head to his hands. As a too-late tear trickled down his face, his final thought was: *Even in my home, Jeremy Lyons wins.*

CHAPTER 54

"JACKIE MAYFIELD'S HOT," PROCLAIMED DANNY DeMarco. Did you see the takedown of Mr. Euphoria?"

"No. I had an early breakfast with a client, and I haven't had a chance to read the papers or even turn on CNBC." Mac pointed to his flat screen.

"The media's goin' nuts. It's bigger than 'Where's Waldo.' So riddle me this, Batman. How does Jackie Mayfield, who lives in New York, get the scoop on an impending arrest in California? She's able to hustle a Fox News crew over there. Elevator doors open to the lobby; two detectives, a big, ugly CEO dude, and two smoking blondes walk out and are caught on tape," Danny finished triumphantly.

"What's the stock symbol for the Euphoria guy's company?" asked Mac, knowing that his stock-jockey partner had checked the pre-opening on the stock.

"CRBE, closed at 24½. The stock is now indicated at 6 to 9."

"Big spread. It'll narrow a bit." Mac looked up and thought for a moment. " I went over this company with R.J. The reason that it came to our attention was the Alzheimer's connection. It was also interesting because the press release discussing the trials seemed to be more aggressively written than most. They were supposed to have a cure."

"Maybe they still do."

"No." Mac shook his head. "If they had a cure, the CEO wouldn't have needed to go rogue. Was anyone else implicated?"

"Not that I know of."

"Any idea how Jackie Mayfield got the heads-up?"

"Yep," Danny answered with a triumphant smile. "Courtesy of 'An Outsider.'"

Mac paused and looked at him curiously. "That's what she said?"

"Yeah. She also said that the Chad Alexander gotcha was a tip from the same person."

"I don't remember seeing that in the news around the time of Alexander's trial," Mac said thoughtfully, "and I read everything about it, because it was local and because I wanted to take a punch at Alexander myself."

"I didn't know about it then either. But in Jackie's interview this morning, she said that she hadn't been authorized to reveal the source until now."

"Calling the source an outsider doesn't identify anyone; it just adds mystery. In fact, it's like writing an exposé and signing it 'Anonymous,'" Mac said. "Obviously, a very well-connected person had inside information on two extremely high-profile incidents in two separate geographical areas and wanted to let the public know about it."

"That sounded like a run-on sentence, Mr. English Major. I think that whoever exposed these bastards is a hero."

"I guess so," Mac said, slowly nodding his head, "unless ..."

"Unless what?"

"No idea of what his motive might be," Mac said thoughtfully, as his mind connected imaginary dots, "but follow me. I've got to run this theory by you, because you-know-who," he pointed to R.J.'s office, "would discount it as paranoia caused by the Stockholm syndrome."

"You're thinking Lyons?" Danny asked. "You're not putting me on?"

Mac raised his hands. "Granted, I'm seeing Jeremy Lyons everywhere, but see if you can refute the logic. Inside information: he would illegally hack into anyone's computer in a heartbeat. Both operations demonstrated perfect timing and flawless execution. The 'outsider' waits until the second incident to take credit, thereby increasing the drama."

"Five bucks says it's not Lyons," Danny challenged.

"What odds?'

"Two to one."

Mac laughed. "How about a hundred to one?"

"Five to one. Final offer," Danny said, folding his arms across his chest.

"Okay." Mac tapped Danny's knuckles with his. "It's a bet I'd rather lose. I couldn't stand it if the world thought that psycho was a hero."

CHAPTER 55

HOTELS WERE A NECESSARY EVIL for Mac McGregor. He was fortunate that his job required a minimum amount of travel. While others in his industry planned exotic journeys to faraway places, Mac was happiest when his feet were in the sands of Bethany Beach.

Yet, every year since 2005, when the conference began, he had gladly attended the Barron's Top 100 Conference. That year Barron's decided to publish a list of the top 100 financial advisors in the country. The stock market and investors were still suffering a hangover from the three-year ugly bear market of 2000-2002, and press was negative on the brokerage industry. The once-envied occupation was more often the subject of jokes than the object of praise. Perceived conflicts of interest inherent in the business, some legitimate, some exaggerated, had added fuel to the criticisms.

Barron's, the most respected financial publisher in the country, came to the rescue like a knight riding in on a white steed. Utilizing formulas created by Joel Little, the industrious and diligent young author of *Financial Winners*, the reporters at Barron's went to work analyzing and ranking the nation's top advisors.

The process began with conversations between the intrepid Little and top management at the various brokerage firms: Who were their elite advisors? How many assets did they have under management? Did they have any client complaints against them? Were their compliance records clean? In the early years the analysis was intensive and included interviews with clients of the advisors to determine satisfaction with service. Little's research was so extensive that the majority of work had been done before the analysts at Barron's did their examination.

The popularity and exposure of the rankings mushroomed. Now there is a top 100 women advisors, a top 100 independent advisors, and even a state-by-state ranking.

By necessity, the analysis became more formula driven. The first conference was held in New York. Invitees included the top 100 advisors and those perceived to be on the cusp, another 400 individuals. Over 95 percent of the invitees attended. The conference was like the Academy Awards for the financial industry.

After his initial ranking as one of the top five advisors, Mac had attended every meeting, and Barron's had allowed him to bring R.J. Brooks along as his guest. R.J.'s intellect and humor made him a welcome addition, and Mac did not have to ask twice.

This year, the conference was being held at the Waldorf Astoria Orlando, and Mac, who was definitely not a New Yorker, couldn't have been happier. The opportunity to spend two and a half days with peers and exchange ideas on best practices and investment strategies was appealing by itself; but add the warm climate, and it was just one step away from heaven.

When Mac and R.J. checked into the massive, sprawling, opulent hotel, Mac smiled to learn that the folks at Barron's had once again treated him well. As a member of Barron's Advisory Council, a group of advisors who discussed the agenda and innovations for the meetings, he was upgraded to a luxury suite. His smile widened as he heard R.J.'s patter with the female desk clerk.

"Oh, no," R.J. protested, "I really can't accept a courtesy upgrade to the Presidential Suite. Any old closet will do for me."

Mac leaned over to whisper to the attractive young woman. She lost none of her grin, as she correctly assumed that he was going to add to the nonsense. "Madam, please forgive him. The young man has recently come out of the closet. Be gentle with him."

Mac snatched his key card before R.J. could offer a retort.

"At least we're never dull," offered R.J. as they walked toward their rooms.

"Life's too short, pal. What's your room number?"

"Nice try. I'm not that easy," R.J. quipped.

"Debatable. Let's have lunch at 12:30. That work?"

"Sure. And perhaps you can rationalize why you bet Danny that your BFF was the outsider." R.J.'s voice went into movie promo mode, "It's bigger than Deep Throat. Everyone wants to know the secret identity, and my senior partner is the only one who knows."

"You're way too young to watch that kind of movie."

R.J. rolled his eyes. "As in Woodward and Bernstein," he said patiently. "But for the record, you may be right."

"Are you ready for your session tomorrow?" R.J. asked as they waited for their lunch orders.

"All over it," Mac answered.

"I would hate to be the panel."

At Mac's suggestion, for the first time an advisor would be leading the session and asking questions to a panel of three advisors from different firms. As the moderator, Mac chose the questions, and he could cut a panelist's answer short if he felt that the responder was not answering the question or was taking too long to make a point. The hour-long session was entitled "Unscripted."

"Will there be paramedics on stand-by?" R.J. asked.

"Hmm. Good idea." Mac turned to his friend. "Do you think Barron's is ready to be a spectator at the coliseum?"

CHAPTER 56

SINCE THE INAUGURAL CONFERENCE, EVERY General Session had kept to the allotted time frame. A large electronic reminder in inescapable view of the moderator insistently emphasized the time that remained.

Mac McGregor was comfortably on schedule, and the ten minutes and nineteen seconds left gave him ample time to play. By request, one of his panelists was Bobby Cohen, a burly, take-no-prisoners New Yorker who represented the independent advisor channel.

Bobby was bilingual, assuming that profanity qualified as a second language. The fact that this venue forced him to abstain obviously inhibited his normally colorful responses. Whenever Mac felt that one of the other panelists' answers was starting to suck the energy out of the room, he would fire a question at Bobby.

This time his friend's answer had been articulate, thought provoking, but, uncharacteristically, a bit boring.

"Bobby," Mac said with feigned surprise. "That was actually a *good* answer."

"Like I haven't been carrying you the whole session."

"Well then, knowing that our peers will hang on your every word, I should let you carry it across the finish line.

"Alyson, Chakra," Mac said, turning to the other panelists, "be prepared to pick up the fumble. Bobby, what is your biggest financial fear for the future, and have you discussed it with your clients?"

Bobby furrowed his face. "You mean other than Gloria spending all my money?"

"Yes," said Mac, laughing along with the audience. The man's delivery had been perfect.

Bobby's concentration was evident, but the unforgiving clock was moving.

"Bobby, why don't I come back ..."

"No!"

The outburst surprised Mac, because his tone had been gentle.

"I've got a *better* idea," said Bobby with a mischievous grin. "You're the financial wizard. You give us the answer."

"Have you forgotten the rules of this session?" Mac asked.

"When was the last time I played by the rules?"

Mac shrugged, turned, and faced the audience. "My greatest fear for the future? Our economy is still in the toilet. The stench is pervasive, and all the politicians are holding their noses and pointing at the other guy."

"Now you're talking my language," Bobby prompted. "So what's the answer?"

"Hopefully, at the break you folks can help me figure out how I lost control of this session." When the scattered laughs subsided, Mac continued. "I don't know the answer, but I know that the fiscal cliff is real. It can't be discounted like Y2K fears. In 2008, for the first time in my career, my clients were really scared. We are three years from the bottom of the market, and they're still scared.

"New home construction in our area is picking up, and my client in the business wants to hire more people to handle the demand. But what if the economy falters? He would have to let them go. At 70, he doesn't have the heart to face that, so he makes do with less.

"A New York client in the vending business wants to hire young adults to help him expand his business. If he pays them fifty thousand dollars, it will cost him close to ninety thousand after taxes and mandatory health benefits. It's just not worth it.

"My clients are suffocating under the blanket of excessive regulations, taxes, and the biggest impediment to growth and expansion, uncertainty." Mac's voice softened. "My biggest fear is that I don't have the answer and I don't know how to help them."

The room was stilled. Mac blinked, cleared his throat, and apologized. "I'm sorry. This isn't about me. We all have the same problems, and we're sure not going to get the answers from acrimonious legislatures or detached pundits!"

He spread his arms. "We're considerably more tuned in than they are," he said defiantly. "*We* recognize the problems. We've been studying balance sheets and evaluating corporate competency all of our careers. Our clients are small businesses: the shop owners, the restaurateurs, the high-tech internet startups. "

Mac stopped, startled. Somehow he had opened an emotional vein, and his frustration and passion flooded out. It was too late to hit the brakes. He slowed his delivery.

"We are the boots on the ground. We are multigenerational listeners. How many of our clients share their hopes, their dreams, and their worst fears with us?"

Unable to control his intensity, Mac felt like he was roaring. "Our clients fear for their legacies – the amount of our national debt that is on the head of each of their grandchildren. They may not have faith in our politicians, but they have faith in us. *We* cannot disappoint them.

"Use your wallet; use your voice; use your network; use your incredible, irresistible powers of persuasion. We can be *re*active or *pro*active toward our fiscal problems. What we can't be is spectators."

Mac looked at the clock. He had one minute remaining. " I'm sorry. I didn't mean to give a speech." He winced. "When you rate this session, please remember that the deviation from intention was Bobby's fault. We have time for one question. Panel?"

Bobby Cohen's mouth hung open, but Chakra Rao asked, "If your friend Jeremy Lyons runs for president, would you consider being his running mate?"

Blood rushed to Mac's face. Forcing a smile, he replied, "I'm waiting for Bobby to run."

At the conclusion of the session, Wesley Graves, the ridiculously handsome editor of *Barron's* and the moderator of the entire conference, took the handoff from Mac with the assurance of a veteran NFL running back. "Thank you. Mac, and thanks to our terrific panel. After that impassioned speech, I feel like shouting, 'Amen.'"

Wesley walked over to Mac and clasped Mac's hand in both of his. "Absolutely loved it, Mac. Great idea and perfect execution. In spite of your 'I have a dream' speech, this will get over-the-top ratings from the group."

"It was fun," said Mac, returning the smile with a vain attempt to achieve equal wattage. "I hope the panel still loves me."

"That I can't promise," Wesley responded with a laugh. "But the audience does. It was interesting, real, and of course, with your sense of humor, no one was texting their office."

"Probably because they were afraid I'd call them out."

"Mac," Wesley said with a concerned look, "the question about Jeremy Lyons was obviously upsetting to you. In Lyons's speech, he sounded like he admired you. Was there a falling out?"

"There was never a falling *in*. He mentioned my name because he knew it would infuriate me. It's a long story, and not a pretty one. The man is not what he seems. Next time you're in D.C., I'll buy you a drink and tell you more than you ever wanted to know about Jeremy Lyons."

Wesley relaxed, patted Mac's shoulder, and said, "I wouldn't miss it. Thanks again, my friend."

Mac walked through a maze of congratulatory folks and shook a lot of hands. He thanked all the well-wishers as he maneuvered back to his table.

As he approached, R.J. nodded and smiled. They were each other's most objective critics, and R.J. gave him a subtle thumbs-up. "If I didn't have all of your skeletons inventoried, your impromptu campaign speech might have even convinced *me* to vote for you."

"Thanks, pal," Mac said as he sat down at the table.

"So I'm going to give you a reward."

"A reward?" Mac replied with raised eyebrow.

"Yes," R.J. answered with a smug smile. "Only one of the four o'clock sessions seemed interesting, so I'm going to take it. While I'm doing that, you will be playing hooky."

As a rule, Mac and R.J. attended different breakout sessions and then compared notes later. "You are scheduled for a fabulous 50-minute massage at four o'clock, compliments of *moi.*" He pointed proudly at himself.

"You're treating?"

"Yes. I'm so grateful that you did not embarrass our group that I arranged for Oscar, a large fella with very strong hands, to provide you with 50 minutes of sensory delight."

Mac gave him the stink eye.

"Seriously, Mac. Regardless of your veneer of cool, this was stressful, as is everything else in your life at the moment. I'm just protecting my investment."

Mac continued to stare at him suspiciously.

"Okay, okay," R.J. said, raising his hands in mock surrender. "The Oscar part is BS, but look." R.J. showed him a confirmation on his iPad: four o'clock with a masseuse. "I can't guarantee her attractiveness. If she looks like Oscar, it's not my fault."

Mac shook his head and bowed. "I accept, grasshopper. It sounds like one of your best ideas."

After reading about what was described as a truly indulgent spa by Guerlain, whatever that meant, Mac thought that he might extend the day by relaxing in the steam room. Not much of a drinker, he didn't mind being late for cocktails.

Just like the rest of the hotel, the spa was a massive facility, ultramodern, fanatically clean, and luxurious. Mac felt slightly out of place as he drank a watermelon-flavored water in his white bathrobe and flip-flops. He wondered why he had never made time for a massage. He couldn't imagine that this type of luxury existed outside of a five-star hotel. Not only were massages supposed to enhance overall health, they were also definitely relaxing.

Exactly at four o'clock, an attractive, dark-haired young woman with smiling eyes introduced herself and led him back to one of the 22 private treatment areas. As he listened to her chatting pleasantly, her cheerfulness made Mac think of a Disney employee, and he wondered if he'd guessed right.

"Please place your locker key in the pocket of your bathrobe, and then you can hang the robe on the hook," she said. "Your slippers can fit under that small table. I will leave you while you disrobe and knock before entering. If you start by lying on your stomach on that table and pulling the sheet over you, that would be perfect." Big smile.

Mac smiled back and thanked her as she left the room. He did as instructed and was lying on his stomach relaxing when he heard a gentle knock. His head was resting comfortably on his folded arms. Without raising his head, he said, "I'm good."

The door opened, and Mac took a deep, relaxing breath.

"Do you *ever* work out?" asked a familiar and chilling voice.

CHAPTER 57

ADRENALINE SHOT THROUGH MAC'S BODY. He stiffened, and with every ounce of determination he could muster, remained lying on his stomach with his head resting on his arms. Naked, vulnerable, he could feel the evil in the room, and he instinctively knew that he could not succumb to it.

Taking a deep breath, Mac casually asked, "Is this your endgame?" He twitched his sheet-covered buttocks for emphasis.

He felt Jeremy move closer. "I really have toughened you up mentally. Now if we can just get you to a gym."

Languidly, Mac rolled over onto his back, turned to one side, and propped his head on his elbow-supported hand. He was relieved that his arm was not shaking. "Are you sure you're not just after a sneak peek?"

Jeremy had on black running shorts, black tennis shoes without socks, and a form-fitting black silk T-shirt. He was perfectly tanned to the point that it looked sprayed on, and Mac couldn't help but be intimidated by his magazine-worthy muscular body.

"You have ten minutes remaining for my little visit, and I'm sure the young lady outside can't wait to give you a happy ending. You *did* ask for this meeting."

"Yeah, I did, and it was probably optimistic to expect that we would both be dressed."

"Would you feel more comfortable if I took off my clothes?" Jeremy asked lightly.

Mac rolled his eyes.

"You really thought that I would physically harm your family?" Jeremy shook his head derisively and moved even closer to the massage table. "Where is your legendary gift of intuition?" He leaned uncomfortably close to Mac.

It was all Mac could do not to recoil.

"Your minute role in my destiny is to be a source of entertainment. You are sport." Jeremy raised his arms and mashed his fists together. He then turned his fists in opposite directions. "How many ways can I twist you and still have you return to your original shape?" He smiled. "I promise not to harm your family. Anything else?"

Mac sat up, holding in his stomach as well as his temper. "Yeah. I'd like you to answer a few questions."

"I will answer one." His face was expressionless; the man was a robot.

Mac tried to form a compound question. "Did you order Max Parnavich to assassinate George Grant so that you could collect his life insurance proceeds?"

"Yes," Jeremy replied unflinchingly.

Mac's mouth fell open. Jeremy had answered with the same equanimity that he'd have if Mac had asked if he was heterosexual. The matter-of-fact answer made Mac's skin crawl and his heart hurt. His eyes welled with tears.

Mac shook his head. "And you want to run for public office?" he spat out.

"If that's a question, I only agreed to one."

Mac breathed deeply to avoid screaming at the sociopath.

"However, I'll indulge you." Jeremy sat on the edge of the massage table and spoke somberly. "That was not my only sin. I regret my past with every fiber of my soul. I am a born-again Christian. God has forgiven me. The rest of my life is dedicated to redemption."

A wave of nausea engulfed Mac. Jeremy was bastardizing Mac's faith. Mac was speechless, too shocked to show outrage.

Jeremy continued. "I would like you to believe me, but it doesn't matter if you do or don't. I know in my heart that I've changed." His left hand went to his heart.

"God may forgive you. I don't."

Jeremy shrugged. He stood up and started to leave the room, but at the door he turned back again. "Your family is safe. Your time here is extended to six o'clock. While they are rubbing the toxins out of your body, perhaps they can rub the hatred from your heart."

"Jeremy!"

Jeremy paused at the door. He did not turn back around.

"Are you the 'outsider'?"

Jeremy opened the door and started to walk out. Over his shoulder he responded, "No one is more inside than I."

Before the door closed, the masseuse stepped into the room and timidly asked, "Was it okay that I let him in?"

Mac told the stricken masseuse that he was sorry, but it wasn't working for him. He dressed and headed back to his suite. To further add to his frustration, he made a wrong turn, and the normal five-minute trek took fifteen after he asked twice for directions. Skipping the massage had been the right decision. No amount of massage would eliminate the poisonous Jeremy Lyons from his life.

Mac walked out onto the balcony of his suite and gazed absently at the golf course below. He searched his mind, trying to find a positive out of this. Like a macho idiot, he had issued a challenge to a psycho who gets off on torture to meet with him in person.

Surprise! The psycho takes him up on the offer and steps in while tough guy is bare assed in a massage room. Mac sighed. It could have been worse, he supposed. Jeremy could have surprised him on the golf course, and he would really have felt inadequate.

A few minutes later, Mac walked back inside and called Joe on his cell. Secrecy now seemed silly, so when Joe answered, he just spilled it out. Joe listened, was intuitive enough not to offer advice, and Mac ended the short call.

Next Mac called Grace. He tried to keep the tension out of his voice, but Grace could see through a wall when it came to Mac.

"I'm so sorry," she said, trying to comfort him. "I wish I could be there with you Do you think we're really safe?"

Mac thought for a moment, and then, with genuine conviction, he answered, "Yeah. He has another game plan for me. I don't believe anything else the man said, but he is too proud to go back on his word. You and the kids are safe."

"That's good," she said hopefully.

Ever since Mac's outburst, the connection between him and Grace had not been fluid. It was like a just-off harmony or a poem straining to rhyme. He knew that it was his fault. He had taken out his pain on Grace, the safest place. His later apologies had been acknowledged, but Mac felt like they were still out of sync. Guilt separates faster than a divorce lawyer.

Into the silence he said, "Babe, I'm sorry for blaming you for this friggin' mess."

She waited a moment before responding. "Mac, if we harbored resentments for every hurtful word we've exchanged over 32 years, we'd never have peace." In a gentle voice, she said, "I've forgiven you. It's time you forgave yourself."

CHAPTER 58

THERE WAS A PLETHORA OF reasons why R.J. Brooks would not want to work anywhere else. Most were obvious: great company, family-like environment, wonderful clients, freedom of choice on investments, strategy, and lifestyle. Only the inner circle would know the kicker. Within their team's tight circle of fifteen, there were no holds barred.

Which is why when Mac walked by his desk at 8:30 in the morning carrying a duffle bag, R.J.'s lips curled into a smile. He waited for Mac to get settled and then casually strolled over to his desk.

"Would you indulge my curiosity?" R.J. asked lightly.

"No."

"Well, then, just follow my thought process to help me see if I'm thinking logically."

"You're not," Mac replied flatly.

R.J. started pacing in front of Mac's desk, assuming a demeanor that he felt was definitely Sherlock Holmes-ian. In contrast, he noted with satisfaction that Mac's demeanor reflected impatient annoyance.

"You are later than usual, agreed?" Not expecting a reply, R.J. continued. "I deduce that the weather is too inclement for you to leave early and hack up the golf course."

"I deduce that you are de-dumb," Mac countered.

"Hardly." Not missing a beat in his purposely irritating plan, R.J. soldiered on. "It is unlikely, though appropriate, that your bag ..." he pointed dramatically at the duffle bag as if he had discovered a clue that was resting behind the back of Mac's desk, "holds a gift for me."

"Actually, it does." Mac reached back, unzipped the bag, and presented it to his partner. "It's a sniff-and-scratch. Insert your head all the way in the bag and give it a couple of big sniffs. You'll want to scratch your eyes out."

R.J. laughed in spite of himself. "Wouldn't 'scratch my nose off' be more logical?"

"You are welcome to take the sniff test to check."

"Okay, so give," said R.J. "From all appearances, you were working out this morning."

"What gave it away?" asked Mac, holding up his arms and flexing them. "The guns?"

R.J. lowered his voice. "And so soon after your nemesis made his unflattering remarks."

Mac rolled his eyes.

"Well, I'm proud of you, Mac. Those of us who have to work out so that they don't get called to go on *The Biggest Loser* tend not to be sympathetic to those of you for whom a weight problem is five pounds. You are our meal ticket. In the words of my favorite Vulcan, I need you to live long and prosper. And if I find a sliver of joy in knowing that you're hating every minute of working out, well, you've always wanted me to be happy."

Mac's half-lidded eyes looked up. "Either big sniff or leave," he said, holding the bag open again.

"Is Lyons really that cut?"

Mac sat back, placing the bag on the corner of his desk. "Let me put it this way. I could work out literally 24/7 for a year, and I'd still be the 97-pound weakling compared to that guy. He is solid frigging granite. If a truck hit him, the truck would be totaled."

It wasn't business as usual. Mac went through his e-mails, obligatory phone calls, and two client meetings, but he knew that he needed to talk to David Grant. It didn't seem right to ask him to lunch or for a drink. How could he tell him that the soon-to-be-Senator Lyons had ordered a hit on David's dad?

He admitted it, David. No, no, he'll never be brought to justice, but maybe he'll be a good senator. Unfortunately, the conversation couldn't be scripted. If the situation were reversed, Mac knew that certainty wouldn't bring closure. It would just feel like an incomplete sentence. Unconsciously he bit the inside of his lip as he e-mailed David to set up a time to talk.

CHAPTER 59

CONGRESSMAN FLOYD CALDWELL, FROM THE great state of Tennessee, was a well-liked politician, laid back and agreeable to everything. Both parties accepted him as an amiable, noncontroversial colleague. Not dissimilar from an employee who wants to remain unnoticed by his boss, Caldwell only cared about keeping his job.

Once, good old boys were coveted. You would pick them first to be on your side, because they would agree with whatever you proposed. In today's Congress, where disparate views were the norm, Floyd Caldwell was mostly ignored. Although he was not classically handsome, his thick, prematurely gray hair and matching gray eyes gave him an interesting look. And the cleft in his chin enabled him to slide into the category of "I guess he's good looking. He's cute."

Who needs Jeremy Lyons? At first, Congressman Caldwell had thought he'd found the golden goose: not only had Lyons funneled $20,000 a month to him, but his benefactor had also introduced him to the hottest women on the planet. So the closet Liberal had liberally indulged himself in the finer things in life.

Standing on his wraparound balcony. looking out at the Kennedy Center, Caldwell again cursed Lyons for abandoning ship. The hypnotic panoramic view of the Potomac River and the Georgetown skyline from his 3750-square foot Watergate co-op guaranteed that whatever woman entered his den of iniquity was going down. For the views. including floor-to-ceiling windows wherever you looked, were just the icing on his over-the-top apartment.

Circular foyer with paneled walls and coffered ceilings; Oriental rugs in the front hallway, custom cabinetry, glass subway tiles, and Italian marble floors completed the picture of decadence.

So what was he supposed to do when the music stopped? Just walk away from the huge mortgage? The association dues were seven grand a month.

So Caldwell did what they all do in one way or another. He peddled a little influence. Penny ante stuff, and not that dangerous. It had helped, but not enough. He was sliding down a mountain of shit and picking up speed.

Fortunately for the congressman, along came Sondra Rochelle. A dark-skinned French woman with zero inhibitions, she helped transition him onto a new gravy train. For him, she was a singer with perfect pitch.

The extraordinarily hot Ms. Rochelle was a vice president at Lockheed Martin in Bethesda, Maryland. The price for Caldwell's new life was sharing a few meaningless tidbits during pillow talks. Sondra's brother, Paul, was also employed at the defense firm. Although Caldwell had no idea which office Paul worked out of, all he cared about was that her brother had no problem greasing the congressman's palm. On purpose, Caldwell and Paul had never met or had an actual conversation, so the connection could never be made.

Caldwell had finagled his way onto the House Permanent Select Committee on Intelligence. In addition to focusing on matters of national security, the committee shared jurisdiction with other committees, including the House Armed Services Committee, and often became the liaison with the Department of Defense. A little inside information can be very valuable when a defense contractor is bidding on contracts, and Caldwell accepted the *quid pro quo* gratefully. There are very few things better than getting paid *and* getting laid.

"Floyd?"

Surprised, Caldwell turned around. Sondra stood there wearing only one of his tee shirts. She smiled seductively at him.

"I didn't even hear you come in," he said, returning her smile.

"I have to sneak around to make sure you're not cheating on me," she teased.

"Who would dare cheat on a ninja," he said, spreading his arms and pulling her into him.

Afterwards, Caldwell lay on his side on the cool avocado green sheets. Sondra lay spread eagle on her back, her eyes closed. She was oblivious and would be unconcerned by lover's worshipping scrutiny of every inch of her nude body.

No question that I would have made a great prostitute, Caldwell thought. *If the link between the sister and brother comes to light, at worst I get a slap on the wrist for having loose lips.* He smiled. *If a judge could see this chick with her clothes off, he would dismiss the case entirely.*

CHAPTER 60

STAGE 3 OF THE OPERATION was proving to be troublesome. Identifying the offenders did not require extensive analysis. It was as if every politician, past and present, were raising his or her hand to volunteer as the target for political misdeeds. Yet even with all the potential candidates, Jeremy Lyons had to find the one who would be a lightning rod.

Jeremy would not do ordinary. It would be an affront to his intellect and to his imagination. The ordinary sins of bribery, blackmail, insider trading, and zipper infractions rang his doorbell like an army of trick-or-treaters. None would create more than flickering outrage.

The task was more difficult because of the success of the first two stages of his strategic plan. That cocky little prick, Chad Alexander, III and the innocent, freckle-faced schoolgirl. Steven Spielberg could not have chosen better characters. Add in the pompous, bombastic epitome of the 1%, Alexander's father, and it was an instant classic. YouTube hits were now over twelve million. It was indeed the gift that kept on giving.

Even Shakespeare could not conjure up a more physically and morally repugnant character than Stanley Lipitz. His horrendous act would be drawn out with excruciating slowness. Innocence would be proclaimed, lawyers would delay; but there would be no plea bargaining. For an egomaniac like the accused, a trial would be the only way to demonstrate his self-proclaimed brilliance and secure his infamy.

So, first, a predator serial rapist who had been exonerated by a shoddy judicial system, then a greedy psychopath who willingly and without remorse poisoned children for profit. The flavor of these exposed transgressions would not disappear quickly.

It had begun with the rape of a woman and progressed to the rape of children's minds. The challenge was to find someone or some group who wanted to rape our country.

Comfortable with solitude to the point where it was usually a preference, Jeremy reflected on his options. Victory would be achieved with or without a final defining event. However, for maximum effectiveness, the margin of victory needed to be large enough to ensure a mandate.

Ideas were interesting, but action was compelling. Every law enforcement agency's mission was to thwart terrorism. They had overwhelming resources to accomplish this objective.

Jeremy smiled. He did have one advantage over the terrorist watchdogs: if he could not uncover a significant impending crisis, he could create one.

CHAPTER 61

AS HE ALWAYS DID WHEN training with Sabine, Jeremy made it a point to get to his gym fifteen minutes early so that he could warm up his aging muscles and stretch before she arrived. Everything, even physical superiority, required both discipline and diligence.

When he opened the door, he was greeted by the familiar smell of vinyl and disinfectant spray lingering from yesterday's workout. The floor and walls of the room were covered in the usual blue mats. Unlike the opulent facility of his Naples, Florida, location, it had seemed frivolous, even for him, to appreciably upscale in a foreign country.

Three of the walls were also covered in thick padding on the off chance he felt the need to teach an unfriendly a lesson. Cushioning helped minimize the chances that a lesson would become terminal. Finally, the front wall had a series of large mirrors as an aid for refining technique.

Jeremy was seated on the floor stretching his hamstring when the door opened and his student arrived.

"Good. You're already here," she said putting her bag on the floor.

Jeremy looked up at her in amusement, pleased by her eagerness. As Sabine was taking off her sweats, he couldn't help noticing the dramatic improvement in women's workout clothing in recent years. Her cropped, fitted tank top and elastic-waist pants revealed the athletic figure that he had personally helped develop.

They spent the initial fifteen minutes with a series of stretches and exercises combined with a standard set of kicks and punches in front of the mirror. When they finished the warm-up he asked, "Do you want me to hold the shield for you or would you rather start with the mitts?"

"Let's spar," she retorted.

Jeremy raised an eyebrow. "That anxious?"

"Not really. I just want to keep pressure-testing the stuff we've been working on. I want to make sure I can use it when I need it."

Encouraged by the enthusiasm of his protégé, Jeremy responded, "Okay. Grab a chest guard and headgear."

The protective gear was hanging from the wall just below the rack with the bo staffs and bokken. She reluctantly grabbed a chest protector and put her arms through the straps.

As he was helping her with the buckle on her back, she complained, "I can't believe you still make me wear this thing! Do you really think I need this?"

"It is not out of necessity, my dear. It is simply that I feel it my duty to preserve what I consider a national treasure."

As they circled facing each other, Jeremy wondered if she would initiate the action as he had taught her. *Always get there first.*

In anticipation of her attack, he rocked back onto his right leg and raised his left knee to feign a front kick. Sabine had seen this move from him before and timed it perfectly. As soon as his foot returned to the ground, she shuffled forward, with her lead hand jamming his arms against his torso, and drove a front punch into his abdomen, followed by a round kick aimed to the side of his head.

After feeling the hollow sensation of air being forced out of his torso, Jeremy recognized the motion of her thigh out of the corner of his eye and managed to get his left arm cover up in time to block the incoming kick. With a quick shove, he countered with a round kick to her leg, followed by a side kick that compressed her chest guard.

Over a series of exchanges, Jeremy was impressed and proud of Sabine's improved transitions and use of angles to take away his advantage in size and strength, not to mention her striking power. She had clearly learned well, but her new efficiency and focus on attacking had him reaching the point of fatigue. She had slipped several of his punches and landed some solid combinations of her own.

Jeremy threw a jab-cross, which she slipped, and drove a left shovel hook into his liver, followed by a hook to the head. He attempted to nonchalantly bounce on his toes, but that shot to the liver sent a wave of pain through his body that he tried to mask. Jeremy needed to end this in a way that she found impressive, and he needed to end it quickly for his own sake.

Sabine attempted a leg kick, but Jeremy quickly lifted his shin to check it. He responded with a patronizing outside crescent kick with his lead leg and suddenly felt the impact on his jaw from her spinning back fist. She quickly transitioned to a hip throw, dropping him onto his back and into a scarf-hold with her in side control.

He reached around her and joined his hands in a Gable grip. He quickly bridged off the mat and rolled over into side control, drawing his knees under him and against her to secure the position. With his weight across her chest he was able to pin her wrist to the mat with his right hand. He quickly slipped his left arm under her upper arm and secured the figure-4 hold. Perfectly executing the Kimura, he lifted her upper arm while her wrist remained pinned to the mat.

Sabine clenched her teeth. Jeremy knew she was trying to withstand the pain of the torque on her shoulder, but it was only out of pride. He had the hold locked. Desperate to end the session, he cranked the shoulder to apply more force and felt the welcome relief of her tapping on his side, signaling her submission.

Jeremy walked over to an ice chest and grabbed two ice-cold bottles of water. He tossed one to Sabine as they gathered for the post mortem.

"You shouldn't have gone to the ground with me," Jeremy said. "In a real situation, stay on your feet after the throw and finish your opponent with a heel stomp or soccer kick."

"I know," she lamented. "I'm so close I can taste it."

He smiled, gave her a nod of acknowledgement, and raised his bottle of water in salute. "There will be a day when the student vanquishes the master; but until then, let's shower, and taste each other."

CHAPTER 62

AS HE PREPARED TO KEY the audio system in the soundproof room, Jeremy reached down and massaged Sabine's shoulders through her partially open black silk robe. "Black on black will always be in fashion," he mused.

The exquisite African-American woman leaned back, closed her eyes, and gently rested her head in his crotch. She was on the floor level, which resembled a cushioned Japanese futon. Jeremy was nude. His legs were spread and outstretched in a large black leather easy chair. The couple was temporarily sated after sharing a post-sparring shower and soapy, languid sex.

"My dear, you give legitimacy to the word 'irresistible.' Couple that with your fluid acting performance, and voila, we're able to take down the poster child for arrogant, entitled rapists," Jeremy said pleasantly, "and Alegria's research uncovered the perfect example of illegal drug trafficking.

"You ladies have left me a hard act to follow," he said, continuing to massage her shoulders. Thus, the final stage before liftoff must be even more dramatic. If you don't mind, I'd like to pick your brain."

Jeremy saw Sabine's smile widen and felt her shiver as she acknowledged the compliment.

"Listen to our old friend Floyd Caldwell and give me your impressions," Jeremy instructed. Eyes still closed, Sabine nodded slightly. Jeremy had previously given Sabine access to edited conversations from his audio recordings. At that time, he had briefed her on the functions of the House Permanent Select

Committee on Intelligence (HPSCI). In Jeremy's mind, the fact that Caldwell was a member of this influential and sensitive committee was proof positive that Congress was clueless.

When Caldwell was a recruiter for Jeremy's operation in Naples, his actions were closely monitored, as was done with every employee. Even in his haste to get out of the country, Jeremy had maintained audio surveillance on any active congressman or senator under his influence. Initially, the purpose was precautionary: the remote possibility had existed that a singing legislator could have sabotaged Jeremy's future plans. Currently, it was conceivable that any information he obtained could create an opportunity.

Sabine had a cunning, instinctively logical mind, and her absorption of Jeremy's teachings had been rewarding. Because it had been Jeremy's intent to get Sabine's read on the Caldwell data, his editing had been minimal.

After listening to the recordings, she offered her conclusions. "If I heard it correctly, the HPSCI and its counterpart in the Senate are like intel oversight masters. It is their responsibility to make sure that the agencies in the intelligence community, such as DOD, CIA, State, Justice, and Homeland Security, are playing within their legal restrictions. So, in addition to receiving a regular briefing on what the intelligence community is looking at, HPSCI members are also privy to threat information. Bottom line: Clueless Caldwell is the perfect mark!"

"I agree," Jeremy said with a nod.

"And Caldwell's lady friend is a professional lover," Sabine added. "The groans, sighs, endearments, pacing, and cries of real or faked orgasms are signs of training."

Jeremy raised an eyebrow a fraction of an inch. "Is that the voice of experience, my dear?"

She smiled. "A fish doesn't need to be taught how to swim."

His eyes glinted with interest. "Go on."

"Caldwell would sell out his country in a heartbeat for her. She owns him."

"But did you hear anything that leads you to believe she's not who she says she is?" Jeremy asked.

"Not at first," she replied. "He's giving her information on defense contracts that may or may not have real value."

Jeremy nodded again, encouraging her to continue. He was impressed with her analysis.

"Also," Sabine went on, "in every instance that has the potential to be a national security issue, she doesn't really ask any substantive questions about his information. This woman takes what he gives her and supposedly just passes it on her brother. It doesn't make sense. Do we know what the kickbacks are?"

"Yes," Jeremy responded. "It seems that our old friend is quite unimaginative. He envisions the former king, that would be me, dead, so he uses the same Swiss bank account and routing instructions. I'm not sure why, but he receives random funds in differing amounts. The total for this year so far is $33,500."

"Not as much as you were paying, but enough to become addictive. Add that to the multi-orgasmic Sondra, and he is reeled in and mounted on a wall."

"I like the analogy." Jeremy paused for a moment and then summarized. "So unless our research proves differently, Caldwell passes on seemingly noncritical information, and in return gets kickbacks and, apparently, high-priced sex."

They were both quiet for a moment. Then Sabine's dark eyes glowed like a cat's. "She's setting him up. For something big."

He waited. Seconds turned into long minutes. Finally, Sabine sat up quickly and her dark eyes brightened. It was as if the proverbial light bulb had gone on. She organized her thoughts for another moment. "It's the National Cathedral!"

"What makes you think that?"

"Play that part again," Sabine insisted excitedly.

Floyd Caldwell spoke in the confident tone of authority. "HPSCI was briefed on the proposed appropriation to beef up security at the National Cathedral for Easter. Actually, there is very little that escapes our purview. Both the FBI and Defense collaborated on the project."

"What happened?" asked Sondra in a voice reminiscent of a star-struck teenager.

"The clergy said no to the extra security, felt it would be too intrusive."

"What do you think?"

"It's no big deal, "Floyd responded. "It's only a small area of vulnerability."

"She asked Caldwell a lot of questions, and her voice was different," Sabine concluded. She paused. "There was a fervor. It wasn't playacting. This was what she was waiting for!"

Jeremy leaned forward and took her hands in his. "Excellent analysis. I believe that you and I see eye to eye on this one."

Her face was radiant with his approval.

"Are you ready for a road trip?" he asked.

CHAPTER 63

STEPHEN STRASBURG WAS PITCHING FOR the Washington Nationals tonight, so the odds of Blake Stone's run being interrupted by early-exiting fans were remote.

Blake was a survivor. A firm believer in "prior planning prevents piss-poor performance," he charted his every move. Although his pedometer/GPS was sufficient to let him know where he was going, he still preprogrammed every step of his runs. When possibilities are limited, the risk of adverse outcomes diminishes: no blind alleys, no congested areas, no repeat runs. Routine is the father of predictability. Random is the survivor's watchword.

Out of necessity, Blake learned to survive at an early age. Like male dogs to a bitch in heat, bullies were drawn to the scrawny, undersized boy. It became great sport to whale on him. But regardless of what they gave him, he gave them nothing in return. He showed no pain, no emotion; knock him down, and he'd get back up. Eventually his battered little face would tighten and his swollen eyes would stare at his attackers. Finally, the bullies would tire of beating the crazy kid who wouldn't stay down.

Later, Blake grew into his resolve. Maturity brought strength, stamina, and a passion for training. Without exception, he sought out and revisited his past tormentors, those who had pounded a small boy, but never into submission. In each case, he extracted retribution, payback. What was wrong needed to be rectified. He became an instrument for justice.

Many are trained in combat, become experts in the martial arts, but the true weapons of retribution have an edge. These individuals may appreciate karma, the symmetry of the universe, and the logic of an eye for an eye. But the edge that keeps warriors like Blake Stone alive is that they never hesitate.

The last leg of his five-mile run took him down South Capitol Street in front of Nationals Park. He nodded, rather than waved, to the smiling parking-lot attendants who acknowledged him. The city is friendly when its sports teams are winning.

Blake wondered what it would be like to attend a ball game, maybe in the President's box in the midst of the Secret Service; otherwise, that wasn't happening. Professional paranoia was his life insurance policy. He carried no weapon on his runs, relying solely on his instincts and training if counteraction was required. It had worked so far.

Blake turned right on N Street Southeast and headed towards First. He was in the homestretch.

His phone vibrated in the pocket of his short-sleeved wind jacket. Only two people had his number: one work and one personal. Work could wait.

He slowed to a jog and hit **Answer**. The slurred voice surprised him. "Pick me up?"

"Where?"

"Mmm ... aah ... Morton's, by the office."

"Give me twenty." He sprinted to his car.

Nineteen minutes later, Blake parked illegally on Connecticut Avenue where a limo waited, inhabited by a dozing driver. He jumped out. Effortlessly, he ran up the escalator and opened the glass doors of the restaurant.

The hostess was momentarily startled to see a man in running shorts in this upscale restaurant. Then she gave him a sad look and pointed to her right.

David Grant sat in the corner in a solitary chair. Bent over, his head was in his hands, and his elbows wobbled on his knees, seeking support.

"Thanks," Blake muttered, and went over to him.

"Let's go, solider," Blake said, taking David's arm as he assessed the situation. It was pitiful. The collar of David's suit coat was turned, his tie was askew. Something unattractive was speckled on his wrinkled white shirt, and his thin, brownish hair showed the results of uncoordinated finger combs.

"No. Changed my mind," came the mumbled response. David grabbed both sides of his chair and scrunched down like he was holding onto the sides of a rescue boat.

Blake leaned down and pinched the back of David's neck.

"Ow!" David's head snapped back, and his hands flew to his neck.

As if the move had been synchronized, Blake simultaneously lifted his friend straight up by his left bicep.

"Hey ..." David's protest was weak as he stumbled and struggled beside Blake. Holding David's arm in a vise, Blake escorted him from the restaurant.

Blake considered it a success to have to pull over only once to let his friend barf his guts out on the asphalt. The only sounds that Blake heard for the remainder of the ride were David's muffled sobs.

Even after a traumatic combat situation, David Grant had never been a binge drinker. Blake's eyes steeled with purpose.

"Where are we?" asked David as Blake tossed him into a tightly made single bed.

"You don't have a need to know."

David looked up with bleary, narrowed eyes.

"Blow lunch on my bed, and you'll die there," said Blake as he pulled off David's coat.

David glared back at him.

"Shower. With or without clothes, your choice."

"I don't need ..."

"Last chance." Blake pulled him up.

"No, no, no clothes." Sometime in the future, David's frantic, uncoordinated striptease might become one of those stories with the life of an Energizer battery. "I'm going, I'm going!" David shouted as he was prodded toward the shower.

"On the floor. Sit. Don't get up," commanded Blake. "I'll make the coffee."

As the cold water hit him, David let loose a howl and a string of invectives that took Blake back to his basic training days.

Minutes later, with a white towel wrapped around his middle and its mate hanging on his shoulders, David gratefully sipped the steaming coffee with his eyes closed. The ever stoic Blake bit back a smile. He wasn't sure if his friend had ever had more than a single drink at any one time. It was tempting to ask him how many it took to get him blitzed.

Instead, he asked, "Is Morton's where the one percent go to get drunk?"

"Fuck you, Snake," David grumbled, not lifting his head from the cup. He held it in two hands like a security blanket.

Blake waited.

David let out a shudder. "My dad's at Bethany Beach, walking his dog on a beautiful morning. The assassin waits, then slams his car into him. Jeremy Lyons is a fucking billionaire, and he kills the kindest, sweetest man on earth ... for money."

Tears like a waterfall ran down David's cheeks as mucus dripped from his nose. "Even in my dreams I can't stop him!"

CHAPTER 64

THE SITUATION CALLED FOR A hurry-up offense. If their suspicions were correct, it was logical that their time frame was abbreviated. The option to brief Caldwell, while appearing simple on the surface, involved too many variables. Intimidating Caldwell into acquiescence would not be difficult. Still, their evidence was certainly not conclusive, and the temptation for Caldwell to warn Sondra might override his fear of retribution.

Sabine called Caldwell at his office with a simple request. It was straightforward and to the point: she asked him to meet her at the Capital Grille at five o'clock that evening. She had a favor to ask of him. The congressman tripped over his tongue agreeing. Just to be seen with Sabine would send his stock soaring.

Located at 601 Pennsylvania Avenue, the Capital Grille is a culinary theme park of dark wood, stuffed game heads, cigars, high-end drinks, fine wines, and dry-aged steaks. Handcrafted mahogany, plush leather, and distinctive art take a back seat to the aroma of sizzling steaks. Even at five o'clock on a Friday, bar space was at a premium.

When Sabine arrived wearing a simple black Armani suit, a cream silk blouse with pearls, and black Louboutin heels, it was as if time stood still. It didn't matter if the men at the bar were alone, in groups, or with lady friends, every eye in the bar followed Sabine as she glided toward the empty bar stool that Caldwell had aggressively saved for her. More than a few women followed the men's lead. She was that stunning.

"Sabine," Caldwell said possessively and more loudly than was necessary, "so nice of you to call me."

She smiled as he took her hand in both of his, and she leaned forward to draw him into an embrace, kissing both cheeks. For a moment, Sabine was afraid that she would have to hold him to keep him from falling.

Caldwell's face was flushed as he motioned for her to have a seat. "What will you have?" he asked nervously.

Sabine swiveled her chair so that her knees were touching his. She gave him a small, seductive smile and then said, "What are you offering? Why don't you just order a glass of wine for me?"

"White or red?"

Sabine shrugged. "You pick, Floyd. I go both ways."

The congressman shuddered, and this time she was afraid he would fall off his bar stool. Caldwell's voice changed pitch as he said to the bartender, "She looks more like a red wine lady to me. The lady will have a glass of Romanée Conti."

"Very good, sir."

"Where have you been, Sabine?" Caldwell asked. "I've missed you. And where is Jeremy?"

"On the campaign trail, I would assume," she said in a voice of disinterest.

The bartender placed the wine and a napkin in front of her. Sabine picked it up and clinked glasses with Caldwell. "To old friends renewing acquaintances." She took a sip, rolled the wine around on her tongue, swallowed, and shivered. "Floyd, you have excellent taste in wine," she lowered her eyes demurely, "and excellent taste in women."

"Sabine, you've captivated me from the first moment I saw you. Whatever favor you need, it's done. How can I help?"

CHAPTER 65

WHEN THE TEMPERATURES ARE REACHING 80 degrees and the cherry blossoms are hurrying out like kids late for class, the concept of global warming gets legs.

The balmy forecast had prompted Grace McGregor to an unprecedented move. Their house in Bethany Beach, Delaware, was going to be inhabited on St. Patrick's Day. But the weather was not her only motivation.

Ever since their blowup, she and Mac had been walking on eggshells. Although the promise to never go to bed angry had worked in the early years of their marriage, it was hard to enforce after 32 years. So her solution was to convince her workaholic husband to take Friday off, leave early in the morning, and spend the weekend in their favorite place.

Like most men of his generation, Mac McGregor had a few rough edges that needed to be smoothed out. The fragile nature of the male ego required that the softening process be subtle, covert, and never admitted. When Grace first met Mac, she had fallen in love with him in half a heartbeat. Although the feeling was mutual, Mac had fought like hell against it. A man with a Volkswagen convertible, a full head of hair, and a guitar on his back was certainly not ready to settle down.

Absolutely the funniest man Grace had ever met, the singing stockbroker also had the potential to be a verbal assassin. She was not sure of its origin, but whenever Mac felt ridiculed or provoked, it was as if a switch went on. With just the right emphasis and tone, cutting words could spew out of his mouth about a mile a minute and shred the perceived attacker.

Once, a friend and co-worker wrote a poem that humorously took pot shots at Mac, and the man read it at a gathering of the top advisors of Johnston Wellons and their guests. Mac stood up, smiled, and asked sweetly, "May I offer rebuttal?" What followed was an extemporaneous dismantling of his friend's self-esteem.

Mac's evisceration of his friend was greeted by a combination of raucous, polite, and/or nervous laughter, and the victim's frozen smile was insufficient to hide his pain. Mac sat down, and Grace could feel the energy coming off of him. As he looked at her, she leaned over and whispered, "You hurt him." A stricken Mac rushed over to his friend and apologized profusely.

Now, as Grace went through the EZ-Pass lane to get onto the Bay Bridge, she looked over at Mac. He was not a fan of riding over the bridge, so she reached over and patted his knee. He smiled weakly in response. Even though their best friends asserted that they'd rather have Grace drive drunk than Mac drive sober, he was fully capable of driving; however, they both preferred having her behind the wheel.

"Bring me up to date on the bane of our existence," Grace asked, partly to distract him. "We're only eight months away from the election."

"I think I'd rather contemplate the collapse of this bridge," Mac replied in a snarky voice. After a moment's silence, he continued, "Let's see. We've already talked about the fact that he gave five million dollars to a charity in our names; told the world about *my* idea to get the economy moving; and now he has a legitimate plan to take some of the risks out of the stock market. Why, I guess that Jeremy Lyons has become my new best friend."

Grace thought for a minute. "Any chance that he's changed?"

"Remember the story of the little girl and the snake?"

She did, but wanted to keep him talking, so she shook her head.

"A little girl is walking in the snow when she hears a plaintive cry, 'Pick me up, please. I'm freezing.' She looks down and sees a snake.

"She says, 'I can't pick you up. You're a snake, and you'll bite me.'

"'I won't bite you,' says the snake. 'Please save me.'

"So she picks up the snake and hugs it tightly. Gradually, the snake unfreezes, due to the little girl's body heat. When the snake gets fully recovered, it bites her.

"'Why did you bite me?' she cries in pain. 'You promised me you wouldn't!'

"The snake replies, 'You knew what I was when you picked me up.'"

Later that night they lay spooned against each other in their king-sized bed. Grace had the feeling that neither of them was ready for sleep. Sex seemed to rev her up, whereas for Mac it was usually a knockout pill. Tonight she was either losing it, or he had something on his mind. When she turned her head back to him, his eyes were open.

Grace had been worrying about Mac's unexpected rendezvous with his nemesis. She didn't know whether it had increased his anxiety or been cathartic for him. She thought it was a good sign that it had not decreased his ardor or his performance.

"Can I ask you a question about Jeremy, or would you rather go to sleep?" she asked.

"Fire away, baby."

"Did you tell David Grant what Jeremy confessed to you?"

"Yes." Mac paused. "I also told Joe. That was much easier. David just seemed to go into a trance. It made me think of him in battle, and how he might have reacted if a comrade got killed: a little tightening of the jaw, but no histrionics or 'I'll kill that bastard' talk."

She nodded. "Is that what you expected?"

"I guess I expected a little more reaction. I really didn't think that he'd get over his dad being killed and the guy who arranged it still scot-free and running for the Senate."

Mac kissed the back of Grace's neck and nuzzled in, a sign that he was through talking. But a few moments later he added, "David thanked me for telling him. But he wanted to know why I chose to ask Jeremy about his dad when I was only allowed one question."

"That's interesting," Grace said thoughtfully. "I would have thought you'd ask about Margo."

Mac went quiet, and she listened to his breathing for a while.

Finally Mac spoke, and when he did, he sounded smaller. "I didn't think Jeremy would answer that question truthfully. It's ... it's too recent. Admission would have invalidated his stated redemption."

"Yet you still believe him when he says that our family is safe?"

Mac hesitated. "Yeah. For some unfathomable gut reason, I do. He's so ego driven that I believe his actions have almost become predictable."

Mac couldn't sleep. Grace snored gently beside him, and rather than continue turning like a fish on a line, he sat up on his side of the bed. No matter where they were, according to Grace's rules, they slept on their same sides of the bed. Unfortunately, at the beach house, that put Mac farther away from the bathroom. Life would be simpler if that were the problem.

The house included a balcony on each floor, so it would have been easy to get up and open the sliding-glass door leading to their private balcony. However, the odds were that Grace would not sleep through that, and Mac was not seeking conversation.

He ran his hand through his still predominantly brown hair, kept short by haircuts at three-week intervals. Mirrors had not been kind to him since he began the slow dance with Jeremy Lyons, so he knew that the circles under his eyes were not going anywhere. Solving problems and finding solutions were his stock in trade. So why did he feel like he was drifting aimlessly?

With his index finger and thumb, Mac rubbed his closed eyes to ease the tension. When that didn't work, he slowly got up, walked around the bed, and headed for his closet. He grabbed a pair of running shorts off the hook, slipped them on, stumbling once, and still in bare feet, opened the door and walked down to the family-room level. Out of the refrigerator that held his supply of bottled water, he grabbed a cold bottle. Familiarity made these movements almost like sleepwalking. Moving through the glassed-in rectangular porch, he opened the door and walked outside into the surprisingly warm night air.

Even one row back from the ocean, the chairs were wet from the mist. Mac sighed audibly, turned around, went to a large drawer in a chest located next to the stairs, and removed a beach towel. As he had been patiently taught, he stretched the towel on a heavy plastic chaise, sat down, and gazed at the star-filled sky. The cloudless night seemed to accent the stars, and when he looked up, he felt like he was fine-tuning a telescope. He closed his eyes and prayed. Not specifically. Just a prayer of thanks and a plea for guidance.

After a while of trying to rearrange what had become the Rubik's Cube of his life, he felt his eyes grow heavy. The endless loop in his brain—protect your family, do your job, appease Jeremy—added an important thought: trust God.

CHAPTER 66

THE HOTEL LOMBARDY IS ONE of the few unobtrusive hotels in the Foggy Bottom business district of Washington, D.C. Normally, guests such as the two people registered as Mr. and Mrs. Lincoln would have stayed at the Ritz, the Four Seasons, or the Mandarin Oriental. However, this couple had no desire to display their wealth, and they enjoyed the relative anonymity of this boutique hotel.

The perverse sense of humor of the male guest was the reason that the unmarried couple was registered as Mr. and Mrs. A. Lincoln. In the process of amassing his fortune, Jeremy Lyons named all of his companies for men who appeared on U.S. currency. At the time he had felt that it was unfair not to spread a few bread crumbs for the inept authorities pursuing him. Old habits were hard to break, and he liked to be amused. It was not unusual that his best audience was himself.

Jeremy looked up from his laptop as he heard the click, and the door to their hotel room swept open. Her smile entered almost before she did, so he knew the meeting had been successful. Not that any other outcome would have been logical. Sabine was irresistible.

As she approached the king-sized bed where Jeremy was propped up with pillows resting against the headboard, she sighed. "God, that was good."

He smiled. "As you expected?"

"The gullibility of your gender is predictable," she replied. "But this man is already having sex with someone way above his pay grade, and he still practically drooled all over me."

"You are unique, my dear."

Sabine laughed. "Is that because I'm just like you?" she asked.

Jeremy removed the computer from his lap and placed it on the far side of the bed. He patted the spot next to him. "Come join me and give me all the details."

"When he said, 'How can I help you?' and I moved closer and said, 'I want Sondra,' I think he came in his pants."

"Delicious," Jeremy chimed in.

"I laid out the whole scenario. I instructed him to leave the door open tomorrow night. I said that I would sneak in and climb in bed with them."

"Did he question how you knew Sondra?" Jeremy asked.

"He wouldn't have questioned me if I'd said we were lesbian sisters. All he cared about was his dream of the threesome of a lifetime."

"Ah, the folly of youth."

"I told him that Sondra and I had met and flirted before, and he still had no questions. I also told him that it had to be a surprise, or I would leave immediately. I would not only never see him again, but I'd tell Sondra that her boyfriend had been cheating on her with me."

"Nice touch," Jeremy said admiringly. "You are indeed a treasure."

Still holding Sabine, Jeremy leaned back and stared at her. "Are you concerned about me?" she asked.

"Sondra will not be easy to break. If we are correct, she will have been trained in interrogation techniques. Pain may still resonate, but death for the cause would be welcomed."

"I understand." she said, matching his intensity with hers."

"I will not be physically with you. You will have only one chance. You must search for a tell—something that would be unnoticed by an amateur." Jeremy pulled her close to him in a fierce embrace and whispered in her ear, "We break her or our dreams are broken."

CHAPTER 67

ELLEN WILLIAMS WAS NOT A natural rule follower. On the surface, that might not appear to be unusual. A significant number of young professionals might fall into that category. However, few are FBI agents. Normally, field agents, depending upon their experience, might be granted a degree of behavioral latitude. But each member of this elite group must recognize that he or she is working for a by-the-book agency.

Regardless of the rigidity of an agent's supervisor, just as in any other walk of life, some people get away with more than others. In Ellen's case, the facts that she was drop-dead gorgeous, imbued with a natural charisma, and everyone who knew her thought she was a superstar in the making enabled her to escape harsh judgment. She never broke rules that would endanger a colleague or a civilian or the Bureau. And in her mind, she had paid her dues.

Early in her career, Ellen had been fortunate enough to be chosen as a member of Special Agent Joe Sebastiano's task force. However, the situation got a little dicey when her first real assignment was to befriend one of Jeremy Lyons's key employees. There is no guide book on how to compromise a member of the opposite sex; it's like Nike: just do it.

As she was the only female on the task force, Ellen did not feel like she was singled out, but Lyons's employee, Frank Griffin, was an incredibly fragile and guarded man. He had been scarred both figuratively and literally by Lyons, and she was supposed to get him to trust her without letting him do the horizontal mambo with her.

Ellen had to admit that the task required some creative thinking and superb acting. And as messed up as Frank Griffin was emotionally, he *was* very easy on the eyes.

The problem was that Ellen really liked Frank, and when she gained his trust, she had to pull the plug. *Here's my badge. I lied to you. Give up Lyons or you're going down.* She did it, but it left a bad taste in her mouth.

Ellen's efforts led to the takedown of Jeremy Lyons's illegal hedge fund operation, but her actions had not been without complications. For the first time in her life, she had thought that she was going to die. Instead, she made her first kill: a suspected assassin.

The trauma of that encounter was still fresh in Ellen's mind when, inexplicably, her source for the takedown, the man she had compromised, allegedly removed all his clothes and took a header off his balcony. Even though Lyons had disappeared and his right-hand assassin was six feet under, Frank Griffin's apparent suicide had Lyons's fingerprints all over it. She still had nightmares of Frank falling six stories.

So, if the Powers That Be discovered that she was fraternizing with another agent and wanted to punish them, she was prepared to argue her case.

Before she became an FBI agent, Ellen had a number of close women friends. But scheduling, the rigors and intensity of her job, and the required secrecy had turned the majority into casual friends. Every time she attended a friend's wedding, she was asked about her relationships. In response, she would simply pat her sidearm and smile.

Although Ellen and Joey McLister, another member of Joe Sebastiano's task force, had previously engaged in some major-league flirting, the Bureau's non-fraternization rules had kept any romantic relationship confined to their minds.

Recently, a number of tragedies had knocked the breath out of the Williams family. First, Ellen's mother contracted breast cancer. She was now in remission, but Ellen had taken some time off to be with her. Then her dad developed early-onset Alzheimer's, and it ravaged his mind with the speed of Sherman marching through Atlanta.

Ellen wouldn't have felt comfortable talking to her parents about her near-death experience, and empathy from her few remaining girlfriends would have been impossible. At least, that was her rationalization. Eventually, she needed more than the Bureau psychiatrist; she needed an agent who'd been there. So she gave herself permission to do what she had wanted to do even before the incident: jump Joey McLister's bones.

To Ellen, Joey would always be her hero. A former golf pro, he enlisted in the Army right after the tragedy of 9/11. After his tour of duty, the FBI recruited him heavily. Anyone who knew him would realize that Joey McLister bled red, white, and blue.

He was her rock. In the year and a half they had been together, they had never even had a fight. The secret of this couple's harmony would make a best seller. In the midst of a discussion, when the tension increased and the temperature rose, both partners would race to see who could get naked first. Arguing under those circumstances was impossible.

Except for the clandestine part, it couldn't have been better. Just looking at Joey made her smile. He was funny, sensitive, and he adored her. If she had just crawled through a ditch full of dog poop, he would look at her and tell her how beautiful she was.

Still, it was hard to put something over on Joe Sebastiano, even though Ellen knew that he had a little of the father-and-daughter complex with her. So even if she and Joey got discovered, she felt sure that their boss would go to bat for them. In the interim, it was don't ask/don't tell.

Ellen knocked on her boss's door.

"Come in," said Joe, looking up.

"Joe, my dad's Alzheimer's group is going to go to Easter services at the National Cathedral. One of the members of the group is a former federal judge, so that's probably why they got a special parking permit. They're going to be able to park their bus right by the church. That is unprecedented," she said sheepishly, "especially for what is the Christians' High Holy Day. But I guess they're afraid that the members might wander off."

Joe nodded as he listened attentively. "Will your mom go with him?"

"No," Ellen replied. "Only members of the group and their caretakers will be on the bus. I'm going to drive Mom separately, and we will meet him there."

"Okay," Joe said. "I think that's great, Ellen. But why do I need to know this?"

"In either an official or an unofficial capacity, I'd like to board the bus when it arrives just to check things out."

He looked at her for a long moment and pursed his lips. "Do you suspect something?"

"Not really," she said, feeling a bit guilty about her ulterior motive. "But the group received special permission. Homeland Security was against it, and the clergy overruled them."

"So do you think Homeland Security will be there?"

"Again, I don't know; but, boss," she said as she pointed to herself with both hands, "who ya gonna call?"

Joe chuckled. "And do you think that it would be wise if I assigned an additional agent as backup?" he asked seriously.

Ellen reddened slightly, but she replied quickly, "If you think that's best, sir."

Joe shook his head thoughtfully and stared at Ellen for an entire minute. "Okay. I'll call McLister. That heathen is overdue for some churchgoing."

CHAPTER 68

FOR SABINE, THE HOURS BETWEEN 3:00 and 4:00 in the morning were the most conducive for an unexpected confrontation. Like a tuning fork that has just been struck, every nerve in her body was humming. As if she were being fed adrenaline intravenously, she felt alive, wired, but in total control.

The glass door was locked, the building only accessible by a key from a resident. It would have been easier to secure a key from Caldwell, but she chose the alternative that she felt would generate the least curiosity. If you're going to be seen, it is better to be open than to look like you're trying to avoid detection. In the unlikely event that there was blowback, who would ever consider the friendly, innocent young woman.

Sabine pushed the button next to the door, and the elderly African-American guard at the desk looked up. Automatically, he reached for the intercom button, but then he looked again at the vision at the door and reconsidered. He got out of his chair with more quickness than normal and walked upright towards her, a curious smile making him look younger. Not totally breaking protocol, he opened the glass door, but did not invite her inside.

She wore a black warm-up suit with the top unzipped and a Georgetown tee shirt showing underneath. With her lustrous hair pulled back in a ponytail, she could easily have passed for a student. The straps of her backpack came over her shoulders, but did nothing to detract from her attributes. Her smile widened in response to his.

"Young lady, it's mighty late for you to be out. Don't you have a curfew?"

She laughed. "I was hoping that you didn't have a date tonight."

The guard laughed so hard, he started choking. When his laughter subsided, he asked, "What's your name, please?"

"It's Sabine. Floyd Caldwell was supposed to ..."

"He did, he did, young lady. Congressman Caldwell gave you the green light." He ushered her in. "Come on in, and if you don't mind me saying, I'da had him committed if he didn't."

"You flatter me," she said demurely as she touched his arm, winked, and walked towards the elevator.

Sabine paused at the door to Floyd Caldwell's co-op. She closed her eyes and breathed in deeply, as if she were already savoring the experience.

Soundlessly, she opened the door and moved slowly to the bedroom, alert to any unusual movement. At best, Caldwell would be sleeping restlessly. More likely, his eyes would be fixed on the bedroom door, and his hand would be fondling his penis. As she entered, she saw Sondra lying on her stomach, arms stretched over her head. For Sabine's purposes, she was perfectly positioned.

Caldwell, who was on his back, raised his head slightly from his pillow. Sabine raised a finger to her lips in response. She walked over to his side of the bed and placed an iPad on the nightstand beside him. She winked in response to his curious gaze. Sabine then pulled a video recorder from her backpack and directed it at Sondra. Caldwell smiled knowingly. The entire time Sabine's eyes never left her prey.

In the dim light of the nightlight, Sabine could see that Caldwell's eyes were filled with lust. She slowly and stealthily moved around the bed. Sondra stirred. Instantly, Sabine was kneeling on her side of the bed, her left arm draped across the woman's neck, firmly holding her head in place.

Sabine whispered in Sondra's right ear, "You have a Taser pressed against your right nipple. Any sudden movement, any attempt to escape my gentle embrace, and I will light you up like a Christmas tree. Nod slightly if you understand."

After a moment, Sondra nodded.

"Can I turn on the lights?" asked Caldwell excitedly.

"First, power up the iPad. There's a Skype message for you."

Although Sondra's head was held down tightly on the pillow, she attempted to turn it to the left as she heard the voice.

Sabine moved quickly and placed her body weight on the woman's chest as she jammed the Taser into her breast.

Sondra responded with a sharp intake of breath and then stilled.

Caldwell looked horror stricken at the vision on the screen as he listened to the chilling voice of the speaker.

"Good evening, Floyd. Have you missed me? Listen carefully, because although you may not realize what you've done, it could still lead you to more sex than you've ever had. Regrettably, it would be prison sex."

Jeremy paused. "Fortunately, you are not our target here. I am afraid that the delectable Ms. Sondra is a terrorist."

Sondra's instinctive urge to escape overcame reason, and she suddenly squirmed and reached for Sabine. Her action was instantly countered with 50,000 volts. Violent twitching shuddered to unconsciousness.

Caldwell's cry was stifled by Sabine. She leapt across the bed and jammed the Taser into his now very flaccid appendage.

Caldwell whispered, "Jeremy, I don't under ..."

"It is not important for you to understand," Jeremy interrupted. Each word came out like a lash from a whip. "Your choice is to follow every instruction Sabine gives you, or to ..." he paused "pursue your own course of action and try to protect your terrorist lover."

The corners of Jeremy's mouth rose to form a contemptuous smile. In harmony, Sabine's mouth looked like a mirror image.

"Decide now," Jeremy hissed. "And if you deviate, it will be a package deal that is sent to the FBI."

"Whatever you say," the congressman wailed as tears streamed from his eyes.

"And, Floyd," Jeremy cautioned, "relive this night only in your dreams. I would consider any discussion of what occurs here with anyone at any time a serious breach of trust."

As Floyd Caldwell's head started to turn towards Sabine, Jeremy's voice stopped him cold. "DO NOT LOOK! There will be plenty of time to act on your voyeur tendencies. At the moment, Sabine is making sure that your little terrorist friend is tucked in tightly. Now, why don't *I* ask the questions, and we can save considerable time. Is that all right with you, Floyd?"

"Ye ... yes," he stammered.

"Do you recall discussions with Ms. Sondra—we will call her that, since her Muslim name, quite frankly, is unpronounceable—in which you discussed security procedures for the National Cathedral?" "Uh, no. I mean, not that I recall."

"Let's dispense with the typical witness testimony. Here, if you lie, we hurt you. Please do not make me repeat the question."

"Jeremy, I'm sorry. I don't remember," Caldwell said in a rush.

"Hmm. Any drugs with your sex, perchance?"

Unable to resist, Caldwell stole a furtive glance at his staked-out lover and mumbled, "Yes."

Jeremy rolled his eyes. "I'm losing my patience. First, keep your eyes focused on this screen and me as if your life depends on it. Second, what fucking drugs did you take, you idiot?"

"Mostly Ecstasy," mumbled the terrified man, whose eyes were now riveted on the iPad.

"Of course," Jeremy said. "And kudos to you, Ms. Sondra. Ecstasy gives rise to a feeling of euphoria and a sense of trust and intimacy. You're not dealing with your garden-variety terrorist, Floyd. If you want to make sure that a mark is smitten with his evil seductress, it's the drug of choice. You see, my unenlightened legislator, significant side effects of the drug include—wait for it—short-term memory loss. If you weren't such a mullet, she might have added benzodiazepine or imidazopyridine to be absolutely certain. But all you wanted to remember were the carnal pleasures." Jeremy paused. "You do know what this means, don't you, Floyd?"

"N-no."

Jeremy shook his head. "You have to love the public. They will elect anyone." He leaned into the camera so closely that his bald head looked like a grotesque skull. "We must extract the information from Ms. Sondra."

Again he waited, allowing Caldwell's imagination to run wild. "I predict that she will be reticent. And it will be *horrifying* to watch. But failure is unacceptable when our country's safety is at stake." He pulled back from the camera and added, "And Floyd, you will be with us ... every ... step ... of ... the ... way."

CHAPTER 69

SONDRA WAS NOT PLEASED THAT she had become the center of attention. The facts that the ligaments in her shoulders were painfully stretched to capacity and that, like a naked X, she was securely tied face-up to the brass bed were of little consequence. She had been trained to endure torture, both physical and psychological. Part of her even relished the challenge. She would not have to hold out for long.

The handcuffs securing her to the rails on the bed were cutting off her circulation, and she tried to wiggle her fingers. Her legs ached, not only from the rope burns on her ankles, but because they were pulled almost horizontal. Yet if she could handle her people's torture, then these infidels had no chance to break her.

When the spectator called Jeremy spoke, she could feel his evil: America's Satan. But instead of frightening her, it emboldened her. It was the black woman who listened to him like he was Allah and looked at Sondra with the eyes of a zealot that made her close her eyes and pray softly against the duct tape covering her mouth.

Sondra heard someone rummaging through a bag. The sounds were unhurried and unfamiliar.

"What are you going to do?" whispered Caldwell in a frightened voice.

It's a trick, thought Sondra as she squeezed her eyes tighter. She felt air moving above her left breast, followed by a drop of liquid on the top of the breast. Her eyes flew open, and her body buckled as the unimaginable pain of blistering-hot fire burned through her outer skin and moved toward her internal organs. Her head thrashed from side to side, and a moment of pure shock overtook her. Then, suddenly, a bucket of ice water was dumped on her chest.

Above her, wearing chemical-tight goggles that had indirect vents and a face shield, stood Sabine. Covering Sabine's body were an acid-resistant long apron and gloves.

Sondra fought not to throw up into the duct tape and drown in her own vomit. She shivered uncontrollably, feeling as if the burning liquid were coursing through her body.

"Do you use sulfuric acid in your country? You must be very careful if you do. See how protected I am?" Sabine asked conversationally. "We have five droppers remaining, filled with acid of increasing strength. Jeremy thinks that you will tell us what we want to know after the second drop hits your right breast. But I think you'll last until a drop lands right here." She leaned down and patted the woman tenderly between her legs.

Sondra's body convulsed in response.

Sabine raised a fist. "Girl power! Stay strong! Oh, I almost forgot. Droppers four and five are for your eyes. And if you win the grand prize, you get to six." She leaned down and kissed the women on her duct-taped lips.

With a look of maniacal pleasure, Sabine squeezed the second dropper. This application was a repeat performance of the first, except this time as the acid burned through to her core, the woman's eyes rolled back in her head, and she went into shock.

For both the first and second applications, Caldwell had been forced to watch and remain silent. The first time Sabine had to hold him up to prevent him from diverting his eyes or passing out. Both times he sweated profusely and became violently ill.

Afterwards, when Caldwell once again collapsed on the bathroom floor, Sabine quietly went to the iPad and asked Jeremy, "Thoughts?"

Sondra's head jerked as the freezing water hit her in the face. All she heard was screaming as her eyes tried to focus while hands slapped one side of her face and then the other. She felt her systems shutting down as pain coursed through her body.

"Wake up, you bitch, wake up! What the hell was that explosion? What the hell was it? You've been out for 45 minutes, and something happened. Tell me, or I'll empty all of the droppers on you NOW!"

Sondra looked toward the luminous clock, not realizing that Sabine had moved the time forward. Then her eyes shone with the passion of martyrdom. She motioned with her head for Sabine to remove the tape.

Sabine ripped it off, glaring at her in fury.

"Too late," Sondra rasped. "Bus parked next to your godless cathedral: 8:05, boom! Praise Allah. I have served him well."

Barbara Sebastiano rolled her eyes at the inanimate object that was incessantly ringing and disturbing her languid approach to getting out of bed. However, in their household, untimely interruptions did not delay movement. It was Joe's work phone, and he was in the shower. She scrambled to the other side of the king-sized bed to grab it.

"Hello?" She looked down at the number and noticed it was blocked. That was strange, because only a few people outside of the Bureau had this number.

"I need Agent Sebastiano immediately."

Barbara wanted to ask the rude asshole to identify himself; but it was duty first, even for FBI wives.

Carrying the phone, Barbara walked into the bathroom and flung open the steam-covered glass door of the shower. Joe's first expression was one of pleasure, a hopeful thought of sharing a shower. It was instantly replaced by a frown as he saw the phone in her hand. He turned off the water and shook his wet hair like a golden retriever. She handed him a towel. He dried his hands while still standing in the shower.

"Sebastiano."

"No questions. Do exactly what I say, and you may be able to prevent a terrorist attack at the National Cathedral. A school bus carrying a group of Alzheimer's patients has received special permission to park adjacent to the church. The driver is a terrorist, and he is prepared to detonate sufficient explosions to kill thousands and destroy at least a portion of the church. His instructions are to detonate the bomb at 8:05 a.m. This is Jeremy Lyons. Do not doubt for one instant that what I say is correct."

The caller disconnected.

Joe stepped from the shower still wet. He immediately texted Ellen Williams and Joey McLister and said a short prayer.

CHAPTER 70

"I STILL WISH YOU'D WORN a bunny outfit," quipped Joey McLister.

"And I think that you have the wrong idea about Easter," chided Ellen Williams in response. "You're just mad 'cause they won't let you ride in the big yellow school bus."

"Maybe I can take it for a spin and pop a few wheelies while you guys are in church."

"And maybe the man who won't pray with me won't get to lay with me."

"Whoa, okay. Just playing here. I can't wait to go to church with you and your family. And by the way, young lady, I was praying for you even before I met you."

The large bus pulled up and headed for its designated parking space. Ellen looked around quickly and then grabbed Joey's hand and squeezed it.

"Think of all the things we can do when everybody's eyes are closed," he whispered. This time, she leaned over and smacked him on the shoulder.

Simultaneously their phones beeped, signaling text messages. Ellen and Joey looked at each other, shrugged, and then read the message.

"Holy crap!" said Joey as he looked at Ellen's ashen face. He started to run towards the bus.

"Wait!" Ellen said sharply as she gripped his arm. "The driver will recognize you as a threat immediately and detonate the bomb.

But he won't suspect a woman rushing in to see her father." Ellen pulled away and walked quickly towards the bus.

Joey matched her stride for stride. "Damn it, Ellen! I'm the ranking agent!"

"Don't pull that shit on me, Joey. I'm the actress. I'm our best chance. I'm begging you! Back off!" She looked at her watch. "We have seven minutes." She turned as she heard the air release as the bus door opened.

Ellen gulped a breath and plastered a big smile on her face as she climbed the steps into the bus. The driver, a dark man with close-cropped black hair, cast her a quick furtive glance and then, attempting to look bored, stared straight ahead.

Although Ellen was looking towards the back of the bus and calling, "Dad, Dad!" excitedly, she noted the sweat beads on the man's upper lip and the fact that the collar of his shirt was too large for his neck. Instantaneously assessing the situation, she ran through the checklist of ways to detonate explosives. She centered herself before her heart beat out of her chest. Both the caretakers and the Alzheimer's patients were looking at her curiously.

Now on the same level as the driver, she turned to him abruptly and said loudly, "Excuse me! Excuse me!" The driver half turned to look at her, and she simultaneously did a shuffle step with her left foot and fired a half knuckle, or leopard strike, which hit him squarely in the Adam's apple.

He gagged, and his hands flew reflexively to his throat as Ellen dove across his body and slammed his head repeatedly into the corner of the window.

"Enough!" shouted Joey, who had boarded the bus when he saw her make her move. Joey pushed Ellen aside, grabbed the unconscious man, and gingerly pulled him from behind the steering wheel.

Ellen raised her hands to the frantic passengers and shouted, "No one move! We're FBI! Everything's going to be okay!"

Miraculously, the bus quieted. Then a frail voice emerged from the back: "That's my girl!"

CHAPTER 71

EASTER SUNDAY, 9:15 A.M.

BREAKING NEWS – TERRORIST PLOT FOILED. FBI STOPS ATTACK ON NATIONAL CATHEDRAL. SCHOOL BUS CARRYING ALZHEIMER'S PATIENTS WAS LOADED WITH EXPLOSIVES.

"Fox News was on the scene after two federal agents thwarted a terrorist plan to bomb the National Cathedral." Jackie Mayfield's face was fiercely serious.

"At 7:50 this Easter Sunday morning, FBI Special Agent Joe Sebastiano received a call at his home alerting him to an imminent attack. Two members of his task force were at the cathedral assisting with security. The following video includes graphic scenes and comments from the reluctant FBI heroes, agents Ellen Williams and Joey McLister.

The two-minute video showed the dazed-looking Alzheimer's patients, mostly smiling at the attention, and a brief glimpse of the captured and bloodied terrorist. The last thirty seconds of the video showed the two young agents, whose only comments were that they were just doing their jobs. Still, the visual of Ellen Williams with blood smeared on her blouse, one arm around her mother and the other around her father, was epic.

When the video ended, Jackie Mayfield spread out her arms as if she were welcoming the world. "Can't we all use more heroes?" she asked softly. "Ellen Williams, whose father was a patient on the bus, boarded the bus under the guise of welcoming him. When the terrorist glanced her way, she struck." Jackie pantomimed a vigorous knuckle strike. "She hit him square in the Adam's apple, and his hands flew to his throat. Then she jumped across his lap and pounded his head into the window until he was rendered unconscious." She shook her head in obvious admiration of the agent.

"If the FBI had not been there, what do you think would have happened to the 80 senior citizens, all cursed with Alzheimer's disease, who were on the bus? And at least half of the churchgoers attending the Easter sunrise service? In addition to the tragic human toll, what would have happened to one of our nation's capital's most beloved churches? There were enough bombs in that bus to blow up a city block." She paused, and her face had a look of utter disgust. "And we've all learned the hard way that the human garbage driving the bus was prepared to die.

"It was not a random call that alerted Special Agent Sebastiano to the terror threat. It was the same 'Outsider' who captured on video the confession of a brutal rapist. The same anonymous source who uncovered the maker and distributer of the illegal drug Euphoria that was killing our children.

"I say, 'Thank God for our heroes.'" She paused again. "And a special thanks to our 'Outsider.' We pray for your continued vigilance and your help." She paused again to let the seriousness of her tone sink in. "Sometimes our intelligence agencies are able to protect us. Sometimes we just get lucky. And sometimes a guardian angel comes to our rescue. Now we can have a happy Easter. This is Jackie Mayfield for Fox News."

CHAPTER 72

"TONIGHT WE HAVE AN EXCLUSIVE interview, one-on-one, with the most radioactive man in America, Jeremy Lyons, author of the number-one bestselling nonfiction book." Brian Woods raised an eyebrow as he looked into the camera, turning his palms over and over. "Or maybe fiction, called *Survival of the Fittest.*"

He leaned into the camera like he was telling the world a bedtime story. "Reported to be a multibillionaire, Jeremy Lyons was one of the world's most successful hedge fund managers." He almost whispered the next few words. "But no one could find him. After a shootout with the FBI in which one of his employees was killed, Jeremy Lyons vanished." Displaying a mouthful of pearly whites, Woods added apologetically, "I can't make this stuff up, folks. It's true."

Of course, to anyone who had paid even the slightest bit of attention to the infamous Jeremy Lyons's story, this was not a news flash. But the erstwhile commentator acted like the guy had discovered a cure for cancer.

Commercial break.

Normally, the McGregor household did not abide commercials. Everything was recorded, at least partially, except for Redskins games, the Super Bowl, and now the Jeremy Lyons special. The large L-shaped couch in their spacious family room was filled with interested parties for this primetime Sunday night special. Special Agent Joe Sebastiano was joined by R.J. Brooks, Artie Cohen, and David Grant. Danny DeMarco lived in Baltimore, so he was watching at his home. Grace McGregor was the only spouse in attendance.

Sunday nights usually meant dinner with the kids, but they understood this break in protocol. As much as Mac and Grace tried to disguise the tension resulting from Mac's forced entanglement with Jeremy Lyons, their children were not clueless.

R.J. broke the silence. "Did it seem to you that Brian Woods was frothing at the mouth?" No one responded. The commercials held no fascination, but the question seemed rhetorical.

The program returned with its dramatic music lead-in.

"Who is this man?" Brian Woods continued. "Is he the man who meant every word of his incendiary book, or is he playing a joke on all of us? Is he the man who was the target of an all-out manhunt by the FBI for eighteen months, or is he the man who gives enormous sums to charity?" His prose seemed to bring an electricity to his eyes. "Is he the man who perfected insider trading and profited mightily from the global financial crisis, or is he the man who wants to cure the financial ills of our nation?"

When his voice reached a fever pitch, Woods threw his hands in the air. He paused dramatically. "One final question." He leaned into the camera. "Is this man the next senator from the pivotal state of Florida?"

The camera panned to Jeremy Lyons, perfectly attired in a dark-blue suit with a light-blue shirt open at the neck. On his left lapel was a replica of the American flag. His composure and confidence were readily apparent.

Grace McGregor looked at her husband, sitting cross-legged on the floor in front of their 60-inch TV. Although there was room on the couch, she knew that he wouldn't join them. All the guests were involved, but to her knowledge only the McGregors had been threatened, and only Mac had been forced to become intimately involved with this abomination.. She wanted to reach down and gently massage the protruding vein on his right temple.

Brian Woods addressed his interviewee. "Mr. Lyons, you are indeed an enigma, sir." Lyons stared at him pleasantly, waiting for a question. "But let's address your book first: real or fiction?" He looked almost lovingly at the man. In Woods's opinion, this could be the most watched show of the year.

"Brian, do you think more books would have been sold if I had said that this was just a novel, a product of my fertile imagination?"

"Uh ... well, no, probably not."

Lyons nodded, as if rewarding a pupil for the right answer. "And since all the proceeds have gone to the Make A Wish Foundation, the objective was to sell the most books, correct?"

"Yes, but that doesn't answer my question."

"No, it doesn't, Brian. But we all need a little mystery in our lives. Besides," he leaned in, "mystery helps sales."

"Speaking of mysteries, Mr. Lyons, it's somewhat of a mystery to us how one speech in Naples, Florida, catapulted you to becoming a strong contender in the Florida senatorial race."

Woods wanted a response, but Lyons greeted his non-question with a calm smile.

Recovering quickly, Woods asked , "Do you think it's because of your economic proposals?"

"I would hope that I have more to offer than just financial acumen, Brian," Lyons said pleasantly.

Obviously agitated, Woods leaned forward. "Let's examine that acumen. How would you solve the spiraling debt problem facing our country?"

"Perhaps it's more accurate to state that the debt is *destroying* our country," Lyons said somberly. "First, the citizens of this country should know that the problem is solvable. Second, it can only be accomplished if we *demand* that our elected officials offer a solution. I do give them credit for trying, but the end result was an abysmal failure.

"On February 18th, 2010, the President established the National Commission on Fiscal Responsibility and Reform, also known as Simpson-Bowles. This bipartisan group's optimistic assignment was to offer a solution to reduce our country's embarrassing budget deficit. Surprisingly, a consensus emerged. Was it perfect? No. But it was a step in the right direction. Why was it not enacted?" Lyons paused . "The President, the Republicans, the Democrats: no one is blameless."

Lyons looked directly into the camera. "Our fiscal house needs independent forensic accountants to examine every program, every agency, every bureau of our government, and determine what adds value and what is waste. Shakespeare said, 'The first thing we do, let's kill all the lawyers.' I would add lobbyists and special interest groups to that figurative mix."

"You certainly don't mince words, sir," said Woods.

"It would be an affront to your viewers, Brian. You asked for my opinion."

Woods nodded. "Are you pro-life or pro-choice?"

"Both," Lyons responded decisively. "The question is a diversion, a political ploy designed to sway votes and divide a country whose heritage was built on unity. It has no place in the discussion of how an individual will govern."

"I can't let you off that easily. The abortion issue is a decision maker for many voters."

"I believe those who vote for me will be more interested in how I plan to enhance their lifestyles than in an issue that is not likely to be altered. When a ship is sinking, the passengers' only concern is saving their lives and the lives of their loved ones."

Shifting gears, Woods asked, "In your prior life, you operated totally under the radar, sought no recognition, and your hedge fund was reputed to have been obscenely successful. How was that accomplished?"

"As you know, Brian, success in any endeavor requires teamwork and usually teachers or mentors." Lyons's hands were clasped comfortably in his lap, and a mischievous smile crossed his lips. "I began my career with the fine brokerage firm of Johnston Wellons. While there, I met a wonderful stockbroker named Mac McGregor."

CHAPTER 73

"YOU'VE GOT TO BE SHITTING me!" Mac screamed and hit the **Pause** button on the remote. Cruelly, his Direct TV had frozen a full-on picture of Lyons smirking. Mac scrambled off the floor, walked quickly to the front door, and wearing nothing but jeans and a short-sleeved shirt, walked out into the unseasonably cold night air. He slammed the door behind him.

Grace got off the couch, walked to the front door and unlocked it. Then she walked back into the room. "Can I get anyone something to drink?"

"Got any cyanide?" Joe asked darkly.

After about five minutes, the warmth of anger no longer insulated him, and Mac was shivering. He felt like a fool. How many times would he let this asshole get to him? He couldn't remember if he had unlocked the door. All he needed was to have to ring the doorbell.

Mercifully, the door opened when he turned the knob. His friends were still sitting in the same place, acting like they were fascinated by the paused TV. "I was getting tired of the commercials" Mac said. "I thought I'd let it get ahead."

"Can we do anything for you?" asked R.J.

"*You* can't, pal, but maybe Joe can. Joe, do you guys have any spare sniper rifles lying around?"

"Yeah, Mac, but you've gotta wait in line." Nervous laughter followed Joe's remark.

"Okay. I'm gonna sit on the couch next to my bride. The TV will only get paused if someone needs to hit the bathroom. And that was selfish. I'm sorry."

"If he had said my name, I'd have shot the TV," quipped Joe.

Mac hit **Play**.

Lyons's face unfroze. "Mr. McGregor was a wonderful teacher and, in fact, I'm trying to convince him to be my campaign manager. Perhaps you can help me, Brian."

Mac squeezed Grace's hand a little too tightly and clenched his teeth, but didn't move.

"One of the problems with our financial system is, of course, the system itself. And," Lyons raised a long finger, "it's the system that I'm going to fix. In my previous occupation I operated inside of it, using every legal means to make money."

"Only legal means?"

"Of course. Otherwise, our fine regulating agencies would have put me out of business."

"They *did* put you out of business."

Lyons laughed softly. "No. That is incorrect. Like many Americans, I got tired of the inefficiencies and overall incompetence pervading our financial and legislative systems. I retired."

With a look of incredulity, Woods persisted. "The FBI and SEC came in and closed down your operations."

Lyons shook his head sadly, as if trying to appease a misguided child. "My associate and I walked out of our private nightclub at about two o'clock in the morning. It was our responsibility to make sure that everything was closed down. Four large men, heavily armed, accosted us. They claimed they were the FBI.

"We had no weapons. I asked to see some identification. They refused. They just kept waving guns at us, shouting for us to lie down on the ground. One even grabbed my shoulder.

291

Fortunately I had a safety system installed at the back entrance to our club."

The camera drew back, showing both Lyons and Woods. Woods was leaning forward, hanging onto every word. Lyons was a gifted storyteller. Mac swiveled to look at Joe, whose face was flushed with anger.

"I pressed the remote in the pocket of my jacket," Lyons continued, "and our assailants were temporarily blinded. In the confusion, my associate wrestled a gun from one of the men." He paused, looked down for a moment as if to compose himself, and then his eyes came back to the camera, full of compassion.

"My associate, a former Navy SEAL, instinctively pointed the gun at the man. I yelled 'Stop!' because I was afraid that someone would get hurt." He lowered his voice. "As we ran towards our car, my colleague jumped in front of a bullet meant for me." Lyons bowed his head. "And he was killed."

Lyons paused in a prayer-like position, then finally raised his head. In a whisper he continued, "I admit it. I fled, left the country. If they could kill a trained combat veteran, what chance did I have?"

After a few moments of silence, Brian Woods blinked as if he had been jarred awake. "That is quite a story, Mr. Lyons. Not exactly the way it was reported."

"You don't have to take my word for the events that transpired. I believe that Special Agent Joe Sebastiano led what we later determined was an authentic FBI task force."

It took considerable restraint for the guests in the McGregor family room to keep their eyes straight. Only Mac canted his eyes towards his friend and thus witnessed the naked fury that consumed Joe Sebastiano.

Brian Woods steeled himself and bore down. He set his jaw. "We've heard your version of why you are no longer managing your hedge fund. What is your response to the allegations that you used insider trading to achieve your enormous profits?"

Lyons gave him an amused look and shook his head slowly. "It was not necessary."

"Not necessary?" Woods protested.

"If a door is wide open, it's not necessary to pick the lock to gain access. On December 8, 2009, the Senate Democrats finally brokered a compromise with the proposed health care laws. We paid for legal access to advance information. As a result, we made a significant profit investing in large health care insurers such as Cigna and Aetna." Lyons paused to let that sink in.

"On January 28, 2010, the Chair of the Senate Banking Committee, now retired, signaled that he would not include the provision to cap fees on credit cards in his bill. It took two weeks for this information to be disseminated. It was a profitable two weeks for our fund. During that time we made investments in Visa and MasterCard. Outrageous, but legal." It was almost like a history lesson: informative, bordering on pedantic.

With an astonished look on his face, Woods sat back. "Any other examples?"

"Yes, but your audience does not need to hear any more about the gross inefficiencies that allow the rich and well informed to legally exploit the flawed system. Instead," Lyons raised a finger and looked earnestly into the camera, "your audience simply needs an independent advocate with insider knowledge of the markets to revamp the system."

"And you're the man to do that?"

Lyons leaned forward, interlocked his fingers, and spoke to the interviewer in a quiet, scholarly manner. "Brian, compare the balance sheet of the United States with that of any number of our well-run corporations. Look at America's best companies: IBM, McDonald's, Walmart, and now Apple. Do they operate with a deficit? When times are lean, instead of undisciplined borrowing, they cut expenses. Yes, they may have to lay people off during extreme economic times, but over any business cycle, they are net hirers. These companies operate out of surpluses. More simply, they don't spend what they don't have."

"We know why those companies are good, Mr. Lyons, but I don't believe that you answered my question. I asked why Floridians should believe that you're the man to accomplish fiscal responsibility."

"Who else?" Lyons shrugged. "Are lawyers or career politicians more qualified? When you manage money for a living and analyze corporate efficiency, you learn what makes financial sense. There is no reason that the skills would not translate to a state or nation. I will lead a task force of objective, unbiased analysts to determine workable solutions for a more prosperous economy.

"I will solicit no donations for my campaign. I will owe no one. I am open to debate, but I will not waste time campaigning negatively. When I am elected, I will proudly represent Florida. However, my first responsibility will be to my country.""

"By your own admission, you will only be one vote out of a hundred senators. Perhaps you can make a difference in Florida, but how can you have an impact on the country?"

Lyons's eyes flashed a glint of evil. "I will be raw meat for the media. I will raise hell until real change happens. Rest assured, Brian, I will not be ignored!"

CHAPTER 74

WOODS NODDED, APPARENTLY PLEASED AT the response to his question.

"We know nothing about Jeremy Lyons. You seem to have no past. Do you intend to run as a man of mystery?"

Lyons smiled wryly. " Seems to have worked for our President."

Digging in, Woods pressed. "Don't you think that the people of Florida need to know about you? Are you going to release your financial information?"

Lyons sat back and allowed a few moments of tense silence to elapse. Then he pounced. "I'll answer your last question first, if I may."

Woods nodded, apparently grateful for a response.

"I believe that being asked to detail my finances is intrusive and unseemly. One of the adverse side effects of our instant information, big brother society is the loss of civility. The very fact that I am capable of personally financing my senatorial campaign tells the good people of Florida what they need to know."

Lyons paused, and addressed his interviewer. "Let me ask you this, Brian. When an NFL team drafts a quarterback with the number one pick, how do they evaluate him?"

Woods blinked, obviously uncomfortable being on the receiving end. "Well, I guess they would evaluate his success in college and his skills."

Lyons nodded. "Exactly. Now, Brian, I have no debts; I owe no one anything. I operate from a substantial surplus. You will not find one of my former clients who lost money. In fact, each would attest that I gave them a superior return on their investments. I believe that I have demonstrated a history of success in business, and I am confident that I have the necessary skills to improve the lifestyles of the residents of Florida. That should be what matters."

Trying vainly to regain control, Woods responded, "I think everyone who has followed your audacious bid to become a senator wants to know why a multibillionaire wants to be an elected official."

Lyons seemed to consider the question. "I have been blessed to have no financial worries. We are an insolvent nation. I want to help us return to a nation of responsibility. Did either of your parents work, Brian?"

"Yes."

"And your grandparents?"

"Of course," was the annoyed answer.

"Why?'

"Because they had to."

Lyons smiled. "And was that a *bad* thing?" He turned to the camera. "You see, the politicians underestimate our citizens. There will be no empty suits when I can do something about it. If a person, man or woman, is unproductive or not doing their job, they should be fired. And I'll tell you why. Because if we tolerate incompetency, we are rewarding failure. And for every person who does not want to work or contribute, there are ten Americans waiting to show what they can do!"

He paused and looked back at Woods. "I'm sorry, Brian. I probably steered you too far off course, but I am passionate about rewarding effort and returning us to a proud nation."

"You sound like a man running for President rather than senator."

"One of a senator's responsibilities is to influence positive change in our country."

"Okay. It still sounds like foreshadowing to me." Woods looked into the camera. "We are trying to unwrap this complex person who is so unique and unorthodox in our world of politics. Sometimes when you unwrap something, you get more than you bargained for."

"I hope that's a good thing," Lyons said humbly.

This time Woods nodded. "One more question before we break. You have been very critical of politicians and our legislative system. Even before you ran for office, your book, *Survival of the Fittest*, primarily detailed your financial legerdemain. My question is, if you are the next senator from Florida, how can you make a difference in what should be a hostile arena?"

"I have no personal agenda. I am beholden to no one. I will not seek re-election. My only objective is to serve the people of the United States. I will make a difference, because the people will require it.

"I would like to guarantee that I can change a culture that allows lawmakers to make laws that are not applicable to them." He shook his head ruefully. "I cannot. But," he raised a finger again, "I will promise to increase awareness of this inequity and be a thorn in their side."

Commercial break.

CHAPTER 75

ARTIE COHEN LOOKED AT HIS friends. "If I didn't know better, I would vote for him. He reminds me of Slick Willie: 'I did not have sex with that woman,'" he said, wagging a finger for emphasis.

Mac thought, *I'm a hell of a host.* "Well, as his campaign manager ..."

Everyone laughed, even Joe Sebastiano.

"The irony is," Mac continued, "that he would absolutely drive the entire Congress crazy."

"And if you disagreed, he'd have you killed," said David Grant solemnly. His comment sucked the brief levity out of the room.

The show resumed. Brian Woods led off. "You sound like you're a Republican, yet you're running as an Independent."

Lyons nodded. "Again, no party affiliation, no conflict of interest, no lobbyists, no undue influence."

"Perhaps we can find out your true leanings if I can get you to open up about your position on social issues, Mr. Lyons."

Lyons leaned in to the camera in Clintonesque fashion and spoke in a voice as serious as a heart attack. "This country does not have time to focus on social issues. I am aware that social issues are important, but political correctness must yield to fiscal practicality. If we do not fix our economy now, then your children," he pointed to Brian Woods, "and all of *your* children," he pointed to the camera, "will not have a country."

There was dead air as Woods absorbed not only Lyons's words, but also the power that emanated from them.

Woods offered a weak smile and said, "I guess I should thank you for that, Mr. Lyons. Just a few more questions, if you don't mind." He looked at his interviewee confidently, as if he actually had control. "You said that you were personally funding your campaign. It should be pocket change for you. Do you plan a big advertising blitz?"

"Have you seen any campaign ads so far?"

"No, I can't say that I have."

"I believe that buying an election is wrong. I will not flood the airways." Lyons smiled. "The good people of Florida have more interesting viewing options."

"Help clarify this for us. You will not *solicit* contributions, but will you *accept* contributions?"

"It is conceivable that some ordinary citizens will send unsolicited contributions. If I do not win the election, those funds will be returned."

Woods had to consciously close his mouth. "So does that mean that you wouldn't accept contributions from political insiders?"

"Absolutely not."

"Other than this program, how will you spread your message?"

"Good question. I believe that not unlike our President, I will get substantial free exposure."

Although he knew the answer, Woods walked in. "Why is that?"

Lyons shrugged. "Because I tell it like it is. Because the country is fed up with our dysfunctional political system. Because when you reporters fact-check my statements, you will find that none of them are false."

"Last question," said Woods. "You told us how you plan to make a difference. We'll buy the fact that although it was certainly not accomplished in a transparent manner, you managed to make a boatload of money. But I think that this is really the critical issue.

Could you expand upon what really makes you different from every other aspiring politician who promises change?"

"Allow me to ask a question first, Brian. What if we gave incumbent politicians report cards on their performance while in office? We're dealing in hypotheticals, so set aside the question of how the standards for evaluation would be set. If that could be achieved, we could readily determine accountability, hold our politicians to the same standards of excellence and progress that we hold our children."

"How would that relate to you, since you've indicated that, if elected, you would only serve one term?"

"Allow me to finish, and I believe that the answer will be clear. Authentic, reliable difference is what the people deserve. If I declare that politics is a dirty business, I doubt that any of your viewers would express shock and awe. We accept the status quo. While our politicians demand transparency from public companies, they give us closed-door sessions in return.

"What if a senator actually read every word of a bill and then picked out every morsel of pork or earmark and asked the legislators to justify its inclusion? More than likely, that independent-minded senator would be ignored until he posed the same questions to his social media army. 'Do you want to pay for this?' should be the question."

Brian Woods looked at him in wonder. "I'm not sure that we should bet on your winning Mr. Congeniality."

Lyons turned to face the camera and then gave a galvanizing stare.

"I am different," his voice resonated, power seeming to build like an orchestral crescendo. "I react to no polls, I have no spin doctors. What I say, I believe. How do we change what is wrong? How do we eradicate injustice? It only takes *one* man to start."

Lyons raised the index finger on his left hand, and the veins in his neck bulged with his intensity. "But he cannot be just a man of words; he must be a man of action! Fixing our financial house is our number one priority, but what keeps us up at night? The fear of being forced to do something against our will? Our children on drugs? Terrorist attacks?"

He moved his head from left to right, as if to make eye contact with every viewer. "In my mind," he concluded thoughtfully, as a conspiratorial smile crept onto his face, "what this country needs is an *outsider*, and that would be *me*."

As Brian Woods's mouth flapped open, Lyons waved modestly, got up from his chair and walked off the set.

CHAPTER 76

MAC POINTED THE THICK, ARCH-SHAPED remote at the TV and turned it off with the resignation usually reserved for a lopsided Redskins loss. As he expected, the room's surprise from Lyons's revelation had not faded. Even though Joe had told Mac and sworn him to secrecy about Lyons's pre-emptive call, there had still been questions as to whether Lyons would reveal that he was the outsider.

"I win $25 from DeMarco, and Lyons ends up being Superman, Sherlock Holmes, and GI Joe all rolled into one," said Mac. No one responded, and Grace asked if anyone wanted anything. When she got no takers, she excused herself and went upstairs.

An almost unnatural quiet in the room made Mac feel like he was at a funeral. As he looked at his friends, he analyzed the situation.

Joe Sebastiano was programmed to let go of his anger and frustration.

Up until two years ago, sustained anger was a stranger to Mac. Now it was like an uninvited guest that refused to leave.

R. J. Brooks and Artie Cohen were Mac's trusted confidantes, but their personal stake was not significant.

The wild card was David Grant, because they all knew that Jeremy Lyons had ordered the execution of David's father. And although the former investment banker did not look the part, David Grant was a warrior.

Mac turned and looked straight at David. "Sometimes I make Jeremy Lyons all about me. I'm sorry. I can't imagine how painful and galling it must be to you that not only is he not behind bars, but he's basking in the limelight." The muscles remained tight in David's face, but he nodded. A moment of silence followed.

Mac turned to face the group. "I need your help." He paused. "It may not be possible to stop his Hitler-esque ascension, but we have to try."

R.J. spoke first. "You were able to get him to admit his endgame. At least his narcissistic coming-out party wasn't a surprise."

Artie interjected. "It had to be a surprise to you when he said your name." He shrugged. "Probably good for business, though."

Mac winced. "I can always count on you to be pragmatic. Any revenues we got from our forced relationship with Lyons would feel like blood money."

"Sometimes it seems like he has already drained the blood from you, Mac," R.J. said softly.

Mac turned quickly towards R.J. A shadow crossed his face. He tightened his lips and willed it away. He remembered his earlier promise of emotional equilibrium and blew out a long breath. "Other than weight loss, suitcases under my eyes, and hair loss, what makes you think that?"

"Hair loss?" said the bald Artie Cohen as he got up to inspect.

"No. I said that for effect."

Artie looked at him dubiously, but sat back down.

"The bottom line," Mac said, "is that I haven't done enough to stop him."

"You felt that your family was in jeopardy," said Joe evenly. "And your self-abuse is neither attractive nor helpful in solving the problem."

Mac's jaw clenched, and he stared at Joe, but did not offer a rebuttal.

"It's not just *your* problem," Joe said with intensity. "It's also the country's problem, and as long as we're playing the me game, he turned *me* into a media piñata. My next assignment may be administrative leave."

The only sounds in the room were those of the men breathing and the icemaker struggling to keep up.

Mac shook his head. "Okay, got it. No pity parties." His eyes still fixed on Joe, he added, "Joe's effectiveness in this has been somewhat muted by Lyons's name-calling. David's ready to go Rambo on the guy. R.J.'s about to challenge Lyons to a vocabulary duel, and Artie wants to ask him about his estate plan."

"I'll bet his federal tax return is pristine," said Artie.

"Where is his weak spot?" asked R.J., ignoring Artie's attempt at levity.

They all looked at Mac.

"His vanity. He thinks that he can control everything. He has a gargantuan ego. When I stood up to him and verbally punched him back, he got pissed. That's when he told me that he was going to be Senator Lyons."

"So besides pissing him off, what else can you do?" asked Joe.

Mac closed his eyes and thought for a minute. "Let's analyze this like an investment problem."

"Or a tactical situation in battle," offered David in a flat voice.

Mac got up from the couch and walked in front of his friends. "He loves the 'Outsider' moniker, which is ironic, because we all know that Jeremy Lyons was the ultimate *insider.* After his *Hallmark Hall of Fame* presentation," Mac said, nodding at the TV, "the whole world will be kissing his ass. I think we need to try to puncture his balloon of adoration."

"How are you gonna do that?" asked R.J.

"I think it's time I did a little investigating on my own."

CHAPTER 77

"HAVE YOU RECOVERED FROM YOUR primetime hangover?" Richard Orth asked Alan Smathers. After a sleepless night of resenting the Fox network's exclusive interview with Jeremy Lyons and swapping expletives, the two men were in the senator's office mapping out a strategy.

"Nope. It's terminal. If my sidearm had been handy, I would have blown the TV into liberal heaven."

"So far, our ads have been positive, emphasizing your character and what you've done for Florida. I guess we'll need to be more aggressive."

"No shit, " Smathers said despondently. He slung his feet onto his desk and laid his neck back against his chair.

Orth waited while his friend worked it out. Two of the man's strengths were that he was a meticulous planner and that he could improvise in a heartbeat.

"Okay," Smathers said sitting up. "Both the network and America's new superhero ambushed us. It was my tactical mistake to not push him earlier for a debate or question his credentials."

"We discussed it," Orth responded. "Lyons was hovering in the polls , but we were waiting for him to either get aggressive or shoot himself in the foot. We took a calculated risk."

"I prefer to think that I fucked up!" Smathers said as he stood up abruptly. "That's what gets my juices going and makes me scream for redemption. You and I are going over every piece of dirt you dug up. I want the ad people in here tomorrow morning. I don't give a shit if it is a Saturday."

"We've held off the press for today, promising a statement Monday, but maybe it makes sense to hit a few talk shows Sunday morning. You and I will decide that after we figure out our attack strategy. I want to set up a debate, and I want it tomorrow! I want to poke so many holes in this asshole that he ends up looking like Swiss cheese."

Orth nodded. "There are still more questions than answers about Lyons"

"Ya think? In the past, the public has allowed some candidates' records to be sealed, but no one is going to buy a guy whose whole life is sealed!"

"I agree with everything you said, but we can't underestimate Lyons. I think he's playing with a stacked deck.""

"How can I underestimate a prick who single-handedly stops a terrorist attack?" Smathers retorted. "I'm going to *overestimate* him, and then we'll have a battle plan to seek and destroy."

Smathers ushered Orth out of his office a few minutes later. Both men were exhausted, and they would reconvene early the next day.

Smathers looked at his watch: 4:40. He rolled his neck. Campaigning sucked. He was looking forward to a quiet dinner with Cindy. She was the best thing that had ever happened to him. He felt a rush of love. Some son-of-a-bitch damn nearly ran her over, and it made his blood boil just thinking about it. A knock on the door caused him to look up. "Senator, there's a delivery for you."

"Thanks, Lela," he said as his administrative assistant handed him a brown envelope. Everything that appeared at his office was scanned, sniffed, and pronounced suitable for opening before it reached the senator's desk. Nevertheless, a strange foreboding came over him and he felt uneasy. Who would send him something late on a Friday afternoon? **Personal and Confidential** screamed at him with its bold lettering.

Reluctantly, his fingers fumbled with the tape. The first of many pictures tumbled out of the envelope. A gorgeous black woman, captured in nude glory, her face shielded. She was draped on a king-sized bed, her head resting on the thigh of an equally naked white woman whose eyes were closed.

Smathers's eyes slammed shut as if he could squeeze the vision from his sight and his memory, but the image was indelible, burned into his retinas. His anger and resolve melted into acquiescence. The other woman was his wife.

CHAPTER 78

"SENATOR SMATHERS, PLEASE."

"May I tell him who's calling?"

"Yes. It's Mac McGregor calling about Jeremy Lyons. Tell him that Sam Golden gave me his private number."

"One moment, please."

Instead of a moment, Mac waited for about two minutes.

"I thought you were one of Lyons's boys," Smathers snarled.

"The polar opposite, senator."

"Didn't he say that you were his inspiration?"

"He's a liar, among other things."

Smathers sighed. "Okay. I got nothing to lose. How can I help you, Mr. McGregor?"

"Before I contacted you, I followed a hunch and called my friend Sam Golden to ask if your office had contacted him. It seemed a logical assumption, since Sam headed a task force to track down Lyons. What you may not know is that I assisted him in locating Lyons's operation. My next call was to Joe Sebastiano, to see if you had contacted him."

"And I guess you're connected to the FBI, too?" Smathers snapped.

"I'm not your enemy, senator."

Smathers let out a breath. "Yeah, I got that. Frankly, I'm pretty raw over this whole thing. How well do you know Lyons?"

"Perhaps better than anyone on the planet, senator."

"You don't really know him until he's stuck a hot poker up your ass!"

Mac exhaled and closed his eyes. He had not wanted his suspicions to be correct, but Lyons always neutralized his opponents.

"I'm not going to give you the specifics," Smathers said. "Suffice it to say that I believe Lyons set up a scenario to ensure my reticence. My well thought-out game plan of exposing him has been permanently shelved."

Mac wasn't happy with that answer. Supposition without confirmation wouldn't cut it with a reporter. He thought about Lyons's MO and took a stab. "Did it involve a beautiful black woman?"

"How the fuck did you know that?"

"He has priors."

"Yeah. He would." Smathers waited a beat. "I'm not a saint, Mr. McGregor, but my wife is. Nothing is worth jeopardizing her reputation."

"I understand, sir. I just needed to find out if Lyons had gotten to you."

"He cut out my heart."

"If it's any consolation, sir, I can guarantee that your wife was set up."

"Thanks. I know. I know her." Smathers paused. "What's *your* angle? Why do *you* want to know?"

"Even though Lyons appears unstoppable, I have to try," Mac responded.

"How can I help?"

"You've already helped, senator. We can't outspend, outmuscle, or out-terrorize the man, and unlike Lyons, we are encumbered by legalities."

"So what's your plan?"

"If I can't break through his armor, I'll shoot for his ego. I'm gonna see if I can get some help from the press."

"No press! If I wanted the press involved, I'd have done it myself."

"Senator, I promise you that no reference will be made to our conversation."

"Okay, McGregor, but I've already got one bullet saved for Lyons. and there're more in the magazine."

"Senator, *I* only have *one* target."

"Tom."

"Mac." Just to be annoying, Mac replied almost before the clipped "m" sound in Tom's name ended. Nothing better than having a reporter's private line. "A man who says his name that quickly and with such a sense of impatience is either on a deadline or engaged in sex."

"Maybe both," quipped his dry-humored friend.

"It certainly seems like an impossible task for a eunuch, but you have surprised me before."

"Actually, I'm finishing up an article about a leading financial advisor's secret life with farm animals." His monotone delivery was consistently unsettling to the uninitiated.

"Tom, Tom Terrific, my friend, I do tend to forget that behind that facile mind and the clever repartee lurks a serious investigative journalist with the potential to maim."

Tom Hessel was a well-respected investigative reporter for the *Washington Post*: bald head; deceptively kind, light-blue eyes; a lean runner's build; never without a New York Yankees baseball cap. Somehow, Tom had sniffed out Mac's involvement in the exposure of illegal hedge fund activities. In return for explicit details, he kept Mac out of the news. Sam Golden, the former SEC Chairman turned advisor to the President, trusted Hessel, and so Mac, in turn, had done the same. From that, a friendship evolved, and whenever the reporter needed a perspective on a local financial figure, he would call Mac.

"So, do you have a scoop for me?" asked Tom. "Nobody calls me just for pleasure. How did you like your pal's speech last night?"

"It's beyond belief that nobody calls you for pleasure," Mac said dryly.

"Come on. Don't try to butter me up. Whadda ya got?"

Mac waited. He knew his hesitation would increase the reporter's interest.

"Tick-tock."

"What sort of latitude do you have in your column?" Mac asked.

"Do you mean will they tell me I can't write something or edit me into passivity? No way, dude. I've got street creds. I believe it, I write it."

"What did *you* think about Lyons's speech?"

"Nice-sounding bullshit."

"How do you feel about telling it like it is?"

"You got facts?"

"An informed source has gone over everything with the FBI."

"Not enough."

"Why does the combative incumbent senator from Florida not go after Lyons?" Mac asked.

"I've wondered that. What's the answer?"

"Pose the question. That's all I can give you."

"Bullshit! I can protect," Tom said angrily.

"Nobody can. It's nonnegotiable."

"Okay, but if you're going to shut me out, I still need more."

"Senator Haywood Cunningham was one of Lyons's recruiters. He's a friend of mine and will talk to you."

"Better."

"My informed source can set up a conversation with you and an informed FBI agent."

"Perfect."

"Tom, you do know that you'll be swimming hard against the current. Everybody else has Jeremy Lyons on a pedestal."

"You're not setting me up, are you? This is not just your personal vendetta?"

Mac thought for a moment. "I would love to see Lyons skewered, make no mistake. But no one will tell you anything that they do not believe is true."

"That works. I've got a 24-hour deadline. Lyons sounds like a closet Republican, anyway. Let's get this arrogant bastard."

CHAPTER 79

JEREMY LYONS WAS NO LONGER just Florida's favorite son. He was now America's favorite son. His revelation that he was the "Outsider," coupled with his dramatic exit from a primetime TV special, at least for the moment seemed to shake the apathy out of the nation.

The Brian Woods interview instantly went viral, with over 13 million hits within the first 24 hours. There was a traffic jam on the blogosphere as everyone wished to comment, and there were more tweets posted on Lyons's performance than for all of the other celebrities combined.

He was a rock star of the highest imaginable magnitude.

Quotes such as "This Lyons never sleeps," "Let's have a Lyons instead of a liar for President," and "Stay straight, or you're Lyons bait" were headlines in every major newspaper. Even Jackie Mayfield's characterization of Lyons as a guardian angel had legs. Jay Leno sang "Someone to Watch Over Me" as a tribute.

Jeremy Lyons became the perfect hero: the man who was tired of all the bullshit and did something about it. A *USA Today* poll showed that if the presidential election were held today and Lyons entered the race, he would win.

Meanwhile, both the Republican and Democratic spokespersons served up quiet platitudes about his contributions in combating injustice. But they were strategically mute on his game plan to change the status quo of Congress. Truth be told, every politician in America was shocked, or perhaps humbled, or just plain scared by the power of the country's new messiah.

Should they befriend him, support him, or just hope that he crashed and burned?

The public had no such questions, and neither the authorities nor civil rights groups introduced the question of vigilante justice. No matter what Jeremy Lyons had done before or how rich he was, he had done some major John Wayne shit, whipping up on rapist assholes, druggies, and terrorists. He was the country's guardian angel and the citizens' avenging angel. He made them feel safe.

Sam Golden had kept his former executive assistant as the sole employee in his small Georgetown office. In the past few years, any work that Sam did could have been accomplished from his home. But it always felt more professional working from his office. Now he wasn't sure why he came to the office at all.

Sam still received calls for advice, to serve on boards, and to speak, but he declined whenever possible. Unfortunately, the axiom was not true for Sam Golden: Time did not heal all wounds.

"Sam, the White House on line one."

Sam raised his head from his hands, grimaced, and picked up the receiver. "Sam Golden."

"Please hold for the President," came an operator's monotone. A minute later Sam heard the unmistakable voice of the Chief Executive.

"Sam, I wanted to call you and tell you how sorry I am about Ms. Savino."

Sam blinked, and his eyes instantly teared. Clearing his throat, he responded, "Thank you, Mr. President."

"Have the authorities determined the cause?"

"No, sir," he said and exhaled.

"It's not often that I feel powerless, Sam."

Sam managed a weak smile into the phone. As much as he appreciated the call and the sincere thoughts, he had no desire to talk with anyone. There was no solace in being reclusive, but the pain of human interaction was still beyond his tolerance. However, this was a man that he could not deny. "Is there any way I can help you, Mr. President?"

The President paused, probably pleased that Sam had given him an opening. They knew each other well. "Sam, I was considering something, and I wanted your advice on whether it made sense and, more importantly, whether it might offend you."

Sam was lost. He decided to remain silent.

"I'm considering having a private meeting with Jeremy Lyons."

Just cut out my heart! Sam's mind screamed. He was dumbstruck.

"The polls show Lyons as the most popular man in America," the President explained. "I've been told that I need to charm him, because if he turns on me before the election, it could be bad news." He lowered his voice. "I won't make the call without your approval, Sam. I know you were frustrated that he eluded you."

It was heartfelt. Sam took deep breaths. Tears ran down his sunken cheeks. "Mr. President," he began, trying to steady himself, "I believe that the man is a crook, probably a killer, and possibly the most dangerous man on the planet." Sam never minced words with his friends.

He gulped a few more breaths. "I don't know if it will help. I don't believe that Lyons can be influenced by anyone. If he acts like your friend, don't believe it. But he will win Florida in a landslide and as an Independent."

Sam ran his hands frantically through his thin hair as if he wanted to pull it all out. He sighed audibly to convey a sense of control. "But you're right, sir. You can't let him be a force for the Republicans. Besides, it is true that you need to keep your friends close and your enemies closer."

CHAPTER 80

MAC MCGREGOR WAS PACING IN his home office, watching dawn struggle through the early morning fog. He wasn't sure what time the Sunday *Washington Post* actually arrived, but he wanted to be all over it as soon as it hit the driveway.

He sipped his ice-cold bottle of water. It was hard to opt for delayed gratification, because he knew all he had to do was go to either his computer or his iPad and pull up the article. But he wanted to see it in print, smell the newsprint, and savor the words.

At 7:15 his resolve weakened, and he booted up his computer. Out of the corner of his eye, he saw the paper fly out of a car window and land on his driveway. He opened the door quietly, so as not to disturb Grace, and jogged out to get his prize.

NO BUSINESS LIKE SNOW BUSINESS
by Tom Hessel

> *Could we all take a breath before we anoint the senatorial candidate who enthralled the nation last Thursday night? Shouldn't we at least try to peek through his cloak of invincibility?*
>
> *When the toughest interviewer on the planet, Brian Woods, serves up nothing but marshmallows, what happens? Jeremy Lyons happens. We were looking for answers. We got evasions, non-answers, edited versions, and pabulum. I'm not buying it.*
>
> *An equitable analysis first requires that we express our appreciation for Lyons's now-disclosed contributions to our society. By means that beg more questions, Jeremy Lyons somehow induced*

an exonerated rapist to recreate the scene of his actual crime. Was the fact that the man ended up in a hospital after being brutalized just a coincidence? For his next trick, Lyons singlehandedly exposed the manufacturer of the street drug, Euphoria, which had been killing children in California.

Finally, in his tour de force, Jeremy Lyons learned of a terrorist attack and warned the FBI, who stopped the attack in the nick of time. If the President wants to immediately appoint Mr. Lyons as the head of the Department of Defense or Homeland Security or even the CIA, his superhero past would make his qualifications unimpeachable.

But we learned of this side of Jeremy Lyons almost as an afterthought. Weren't there all kinds of questions swirling around our heads before his walk-off revelation? During the interview, Mr. Lyons referred to FBI Special Agent Joe Sebastiano, who actually led the task force that attempted to arrest Mr. Lyons and his associate. In the confusion of a firefight, Lyons escaped and fled the country. Although the FBI, in cooperation with other authorities, pursued the Florida senatorial candidate, he could not be located.

Why has the government not charged Mr. Lyons, now that he has returned to the United States? There is no statute of limitations on the original charges. The uncomfortable answer is that the government's key witness was an apparent suicide victim. After receiving immunity from the FBI, Frank Griffin promptly decided to shed his clothes and dive off of his sixth-floor balcony. The Naples, Florida, police have no evidence to refute that theory.

Concerning his suspect past, did Jeremy Lyons tell us why he created centers of influence, including former senators, to persuade rich people to invest with him? Did he tell us that he guaranteed his investors 20 percent a year? Warren Buffet can't do that, so what's the catch?

Is there a common thread among these ultra-rich investors? How many were either Chief Executive Officers or Chief Financial Officers of public companies? The answer is: all of them were either corporate officers or major-league centers of influence.

Because Lyons was under no obligation to discuss who his clients were or what he was buying and selling, let's examine what we do know about his operation. Ten CEOs and two CFOs of public companies admitted that they discussed privileged information outside of the boardroom. Coincidentally, all these company officials were males. Equally as coincidental is that all of their unauthorized conversations were with females alleged to be of exceptional beauty.

This reporter interviewed one of the former senators recruited by Mr. Lyons's organization. Senator Heywood Cunningham, a former major player on Capitol Hill, had the cushy job of approaching high-ranking corporate executives and giving them an offer they couldn't refuse. Senator Cunningham never met Jeremy Lyons, and to his knowledge, neither did any of the recruits.

All of Senator Cunningham's conversations were with Max Parnavich, the ex-Navy SEAL who was Mr. Lyons's associate. Mr. Parnavich was an extraordinarily menacing man, seemingly more prone to intimidate than entice. In his hour of glory, Jeremy Lyons failed to disclose that Mr. Parnavich was dishonorably discharged from the SEAL program for the use of excessive force.

The FBI was prepared to arraign Mr. Parnavich on charges of multiple murders and torture; however, the disgraced ex-Navy SEAL died, as was so aptly stated, taking a bullet for Mr. Lyons.

Finally we come to the reigning senator from Florida, Alan Smathers. This war hero fought and clawed his way into office. Envied for his ability to pitch what seemed like a 24/7 campaign, capped by a debate performance that was fit for the national stage, Smathers routinely eviscerated his opponents' positions and arguments.

Fast forward to his current re-election bid. Behind in the polls, he hasn't questioned Lyons's credentials or demanded a single debate. Smathers has one of the more respected war chests, but apparently no systematic plan to attack. Lyons's primetime speech, which seemed patently unfair to this writer, since there is nothing scheduled for equal time, should certainly prompt the Republican senator into action. Stay tuned, Florida.

In our times of full disclosure, aren't we entitled to a few more revealing answers from our political leaders? On the issue of his beliefs, Mr. Lyon is refreshingly forthright, unhedging, and passionate. Still, his past remains murky and troubling.

So how 'bout it, Mr. Lyons? Will you clean the snow off the windshield of your past so that we can have a clearer view of your candidacy? Clarity is important, Mr. Lyons ... even for superheroes.

CHAPTER 81

IT WASN'T AS IF MAC objected strenuously to a change of seasons; he just objected to days below 50 degrees. Today was downright cold, with the temperature just above freezing. However, after reading Tom Hessel's article in the Sunday paper, he was so fired up that he could have frolicked outside in the nude.

In order to burn off some energy, Mac was on a solo mission on the canal. A combination of the weather and the early-morning time persuaded Grace to remain behind with the promise to make pancakes. It took him less than five minutes to suit up.

Mac's twelve-year-old sports car did not handle the bumps and potholes as easily as Grace's minivan, so he very tentatively maneuvered his car down the dirt road to Pennyfield Lock. Parking was easy, because at 7:40 on a cold Sunday the lot was empty. He got out of the car and clicked the remote to lock it. Layered up, complete with Redskins ski cap pulled down over his ears, he bent down and re-laced his shoes.

Because he'd decided he was going to run some today instead of just walking, he placed a leg on the rail of the wooden bridge leading to the towpath and executed a half-assed hamstring stretch. He repeated the semi-exercise on the other leg. As he paused a minute to absorb the beauty around him, he thought that it felt like the sun was reluctant to wake up, its reflection faint and scattered on the water.

Mac turned right, and his leisurely walk shortly turned into a fast walk and then a comfortably paced jog. As much as he loved music, he chose to be unencumbered by electronics, so his iPhone was zippered in, but turned off. Today he just wanted to picture Jeremy Lyons's face when Jeremy read Tom Hessel's article. Grabbing flesh down low on his thigh, he hollered to the empty path and surrounding trees, "I've got your 'Outsider!'"

Lost in thought, Mac hadn't noticed the figure in black jogging toward him. As he got closer, he decided he would have noticed her even if he was in a coma. Normally, he would have bravely attempted to represent his gender well by keeping his eyes on her face. But her aversion to cold must have been worse than his. A black ski masked covered her face.

In a store or a bank, the ski mask might have been threatening, but on the canal in frigid weather, it was almost normal. Another 20 degrees colder and it would be mandatory. Still, in this case, when there were apparently two perfect breasts highlighted under a tight, black knit jersey, any sins of fashion would be forgiven. In his walk/run/walk/run cycle, Mac had definitely finished the run portion; but it would have been too wimpy to stop running and let her hear him panting.

Mac smiled when her dark eyes got within about ten feet of him. As they passed each other, she swerved, and her shoulder hit him just under his shoulder blades with the force of a cross-body block. He lurched back violently, trying to regain his balance. At the edge of the canal, he put his hands on the ground and was just able to right himself before falling into the water.

"You knocked me off my stride!" she yelled.

"Excuse me?" he replied angrily.

She stepped closer, crowding him. "What? Were you looking at my boobs or something? Is that why you bumped into me like a drunk?"

"Listen." Mac had his hands in a placating manner. "Let's both just be on our way."

"Is this what your white-bread ass was dying to see?" she asked, and in one motion she pulled up her jersey and let her milk-chocolate breasts spill out.

"I'm out of here," Mac said, turning to leave. As he stepped forward, she grabbed his shoulders and leg-whipped him on the back of his knees. He fell forward, and his knees and hands hit the tiny rocks of the towpath simultaneously. Before he could move, another powerful kick caught him in the left ribcage, and he collapsed on the ground with a cry of pain. As he rolled to the right to avoid the onslaught, she dropped heavily onto his chest. Air rushed out of his body, and a feeling of panic consumed him. She leaned down and whispered in his ear, "Are we *clear* now, bitch."

CHAPTER 82

"WHAT THE F ...?"

Mac held up his hand as he walked gingerly to his desk. Well aware that he looked like the loser in a twelve-round bout, he was sure that he actually felt worse than he looked. "I am aware that inquiring minds will want to know the details," Mac said painfully into R.J.'s concerned countenance, "but I prefer to discuss it in our Monday morning meeting rather than to have to repeat it fourteen times."

R.J. pursed his lips and gave him a look of frustrated acceptance. Not only did he prefer being in the know, but patience was not his strong suit when it involved one of the group.

"Actually, if you do want to help," Mac added in a tired voice, "you could conjure up a more creative reason than what actually happened."

"Happy to oblige. Perhaps you could give me some indication of which trash compactor you fell into?"

"No. That would spoil the surprise."

Monday morning meetings at 8:30 sharp were a ritual for Mac's team. For all of these weekly meetings, anyone who was a minute late became the target for a tag-team abuse-a-thon.

Today, however, the normal convivial atmosphere of the meeting was subdued, and until the team got an explanation on Mac's condition, even insults were put on hold. Everyone looked at him curiously, with a mixture of concern and, in David Grant's case, fury.

Mac tended to be the big-picture guy, outlining philosophy and business-development ideas, and providing overall direction.

Typically, he stood and led the conversation, then turned it over to the partners and associates to discuss other areas. All fourteen team members were gathered in a loose semicircle around his desk. A few were half-sitting on neighboring desks, but most were standing.

Due to his discomfort, Mac remained sitting for this meeting and spoke from his chair. "We have a meeting tomorrow with a referral," he began.

"Unh unh," interrupted Lena Brady, wagging her finger at him. "No business until you tell us who gave *you* the business."

Mac knew he had no chance to delay an explanation, but he enjoyed watching Lena put on the attitude. He smiled weakly. "Would you believe that I got mugged on the canal by a beautiful woman who first flashed me her breasts?"

"I don't *think* so," said Lena, her hands jauntily on her hips.

"Then I got nothing. Let's move on."

"Mac, we're worried. Please don't make a joke out of it or devalue our concern for you," R.J. admonished.

Mac rolled his eyes. "Will you not grant me an ounce of pleasure over getting my ass kicked by a woman?"

R.J. turned away in disgust.

"What I just told you is absolutely true," Mac said painfully as he leaned across his desk. "I'll give you my version of why a stranger with no provocation practiced her martial arts on me."

R.J. had turned around, and every eye was riveted on Mac.

"Most of you have probably read Tom Hessel's article on Jeremy Lyons in the *Post*."

Heads noted in response.

"What do you think Lyons's reaction would be to Hessel's particularly unflattering analysis? Would he assume that the reporter assembled all the information himself, or would he think that Hessel got some inside information from this fella here, now nursing two cracked ribs, a plethora of cuts and abrasions, and a swollen lip?" Mac pointed to himself with both hands.

"So he retaliated using a woman, knowing that it would be awkward for you to discuss it publicly, and there were probably no witnesses anyway," offered David in a flat voice.

"Not at that hour of the morning," said Mac. "It may sound like an excuse, but that was no ordinary woman. She was trained in martial arts, and she attacked and laid me out before I knew what was happening."

"When did it happen?" asked David.

"Early yesterday morning."

"So someone was watching your house. Do you always jog in the same direction?"

"No, Detective Grant," Mac answered wearily. "Not interested in analysis."

For about a minute, no one spoke. Then Danny DeMarco, who obviously was out of patience, quipped, "Was the flash worth the pain?"

CHAPTER 83

BY THURSDAY OF THE SAME week, Mac was either feeling better or the novelty of the pain had worn off. All morning he had been grinding at his desk, and, at a minimum, he needed a stretch. He got up from his chair, stretched like a big tabby, rubbed the back of his neck with his right hand, and headed towards the men's room.

As Mac walked by David Grant's desk, he noticed that David was off the phone. Mac's bathroom break was more precautionary than necessary, so he stopped and asked David a question. "We have an 8:30 meeting with a potential new client tomorrow. Are you good?"

"Uh, Mac, I'm going to be in a little later tomorrow. Can you get somebody else?"

"Is that on the calendar?" Mac asked, raising an eyebrow.

"Sorry," David said, grimacing. "It just came up."

"Does that mean that you're *finally* going to consummate the marriage?"

David reddened, which in most environments would be considered endearing. In Mac McGregor's group, it was chum in the water.

David, sensing his vulnerability, replied quickly. "I don't think so. My two kids would think that was gross."

"Hmm. It must already be awkward that they both look so much like Danny Demento."

David laughed. "Exactly. I have to make sure they never see him."

"Actually not a bad idea, regardless," Mac responded sagely. Because privacy was overrated and rarely respected among them, he queried further. "So, is it a client breakfast?"

"No," David answered. "My unit from the army is having a mini-reunion tonight, and I'm afraid that I'll do more harm than good in an early meeting."

"And that's different ... how?"

David laughed again, then took a white handkerchief out of his pocket and waved it in the air.

Mac smiled and started to walk away when another thought hit him. He turned back to David. "Hey, is Blake the Snake going to be there?"

David waited a beat and then answered, "Yes."

"Give him my best. I could have used him on my canal walk. I'll bet he could've kicked that woman's ass."

David's eyes narrowed, and he looked straight into Mac's. "Boss, he can kick anybody's ass."

CHAPTER 84

AS THE BLACK SEDAN WITH tinted windows navigated Washington, D.C., traffic, Jeremy Lyons leaned back into the cushioned seat, folded his arms, and crossed his legs at the ankles. This ride was an unexpected, unlikely, unprecedented augmentation of his plan. A one-on-one unscripted interview with the President of the United States. *Jeremy Lyons is in the house!* He smiled. It could also be interesting.

As Jeremy had assumed, his victory in Florida was now assured. When he revealed on national TV that he was the "Outsider," every woman who had ever been abused, every drug-hating parent, and every gun-toting good ol' boy had their champion. The opposition had been neutered.

After his election, he intended to move quickly to revolutionize the Sunshine State. His fellow senators would be looking at him curiously, expecting him to bide his time, learn the ropes, and then make a few false starts. Novices in the art of war, the last thing they would anticipate would be an immediate full frontal assault on the Senate floor with the accompaniment of a full media orchestra pummeling them at every indecisive moment.

Jeremy thought about how he would like to address his fellow senators:

Fait accompli, my esteemed colleagues. Get on board or get out. I am the Pied Piper of Responsibility. Follow me, or your constituency will chew you up and spit you out. You have been lulled into a false sense of security by the countless pretenders before me who promised bold action and change, only to be discouraged by the old boys' network or lengthy filibusters. I will not be coddled or contained or even influenced. I will not compromise or offer you the traditional due respect. You must earn my *respect by putting your country ahead of your constituency, your party and, yes, even your re-election.*

There are no undercover Secret Service agents in the nation's capital. At least that's what Jeremy assumed as he studied the large neck of the pasty-white driver of his sedan. The cheap gray suit, closely cropped hair, slightly frayed white shirt, red tie, and telltale ear buds were dead giveaways.

As he studied the driver's wide shoulders and silent demeanor, Jeremy wondered if the man had sized up his passenger. Is there an automatic threat assessment? Not that the agent would have ever given it a thought, but he would certainly assume that he could subdue his passenger if there was ever the need to do so.

For obvious reasons, Jeremy's host did not want to advertise that he had requested a one-on-one meeting with an Independent senatorial candidate. Still, Jeremy did not doubt that the man would have a plausible explanation in the event that the private meeting accidentally became public. This President could spin a top with his words.

One of the interesting questions was whether the President requested this meeting as a result of his party's urging or if it was his personal curiosity. When he received the invitation, Jeremy's first inclination had been to refuse. If he had been able to have video surveillance of the Oval Office, he would have turned down the President's offer in a heartbeat. A video of the shock and awe of the reaction to someone stiffing the leader of the free world would have been the highlight of Jeremy's home movies. Well, perhaps not the highlight, but at least it would be splendid comic relief.

However, at the urging of Sabine, who added the incentive that they would have a lovely dinner at Mac McGregor's favorite restaurant after the meeting, Jeremy accepted. As Sabine also pointed out, rarely does a new home inspection take place five years before occupancy.

CHAPTER 85

JEREMY LYONS WONDERED IF IT was presumptuous to be thinking about changes in the decor as he sat with the President in the Oval Office. Apparently, each President feels compelled to put a fingerprint on the room by choosing new furniture and drapes and designing his own oval-shaped carpet to take up most of the floor.

Jeremy would not feel compelled to engage in what he considered one-upmanship. In fact, he would make a point about austerity and not change the decor at all.

At the moment, Jeremy was half listening to the leader of the free world as the man tried to charm his way into the Florida senatorial candidate's psyche. Exuding a warmth that made Jeremy uncomfortable, the President had given him a quick tour of the Oval Office. Politicians tend to assume a closeness on first encounter that, in most instances, is flattering to the recipient – not in this case. Pointing towards the three large windows overlooking the South Lawn, then asking Jeremy to join him on the obligatory short stroll through the Rose Garden, the man was the perfect host.

Later, as they sat in chairs facing each other, Jeremy declined the offer of a beverage from the White House butler. Instead, he sat patiently and confidently, waiting for the President to begin the conversation.

"You're probably wondering why I called this meeting," the President began amiably.

"I don't often wonder, Mr. President."

"Jeremy, if you can read minds in addition to your other apparent super powers, you can really be valuable to our country."

Jeremy responded with a half-smile, but remained quiet.

"I don't suppose I could entice you to run one of our intelligence agencies," the President said, only half joking.

"I believe that I am more suited to be accountable to my entire constituency than to one person."

The President maintained his broad smile as he appeared to absorb his guest's response. He leaned forward, and his tone was TV-worthy serious. "I do want to thank you for your service to our country. The rape case may have been an isolated incident, but identifying the manufacturer and distributor of the drug Euphoria was a gift to all our children."

Jeremy nodded his acknowledgment.

"And I'm not sure you'd tell me, or that I even want to know, how you uncovered the terrorist plot on the National Cathedral."

Still receiving no response, except for his guest's half smile, the President added, "In fact, one of our agencies picked up a terrorist and was able to extract some valuable information. This detail is not known to the public, but I felt that you had the right to know." His words were pointed.

"Thank you for that information. It is good to know that our agencies are on the ball." Jeremy's response walked that fine line between respect and sarcasm.

The President smiled, but the seriousness of his eyes belied his casualness. "I have to admit that one thing did give me pause in the recounting of your extraordinary contributions. In each instance you alerted Jackie Mayfield of Fox News. Did you have a previous relationship with her?"

Although the question felt a bit intrusive to Jeremy, he answered without emotion. "No. I had never met her."

"Well, I hope that is not an indication of your political leanings."

"Mr. President, I am an Independent. I don't lean."

"Glad to hear it, Jeremy. I do believe that you will be the first Independent senator from Florida, and I would love to work with you in the future." He smiled again, and this time his eyes went along for the ride.

"Thank you, Mr. President," Jeremy replied.

Jeremy watched as the man steepled his hands and then rubbed them together.

The President leaned forward again and looked at him with earnestness. "In the next four years, I will need some help from the moderates in Congress in order to get this country back on track. You are a man of ideas. My people are currently evaluating your idea about how to invigorate the real estate market. I also believe that you are a man of vision, and I know that you can be a leader in the Senate."

He paused, but Jeremy knew that the man was not waiting for a response. He was adding weight to the moment.

"I would like to know that I can count on your support."

Jeremy let the eye contact marinate for a few moments before speaking. "I will not be an advocate for any fringe political philosophies, if that is a concern. Nor will I be a spokesman for any party. However, I will support any President whose agenda is restoring our country's fiscal sanity."

His host nodded as if he had gotten a satisfactory answer.

"Outside of your book, which may or may not be fiction, no one seems to know anything about you," said the President. "It's hard to believe that in our media-saturated world, a candidate can remain a mystery. What is your secret?"

"No secret. I simply refuse to allow an unnecessary invasion into my personal life. I am happy to reveal my birth certificate,"

Jeremy answered, "as well as my charitable contributions. But what relevance would my tax returns have on my ability to govern?"

"You don't have to convince me, Jeremy. I'm just surprised that for now the press and the public are giving you a pass. Knowing their short attention span, your lack of intrusion holiday may also be short lived."

"Mr. President, the *desire* to know is merely baseless curiosity; the *need* to know is often required. The people of Florida *need* to know that everything I say, I will do, and I am happy to elaborate on my platform. If one were able to examine even a moment of my life, they would see that I have always done what I set out to do."

The President gave him a skeptical look. "So you really expect to keep your personal life and your history private?"

Jeremy nodded. "No one *has* to vote for me, and I believe that a certain degree of privacy is civilized."

"I'm surprised that you weren't asked the question by Brian Woods, but you must be the only aspiring politician that's written a book advocating that the end justifies the means."

"Did you read my book, Mr. President?"

"I was briefed on your more philosophical positions,"

Jeremy nodded. "A politician would not espouse that belief or truly be candid about what he or she really believes. That philosophy would more likely be attributed to a successful general. May I ask you a question, Mr. President? If a terrorist held your daughter hostage, would you torture him to save her?"

The President furrowed his brow. "You know I can't answer that. Let's change course."

The President's next question changed the dynamics of the conversation. "Do you feel that the article by Tom Hessel in the *Post* will damage your aspirations?"

Jeremy's eyes narrowed. "Nothing will derail my aspirations. I believe that it was drivel, prompted by a ..." he paused, "former friend."

"Do you believe that the article was politically motivated?"

"No. It was a hatchet job, based on rumor and innuendo. No politician would *dare* suggest that article."

The President nodded as if he understood. The nod felt condescending to Jeremy and increased his annoyance.

Before the President could respond, Jeremy added, "It will not be the last attempted character assassination of me. I am sure you are aware that the press often get it wrong.

"Of course," the President agreed, smiling uneasily at the man's intensity. "Last question: I don't believe that I've ever seen a more meteoric rise in the political arena. And your candor is a refreshing change from the bluster that we hear from the opposing party." He smiled now as if he were facing a bank of cameras. "No disrespect. Was this simply your being in the right place at the right time, or was this your plan all along?"

Jeremy met the President's eyes. "Everything I do is planned, Mr. President."

The President nodded sagaciously as if Jeremy had said something profound. Then his body language changed. He smiled and telegraphed that the meeting had entered the termination phase.

Before the President could speak, Jeremy looked at his watch and said quickly, "Sorry. I have a previous engagement, Mr. President. I'll have to cut our visit a little short."

Jeremy noted a slight tightening in his host's jaw.

The President stood and extended his hand. "I understand. I'm well aware that the political process takes a toll on our free time."

Jeremy rose and gripped the man's hand firmly. "As do beautiful women. Mr. President."

CHAPTER 86

EXITING THROUGH THE WEST WING entrance, Jeremy acknowledged the friendly goodbye from a Secret Service agent. He wondered if the man was sufficiently intuitive to suspect that he had just met a future POTUS.

As he walked toward Pennsylvania Avenue, he noticed that a news crew, apparently the White House correspondents crew, was hovering to his left. Before joining them, he walked to the waiting car and dismissed the driver.

Certain that no official announcement had been made of his meeting, Jeremy considered the fact that either this was a leak or he was being expertly shadowed. He dismissed the latter thought, and when he saw the FOX cameraman, he broke into a smile. Jeremy Lyons was well aware that to the press, he was a full-course buffet.

"Mr. Lyons!" cried an attractive Asian woman. "Were you meeting with the President?"

"Did he tell you that?"

"No, but ..."

"Then how could I, a lowly citizen, be so presumptuous to discuss it? Turn off your camera for a moment," he commanded.

"Stop recording," said the reporter, turning to her cameraman.

"Let's have a brief, off-the-record conversation, and then you can turn the camera back on" said Jeremy."

"Okay," the reporter replied eagerly.

"How did you know that I would be leaving the White House at this time?"

"A source."

Jeremy nodded. "Do you believe that your tip came from the Administration?"

She thought for a moment. "I'm not sure. My instincts say no. I didn't take the call, but the caller was an unidentified male, and he was calling from a blocked number. I was told that he sounded very professional. He called, gave the information, and disconnected."

"Okay, you can turn the camera on again."

For the next three minutes, Jeremy fulfilled his part of the bargain and succinctly answered the reporter's questions. He had stipulated that she not ask him any questions about the alleged meeting, and he told her what her last question would be. With eyes that reminded him of a predator who had finally snared her prey, she asked her final question: "So, Mr. Lyons, what *was* your reason to be inside the White House this evening?"

Jeremy gave her his best little-boy smile and then replied in a humble voice, "House hunting."

Jeremy's mind raced as he walked briskly towards his destination.

I would not be surprised if my parting comment allowed the interesting woman to achieve at least a mini-orgasm. At least her scream of "Yes!" as the camera went dark had the requisite sound to substantiate my theory.

Perhaps the President will be more judicious in future conversations with me. As I suspected, dismissing the White House driver and choosing to walk the short distance to the restaurant was the right move. It would have been bad form to exit the car and then give my host a parting shot.

I will need to pick up the pace. I am now seven minutes behind schedule. I abhor tardiness. It is the classic ingredient of the self-absorbed.

CHAPTER 87

THE FIRST STEP IN PLANNING a successful operation is to analyze the primary variables. In this case, the variables were automobile and pedestrian traffic, potential alternate routes, weather, and the tendencies of the target.

The second step is to attempt to control or influence the variables. The first three variables were off the table, but a well-placed phone call to the press dramatically increased the probability of the fourth variable being eliminated.

Recon had not been difficult. Fame and its temptations tend to lessen healthy paranoia. Without constant training, even the most careful man loses a step. Routine is the Achilles heel of most targets, which is why termination of a professional requires not only study, but a degree of luck.

The driver was dressed in a shiny blue suit, a white shirt with a frayed collar, and a thin, nondescript tie. He waited. In his right hand he held a flip cell phone to his ear. The batteries had been removed. As pedestrians neared, he lowered his head and pantomimed an animated conversation. It wasn't a problem; he had waited many times before.

Contrary to their recent criticism, the Secret Service of the United States is a tight-knit, highly professional force of elite operatives. The driver appreciated their loyalty and their service to the country, and the fact that only in Washington would a parked Secret Service vehicle not cause unwarranted attention.

His supercharged, six-year-old, black Suburban was parked on the south side of H street facing Jackson Place, in the last legal parking spot. From the passenger-side window, the driver could see the venerable Decatur House, which had housed statesmen and Presidents. Hopefully, it would witness another historic event. At exactly 1830 hours, the driver started the engine, and the specially designed vehicle idled quietly.

As Jeremy Lyons approached the gate, the officer escorting him motioned to the booth, and the gates that opened onto Pennsylvania Avenue. Primarily as a response to the Oklahoma City bombing in the same year, in 1995, the United States Secret Service closed off Pennsylvania Avenue to vehicular traffic in front of the White House. As a result, tourists were able to gather in front of the White House fence to take pictures. One young man snapped a series of shots of the athletic-looking man who had been talking to the reporters.

The cool, late spring evening had experienced intermittent bouts of fine, light rain. Pedestrians' umbrellas had been closed for most of the early evening, but remained at the ready. For the moment, the street showed only slightly discernible effects of the earlier rain.

Jeremy felt, rather than observed, the curious glances of the onlookers as his long strides carried him away from the White House. After heading west on Pennsylvania Avenue, he turned right onto Jackson Place, maintaining his rapid pace. That route was the most direct, and he would resist the temptation to scout out Lafayette Park for the future site of his statue.

Jeremy checked his watch and thought about jogging, but that crossed the appearance line from purposeful to desperate.

Every previous assignment had come from the chain of command or a commander on the scene. This mission was unauthorized; it was off the grid. God did not ask him to do it, nor had anyone suggested the mission to him. No commendations, congratulations, or acknowledgements were in order. The soldier shook these thoughts from his head. Retribution, payback was required; he would not hesitate.

Under his latex gloves, the Suburban driver's knuckles itched. He gave a grim smile. A shrink would say that the discomfort was psychosomatic. He preferred his own interpretation: it was an omen. His heartbeat was steady. The cell phone was in his coat pocket. He was at peace. If history held true, then once again what goes around would come around.

Jeremy was close now. In just a few blocks he would cross H Street. At that point Jackson Place turns into Connecticut Avenue, and the Equinox restaurant, where he was meeting Sabine, is straight ahead. He estimated that he would be three minutes late, which was unacceptable. But there had been extenuating circumstances, and Sabine would agree that the "house-hunting" quote, which would surely go viral, was definitely worth the wait.

Energy flowed through him, and his eyes shone with intensity as he came closer to his destiny. There were no obstacles that he could not conquer. Jeremy Lyons was unstoppable.

The man in the Suburban had slumped down so that only his eyes were above the dashboard. A fine mist began to fall on the windshield. The vehicle was already in gear.

Jeremy and two other pedestrians were waiting to cross the street. Impatiently, Jeremy glanced at the Suburban. He looked up angrily and started across the street. The other two pedestrians waited for the walk sign. Jeremy was halfway across the intersection when a sound made him look up.

A burst of adrenaline flooded his bloodstream as his sympathetic nervous system ratcheted into overdrive. His pupils expanded as if to supercharge the amount of information being sent to his brain. The rapid increase of stimulus created the extremely realistic illusion of time dilation. As his brain processed the black Suburban accelerating towards him, his blood vessels constricted, and his heart pumped furiously, igniting his muscles to move. His athletic calves coiled and released in lockstep to propel his body out of the way of the encroaching threat.

The driver had anticipated the reaction and guided the lethal mass into the new path to complete its objective. The Suburban hit Jeremy's left side. The force catapulted him across the windshield, and his body slid over the roof of the speeding vehicle. His brain continued to process the influx of data, and he was acutely aware that his pelvis was smashed, his foot was in a location not obtainable through any amount of yoga training, and he was gliding through the air upside-down. Instinctively, he tucked his head. To the horror of spectators, Jeremy Lyons landed behind the vehicle with a sickening thud.

The driver did not pause, did not look back. He slid his fingers off the wheel to turn on the wipers, and the smear of red began to fade. Although the target was extremely fit, the driver nonetheless estimated the probability of death at 80%. If Lyons lived, it was meant to be.

He turned right onto 14th street. At the light, he rolled up the latex glove on his right hand, closed his eyes, and brought the tattooed knuckles to his lips. When the light changed, he headed towards Reagan National. There was another mission waiting for him, and this one was authorized.

CHAPTER 88

AS SABINE EXPECTED, THE QUESTION she asked the maitre d' of the Equinox restaurant had not elicited a helpful answer. It was the McGregors' favorite restaurant, but they were not expected to dine there that night.

Sabine had secured one of the few booths to ensure privacy. Although their reservation was for seven o'clock, she had arrived fifteen minutes early, because she never kept Jeremy waiting. Smiling, she took a sip of wine, leaned back into the booth, and thought about the reaction that Mac McGregor would have if he saw them there.

At precisely 6:57, she received a text: "ETA + 3. Pls dont punish." Her heartbeat accelerated, and she responded quickly: "No promises."

Sabine nervously looked at her watch: 7:10. Jeremy was never late. The fact that he had a meeting with the President would not have affected his punctuality. He would still have been in control.

Sabine's hand was shaking as she swished the wine in her glass, and a premonition, a wave of dread, passed through her. She shuddered. Something must have happened.

Almost as if on cue, she heard the sirens. She threw a twenty on the table and rushed out the door of the restaurant. She bent down, tore her heels from her feet, and started running down 18th Street towards the White House.

The revolving lights on top of the police cars caused her to gasp for breath as she sprinted toward them. The sirens of two emergency vehicles pierced the air as they sped by her. A large area was cordoned off. Police officers formed an immovable circumference around the scene of an accident.

Terrified, Sabine cried, "Let me through!"

"I'm sorry, ma'am," said a large policeman, holding his arms out to restrain her.

"I need to speak to the officer in charge immediately. Is that Jeremy Lyons?"

"Ma'am, I'm not sure who the victim is."

Sabine shoved the policeman's arm away and started towards the scene. "Ma'am!" the policeman shouted, grabbing her right arm tightly.

Effortlessly, she jerked her arm towards his thumb, breaking his hold.

"IS HE DEAD? DO YOU EVEN KNOW THAT?" She lowered her voice. "Find out if he is alive and if it is Jeremy Lyons. He just came from a meeting with the President of the United States. Find out now."

The officer blanched, looked at the crazed woman warily, and called a fellow officer over. "Do we have an ID on the vic?"

"Yeah. It's Jeremy Lyons, the guy running for senator who's been all over the news."

"STOP!" Sabine pointed at an EMT who had jumped out of an ambulance and was kneeling over the body, "I WANT THE OFFICER IN CHARGE – NOW!!" Sabine screamed as pedestrians came closer to witness the spectacle.

The man bending over the body stood up when he was approached, shook his head, listened for a moment, and then walked over to Sabine. "I'm Lieutenant Capadanno, ma'am."

"Was it a hit and run?"

"That's inconclusive at the moment."

"Bullshit, Lieutenant," she hissed. "Is there a car with pieces of him stuck to it in the area? Please just answer my questions. I want to see him," she said, moving towards the body.

"I'm sorry, I can't let you!" said the lieutenant as he moved in front of her. "This is a crime scene."

Sabine shook her head in disgust. She lowered her voice. "Officer, Jeremy Lyons just came from a clandestine meeting with the President. Does this *accident* appear suspicious to you." Her anger was palpable.

The lieutenant's stoic cop face lost a little of its composure, and a tic appeared above his left eyebrow.

"I'll take care of this," she spat and abruptly turned her back to him. She called a preprogrammed number on her cell and spoke softly, but efficiently. Turning back to the officer, she informed him, "You will be instructed to stand down. The Secret Service is assuming control of the situation and will be here momentarily.

"NO ONE TOUCHES HIM!"

CHAPTER 89

AS MAC WOULD HAVE EXPECTED, Joe Sebastiano was the first call. It was 7:45 at night, less than an hour after the incident and about thirty minutes after the details had gotten sorted out.

"Jeremy Lyons may be dead," said Joe.

Mac blinked and sat down on the nearest chair.

"He was struck by a hit-and-run driver less than an hour ago." Joe's voice was emotionless, like a reporter who was giving the news without adding inflection or emphasis.

Mac tried to feel compassion, but mages of mourners at George Grant's funeral mixed with the look of hopeless devastation engraved in Sam Golden's face. He exhaled. "Do you know the extent of his injuries?"

"Nobody knows anything. It's like a blanket of secrecy. You'd think they hit the President," Joe answered.

"Are you sure this wasn't an accident?"

"Positive."

"God, Joe, think of the irony. Jeremy acknowledged that he was responsible for the hit and run on George Grant, and now the same thing happens to him."

"Any idea who would want him killed?" Joe asked.

"*Yes!*" Mac thought somberly. If his gut feeling was correct, he was right in the middle of this assassination attempt. He was complicit, an accessory. If Blake Stone was the weapon, Mac McGregor had fed him the ammunition.

"Is your list of suspects that long?" Joe sounded annoyed.

"I'm just trying to make some sense of this," Mac answered evasively. "How the heck would I know who tried to kill him?" He gave a hollow laugh. "It's nuts. I have no idea how to handle this news. "

CHAPTER 90

"SAM GOLDEN ON LINE ONE."

Mac closed his eyes. After Margo's death, Sam became a recluse. One day Mac had impulsively stopped by Sam's office to take him to lunch. He stood in the doorway and saw his friend's tall, skeletal frame hunched over his computer. Sam's unkempt hair, wrinkled dress shirt with the sleeves rolled up, and loosened tie thrown over his shoulder gave such a poignant picture of hopelessness and depression that Mac couldn't bear to interrupt. He turned and walked away.

Reluctantly, Mac picked up the phone. "Hey, Sam."

"Do you think he's dead?"

"All I know is that he was splattered on the sidewalk," answered Mac. "I thought if anybody could find out, it would be you. Do you know why he was meeting with the President?"

"POTUS was just sizing him up, nervous about Lyons's sudden rise in power, looking for an ally." Sam's clipped response confirmed Mac's assumption that Sam had been aware of Jeremy's visit.

"You think he had Margo killed?" Sam asked.

Mac paused. What he thought shouldn't have mattered to Sam, but he knew that it did. "I don't believe that her death was an accident," he said as he tried to form on actual answer. "Lyons was a man who hated loose ends and planned for every contingency. As much as he tried to convince me otherwise, my gut tells me that he considered people as inanimate objects."

"So that's a yes."

"Not exactly, pal. Jeremy seemed surprised and upset when I screamed at him, accusing him of killing Margo."

"You never told me that," Sam interrupted.

Mac considered his response. "Sam, I love you. But I didn't know how to heal you. There are a lot of things we haven't discussed. Jeremy's pattern is to have an assassin as his second in command. Even though he never gets his hands dirty, he's definitely the architect."

"And yet, he would have been a senator," said Sam sullenly.

"And maybe President."

"You've got to be kidding me!"

"He punished a rapist that the justice system misfired on, arranged for the arrest of the producer and distributor of a drug that killed kids, and stopped a terrorist attack on the National Cathedral. America is desperately looking for a hero. I think he'd have won as a write-in."

"Eloquent, strangely charismatic, full of logical ideas, and with the balls to push them through," added Sam begrudgingly.

Mac was quiet, and Sam spoke again. "But in this case, I do come to bury Caesar. There is no remorse on my part. Either dead or comatose for life works for me. I believe that he killed Margo and, in turn, killed a part of me."

CHAPTER 91

THERE WAS NO EBB IN the media frenzy. Lack of access was catnip to print media, cable, bloggers, and conspiracy theorists. Jeremy Lyons, the man who had captivated the world's attention, had been struck down by a hit-and-run driver. Was he alive? Was he dead?

Various cell-phone videos gathered from moments after the accident showed the mangled body grotesquely splayed on the asphalt. The police had immediately cordoned off the area, but a striking African-American woman swooped in, gave the policemen hell, and seemed to take charge. There were also photos showing the Secret Service arriving and a helicopter removing Lyons from the scene. The woman had been allowed to accompany him.

Reports stating that the patient arrived at Bethesda Naval Hospital in critical condition had been confirmed. Since then, no further information had been made available. Flaying the skin off a reporter was preferable to total information shutdown.

The White House issued a statement that the Florida senatorial candidate had met with the President shortly before the incident and that all attempts were being made to find and arrest the driver of the vehicle. The assertion that the purpose of the meeting was just social only ramped up suspicions. Why did the President have a secret meeting with an Independent candidate for the Senate?

Four days later, the dearth of news had almost pushed the mystery to the back page. Then a headline appeared in the *Washington Post*: "JEREMY LYONS DISAPPEARS." The accompanying story quoted a "reliable source," which stated that Jeremy Lyons, still in critical condition, had been taken from the intensive care unit of the hospital.

There was blood in the waters. Brian Woods's face was crimson as he verbally assaulted the White House spokesman. "Do you expect the American public to swallow the 'I see nothing, I know nothing' story from the administration?" "It's the truth!" the bespectacled man said, his lips firm in defiance.

"Do you deny that the Secret Service transported Jeremy Lyons to Bethesda Naval Hospital after the assassination attempt ?"

"No," the spokesman said dejectedly. "But Mr. Lyons is a private citizen and ..."

"A private citizen," Woods interrupted, "who is the most loved politician in the country, who had just left a secret meeting with the President. It's just too damn convenient." He shook his head in frustration and stared at the representative. "Re-election just got easier," he snarled.

"What are you insinuating?" The shock on the spokesman's face would go viral.

Woods caught himself and backed off. "Our Commander-in-Chief has the best resources in the world. Find Jeremy Lyons."

CHAPTER 92

EUROPE, THE UPCOMING NOVEMBER ELECTIONS, Kim Kardashian. It was as if nothing on the planet mattered except Jeremy Lyons.

Mac McGregor was as clueless as everybody else, and his team instinctively knew that it was not a topic he wanted to discuss. Unfortunately, his vacation from Jeremy would be short lived.

"Mac, it's Alcina from the Lahr account, and she wants to talk to you."

"Me?" Mac answered without thinking.

Wade Larson, who had been the only continuing contact with the client, simply nodded.

The coverage on the Lahr account was unprecedented for their group. All substantial accounts had two partners assigned to them, and an account of this size would have also included Wade to make sure that there were no administrative glitches. Furthermore, Mac and the assigned partner would have had either periodic meetings or conference calls with the client. In this case, the client had his own performance monitoring system and requested no meetings or updates. Fortunately, the account had performed much better than the overall stock market. An unusual arrangement to be sure, but the client always drives the bus.

Mac motioned for R.J. to join him on the call. "Good afternoon, Alcina. I have my partner, R.J. Brooks, on the phone with me. Is it all right that he joins us?"

"Of course," she replied in a shaky voice.

"I'm sorry. Are you okay?" Mac asked.

"Not really," she replied, choking on the words. "Mr. Lahr has a message for you."

Mac glanced at R.J., who shared his befuddled look. Moments later, they heard the British accent.

"Mr. McGregor, I believe that we may have something of a sticky wicket. You see, the only way you are hearing this recording is if I am no longer of this world or am incapacitated."

After a pause, the voice changed. "I'll allow a moment for you to dry your eyes."

Mac shook his head in wonder.

"For someone they call 'The Wizard,' old boy, you are not overly perceptive."

Hearing Jeremy Lyons's voice triggered what felt like an emotional overload to Mac.

"You get a call from a stranger, who after a five-minute conversation wires you $100 million. No information on Google or anywhere else on the Internet. Albert Lahr does not exist. Yet, the minimal requirements of the know-your-customer rule check out with you and your firm. No further direct contact — that is, if you don't count our weekly chats — is made with the principal. And in your only conversation with the delightful Albert Lahr, I foreshadowed my identity with the comment, 'I never lack courage.'"

Lyons emitted a loud, obnoxious sigh. "Mac, if you're not there yet, I have seriously overestimated you. Bert Lahr, who played the Cowardly Lion in the 1939 classic *The Wizard of Oz*, at your service. I will pause for the applause."

Mac and R.J. exchanged a glance.

"Enough of my cleverness. Let's go on to the sticky-wicket part. First, I hope the fact that I gave you absolute discretion with my money and insisted that your fee be doubled demonstrates my genuine affection for you.

"Second, it might be awkward for you to continue to manage the funds, as your sense of values may prohibit you from receiving revenue on what you consider ill-gotten gains. As you are well aware from my financial bible, *Survival of the Fittest,* I would never be burdened by something as plebeian as a conscience.

"Ah, I will miss one of the clever rejoinders that you would normally insert here. However, if your righteous indignation causes you to relinquish the management responsibilities and forego the fees, my associate, Alegria — you know her as Alcina — will be happy to facilitate the transfer of the funds.

"At some point, all of my meager assets will be converted to my Change the World Foundation. You see, you have had a positive influence on me.

"For example, you taught me to be open and honest with my dear friends, so I will give you a final piece of inside information. Because you mistakenly tend to suspect the worst of me, you may think that I staged the terrorist attempt on the National Cathedral. Not so. After I uncovered the plot, all that was required was a bit of creative persuasion and the ability to make time fly.

"Finally, I do regret that a rogue associate of mine pushed you around a bit on your canal. For some reason, my people tend to be overly protective of my good name. For everyone's sake, I would hope that your crack investigative reporter friend, Mr. Hessel, will let sleeping dogs lie. Or in my case, sleeping legends.

"And, Mac, in the event that I have gone to my final reward, I will wait patiently for you to join me. Ta ta."

CHAPTER 93

THE CHAIR WAS NOT BUILT for two, but neither Mac nor Grace was complaining. It was an early Saturday morning. He still had on pajama bottoms, and she was still in her nightgown.

Grace sat on Mac's lap with her arms around him as they looked out through what he called his big-ass windows. As they shared the beautiful sights of the sun-kissed morning, their gorgeous red maple, dressed in full regalia, its graceful trunk spreading like a large family tree, seemed to bow in response to their reverence.

For the McGregors, it was like they had been holding their collective breaths for so long, and now they were able to gratefully exhale.

"So what are you going to do?" Grace asked.

Mac gave her an amused look. She asked about his business about as often as he asked her about decorating. "My team has rationalized the situation perfectly," he said as his eyes twinkled. "First, the performance of the account has been excellent. Second, who better to manage these assets when the ultimate purpose is charity? Third, Lyons owes me."

"That last one's easy for me to agree with," she interjected. "So you'll continue to manage the money?"

"If I had known that it was Jeremy's money originally, it would have been poison. But I have reduced the fee, so that the charity's cost will be less than other advisors would charge, so I think I'm okay with it."

After a few moments of contented silence, Grace took Mac's hand and asked, "Is Jeremy Lyons really out of our lives?"

Mac became pensive. *Yep, I had him taken out, started the ball rolling by telling Blake Stone that I'd do it myself that I had the stones.*

It had been hard for Mac to reconcile what he believed was his part. Eventually, rationalization provided a balm to assuage his guilt. He had been swayed by Jeremy's public charisma and his political philosophies. But the man was evil to the core. The image that one day this callous, unethical sociopath would be in the ultimate position of power and have his finger on the button of mass destruction ...

"Knock, knock. Anyone home?" Grace's gentle tapping on his temple brought him back to the moment.

"Dead or alive, I think Jeremy is out of our lives. Raising his voice, Mac added, "I hereby declare that the Jeremy Lyons affair is over."

Grace wrinkled her nose and looked at him. Then she raised her index finger, smiled, and started singing: "I'm gonna wash that man right outta my hair."

"What are you doing?" he laughed.

"Well, it's not over till the fat lady sings."

"That does it." Mac wrapped his arms around her, cradled her, and picked her up.

"What are *you* doing? You'll hurt your back!" Grace squealed as Mac carried her towards the downstairs guest bedroom.

"Nope. Been working out, girlfriend. And I'm about to show you what I do to fat ladies."

CHAPTER 94

JEREMY LYONS WAS IN A prolonged coma. Two months without a flicker of a response. Yet Sabine was undaunted. She would never concede that he was in a permanent vegetative state.

It was imperative that she first prevent infections such as pneumonia. Also, in order to prevent joint or muscle deformities, a strict program of physical therapy was required. The best minds in the field would ensure his nutritional intake; Sabine was in charge of the nutrition of his soul.

In most cases a coma is a temporary condition, rarely lasting more than two to four weeks. After a patient emerges, the prognoses vary. It all depends on the severity and location of the brain injury.

Sabine would not allow Jeremy Lyons's muscles to atrophy. Nor would she entertain the possibility that he would not fully recover. His heart was still strong, and soon his brilliant mind would fight through the veil of his unconsciousness.

Jeremy had even prepared for his care and treatment in case he became incapacitated. He understood the danger of being a reformer, a visionary, a messiah. In an attempt to achieve his ultimate goal, he would have made the ultimate sacrifice, as Sabine well knew. But it was way too early. Premature martyrdom was like a pebble in a river: its effect faded far too quickly.

The facility Jeremy had built was a testament to his foresight and genius. In the United States and in Europe, there are private hospitals that cater to the wealthy. Luxuries include marble bathrooms, flat-screen TVs, a personal butler, a chef, and, of course, an extra-attentive medical staff. All of these are available at a very steep price to the 1%.

Even though this particular facility's state-of-the-art equipment, laundry list of luxuries, and medical expertise were unequaled, it was Jeremy's private facility, and it would never make a Google list.

Except for the gentle, rhythmic movements of his chest, Jeremy appeared lifeless. He lay on his back with a single white sheet, changed several times a day, covering him from the waist down. No hospital gown. The still muscular, hairless body under the sheet was naked.

Aside from the doctors' visits, which were precisely scheduled by Sabine, Jeremy's regimen did not change. Although two registered nurses were housed in the building, Sabine was his primary caregiver. She was convinced that the monotony of routine would serve as a healing balm for him.

Stimulation for coma patients has been as rudimentary as talking, touching, and pinching. Advanced technologies such as neurostimulators include such devices as transcutaneous electrical nerve stimulators, or TENS units, which are used primarily to check motor and sensory responses. They send electrical impulses to whichever muscles or nerves are being checked.

Two of the world's finest neurologists had agreed to take sabbaticals from their jobs, friends, and families. Once the contracts were signed, the specialists became virtual prisoners; they did not have leave privileges or visitation rights. They had not agreed to these stringent terms out of duty or patriotism, though certainly the amenities were beyond first class. The motivation was obvious: money.

When the doctors were permitted access to the patient, they ran EEGs or MRIs to analyze the effects of certain stimuli on his comatose brain. Often the neurologists injected contrast fluids that could light up parts of the brain in response to stimuli.

During all of this, Sabine was in attendance. After only one demonstration from the doctors, she was able to properly use the exercise equipment available for Jeremy. She would position his limbs into machines that increased blood flow and helped maintain a degree of strength and flexibility.

Sabine ignored the doctors' obvious discomfort as she ministered to Jeremy. She would whisper in his ear while she gently caressed his penis and testicles, then leaned over and rubbed her naked breasts on his face. It was difficult for them to hide their arousal when Sabine pulled back Jeremy's sheet and gave him a long, sensuous full-body massage. Often, she took his flaccid penis in her mouth. Sabine's complete lack of modesty and total adoration of Jeremy were far outside of the doctors' medical expertise. As was this goddess far outside of even their most erotic fantasies.

It was the nightly ritual that was strictly off limits to everyone. Even Alegria, who continued to search tirelessly for new science and clinical trials for awakening comatose patients, was not authorized. Sabine sat with her legs crossed at the top of the bed. Fresh from showering, she wore only her favorite scent. She laid Jeremy's head on a pillow on her lap and read to him his own words, the summation of the entry in his journal entitled "Gift for America."

Sabine reached over and placed the journal in the nightstand. She leaned down and kissed Jeremy's cold lips. She flicked a remote, and the 50-inch flat screen above them came to life.

She narrated in low, seductive tones as her work came to life. "Frank Griffin betrayed you. Like a rotten slab of beef, he hangs over the balcony of his apartment. I lean down. I grab him. I thrust upwards, propelling him through the air as he plummets to the death he so richly deserves."

Sabine's breathing became more ragged, and she felt moisture between her legs. She laid her hands gently on Jeremy's face. leaned close, and whispered, "This one I've saved for you, my beloved. It's a surprise. Margo Savino betrayed you ..."

EPILOGUE

"WE MUST BE GETTING OLD," Grace McGregor said to her husband.

"Wash your mouth out with soap, girl!"

"See? Who says that? No one under 80."

"I marry the past with the present in order to weave history into modern-day culture."

Grace looked at him skeptically. He was lying on his side on the couch. It was ten o'clock on Halloween night, and they were both trying to summon the energy to get up and go to bed. "Do you even know what you just said?" she asked.

"Of course not," he said airily. "Inane prattle is my stock in trade."

Grace shook her head dismissively. "My point was that we bought all this candy, and we only had five trick-or-treaters. I feel cheated."

"Fear not, fair damsel. I will accept full responsibility for the remainder."

"Some things never change," she said. "You used to take the kids out while I held down the fort. The neighbors would all get a kick out of you begging for candy right up there with the kids."

"And they were well advised to pay tribute. I can be very tricky."

Grace sighed. "I do miss those times." They shared a few minutes of peaceful silence. "Do you realize that it's been over a month, and no one even knows if Jeremy Lyons is dead or alive?"

"Uh ... you do know how to break a mood, girlfriend. No treat for you tonight."

She laughed.

"I also realize," Mac said, "that in less than a week, Florida may elect a corpse as senator."

"I wonder if that would increase Congress's approval rating," Grace mused.

Mac snorted. "I guess there's some truth about married couples starting to act alike. On that note, my little cynic," he reached over and grabbed her hand, "let's go to bed."

The ringing phone sent a shiver through Mac's heart. The first thought of every parent is the children. Mac looked at the clock, 11:55. Grace picked up the receiver.

"Hello? Yes, it is. Uh ... okay, just a moment."

The lack of urgency in her voice allowed his heartbeat to settle. "Who is it?" he mouthed softly.

Grace put her hand over the mouthpiece and whispered, "It sounds like a very elderly man. Probably a client."

As he reached for the phone, Mac's mind automatically ran through possibilities.

The voice was so soft that Mac had a hard time hearing it. "Mac McGregor?"

"Yes," Mac answered, sensing familiarity.

"Trick or treat."

ACKNOWLEDGMENTS

THE ONLY DOWNSIDE OF ACKNOWLEDGING all who help an author is the fear that someone may be inadvertently left out. If I did err, please let me know and you will become an enviable character in my next book.

In my previous novel, I began by thanking God and I continue to express my gratitude daily. It is with an ever present sense of awe that I treasure my blessings of health, family, and friends.

In addition to my patient and ever accessible editor/sister Kay, I was fortunate to acquire another partner for this book. Mary Perry, also an editor and retired military attorney, signed her emails as my humble researcher, and was very valuable in that role. She supplemented her knowledge of the intelligence community with treks to the courthouse, and the Lucky Lounge to add authenticity to my descriptions. Later she volunteered for the role of business manager. I love to write; the details and mechanics of publishing, not so much.

New authors are definitely a work in progress. One of my first goals in writing my second novel was to streamline. To that end, I lucked into a transcription service owned by a lovable lunatic, Brenda Rutgers.

About three months before sending my first draft to two of my real author friends, David Baldacci, and Kitty Kelley, I asked my older son Jamie to read the manuscript. He read it, and attacked with a vengeance. Now every parent of adult children knows that to get one of your kids involved in your passion is better than a hot fudge sundae. However, if it involves creative writing, be very, very careful. Pulling no punches, it felt like I had yet another editor, only this time he was suggesting plot changes, deleting paragraphs, and countless rewrites. We all want our children to be happy, but gleefully telling their father what to do was perhaps not one of the ways I anticipated bringing him joy.

One of the perks of my day job is that it gave me the opportunity to work with and develop a friendship with Kitty Kelley. A gifted writer, she is an even better friend. When I asked her to dissect my manuscript, she was as thorough as she is in her research. I owe her quite a debt for her astute observations and critiques.

One of my business partners, AJ Fechter, has once again added his valuable insights to my work. Anytime I feel like a paragraph is close but not there, I ask AJ, the consummate wordsmith, to fix it for me. Patrick Duffy was nice enough to share his martial arts expertise, and the real James Kersey helped make sure that I didn't have too many legal errors. I also need to thank the inimitable word doctor, Linda Cashdan for help and Marina Ein, be still my heart, my new publicist.

I dedicated my first novel, *Insiders,* to my wife, Jo Anne, who is the center of my greatest blessing, my family. Because they are destined for stardom, I must also thank Caitlin, Jackson, Sophie, Charlotte, Anthony, and baby Roe who make me smile.

I am grateful to all of my friends who bought multiple copies of *Insiders* to give as gifts. I appreciate your confidence, approval, and support. I would encourage you to continue this noble practice because any profits will go to charity and because if you don't, I would likely depict despicable characters with alarming similarities to you in my next novel.

AUTHOR'S NOTE

IN MY FIRST NOVEL, *INSIDERS*, my goal was to wrap a thriller around the problems that existed and still reside in our financial markets. The writing experience was harrowing, humbling, and at the conclusion, cathartic. *Inside Out* gave me the opportunity to explore a dysfunctional political system and question whether we have the ability or the will to fix it. Even more intriguing to me was the thought that a charismatic, unprincipled leader could manipulate and galvanize a constituency.

For this novel, I have allowed myself to be pulled, kicking and screaming, into the world of social media. As such, I will look forward to responding to readers' comments and questions. The elections are over, but the problems still remain.

ABOUT THE AUTHOR

MARVIN MCINTYRE IS A NATIONALLY acclaimed financial advisor with over 40 years of experience. Since *Barron's* began ranking the country's top financial advisors, McIntyre has been listed in the top 100 advisors, rising to number 3 in 2008. In addition to managing wealth for ultra high net worth families and advising corporate clients on a broad spectrum of financial issues, he has been a featured speaker on radio and television, covering investments and the markets. He is affectionately known by the nickname "Financial Wizard" because of his candor, acumen, and humor. After exposing the financial system in his debut novel, *Insiders*, McIntyre now dissects our flawed political system. A native Washingtonian, graduate of The Citadel, and Vietnam veteran, McIntyre donates the profits from the sale of his novels to charity.

Made in the USA
Lexington, KY
08 June 2013